CYBER WITCH

CYBER WITCH: 2082 BOOK 1

EDDIE R. HICKS

Cyber Witch

Cyber Witch: 2082 Book 1

By Eddie R. Hicks
Copyright © 2019 Eddie R. Hicks
All rights reserved.

This is a work of fiction. Names, characters, businesses, places, events and incidents are either the products of the author's imagination or used in a fictitious manner. Any resemblance to actual persons, living or dead, or actual events is purely coincidental. This novel contains scenes of graphic violence, explicit language and sexuality and is intended for mature readers.

Cover Art by: Ravven

V 1.03

CONTENTS

PROLOGUE

WALKER

Walker's computer terminal sent emergency alerts. The kind of alerts that told you to drop what you're doing and run for the nearest exit.

Had he not stayed behind in his lab to back up his files, he'd have made it to the fire exit. Walker worked hard on this project, and it was going to change everything. He went for the door when his computer sent the confirmation the backup was nearing completion and mentally prepared himself to venture outside into the sweltering heat of Indonesia. The heat was too much for his aged body.

He wasn't sure where the lab was exactly, Zhang Industries valued its secrets more than anything. Typical corporation. Walker had been blindfolded during his flight from Sydney to here. He knew the lab was in the middle of some Indonesian jungle and that was about it. He hoped the corporation would fly in a rescue team soon.

Screams bellowed from the halls, a mixture of English, Indonesian, and Chinese voices. Their shouts for help froze Walker's finger still, it was inches away from the wall door control panel.

Maybe leaving the main central lab was a bad idea. He opted to put his ear to the door. His ears picked up more shrieks, burning computer terminals, and exhaust pipes spraying their cooling contents outward. There were popping sounds, like echoing gunfire. Nobody was screaming after the gunfire stopped blasting.

This wasn't your typical lab accident. It was an attack. The corporation wasn't going to be sending help, not while the Federation military sprang into action in response to the sounds of violence beyond the exit.

"You, wait there." A woman's voice spoke beyond the door. He didn't recognize the voice, though he recognized the accent. North American, west coast, he reckoned. "Open the fucking door."

Now Walker was truly regretting not leaving the lab when he had the chance. Someone outside wanted in. He backed away from the door, his eyes gazing at the various computer workstations and testing pods; one of them should provide cover.

The doors slid open and ahead of it stood a corporate PMC, his body covered from top to bottom in black and gray combat armor, in his hands, an SMG. Behind the PMC stood a woman with blue eyes, thin curly golden-brown hair, and wearing a white lab coat, stained with red handprints. She was something to look at, though. Her hands were also glowing white. Walker's throat tightened; she was an imaginary witch.

The witch stepped ahead of the PMC and instructed him to shoot himself. So, he took off his helmet, put a gun to his head, and pulled the trigger. His brains came out the other side, splattering across the door that had slid shut during the middle of the act. Walker wanted to run, he really did, but when the witch faced him, ordering him to stand still and not move, he did. He had to; her telepathy told him to. He became her mindless puppet.

"Take me to the prototype," the witch demanded of him.

Walker's mind-controlled brain obeyed, and he nodded. "As you wish—"

"Did I give you permission to speak?"

"No, of course not."

He escorted her into the lab, a chamber full of decorated tables, computers, unfinished robotic devices, and a tube-shaped pod at the far end of the chamber. They made their way to the back and stood facing a cylindrical tube large enough to fit a large man inside. Most people wouldn't be surprised if there was a man inside it as there was something that had legs, arms, body, and head beyond the tube's frosty glass-like exterior.

She gave the tube a look up and down, then let out an impressed whistle. "You guys have been busy."

"It will change the world once it's complete."

"I'd bet," she said, placing her hands on her hips. "Now, I want you to tell me everything about it."

"Everything?"

"I'm a quick study." Her index finger tapped the side of her head. "Show me all the reports, diagrams, blueprints, everything you know and have on those computers."

Walker obeyed. He keyed in his password, bringing up exactly what she requested, the files he had saved to backup. The witch leaned in, viewing the screens as their blush light shined across her pale face.

"Am I free to go?" he asked.

"There's one last thing I'll need from you once I'm done here," she said as she continued to browse and commit everything on the screen to memory. "Place the facility on auto-destruct."

"As you wish," he said and went to key in the command on a rear computer terminal. "Anything else?"

She grimaced, reaching for a pistol strapped to her thigh, holding it to her face. She handed him the gun. He felt his heart beat in his neck.

"Open your mouth," she said and watched as he held the gun

and opened his mouth wide open. "Put the gun in it." The barrel of the pistol found its way into his opened mouth.

He couldn't resist the witch. She had total control of his thoughts and body. "Please ...please don't," he said with a mouth full of a pistol barrel.

"I don't want to do this," she said, facing away from him. "Believe me, I don't. But I have my orders. If I don't carry them out, someone else will ...after they punish me."

"There's ...always another way."

She didn't believe so. "Pull the trigger."

A bang echoed and the contents of what existed at the back of his head made the white lab walls behind him sticky with crimson and gore.

The witch continued her task, committing the data to memory as the self-destruct alarms blared.

ONE

ESTRELLA

A storm was about to roll in.

How bad of a storm? Estrella didn't know. She focused her mind on other things, like how she would make rent this month. Being broke as fuck sucked.

She walked ominously through the crowded streets of downtown Buenos Aires when the downpour of water fell from the skies. The clouds overhead grew thick and dark, making the sun vanish. You couldn't tell the difference between night and day. The metallic urban jungle around her didn't help.

Neon signs flashed on automatically, controlled by their light sensors, the storm tricking them into thinking it was the evening when it wasn't. In reality, it was still the middle of the day. Nobody was looking for a spin in the casinos or seeking the titillating flesh of dancers on stage in the clubs. People were busy at work, feeding the corporations that ran the globe, earning pay that'd be invested in the splendors surrounding her, all owned by the corporations. It was a fucked-up cycle. The local arcades were populated however, mostly kids skipping school to play videogames. She did the same back when school was a burden in her life. Videogame music and sound effects echoed at her side as she walked past and splashed through the puddles.

Looking up, Estrella saw countless people walking across the overhanging bridges connected to the upper levels of the city. They deployed their weapon of choice to combat the heavy rainfall, mostly translucent umbrellas. Her weapon of choice was a transparent rain jacket, umbrellas made you vulnerable. Much easier to reach for a gun when your hands were in the pockets you stored it in. That and it helped make her look human as she kept both her hands at her sides, buried into the jacket's pockets.

Estrella's left arm was synthetic, though it was hard to tell from afar, and as for her right, it was wrapped in an NC gauntlet. Humans never had that combination of tech on them, neither did imaginary witches, often referred to as IWs, since imaginary witch was a bit of a mouthful to say. Shades covered her synthetic eyes, now radiating with an emerald glow thanks to the low lighting brought on from the darkened clouds. The navigation data overlaid on her eyesight guided her through the urban sprawl to her destination, her boots splashing through rain puddles reflecting the glow of neon that wasn't there two minutes ago. She chewed the bubblegum in her mouth during the walk, occasionally blowing pink bubbles.

She arrived at The Den half an hour later, a popular hangout stop for mercenaries. The drinks were cheap, and the job board always had high-paying gigs. Her boss Ricardo was always here when they weren't any jobs. If he wasn't, then she'd be kicking in the door of every brothel on the east side until she found him. And she would find him too.

The Japanese words and logo for the Yoshida Corporation flashed on a sign outside the establishment, one of many businesses they owned. The same logo was etched into her NC gauntlet and probably stamped on the inside of her synthetic arm and skeleton.

A doorman stood at the entrance as Estrella approached. He

looked at her strangely, like she didn't belong there, so she shed her somewhat fake appearance. She took off her jacket, pulling the hood away from her headfirst. Her long black hair was free to embrace the warm wet downpour from the heavens. She lifted her shades to the top of her head, unmasking the emerald glow from her synthetic eyes, and her black eye shadow and lipstick. She blew another pink bubble, and it popped. She resumed chewing it.

The doorman knew what she was at that point. His wide eyes said it all. But, just to make sure, she formed her hand, wrapped in her NC gauntlet, into a cup, flashing her holographic ID card. There was no question who she was, Estrella was an RW, a real witch, and she belonged with the mercenaries.

"I'm here to see Ricardo," Estrella said, lowering her hand.

The doorman looked puzzled, narrowing his eyes at her. "Que?"

"Estoy aquí para ver a Ricardo," she repeated.

"Si, si!"

The doorman waved for her to enter the establishment. Rainwater became a thing of the past as a dry and air-conditioned environment replaced it. She moved past the crowds of mercenaries. She could smell the alcohol on their breath as they spoke, and the lingering scent of stem cell burgers and overcooked fries from the kitchen. It wasn't hard to tell who was human and who was an RW like her; just look for the NC gauntlet, synthetic arms, and eyes. It was the international sign that someone traded their humanity for money and cyberware so powerful it might as well be called magic.

Ricardo was at the back, sitting in a private corner reserved for hotshots like him. Three rounds of empty beer glasses stood on the round table in front of him. He was your typical mercenary boss in this part of the city, sporting a brown jacket full of rips and tears, probably a hidden weapon or two when he wasn't asked to leave them at the door. Then again neither was Estrella, but she was a different case. RWs couldn't harm humans.

So she wanted the doorman to think.

The optical scanners in Estrella's eyes ran a facial scan of Ricardo, not that she needed to, but it was always good practice to make sure you were about to confront the right person. The data displayed over her eyesight.

Name: Ricardo Cortez

Age: 34

Species: Human

Occupation: Mercenary

Notes: Frequently visits underage prostitutes

She grimaced at the last line of data. That was new. The corporations harvested new private data from Ricardo recently and chose not to forward it to the police. She wasn't surprised. Richard sat with a brutal-looking bodyguard with a fierce crimson mohawk on his shaved head and enough nose piercings to hide the fact he even had one. Some young girl cuddled with Richard wearing booty shorts, fishnet stockings, and a bikini. She was most likely found in the red-light district, and Estrella had serious doubts she was older than sixteen. She grinned and scanned her too.

Name: Alexis Castillo

Age: 18

Species: Human

Occupation: Streetwalker

Notes: Error, please try again later

There was no point in trying again later. Error messages like that were typical signs someone paid a hacker to alter their profile, a bad hacker at that. The good ones would have doctored notes and would have charged Alexis, if that was even her real name, extra. Streetwalkers with fake IDs were usually underage. This meant Ricardo committed three crimes. Estrella's actions would be just.

Additional scans displayed lines of text over her eyes. The scans suggested everyone at the table had more than one drink each, and that no weapons were detected, though it was possible they had something hidden within their body armor. *Well, here it goes,* she echoed internally. Estrella gave Ricardo the worst scowl he'd ever seen. "Ricardo!"

Ricardo slouched back in his chair, looking up at Estrella and smiled. "Estrella Rodriguez in the flesh!" He rubbed his hands together, standing up to greet her with open arms. "Soon to be number fucking one RW in the city, what can I do for you?"

Estrella clenched her fists. "Stand still and put your hand on the table."

"Que?"

"Just do it."

"What's this about?"

"Just do it, motherfucker!"

He grinned, looking back at the underage girl he was sitting with. She shrugged. Ricardo did as well and then rested his palm on the table as requested. Estrella reached for a concealed dagger strapped to her leg using her cyber speed, impaling his hand to the wooden table. Ricardo screamed.

His bodyguard rose, and the chair he sat on crashed backward. He went charging for Estrella. She struck him hard across the face with her right hand, wrapped in the silver-studded NC gauntlet. If it had been her synthetic hand, he wouldn't be standing or holding a hand to his nose which was now leaking red.

Ricardo examined his hand that was stuck, held to the table by Estrella's dagger after stabilizing his balance. He watched the red that plumed on his fingers, she looked at the fury burning in his natural human eyes, something she'd be doing if she still had them. The girl he was with, Alexis was it? Estrella had forgotten already, went into a frenzied panic. Estrella told her to scram, and she did, heels clicking, into the bar behind Estrella.

A downed bodyguard on one side and Ricardo's stabbed hand

on the other. It was her and Ricardo now. She placed the swarm of nanites within her body on full alert.

With gritted teeth, Ricardo yelled. "What the fuck, Estrella?"

"You don't like to listen do you?!" she retorted.

"You fucking bitch!" He staggered, unable to move with a dagger through his still-bleeding hand, holding him in place. "You fuckin' real witches aren't supposed to harm humans!" He tried pulling the dagger out from his hand. It didn't budge. Estrella basically nailed his hand to the table with it. He groaned. "I thought that AI in your head prevents you from attacking us?"

She sneered. "I changed the rules."

Ricardo's downed bodyguard got to his feet in a daze from her punch. Estrella saw the guard reach for a pistol. By the time he aimed it at Estrella, she held her gauntleted hand out, and it was glowing blue. Holographic pentagrams spun in circles on her gauntlet, the utility nanite swarm within her was seconds away from behind deployed and had been before the bodyguard touched the material of his pistol.

The bodyguard backed off like a scared puppy. Estrella was a pissed-off witch. You don't point pistols at people that were designed and built to fight users of special abilities. Just ask the two dead warlocks lying in the city morgue.

The patrons sitting at the bar got silent during the confrontation, probably watching it unfold like it was a sports game. There was an estimated three minutes before the doormen up front caught wind of her actions. She asked the AI wired into her brain to watch her back. Estrella was running out of time.

She placed a pistol on the table. It had old bloody fingerprints on it. Estrella pointed a finger at it. "Know where that came from, Ricardo?"

"Should I?"

"It belonged to your recent murder victim."

"Fuck off! I ain't no murderer—"

"Oh yes, you are, man. Her name was Lee Yu-Mi."

"Yumi?"

"Yes, you fucking killed her."

"Bullshit! She was weak and fell in combat."

"She was my partner," Estrella said angrily, "my best friend, my roommate, and a D ranked RW. We told you she wasn't experienced enough for the mission. You didn't listen. Yumi begged you not to send her. You didn't listen. Yumi and I came up with a list of other teams you could have sent and were more experienced than her. Yumi was scared and felt her lack of experience would get her killed during the mission. And guess what happened? She fucking died. You're a murderer, Ricardo; you sent her on that mission hoping she'd die."

"You guys know the risk of our work!"

"And you knew corporate fuckwits would send you a replacement for her as part of the warranty you got on us RW units. Cheaper for you to have your weak RWs killed, and hope you get a free replacement that's stronger and more experienced from the almighty corporation."

Ricardo was committing warranty fraud, a murderer, and screwing underage streetwalkers. Estrella was okay with putting a bullet through his head. She grabbed Yumi's pistol off the table, then grabbed Ricardo by the neck, using her synthetic left hand. The mechanized joints within it whizzed as she tightened her grasp onto him.

"Oh, and you didn't pay me," she spat and put the firearm to his head.

"I paid you!"

"You didn't give me Yumi's cut or send it to her crying family. You pocketed it."

"Because half the witches I asked you to bring in alive ended up dead."

"Because people were shooting as we walked in. What did you

expect us to do, ask them nicely to stop?" She tightened the grip on his neck while bringing her gauntleted hand holding the pistol closer to his face. "I didn't sell my humanity to Yoshida for this shit, and Yumi didn't sell hers just to be erased, because you saw her as useless and wanted a free replacement unit."

Ricardo smirked smugly. "You girls should have taken up pole dancing then."

She flicked off the pistol's safety. "Any last words before I deliver justice?"

Ricardo smiled. "Yeah, look behind you."

Estrella's body twitched violently. Holding onto Ricardo became an impossible task. Error screens populated her eyes and she lost the means to communicate with the nanites swimming in her body. That meant she couldn't use her abilities, the one thing that prevented the bodyguard from taking action against her.

She fell to her knees and heard Ricardo laugh. The last status report from her AI reported that a surge of electricity entered her from behind. Her AI also failed to warn her of the ambush. She wondered if the modifications she made broke it. The energy surge was on the same level as a Taser, most likely from the doorman when that running girl ran past and told him. Next time, she won't give people she hated the chance to utter last words.

If there was a next time.

Her hacked AI was bound to be discovered now.

Her last sight of the establishment she was in was the TV screens hanging on the wall behind the bar. The news was playing, a headline mentioned something about the jungles of Indonesia catching fire mysteriously.

Estrella's vision went black amidst the various error screens obscuring her vision. It looked like someone powered down a computer screen.

TWO
RAY

Everything looked like a blur at first, most things do when you open your eyes for the first time, after a long unexpected sleep. It took three seconds for Ray's vision to clear, and three seconds more for him to realize he had been asleep, but at the same time not. It was hard to explain the feeling. This had been his first time doing this in years.

He rolled off the couch he had fallen asleep on. One half of his mind was surprised to notice he dozed off, and the other half was astonished that recalling what happened seemed so ... real. Ray let that half shut down. He didn't want to spoil what was to come next.

He was in his apartment out in the heart of downtown Los Angeles. Evening had fallen upon the city, turning the once sunny skies that hadn't seen rain in over a year into cloudless darkened skies devoid of the pinpricks of stars. Not that you could see the sunlight if you were on the streets below. The endless lines of towers and apartments, miles long, upstaged that.

Ray faced the window grimacing. His place, on the 80th floor, never provided a room with a view, unless watching other high-rise structures close by was your cup of tea. It wasn't for Ray. He missed being able to look out a window and have sunlight enter his place during the day. It's like the people that built the city didn't want anyone to see sunlight.

Sunny LA my ass, Ray hadn't seen direct sunlight in weeks.

The view of the city in the window got obscured by the reflection of a woman. She approached him from behind. The white and silky gown she wore didn't do much to cover her bra, panties and garter belt set, and stockings, and he didn't care. Her golden-brown, light curly hair draped over her shoulders. She brushed it away before wrapping her arms around his body, resting her chin on his shoulder.

"Don't you have to work in the morning?" Arianna said to him.

He reached down, holding Arianna's soft hands as she continued the embrace from behind. "Don't you have a flight to catch?"

"Yeah."

She pressed her pink lips against his neck. Ray wasn't a fan of neck kissing, neither was Arianna. This was her way of saying turn the fuck around so we can do this the right way. So, he did, and then they did things the right way, a two-minute long make-out session. It was just how he remembered they did it. He felt the increased blood flow into his penis.

Arianna tilted her head away from him, a gap formed, separating the lips of the two lovers. "Come to bed, Ray."

Ray glanced behind Arianna, looking at the travel luggage bag that remained open. It was free of clothes. "Shouldn't you be home, packing?"

"It's just a business trip to the European Union," Arianna said. "In and out, don't need to bring much."

She pushed on Ray's chest, and he fell backward onto his bed. A grin spread across his face; he always forgot how strong those skinny arms of hers could be. She crawled over the top of him on all fours. Arianna's opened gown made it easy for her to peel it off her body like she was shedding skin. A push of a magnet keeping her bra connected released her pink-nippled breasts from their captivity. Ray slipped his trousers off, releasing his erect penis from its prison.

He looked up at Arianna's natural curves, now exposed to the flashing neon glow from outside, illumining her body as each of her garments come off. One by one, she flung them in the corner. She hovered above his penis, her knees skinning into the fabric of the sheet and mattress. Arianna looked down at him, smiling and giggling with excitement, this was going to be their last night of fun before she went away.

Ray's world froze, even the lights outside that had been painting her pale body with various tones of pink and purple neon colors stopped, as did his own body. The entire world was put on pause, and he fucking hated it.

"Yo! Holmes," the sound of a male voice spoke. "You got an incoming phone call, ese."

Ray groaned internally. "Ah, man ... Fuck!"

The apartment vanished in a burst of light. Arianna's idle body, the bed, even Ray's body that was seconds away from penetration deep beyond her beautiful pussy hair.

Ray's eyes opened, this time for real. He was reclining on a chair, in a room with walls made of concrete, shaking with vibrations from the loud music played from beyond it. He was back in the real world and out of the world of his past.

Ahead of him stood Garcia wearing a tank top with an unlit joint in his mouth, tattoos of pentagrams decorated his muscular arms. Ray shook his head at the telepathic warlock who had interrupted his psytrip session as he reached for his phone stuffed in his business suit pocket.

"You like?" Garcia asked him, holding a palm size memory sphere for him to look at.

"Yeah, yeah, I'll take it."

Garcia tossed the sphere, and it arced toward Ray. He caught it with his free hand, while the other held his phone still ringing its tone. Before he answered the call, or checked to see who was calling, Ray accessed his banking information with a payment app. Garcia did the same with his phone. A screen appeared asking Ray to pay 120 Alliance dollars for the memory sphere. His thumb tapped the confirm button. Garcia smiled when his phone beeped the confirmation message.

"Got a two for one deal going on now too," Garcia said. "Wanna go back to high school and fuck the prom queen again?"

"Never did that."

"Whatever man." Garcia put his phone away and held his hand out. A cigarette lighter flew into it from the counter. "Anything from your past, I'll recall for you."

"I'm fine with this for now."

Ray held the phone to his face, the real cause of the interruption to the service he was paying for. The caller ID from the blaring phone displayed the name Steven Jarrod and his Los Angeles area code number. The editor-in-chief of the Alliance Star newspaper. Leave it to a late-night call from your boss to blow your memory recall experience.

He thumbed the answer call button. His transparent plastic phone turned into the image of a middle-aged man with a fading hairline. "Ray, what are you up to?"

"Stuff," Ray replied, shrugging.

He'd rather not say. This was the Pause, Play, Rewind. Most people that came here were there to record new memories and then save them, not recall them. The telepathic women faking orgasms in the rooms at the far side of the hall could attest to that.

Steven, on his end of the phone call, aimed the camera on his phone at a computer screen for Ray to see. What Ray saw was a news broadcast from the European Union, depicting police and ambulances bathing a hotel with their siren lights. The text crawl on the screen was written in German.

It made Ray's heart thump with fear.

"Terrorists hit the EU today. Some hotel in Munich got attacked," Steven said bringing the camera back to face him. "You got any contacts down there?"

"None," Ray said, his mind drifting to Arianna. She went to Munich on business. "Except for—"

"Arianna, your girlfriend, right?"

"Yeah ... Fuck."

"I'm sure she's okay, she works for Yoshida, right?"

"That's right."

"Forget that story about the jungle fires in Indonesia. That shit's old news. We need to be the first to report this."

"Are you sure? My source is certain an explosion started those jungle fires."

"And even if they were, he'll never get past the Federation's veil of censorship to confirm that. Fuck the Indonesia story, find out who these EU terrorists are."

"I'll see what I can do."

"Call, email, text every fucking contact you have in the EU. Give me everything you can."

Ray stood up to leave, keeping the phone's camera on him, hoping the concrete wall behind wouldn't give away where he truly was. "Understood."

"Every fucking paper and news outlet in the Alliance will be on this soon, so make it fast!"

His call ended, and the phone returned to its natural form, a rectangular transparent object. Ray slipped both the phone and memory sphere into his pockets. If he wanted to return to that steamy night he and Arianna shared, he'd need to present it to a telepath, like Garcia. The Pause, Play, Rewind was full of them,

IW class witches or warlocks that used their special gifts to provide a service.

Walking out from the room, down the narrow halls, Ray could hear behind closed doors others paying a telepath to recall old memories or make new ones. Some people broke down, when they suddenly found themselves back in time, reunited with loved ones that had long been dead. Others wept tears of joy when they relived happy moments that had been forgotten.

With a few extra dollars, you could even live in memories that weren't yours. The memory sphere wasn't exclusive to the brain it originally came from. Arianna was known for gifting him memory spheres she bought, so Ray could sense the emotions she felt when they went on dates. Why tell someone you love them when you could have them go through what you felt about them? Just pay two hundred dollars for the service to extract the memories and transfer them to the sphere.

A warlock doorman stood with their pentagram tattooed arms crossed when Ray approached the exit. He shouted to Ray as he reached for the handle. "Yo."

Ray faced the warlock doorman; he was pointing at a box. It was a sad looking box, made of haggard cardboard full of rifles, pistols and shotguns. A sign on the wall above it read 'no weapons beyond this point.'

"Don't forget your gun," said the warlock doorman.

Ray shrugged. "Didn't bring one."

"The fuck? You crazy man? Never leave your home without a gun! Even us powered folks need 'em."

"I'm from district three," Ray said. "Never needed it and it's not that late."

"Fuckin' district three humans, I swear. One day, you're going to regret not keeping a gun on you in the streets."

Ray grinned and left. Outside, the humid evening air of Los

Angeles hit Ray in sync with the sea of neon around him, like the Pause, Play, Rewind sign above the door he walked away from.

"Get your fucking hands up!" The voice of law enforcement personnel yelled in his direction.

Ray's heartbeat sped up. Two policemen had their pistols drawn, approaching the building he left. Darkness had fallen in Los Angeles, and Ray hadn't realized he was inside so long. If he did, he would have left earlier. Or brought a gun with him.

The streets weren't safe for him at night. They weren't safe for anyone, honestly.

THREE
ESTRELLA

When Estrella awoke, she found herself on a medical table. Her slender body was stripped naked, and she lay back down with her bare chest and trimmed pubic hair facing up to the ceiling. Her fusion of state-of-the-art technology, and what remained of her humanity, was exposed for anyone to see including the barcodes tattooed into her right thigh.

She went to move her arms, but restricting bindings kept them in place, the same with her legs. Repeated attempts to break free yielded the same result, her breasts shook with each jerk of her body while seeking escape.

She couldn't see much of the room, just the ceiling covered in darkness, and the logo of the Yoshida Corporation on the wall, barely visible. She tried activating her night vision, but an error screen denied her. It informed Estrella she wasn't connected with her AI, and that she should report to a service tech to have it looked at.

Yeah, a little hard to do that right now ... she stared at the bindings keeping her arms and legs to the table. They left Estrella with little choice but to lie back. She felt the soft fabric of her long black hair press against the flesh of her back, right down to her ass. It was that long.

"Ah, welcome back real witch unit seven, eight, three, nine, two."

She moved her face from left to right looking for the source of the voice. She found it; the speakers on the wall while a mechanical arm lowered from the ceiling and slowly inched toward her face. A maintenance AI.

"How long was I out for?" she asked the ceiling arm.

"Approximately two days, six hours, seven minutes," the maintenance AI said.

She growled at that statement. "I can't access my AI, Reeves."

"We have removed your AI."

"I can see that. Why?"

"It will be replaced shortly with a new one as there was some damage done to it, likely because of unauthorized modifications which enabled you to willfully assault a human."

She grinned. "I may or may not have been responsible for that."

"That is the consensus of the audit recently conducted on you. You are under a great deal of stress. You will be reassigned."

"I didn't ask for a fucking new post!"

"We at Yoshida Corporation value the hard work and contributions all employees and RWs make and understand that at times things may become stressful in this competitive business world we live in."

Blah, blah, she thought, it was the copy and paste company statement for situations like this. "Oh, here we go," she said as the arm made its way to the back of her head.

It peeled off the skin on her left temple, giving it access to the wires and parts that made her AI and neural implants work. What it did next, she couldn't tell, only hear, and what she heard was the buzzing sound of drills, and the pulling and inserting of computer parts. She couldn't feel it; the maintenance AI had deactivated her sense of feeling at that point, her whole body turned numb. It felt great all things considered, the nasty draft blowing against her and tickling her exposed nipples couldn't annoy her anymore.

"Your assault and attempted murder of a valued client of Yoshida, suggests you've become stressed. This is most likely because of the ongoing combat with IW gangs you've been asked to take part in with the mercenary groups in Buenos Aires, and the loss and feelings of grief for your partner and roommate, Yumi. We feel a different assignment is necessary, one with fewer responsibilities and away from anything that may remind you of Yumi."

"My family lives in Buenos Aires!"

"We are aware of that and will ensure your new assignment will be within the borders of the Alliance of the Americas."

"Where are we going?"

"Please remain still."

"Answer the fucking question!"

"Please remain still; we need to install your new AI assistant."

Estrella wanted to say more, but she felt her motor functions seize up, as her neural network underwent a brief reboot. Her new AI had been successfully installed and synced with her brain and cyberware. New status screens populated her vision, a text crawl of numbers and computer code rained down.

Greetings Estrella, a voice in her head said; it had a British accent. It was a nice touch by whoever programmed it. *My name is Geoffrey; I will be your new AI.*

Great, maybe you can tell me what the fuck is going on.

You hacked your previous AI, removing its ability to restrict unprovoked violent acts toward humans. With that protocol gone, you assaulted a client of Yoshida who had your body on lease for their business. You also assaulted another man under his employ. Both were human, and that is unacceptable, you were repurposed to protect humans, not harm them. Yoshida believes this is a result of

stress and will transfer you to a new city to assist their law enforce-
ment combat unregistered imaginary witches and warlocks.

No, no, my family lives in Buenos Aires.

I understand, but the Yoshida Corporation has made the
decision.

What about Yumi?

I am unfamiliar with that name.

Lee Yu-Mi, she was an RW like me.

Scanning. Ah yes, Lee Yu-Mi, she is listed as killed in combat.
They will harvest her cyberware parts as they are corporate property.

That's the problem, how are you going to bury a woman who had
almost half her human body ripped out to get augmented?

What remains of her body will have to be laid to rest.

That's fucked up man! Bury her with her parts. Don't let her
family's last memories be a woman missing her bones, arms, and—

It is company policy to harvest all cyberware from fallen RWs
unless a third party is willing to purchase them for a proper burial.
Are you offering to pay for that? They are very expensive.

After the botched job, Ricardo withholding Yumi's cut of the
cash, and Estrella giving the last of her money to her aunt to pay
rent, her answer was a reluctant no.

After a lengthy diagnostic and various tests of Estrella's cyborg
skeleton, left arm, and AI were completed, she was forced into the
processing chamber. The chamber was dimly lit and populated
with a dozen naked men and women like her, all of them featuring
synthetic left arms, data ports on the sides of their heads, and dots
of silver covering their right arm. They were real witches or
warlocks, some were new recruits, and others were like her, undergoing upgrades for a new assignment.

Nobody was ashamed at their full-frontal nude form as they all
featured bodies the advertisements of the nation told people they
should have. Body modification and genetic retuning was big business. The naked men standing around her had penises no shorter

than six inches, while the women had breasts swollen to a C cup or larger. Everyone had to have the perfect body according to the media. If you didn't have one, then ads harassed you daily until you spent money to get it, after that they hounded you to buy sexy clothes and shoes to show it off.

Estrella, along with the men and women, were asked to stand on a conveyor belt which carried them deeper into the facility. Robotic arms ahead lowered, while red laser scanners took slow detailed analyses of their form and cyberware, casting gridlines of red over the naked group. Once completed, new robotic arms moved forward, pricking the arms of everyone, and injecting a silver-colored fluid into them, nanites, the powerhouse of RWs.

She got her injection of life-support nanites when it was her turn. A crawl of computer text over her eyes confirmed the injection was a success. The tiny robots traveled throughout her circulatory system and went to work, ensuring her body continued to not reject the synthetic tech within her. She saw windows to her left and right. They were operation rooms where naked men and women lay on beds. Men in lab coats used surgical equipment to remove their arms from their bodies, others had their bones pulled out, in preparation to have it replaced with a cyborg one. It brought back memories of the day Estrella sold her body to the corporation when she and her family had hit rock bottom.

A robotic arm held a network cable to her when the assembly line to receive upgrades ended. She took the end of the cable as instructed by the digital voice, plugging it into one of the three network plugs on the side of her head. She jacked into Yoshida's software update server and saw a progress bar move from left to right. A flash of computer file names and directories flicked above it.

Please standby, her AI said. *Downloading a new operating system and receiving the destination to our new assessment.*

Where is that? Please don't say, Los Angeles.

It is Los Angeles, unfortunately.

Fuck me sideways!

Unable to comply.

Not literally.

Ah, that was an idiom. I am unfamiliar with that one.

I hope you're a fast learner, there's plenty more where that came from.

Indeed. Your body is the first one they have installed me in. I will look forward to what we can accomplish, and learn, together.

FOUR
RAY

Ray kept his face away from the two cops. The two uniformed men remained standing, pointing their pistols at two thugs with ripped jeans and sleeveless tops. The fists of the two men flared with tiny sparks. They were gathering energy for an electrokinetic attack; they were warlocks, IWs. The two IW thugs refused to comply with the cops; they had special powers, and the cops had guns. The two cops remained where they stood. They were outmatched.

A third nonuniformed man approached. He wore the silver and shiny NC gauntlet on his right hand. It was an RW, a cyborg warlock created to keep the local IWs in line. The sparking fists of the two IW thugs went to the air when they saw the RW. The cops pushed them to the hood of their vehicle, placing them in handcuffs. The thug IW duo roared, cursing the police, and then threatening the RW with death. Ninety-five years later, and people in LA were still yelling 'fuck the police.'

IWs in cuffs, regardless if they were a shifter, telepath, warlock, or witch, were typically unregistered with the Alliance government and oftentimes were extremely violent. Use of IW powers was illegal without a permit, as was training to hone one's supernatural abilities. Unregistered IWs had a tendency to break all laws regarding that.

Ray power-walked to his car. If they had called an RW to back up cops, then things could get messy real quick. He'd written his fair share of news articles about innocents getting nasty burns over their bodies when they stumbled into the crossfire between the police, RWs, and rowdy IWs that didn't want to be hauled downtown.

The world of today, nearing the end of the century, was way different from the start.

His car was parked a block away, forcing him on a long walk along the unkempt sidewalks. It wasn't a pleasant experience, since Ray was human. Everyone around him were witches and warlocks; he was in the heart of the IW district.

Two women, no older than twenty, whistled at Ray, their faces covered in black and gold streetwalker war paint. They were wearing black fishnet stockings and shorts so short you could see half the mold of their ass cheeks. And if you were looking at their chest, rather than the ass, then you'd be able to catch a glimpse at the full shape of their nipples, bleeding through the loose-fitting tank tops they had on. One of the working girls had fox ears and a tail; she altered her DNA with a quick wave of her hands.

She made a duckface motion with her lips when Ray saw her. He kept walking as she changed her appearance. She lost the ears and foxtail, becoming an Asian woman, then a gorgeous African woman, a Caucasian woman with blonde hair, a stunning Persian. Her biokinetic skills let her become any ethnicity she wanted. Sex with biokinetic prostitutes was in high demand.

The foxy streetwalker was back to her previous look with the fox ears and tails when she called out to Ray. "Hey, you human?"

"I think he is," her partner said.

Foxy smiled at Ray as he looked back at them. "Ever fucked a witch, big boy?"

Ray shook his head, keeping his movement toward the parking lot. "I'm good, thanks."

"Let me suck your dick once," Foxy said. "I promise you'll never look at a human girl again!"

Ray chuckled. "I'm fine, really."

The second streetwalker snapped her fingers, it made her hands flash with blue light brighter than the neon one's decorating the district. A small gathering of rain clouds appeared above her, drenching her body wet, then vanished with the flick of her glowing hands. She ran her palms over her chest, across the soaked tank top. It was hard for Ray not to peek at the full shape of her augmented breasts visible from the hydrokinetically drenched top.

"You sure?" she said. "You can have both of us, two for one deal tonight."

Ray turned away, keeping to the straight and narrow path to his car. "Everyone seems to be holding those."

"We can have a telepath record it too," Foxy shouted. "Pause, Play, Rewind is back there."

Smile and keep walking. The more he spoke to them, the more they'd tried to lure him back. Not that he'd ever do it, Arianna was the only woman he needed in his life, and she was human. Nailing a woman with strange powers in the bedroom didn't sit right with him. What if they make his dick shrink as a joke? Or worse? There was a reason the world put all IWs on a tight leash after the third world war. And he saw it as his trek to the parking lot continued.

A warlock doused his body in flames and entertained a mass of girls with his pyrokinetic ability to juggle burning pieces of wood. Telepaths performed tarot card readings at tables near the streets. Dance clubs released loud vibrations from their music and signs out front stated humans weren't allowed inside. Anti RW graffiti was spray-painted across several grimy buildings as trash crunched below Ray's feet.

A hologram poster read: **Want safe streets? Then make**

haste and report all unregistered users of magic. A tips number flashed below as Ray moved past it. It was one of many holographic banners speaking to the masses.

Next Friday Breaker vs. Xray in a flaming cage deathmatch! Come watch the action live at Josh's Beer shack!
Hot biokinetic girls on stage tonight! You'll never believe how low they'll go!
Is your spouse cheating? Text telepath Nikki today for a free estimate.
Walking home alone? Missed the bus and got to wait for the next? Swing by West coast Gunsmiths for ammunition. Always keep a full load in your gun at all times.

The billboards and signs went on for days, adding their luster to the neon brightening the buildings, streets, and sidewalks.

A sense of safety calmed Ray's head when he sat in his car. It activated with the insertion of his keycard, and a three-second retina scan temporarily blinding his vision with six green lights from the scanner. With the car in motion merging into the traffic of the city, he switched on its autopilot and reached for his phone.

He made a long-distance call to Arianna, something he'd avoided doing when news of the terrorist attack that hit the EU was made known to him. He wasn't ready for the bad news if there was bad news to be shared. Her voicemail sounded. She's just sleeping he told himself. It was, after all, past midnight in the European Union.

The beep sounded the cue for him to leave the message.

"Hey Arianna, it's me, Ray. Of course, you didn't need me to tell you that, since you could tell by the sound of my voice, oh and caller display. Yeah, I'm probably rambling. Anyway, I heard of the terrorist attack in Munich, just calling to make sure you're safe 'n' shit. You not picking up is worrying me ... then again, time zone difference, yeah. Anyway, just give me a call back when you can. I love you, Arianna."

The call ended with a prompt asking him to confirm if he wanted to leave that message or record a new one. He gazed at the screen for two minutes wondering if she'd ever pick up the message.

The automated computer voice of his car informed him they were leaving the IW district and entering the human one. That meant his car had been driving for twenty minutes. Ray was looking at his phone with the car autopilot on for that long. He shook himself out of the trance, hit confirm, and put the phone away, ready to accept manual control of the car back.

Outside the car's windows was the Los Angeles freeway populated with cars and trucks, helping dot the darkened roads with their headlights. Gone were the flashing shows of IW powers, cops, and RWs looking for unregistered IWs. Those sights were soon to be replaced with humans on the streets and RWs making sure IWs stayed in their place when he arrived in the human districts. All the negativity he was exposed to earlier was gone, except the thought of possibly losing Arianna to an overseas terrorist attack. There was so much he wanted to do with her, so much he put off because he thought he'd have all the time in the world to do it.

Ray had to take control of the situation.

"Computer, show me the location of the nearest jewelry store."

His dashboard's computer screen illuminated. A detailed top-down map of Los Angeles appeared. His location displayed as a flashing dot on the freeway, as the nearest shops requested showed as pulsing red dots. Tapping the dots changed the screen, showing photos, addresses, customer reviews of the jewelry stores. He browsed their catalog carefully.

They sell engagement rings.

Ray pulled out his phone again and selected his schedule planner app. He thumbed in a note to browse the store and purchase a gift he'd long put off for Arianna. A surprise for her when she returned to Alliance soil.

Assuming nothing happened to her overseas.

FIVE
ESTRELLA

LAX and the pretentiously tall structures that made up Los Angeles was a depressing sight. It was confirmation Estrella's forced reassignment was real, and not a joke. She was in LA, there was no going back home so long as Yoshida's decision still held.

Out there in the jungle of skyscrapers and neon, was the notoriously huge IW district she heard so much about, the district that sent a lot of RWs home in body bags. The LAPD was going to make her spend every day there, now that her body was leased out to them, she figured.

She sighed a sound full of dejected emotions and wondered what she'd be doing if Yumi was still with her. Probably smiling.

So ... which way to the LAPD? She asked her new AI, Geoffrey.

Processing, please standby. A map of the city appeared over her eyesight. Red lines were drawn on the map by Geoffrey, traveling from LAX's location to the police headquarters they assigned her to. *This is the most efficient route to it.*

Who do we report to again?

A profile dossier replaced the map. It showed the ID photo of a uniformed cop, a man in his mid to late twenties—short brown hair, emotionless gaze—listing his age, height, name, service record, and education. Geoffrey had everything on him; even his address and phone number. She was surprised it didn't list his hobbies and turn-ons.

This is Marcus Desmond, Geoffrey explained so Estrella wouldn't have to read the file. *He is an officer, part of the Los Angeles IW crimes unit.*

All right.

Hmm, it would seem he is not at the station. Marcus has been called to the scene of a crime in progress, possibly IWs involved.

Locate it. Marcus's profile vanished, and the map of the city returned to her vision. The red lines carving a path to the HQ changed. She gave the updated map an inquisitive glare. *It's not far away. Let's give them a hand.*

It is likely they called RWs to the scene already.

Last time I checked LA is short-handed in the RW department. Estrella put her hands on her hips which were wrapped in tight black shorts. She wondered if the people walking past her were noticing her facial expression changing because of the silent internal conversation she was having. *That's why they hauled my ass out here, and you know it.*

Following the map floating in the vision of her synthetic eyes, she moved away from the airport, walking to the nearest public transportation train. *You were assigned here as a part of your stress management.*

No, it was punishment. I ain't got any fucking stress problems. This is LA, the highest concentration of IWs in the Alliance. They need RWs because they always end up dead.

You are about to engage in risky behavior which could be attributed to stress.

She snickered out loud, drawing the confused glares of the surrounding people. Their confusion faded when they saw the silver NC gauntlet on her right hand, her eyes emitting emerald light, and the black faux leather bustier. They knew a synthetic witch with an AI implanted in her head when they saw one.

I'm about to make a good first impression, she continued. *The sooner we please these people, the sooner we get a choice of a new assignment, meaning I can go back home.*

———

The subway station Estrella crawled out of deposited her in a neighborhood in dire need of a cleanup, and maybe a recycling truck to remove the mountain of rubbish building up. Every pad had security bars over their windows, more upscale ones had the laser upgrades securing windows, though Estrella only saw two of those. Quadcopter drones raced overhead, and they all bore the logo of the LAPD. She was getting close, just follow the drones. A gathering of LAPD and a few unmarked cars idled outside one small apartment, and the drones she saw earlier all floated next to a window on the thirtieth floor, or was it the twentieth? She didn't have time to count or scan.

Time for first impressions.

She marched forward, stepping under the police tape as if they invited her to the gathering of uniformed men and women. They shot her a look, the kind that said who the fuck are you. Those looks dissolved when she used her synthetic arm to flaunt her NC gauntlet.

Estrella neared the group of cops looking at a mobile computer screen. "Someone call for RW support?"

"We did," one cop replied. It was Marcus, though he was sporting a thin beard. His profile picture needed an update. Marcus winced at Estrella after examining her frame, the bustier, shorts, and exposed midriff. "But ... not you ..."

"Name's Rodriguez," she said, offering a silver gauntlet hand-shake. "Just transferred here from Buenos Aires."

They shook hands as she cringed internally at the usage of the word 'transferred.' She was punished and made to work here.

"Ah, the new girl," Marcus said. "Looking to get started already?"

"Might as well."

Marcus pulled out his phone, fingering a number he had on speed dial. "Taylor," he said as the person he called picked up.

A woman's voice replied; a soft and sweet New Zealand accent. "Yes?"

"You're on standby," Marcus said to the woman, evidently named Taylor. "The new girl showed up. She wants to dive in."

"Understood," Taylor replied.

Marcus ended the call, putting his phone away and facing Estrella.

"That's assuming we really have an unregistered IW inside," Marcus said. "Could just be a bunch of fucking gangbangers."

She looked up at the tall man with a wince. "And if it is?"

"Then you could go home."

"Fuck that, you know all the trouble I went to get here?"

"You're not a cop, I am—"

"Yeah, yeah I know the drill," Estrella interjected, with an eye roll. "Cops catch the bad guys; RWs catch the witches and 'locks because cops aren't strong enough."

The two returned to the mobile computer screen that held the law enforcement personnel's attention. It displayed shaky but reliable video feeds from one drone, and it looked like it entered the building undetected.

Marcus whistled loudly. She thought it was at the video until she saw his eyes locked onto the silver glittering gauntlet on her hand. "That a mark two?" he asked pointing at it.

"Mark three Nano Control gauntlet," she corrected him, giving the gauntlet an up and down stare.

Three point two to be exact.

Thank you ... Geoffrey.

They continued watching the live drone feed like it was a thriller movie. The drone inched deeper through the halls of the apartment on the floor the call came from. It drifted past the door to the unit which had been unlocked and left ajar.

Slowly, the drone flew in, scanning the area, snapping photos of overturned furniture and pictures off the wall lying on the floor with shattered shards of glass scattered about. Four trench-coated men moved about like they were searching for something. A fifth one stepped into view holding an automatic pistol.

"Got five targets, all male," said the drone operator. "All heavily armed."

Estrella moved closer. "I take it they don't live there."

Marcus snorted. "Nope."

"Any hostages?"

The drone operator fiddled with his controls, taking careful manual control of the drone. "Standby."

He moved the drone closer, its camera capturing and displaying the maneuver. With it flying high, close to the ceiling, Estrella caught a better glimpse of the men searching the unit. They were bald with the tattoo of a skull on the back of their head. The images were haunting to see. She had a flashback to a moment of her life she tried hard to forget. Her breathing didn't feel right.

Bald men with skull tattoos on their heads. Their hands delivering pain to her body, their hands forcing her young fragile form into doing things she didn't want. Their hands tearing her clothes—

"Fuck! They fucking shot it!"

The sudden outburst grounded Estrella's head in the present. She wasn't in the past. She wasn't suffering at the hands of the Bald

Skulls gang, a gang she put in the hole when she was of age to trade her humanity for high tech witch powers. Yet, everything on the screen, before it turned to static, suggested they were alive and kicking.

"How the fuck did they do that?" Marcus asked. "That was a recon drone; the fucking thing was the size of a fucking marble!"

Estrella knew the answer. She stepped forward drawing all eyes on her. "Because those are the IWs."

The drone operator shook his head. "To be fair, I clipped the side of the wall. They might have heard it—"

"No," Estrella cut in, the fury in her voice made Marcus' eyebrows rise. "He shot it because his electrokinesis would have sensed it."

"We don't know for sure," Marcus said.

She waved him off and marched to the apartment's lobby. "I'm going in."

"Stand down RW, we need to be sure here," Marcus roared at her. It didn't stop her boots from moving. "If those are humans and we let your kind handle them—"

"My kind?" That got Estrella to stop, as she spun on her heel facing Marcus with rage.

"You're a witch. Witches fighting humans regardless if they're an RW or an IW is bad," he said.

"My AI prevents me from harming humans." Estrella knew all about that.

"Unless you're threatened first, then your AI lets you loose. Let's get confirmation on what we're dealing with!"

"Go get your fucking confirmation." Estrella's back was once again turned to Marcus and the flabbergasted cops. She ran into the lobby. "I'll go get mine."

"Rodriguez, get back here!"

His words couldn't stop her. These men were supposed to be dead. How the fuck did the dead come back and follow her to Los

Angeles? Marcus came into the lobby screaming for her to stop. She replied with a middle finger as the doors of the elevator she had entered slid shut.

The elevator rose to the floor where the action was at. Estrella brought her synthetic arm to her face, sending a command to it. It split open like a storage cabinet. Inside were various items she kept on her, amidst the network of wires that traveled to and from her hands, up the length of her hollowed-out arm, and into her body.

One of those items was a semi-automatic pistol folded up for easy storage. She pulled it out and watched as her arm returned to its previous state, fooling the masses from afar that it was flesh, blood, and bone. Three folds of the pistol returned it to its ready-to-kill mode. Its targeting screen flickered on, listing its current ammo count. Ten rounds and three clips were looking to kill.

Perhaps you are being too rash? Geoffrey internally voiced.

It's the Bald Skulls gang, Geoffrey.

I am unfamiliar with that group.

Was a small gang of warlocks and telepaths out in Buenos Aires. I doubt your database would have anything on it. I killed them last year.

If that is the case, then should we not share this intel with the local law enforcement?

Do you seriously think they'll follow the whim of the new RW that moved in without proof? The elevator came to a stop, and its door parted. Dank and rundown halls awaited her as she bolted out, searching for the room. *Besides, they were taking too long, these guys don't fuck around.*

Do you know how they operate then?

I have firsthand knowledge.

Were you a member?

A sudden flashback before her eyes sent her back to the past once again. She was a little girl crying, pleading for the pain to stop, begging for the gang members to explain what she did wrong. Was it PTSD? Or lingering telepathic mind invasions? She didn't know, just that both were just as deadly if they popped up in the middle of a gunfight. Both were also a good way to make her early impressions on the first day on the job look bad, more so than she already had.

Estrella brought her thoughts out of the horrific flashback. *Jesus fuck Geoffrey you always this chatty?*

I am still building a personal and psychological profile of you. So, in essence, the more we talk, the better I will be able to help you.

How about you assist me with some tactical data?

As you wish.

A blue wireframe digitized ahead of Estrella, forcing her to stop. She watched as the wireframe forged into the shape of what looked like a cat, and after three seconds, the wireframe model fully rendered into a black cat with haunting yellow eyes looking up at her.

She grimaced at the holographic cat. *That you Geoffrey?*

I have chosen this image for my exterior appearance. What do you think?

Estrella shook her head, and pushed forward, keeping the semi-auto in her hands pointed at the floor. *You're a fucking cat ...*

And you're a witch. I am not only your AI but your feline familiar as well.

The silent conversation with her AI, now being projected as a cat that scouted ahead, made her snicker. *Funny.*

I thought you'd find it so. Now, as for data? Arrows appeared in her vision, it was the route the holographic cat made, a pathway for her to follow in the halls. *This is the optimal path to the apartment unit.*

Two minutes later Estrella found the opened door to the unit seen from the now fallen drone. She double-checked the readiness of her weapon, it was good, then double-checked the readiness of the single nanite swarm swimming within her body. An overlay screen revealed they were ready with her body at an 84 percent battery charge. She leaned against the right side of the door frame as Geoffrey in his holographic cat form slithered into the unit undetected.

Processing threat assessment, Geoffrey projected. *Please standby.*

Worrying thoughts clouded her mind. A mini window showed what Geoffrey saw and scanned. She saw what he saw from the ground because of the cat form he took, and she could see the figures of the five gang members searching the living room, kicking in door after door within the unit. Geoffrey highlighted their appearances red, allowing her to see them through walls, or cover. Their weapons got scanned next, and overlays appeared informing Estrella of the gang members estimated ammo count—

A firm hand clasped onto her slim shoulder. Sweat dampened her forehead, and fear made her breathing unstable. The hand yanked her back, away from the doorframe. She responded by jamming the barrel the semi-auto into the face of the hand's owner.

Then she lowered it with a loud grunt.

"I'm on your fucking team, Rodriguez!" It was Marcus, stepping back with his hands raised, his eyes locked onto her weapon.

She beamed. A cop raised their hands to Estrella without her having to say a word. She found it amusing. "How are you gonna come up to me like that and not say a thing?"

His face contorted. "Because I don't want to blow your cover?"

"If you're here to convince me—"

"I'm here to make sure the new girl doesn't get her brains blown out."

Threat assessment complete, five B ranked warlocks, Geoffrey's voice in her head revealed. *You were right in your assumption, these are unregistered IWs.*

Estrella nodded to the flickering holographic cat as he exited the suite. "All right, my AI just confirmed these are IWs, all ranked at B," she said to him. "Satisfied now?"

Marcus' lips twisted. He reached for his sidearm. "What rank are you?"

She made the same twisting of lips. "C."

"Then, no," he said and took cover to the left side of the opened door. "I'm not—"

"You hear something?"

The voice came from inside the unit. One of the gang members was closer than she thought.

Looking at the wall behind her, she saw two red, highlighted figures move from the living room with weapons forward. They were trudging to the front door she and Marcus were squawking at, evidently, squawking too loud.

She placed her back to the wall again, inching her way left to the right side of the door. She lifted the semi-auto, and could see the shine of its barrel.

"No turning back now," she whispered to Marcus.

One Bald Skull gang member approached the door, ready to search the halls, oblivious of the cop and synthetic witch with weapons drawn with their backs to the left and right walls next to the door.

The first Bald Skull gang member exited the apartment, his gaze shifting to the right. His gun rose to greet the cop he was surprised to discover there. The Bald Skull gangster's hands glowed purple and sparked, charging his body with electrokinetic energy.

Estrella plugged two rounds through the tattooed skull into the back of his head. The holes were wide enough to show Marcus's stunned face, and the chunks of brain matter and blood splattered across it.

"Oh fuck!" Estrella heard another gang member shout from the unit.

She faced the wall again. The four remaining members grabbed their weapons and stormed to the unit's entrance. Two of them were near the front door, their heads bobbing up and down, communicating to each other.

Warning, you have alerted them of your presence.

Yeah, no shit!

SIX
RAY

Ray's smile was as bright as the setting sun on the horizon. He entered his place of Zen, the outskirts of Beverly Hills, one of the few places in the region where one could get sunlight, and one of the few places in the nation where actual houses existed. Constructing anything that wasn't a densely packed high-rise, on a planet packed with over ten billion souls was often frowned upon. You can shove more people into an apartment than you could with a one or two-story house. Tackling overpopulation starts with you, as the commercials would say.

This was assuming you weren't a celebrity or worked for the corporations that ran the world. If that was the case, you did whatever the fuck you wanted. Humans and IWs owed their continued existence to the one percent as far as they were concerned.

He stood next to his car parked at the side of the road in a quiet residential neighborhood, indulging in the January air that blew through his chestnut hair, making it wave about. The palm trees around him rustled when the winds passed; he liked that sound. Looking east he saw the mammoth high buildings that blocked out sunlight elsewhere beyond the bubble of Beverly Hills.

The house he approached had two stories, unlike its adjacent neighbors, which were expensive one-story dwellings. The garden he had to pass through to get to the front door was immaculate, perfectly trimmed bushes forming a wall separating the front lawn from the sidewalk. Trees that he didn't know the names of lined the path leading to the entrance of the home. The vibrant green grass on the lawn and its height were consistent throughout. He imagined the same could be said for the grass in the backyard.

A gardening robot greeted him by name. Ray was a common visitor to this household. It made him smile, the machine finally recognized him. It only took thirty visits to do that. The new software update must be working. He checked his phone as he neared the front door, his eyes searching for missed calls or text messages from Arianna. There were none. This wasn't normal for her.

The article he wrote on the terrorist attack in Munich had him worried. Turns out IW terrorists of a strange and unknown group targeted a hotel using their powers. The bodies of those killed were still being collected, what was left of them that was, and that was the scary part. The pictures his source shared with Ray depicted bodies with their limbs pulled off and thrown against walls. Other victims were reduced to piles of ash, and that was before one of the hotel rooms caught on fire. IW abilities were powerful, but not that powerful. This was a new weapon in use as far as Ray was concerned, and the people responsible were still at large. Arianna needed to come home now, especially if these terrorists were targeting EU hotels at random.

She's a busy woman and didn't have time to call. Get a grip, man. She'll be all right.

Ray got a grip, shaking off the doom and gloom.

He rang the doorbell, summoning a small drone out from a hidden hole in the wall. It was no bigger than a bird. The drone floated ahead of Ray and scanned him by running blue and white beams of light across his body, starting from his face down to his feet. Once the drone confirmed his identity, it activated its holographic recorder, projecting Ray's likeness to whoever came to answer the door.

Ray gave the tiny disk-shaped recorder a smile, then a wave. The door opened, and a man in his sixties with silver hair and aged, withering skin stood at the entrance, wiping his hands clean with a towel, Norris Kounias.

"Ray," Norris said to him with a half grin. "What brings you here?"

"Was hoping to chat with you."

"Couldn't you just send me a video call?"

"Naw," Ray said, with a swift shake of his head. "This was something I wanted to do in person."

Norris invited Ray in, shutting the front door behind them along with the light from the golden setting sun. The two men walked away from the foyer, and through the house built like a palace from the early 2030s. Ray spotted Norris's wife, Maria, in the laundry room as they walked past. She was transferring soaking wet apparel from the machine into the dryer and gave Ray a wave with one free hand. He waved back.

In the kitchen, Ray saw why Norris had been wiping his hands clean. A sink full of dirty dishes ready to be cleaned and rinsed was the object of his attention until Ray rang the bell. The LED screen on the dishwasher continued to flash an error message. It was the same one Ray saw during his last visit.

"All right, hit me," Norris said, taking a seat at the kitchen table. "What do you want to talk about that's so important you had to drag your ass here?"

Ray's face turned a shade of red. He clenched his fists and braced himself to reveal the news. "Well, it's about your daughter, Arianna."

"She's overseas on business, and you know that," Norris said. "Well, I hope you do."

"Oh, I do."

"Good, you'd be a fucking terrible boyfriend to her if you didn't and came here asking me what happened to her."

"Well that's the thing; I did come here to ask you something about her."

Norris lifted a silver eyebrow. "And that is?"

Ray felt his heart race. *This is it,* he thought. *You can do this, man, you've been going over how to approach this all fucking night.* "Call me old-fashioned, sir," Ray finally spoke. "But, as Arianna's father, I'd like to ask your permission to ..."

Ray paused. His nerves were getting the better of him.

"To what? Spit it out, boy."

He took a long deep breath. "I want to marry Arianna."

Norris burst out laughing, slapped his hand on his leg, stopped, looked up at Ray, and then laughed again. *Well, that's a no. Fuck me.*

Norris stood from his seat, walking past Ray, and moving to the fridge, still laughing. The feeling of defeat hit Ray in the chest hard. He stood still and embraced his epic loss, unable to turn and face Arianna's laughing father.

When Norris returned to the table, he held two cans of beer. He offered one to Ray. He looked at it and winced briefly, shaking his head. "Oh, I—"

"Ray, shut the fuck up and drink it," Norris cut in and forced the cold can covered in condensation into Ray's hand. "I don't want my daughter marrying some pussy-ass man. So, man up and drink. Prove to me you're worthy."

A ray of hope materialized. Without a second thought, he found the pull tab on the can with his index finger and cracked it open. The hissing sound of the can followed, then a second one when Norris opened his. Ray hesitated for a moment to drink. Not because he didn't like to, but because he was supposed to go to work soon. Returning to the job after a break with a beer in you was a bad image. But if this was what it would take to get Norris' blessing.

Ray downed the cold golden colored fluid within the can and then pulled it away from his lips with a proud grin. "Did I pass the test?"

"Well, I guess." Norris shrugged, before sipping his beer. "I've never seen Arianna so happy over the last five years, and I'd be lying if I said you had nothing to do with it."

Ray's chest warmed upon hearing those words. "Thank you!"

"You encouraged her to work at Yoshida when she thought she wouldn't get the job. Fast forward to today, and now she's some big-time manager broking deals out in the EU. And this house? Fuck, we didn't earn it, but Yoshida likes to treat their employees."

"So basically, you're saying my personality indirectly got you all this."

"I'm saying you made my daughter happy. Happy people are motivated to do stuff with their lives." Norris's facial expression underwent a change. It was a concerning thing for Ray to watch. "Which brings me to you, Ray."

"What about me?"

Norris placed his beer can on the kitchen table and faced Ray with arms folded over his chest. "What are you doing with your life? Still wasting it at the Alliance Star?"

"It's the biggest news outlet in the city."

"Are you proud of what you do?"

"Being a seeker of the truth and reporting it? Yes!"

Norris snorted. "Don't make me laugh."

"I think I did that earlier."

"Yeah, so don't make me do it again," Norris said. "Truth and the news aren't typically things that go together."

"I don't report fake news."

"Everyone does and has been since the turn of this century. People don't have time to read newspapers magazines or tune into a news station at a specific time. Easier to check your social media feeds and follow the rabbit hole of links."

Ray took a final gulp of his drink. "Some people do, that's why we still exist."

"That number is dropping." Norris waved an index finger at Ray. "The only reason print news isn't dead is because of the third world war. People figured out real quick you couldn't read the news when your city was without power for weeks. But the war is over and has been over for decades. Your sales dropped and now you got corporations and government bodies spending money to keep your business afloat, for a price, to make them look good."

"I'm not like my colleagues," Ray said as his now empty beer can joined the one Norris left on the table. "I will get the truth out, regardless of what my editor tells me. And, if he says no, I still have my blog, which has quite a few followers I might add."

"What? That old hacker page you used to run?"

"Well, the page is gone, but I still maintain the blog and archived all the leaks I came across or hacked during my younger days."

"Just watch yourself, Ray." Norris' tone changed to a concerned one. "We live in an age where telling the truth will make you a homeless person dwelling in the streets, or a dead body on the roadside."

"My days of hacking and reporting the edgy corporate secrets are over," Ray said. "I just report hard news and make sure it's the truth, no matter how painful it is to accept."

"I don't want my daughter to be a widow, and I don't want to see her career at Yoshida end because you said something they didn't like. But ... I also don't like a person that deceives the masses, which is exactly what you will have to do to prevent one of the above from happening."

Norris might as well just come out and said it. Quit your job because I don't want my daughter marrying your kind. Not likely

Ray would do that however, he wasn't qualified for anything else in life. Maybe coding, but that doesn't pay the bills, not out here in LA at least.

Speaking of coding. Ray tapped the side of the error messaging dishwasher. "Still giving you problems, huh?"

Norris nodded, standing behind Ray as he kneeled, searching for the dishwashers control panel. "Yeah, some tech said it crashed during an update. Going to wait for someone to come and repair it."

"You know, I could write a temporary fix if that's the case."

"Really?"

"It's Yoshida tech. If I can hack it, I can also reprogram it, or in this case program a software patch to fix it—"

The ringing of Ray's phone interrupted their chat. He pulled it out, raising its screen to his face, the name Piper Taylor flashed on the caller display. His eyes opened wide.

"Sorry," Ray said as he hastily got back to his feet. "I got to take this!"

Ray took the call and stepped out of the kitchen into the hall. Piper's face and black pixie cut hair appeared on his screen.

"Ray, what are you doing?" she asked in her kiwi accent.

"Talking with my future father-in-law."

"So, you did it, huh?"

"Haven't asked her yet, just was asking for permission."

"Great. So, news tip coming at you. There's a hostage crisis going on and it might involve warlocks."

"Oh, really?"

"Bunch of IWs stormed an apartment, shots fired, don't know the rest. I was heading there but was asked to be on standby. Some new RW on the team named Estrella Rodriguez wants to try her hand at this and will probably fail. Either way, this might be a story for you."

"I'm on it." When the call ended, Ray returned to the kitchen, placing the phone back in his pocket, facing Norris. "Hey, listen, man, I got to go. Thanks for the beer."

Norris gave him an approving nod. "News scoop?"

"You know it, and I assure you, it will be the truth as long as I'm writing it."

SEVEN
ESTRELLA

Being pinned down by bullets shot from the weapons of warlocks was no fun. Stressful too, but mostly not a fun experience. The slugs that came plowing at them, out from the opened apartment suite door didn't travel in a straight line. They curved as they passed the threshold into the halls, bullet bending as they called it.

Why aim your weapon at your target when you have the powers of an IW? Just shoot and use your gifts to make bullets make a sharp turn in midair. It wasn't safe for Estrella and Marcus to remain with their backs to the wall next to the door. It wasn't cover, maybe if they'd had been engaged with human targets, yes, but bullet bending warlocks?

New overlays flashed ahead of Estrella's vision as her combat HUD activated.

Geoffrey detected one warlock that covered their body with an electrokinesis sphere. The British sounding AI voice revealed the findings in her head. *I am detecting the presence of a defensive electrical barrier.*

Well, that's just fan-fucking-tastic.

The current weapon's load out of you and—

Yeah, yeah, our bullets are just going to hit that barrier now.

There was a delay in the rate of fire. Estrella's graphical overlay informed her that the two targets inside were most likely reloading. It was time for her to act, and she had until they finished reloading to do it.

She dropped down, searching the body of the first warlock she put down. Traces of its brains and blood still made a mess of Marcus' face. From the dead hands of the warlock, she pulled his rifle and stared toward Marcus and his hands holding his standard-issue police pistol, a LY-65 semi-auto. Marcus was seconds away from returning fire. He needed to not do that.

"Give me your gun," she said to him.

Marcus looked at her, his eyebrows lifting with confusion. "What?"

"It's useless against an electrokinesis barrier."

There was a moment of hesitation, but Marcus caved in and hurled his sidearm in the air, sending it spiraling into the cyborg speed and reflexes of Estrella's synthetic hand. Three weapons lay before Estrella, her semi-auto, Marcus's sidearm, and the dead warlock's rifle. She glanced at her NC gauntlet while commanding the utility nanite swarm within her to remain hot.

Geoffrey, I need a shotgun with a big boom that could break the barrier.

I got just the thing, please standby.

A blue and white display flashed in her eyesight, visible only to her, listing a small menu of nano printable weapons her AI could produce on the spot, given it had access to enough raw materials. Like the three weapons at her knees. She selected the sleek, light-weight, black, and shiny Equalizer, a 12-gauge shotgun.

A second notification appeared, a warning stating it would consume at least one utility nanite swarm to nano print. She selected the confirm button.

Nano printing weapon, please stand by.

Light dazzled her NC gauntlet as she waved it above the three weapons on the floor, and a single swarm of utility nanites within her body pooled into her right arm. Tiny distribution tubes within her gauntlet pricked the flesh on her arm like needles. They collected the nanites, sending them into the gauntlet, then out of it like a spray from an aerosol can, onto the weapons below.

Atom by atom, molecule by molecule, the three weapons were dismantled, seemingly liquefied into three blobs of gray goo. The three blobs of goo came together, forming one large blob, and then formed into the shape of the 12-gauge shotgun. In three seconds, Estrella turned a rifle, and two semi-autos, into a shotgun. Marcus looked on with intrigue. It looked like she performed a magic trick. But to her and the AI in her head, it was state-of-the-art nanotechnology at work. Basically, tech magic.

Estrella got to her feet with the newly forged shotgun held firmly in her hands.

Marcus pointed at it. "I'll never understand how your kind does that so easily."

She smiled at him. "Magic."

Alert, Geoffrey cut in. *Utility, nanite count is low.*

Like a gun, Estrella's RW body needed to be fully loaded for dangerous situations, loaded with nanites. The swarm used to forge the shotgun were dead, their batteries drained to perform the complex task. She split her synthetic arm open, accessing its small storage space, and pulled out a fresh nanite tube, it was one of five she had remaining.

A switch on the side of the tube deployed a syringe injector. She took a quick deep breath, bracing herself for the sudden pain that was about to commence, and stabbed her thigh with the device. A single swarm of nanites entered her body, and Geoffrey established a connection with them, relaying the message to her.

Estrella readied her second magic trick for the night, after browsing through her list of pre-programmed commands to issue to nanites. She grinned at the new screen that clouded her vision.

Overdrive

Nanites alter brain chemistry while enhancing cyberware to slow perception of time and increase movement speed.

Min. nanite swarm(s) required: 1

Nanite swarm(s) remaining: 1

Geoffrey hit me with an overdrive boost.

She felt the newly injected nanites go to work. They quickly swarmed to various parts of her body, making slight alterations to her synthetic bones, adjusting the chemistry in her brain, and releasing combat enhancement chemicals into her blood. Estrella's world froze in time.

Marcus's lips were open but remained that way. It looked like he was trying to say something, a warning perhaps? Too late now, the overdrive was active, and any words said during this mode would come out like long grumbles of sounds.

Estrella went charging into the unit with a raised twelve gauge, cocking it as she went. A single shotgun shell was inside the weapon, waiting for the trigger to be pulled. She came within firing range of one of the two bullet-bending warlocks.

She saw the electrokinetic barrier, a bubble of electrical bolts cocooning the bald warlock gangster. She kept running at the warlock, he too looked like he was frozen in time, as was his partner, still reloading his weapon to the right of her. In reality, Estrella was moving fast, so fast that bullets shot at her moved slow enough for her to sidestep them and watch as they inched past her with translucent shockwaves in their wake, smile, then return to her charge at the warlock.

She was a 100-pound woman, holding a 6-pound shotgun, moving faster than bullets. At those speeds, she didn't need to shoot the warlock in the chest, to penetrate the electrokinetic barrier, although she did, as her fist driving into his face would have done the trick. It also would have hurt like hell and require her nanites to work harder to reduce or repair any damage to her.

The now-dead warlock was flying backward, bits of gore ejected out a huge exit wound in his back made a grisly mess of the wall behind him. Like everything else around Estrella, the warlock's body moved backward slowly, his screams sounded like a long grumble, and the blast of the shotgun sounded like a rocket ship taking off into space.

A second cock of the shotgun primed it for its second shot. She spun to the right, spotting the next warlock, his hands still inserting the clip into his pistol. She lifted the shotgun's barrel, lining up the perfect headshot. She pulled the trigger. Another loud rocket ship roar echoed, and another slow-moving shotgun shell ejected.

She saw in slow motion what happened to someone's head when they took a close-range 12-gauge blast to the face. It broke apart into nothing, face vanishing, then the forehead, ears, everything just battered into pieces of flesh, bone, and pink with a spray of red traveling in directions away from Estrella. It was disgusting, yet satisfying, continual vengeance for those that lost her lives to the gang. Her parents would be proud if they were still around today.

Nanite swarm efficiency is down to 46 percent, Geoffrey reported.

Understood, cancel overdrive.

Estrella exited the bullet time world, returning to the normal one. The two bodies of the gunned down warlocks finally fell to the floor, painted with gore and crimson. There were still two warlocks in the unit, and she needed to conserve her limited stock of nanites. She pulled out a second nanotube, injecting herself with it; there were now a swarm and a half of nanites swimming inside her body.

She repeated the task twice more, littering the floor with spent nanotubes.

Nanite swarm(s) remaining: 3.5

Bullets from a washroom came flying at her; she dove into cover behind a couch in the living room, cocked the shotgun, and returned fire with a thunderous roar. The warlock hiding in the washroom vanished behind the wall, evading her weapon's less than effective shots, given the long-range. Estrella continued cocking and firing anyway, the warlock continued bending their bullets from their cover, sending the stuffing inside the couch up into the air.

The shotgun wasn't going to do shit, and neither would Marcus's help as she had to use his gun to nano print it. She tossed the twelve gauge to the floor, pushed her right hand dressed in the NC gauntlet forward, and selected an offensive nanite ability from her internal tactical menu.

Incinerate

Nanites burns selected target from the inside out

Min. nanite swarm(s) required: 3

Nanite swarm(s) remaining: 3.5

She released a spray of nanites from the gauntlet, flying through the air. They were almost invisible to the naked eye, and not detected by the bullet-bending warlock still hiding in the washroom.

Like a swarm of microscopic angry bees, the flying nanite swarms found the hiding warlock and entered every orifice in his head. Once inside his body, the three swarms executed their pre-programmed instructions, making every particle in the warlock's body they found spin fast. Screams of horror left the washroom, and soon afterward came a warlock engulfed in raging flames, flailing his arms about to pat them out.

He tried to roll the flames out, and when that didn't work, he screamed for help, but none of it came. IWs knew never to touch a comrade-in-arms whose body is under attack from an RW nanite swarm or three. Estrella could easily make it spread like a virus if there were enough swarms with battery power left. She was saddened to see that nobody fell for it. There was a moment of silence as Estrella's eyes scanned the unit, searching for the last remaining red wireframe figure. She couldn't see it. It made her breathing unstable. Geoffrey scanned and highlighted five targets, four of them were down. There was another at large and it broke out of the threat detector highlight.

She needed Marcus for this and gave him the all-clear to run in. He took cover behind the bullet hole covered couch with her. During his charge to the couch, she injected herself with her last nanotube, and then waved her glowing gauntlet above the shotgun, spraying it with a fresh nanite swarm. The shotgun turned to gray goo as she selected an SMG from her weapons screen, a Stellaris 77.

She asked Geoffrey for two of them.

"This isn't what I came in with," Marcus said reaching for one of the two SMGs Estrella nano printed.

She beamed, reaching for the remaining weapon. "Nope, I made it better—"

Gunfire roared, cutting her off. The bullets weren't curved and traveled in a straight line. The warlock's gifts were in the cooldown phase.

IW powers had a limited window. They could use their abilities so long as the glow in their hands remained. The moment it faded, and they entered a phase known as the cooldown, where a period of time passed before they gathered more strength to use their powers again. She always viewed it like drinking a glass of water. Once the glass was empty, you had nothing left to drink unless you refilled it. How long it'd take one to refill that glass of water depended on them. IW abilities were similar, they charged up, unleashed their fury, got drained, then had to gather more power to strike again. Bullets that didn't bend and curve were a sign to watch out for. Estrella had a minute or two before the warlock was using its powers again.

She and Marcus rose from their cover, SMGs in hand. A rapid-fire release of bullets punched holes in the walls and sent the last remaining warlock spinning in circles through the air in a bloody mess. There was still nothing on her combat tracker, despite having visual confirmation the final hostile was downed. She didn't like that feeling at all.

The two cautiously moved from the living room deeper into the unit with their drawn SMGs leading the charge. The last warlock lay in a pool of blood. Marcus went to search the body. Estrella slowly backed away from the blood soaking the floor. Her footsteps weren't splashing through it, neither was Marcus.

She winced and backpedaled onto the floor free of bloodstains. She left no red boot prints. "Fuck!"

Marcus faced her. "What's wrong?"

Shit, how did I miss that? "Back up!" She roared, her weapon rising, while moving to look for the threat that still loomed. "That was a doppelganger!"

Marcus joined her in the search with weapons. The body on the floor was an illusion, mental manipulation. It was a trick to bait them right where the trickster wanted them to be, and that was out in the open of the unit, out of cover.

He's a fucking telepath, Geoffrey, she internally spat. *You said these were 'locks?*

It would appear he was deceiving my scans.

And why he vanished from the combat tracker—

A bald figure wearing a trench coat appeared from one bedroom, shooting. It was the last hostile target. The telepath whom she thought was a warlock. It'd explain the lack of bullet bending as his magical focus was spent telepathically tricking the minds of the two. He wasn't on cooldown at all.

Marcus' gun clapped first, tagging the last target. It turned into a puff of blue vapor. He grimaced. "What the fuck is going on?"

Estrella saw the target reappear. She took aim and put two bullets through its head. It turned into a puff of blue vapor too. "He's fucking with our head!"

Get back into cover and reassess the situation. That's all they could do.

Geoffrey?

Attempting to match his brainwave patterns.

Telepaths were dangerous only because they could get in your head and make you see what they want you to see, that was until an AI like Geoffrey could block it. A scanning progress bar moved from left to right across her vision, Geoffrey was building an algorithm that'd block telepathic thoughts from the target in question. Marcus, being human would still be a victim of course. He'd have to follow Estrella once the block was in place as the fake illusions would be visible to him.

At least, that was the plan which had to be altered when two bullets ripped through Estrella's torso, and one through her left shoulder. The pain mixed in with the force of three back-to-back trucks pushed her to the floor. She tried to ignore the pain and tried to tell herself that the warm fluid trickling across her skin from the source of the pain wasn't blood gushing out. She struggled to tell herself that the next sounds of guns fired and screams of pain weren't Marcus getting shot when he tried and failed to help her.

She wasn't fooling herself, the critical warning screens flashing over her vision made sure of that. But on a good note, Geoffrey had successfully learned of the telepath's brainwave frequency and blocked him fucking with her mind.

Track him, she asked of her AI.

The telepath's figure was highlighted red once again as he walked with confidence toward a downed Marcus. Despite lying on the floor, looking up at the ceiling, spilling Gods knows how many liters of blood; Estrella could see the head of the telepath looking at Marcus via a secondary screen. She saw the telepath step above him grinning and aim his pistol down at his face. She discreetly reached for her fallen SMG, taking aim with it, while keeping her face to the ceiling. The secondary window was a godsend.

A single bullet to the neck ended the threat. The telepath didn't see it coming, visually or mentally. He went down with his hand trying to hold in the red that wanted to come out. It did by the time he crashed to the floor. The telepath's life faded as three long red squirts shot out from the gunshot hole through his neck.

Estrella sighed in relief and went searching for the strength needed to stand up and ignore the pain. She couldn't find it. Geoffrey opted to remind her why. *You have approximately three minutes to live. Nanite first aid is recommended.*

She selected it from her menu.

First Aid

Nanites administer first aid treatment. Extent and speed of healing varies on the number of nanite swarms used.

Min. nanite swarm(s) required: 0.5

Nanite swarm(s) remaining: 0.5

Get those nanites working!

I am however there is not enough. Due to the extent of your injuries, I require two nanite swarms. There is only half a swarm within you.

Estrella was bleeding out. She reached for her storage compartment when her synthetic arm split open. There were no spare nanotubes left. She was delaying her death with the half swarm mending her gunshot wounds.

When Estrella's wounds began to partially seal, and reduce the pain, she crawled across the floor, leaving behind a smear of red in her wake. She found the burning body of the warlock she incinerated earlier. Her optical scans showed the nanite swarm that ended him was still functional.

She kneeled next to the smoldering body and held her breath from the smoke and the scent of cooked warlock flesh. Her NC gauntleted hand hovered above the corpse and issued recall commands to the nanite swarm inside the body. They rose away from the smoking body, flying into her gauntlet, it looked like a spray can working in reverse, her gauntlet being the can.

Nanite swarm(s) remaining: 2

The two salvaged nanite swarms worked rapidly to mend her body. They were given permission to burn out what little battery power they had left to finish the job as quickly as possible. The swarm stopped her bleeding and repaired damaged organs and flesh. Blood that made a mess of her skin and black outfit moved in reverse, trickling back inside her. She'd order the blood she spilt on the floor to do the same, but that'd require a third nanite swarm, she didn't have that.

She was down to a swarm and a half when the process was halfway finished. She found Marcus' body on the floor, unmoving, and slowly bleeding out. Her synthetic eyes looked up and down his body, taking in his condition.

He will not survive, Geoffrey revealed. *I'm sorry.*

Let me heal him.

Unable to comply, insufficient nanite swarms.

Give him one full swarm of mine.

That would greatly reduce your healing. The nanites have not finished repairing your body.

I'm stable enough to live now, he's not. We're healing his ass.

Understood, canceling current healing on your body.

Estrella's NC gauntlet lit up with light as it gathered one full swarm from her body. She held her hand covered in the gauntlet above the red gushing wounds on Marcus' body, spraying it with nanites with orders to stabilize him.

Nanite swarm(s) remaining: 0.5

Will he live, Geoffrey?

Yes, this should stop the bleeding and repair damaged organs.

Marcus would live to be the cop half the city hated to see, and others have loved when they made that emergency 911 call. He still lay motionless on the floor, likely passed out from the pain. Estrella was the only one standing in the unit, and the only one available to search for clues as to what the Bald Skulls gang was doing.

The gang was searching for something, or someone. Estrella went searching for it, limping her way to one bedroom none of the gang members had the chance to kick in. She pushed the door open and frowned. Three people were inside, one man and one woman, both of them holding onto the shoulders of a frightened child, likely their child.

This was their home until the gang kicked in the door looking for them. She saw a bit of herself in the child's eyes, she was the same age as the kid when the gang kicked in the exit to her family's place and gave her a gift she didn't ask for; a ruined life and shattered childhood.

The three looked at Estrella, but none of them seemed glad she was there. It might have to do with the fact that she still held the SMG in her hands. She slowly lowered it, but not fast enough for their kid. In a panic, he picked up and threw the clock on the wall at her ... just by waving his hands that glowed white. He didn't touch it physically; he touched it with his gifts.

Estrella's eyes narrowed, running facial recognition scans of the kid and his parents. Their names and ID appeared, it listed them as humans.

That child is an IW, Geoffrey commented. *It is likely his parents are as well.* IWs with human IDs meant one thing. They were unregistered. *We must detain and report them to the police department at once.*

She did something else, placing the SMG on top of a dresser. "Easy guys, I'm not here to hurt you."

The frightened father stepped back as Estrella stepped forward, dragging his wife and son with him. "Who ... who are you?"

"I'm an RW working with the LAPD," Estrella said to him. "We heard there was trouble here. Any idea why these IWs came after you?"

"No idea, we're just humans trying to make a living."

Meaning they were unregistered IWs living in secret. She caught the kid using powers, and their names didn't show up in the registered IW database when she logged in and accessed it. She double-checked to make sure their IDs pulled from the facial scans listed them as human. It was the job of an RW to kill or capture all unregistered IWs, gangbangers or not, and that included this family.

But why would an IW gang attack them? It made little sense to her. IWs always looked out for their kind, especially the unregistered ones.

Perhaps it was mistaken identity.

That telepath should have sensed they were IWs. No, they attacked this family for a reason, and they didn't care that they were fellow IWs.

I presume this behavior of this particular gang is not typical then.

They hated humans and made sure all their victims were them. This goes against their code ... fuck, them being alive still goes against how I thought life and death worked.

She heard Marcus groan from the halls, so he was coming to. The sound of his slow limps grew louder with each second. Estrella had a choice to make, hand over the family to Marcus to arrest them or do something that went against her obligation as an RW.

Her eyes scanned the walls ahead, confirmation messages revealed a neighboring unit laid behind the wall. Her NC gauntlet hand came to rest on the surface of the wall, and a command sent the remaining nanites within her into the wall. Standing back, she watched and waited as the wall turned into gray goo, and dripped down to the floor, creating a circular hole in the wall. The hole was a passageway into the vacant neighboring unit.

"Go," Estrella said to the family of three, pointing at the new hole in the wall. "Stay low until the police are finished investigating."

The family moved through the hole in the wall. Once clear, Estrella's gauntleted hand extended, communing with the half swarm of nanites, ordering them to take the gray goo at her feet, and reconstruct the wall it dissembled atom by atom. By the time it was done, the hole was gone like it was never there to start with. The half swarm returned to her gauntlet, the pinpricks within it stabbed her hands and arm, injecting them back inside her.

She turned away from it, her mind quickly going over what to say to Marcus when he entered. She aided in the escape and concealment of an unregistered family of IWs. That could land you twenty-five to life in prison if you were human. If you were an RW, that was a defective product label stamped on your forehead and a one-way trip back to the factory that augmented your body.

She was fucked if somebody found it.

EIGHT
RAY

Ray missed it. The blood, death, and destruction, an epic battle waged with a newbie RW and a cop. He missed it all because of the fucking traffic.

By the time Ray arrived at the apartment Piper had tipped him off about, EMTs had carried out five body bags from its lobby. He pulled his smart glasses out from his pocket, placing them on. Holographic overlays confirmed they were recording everything he saw, as he tapped the left control pad of the glasses, ordering them to analyze objects he stared at for periods longer than five seconds.

The cops were silent, especially when Ray approached and asked if they cared to comment on what happened. They didn't, but that didn't stop him from snooping around. Something major went down, and the city of LA had to know.

He spotted a woman leave the lobby, she had long black hair, black makeup, bustier top, and shorts. Had to have been a witch, they always loved to dress like that. The NC gauntlet on her arm suggested she was an RW. This must have been the new girl Piper spoke of. Rodriguez was it? He double-checked his tablet pad, searching for the quick notes he made. Estrella Rodriguez, that had to have been her.

Ray glared at her, holding the stare for five seconds, the holo screens of his smart glasses did the rest, accessing the local public Wi-Fi, pulling up everything it could on an RW named Estrella Rodriguez. A news report from Buenos Aires appeared on the lenses talking about Estrella, but it was written in Spanish. He didn't understand a word of it. What he did know was that Estrella came here to LA from Buenos Aires recently. She had to have been forced into that, no RW requests a change like that. Everyone knew the RWs Yoshida provided the LAPD had a short life expectancy—

His glasses flashed with a critical discovery. Zoomed in images of her NC gauntlet enlarged showing the red stains on it. Five body bags and an RW with her hands covered in blood meant either a violent battle with IWs, or an RW was forced to kill humans. Either way, this was breaking news. RWs were forbidden from engaging human targets unless they had no other choice. RWs were supposed to prevent human life by being taken by IWs, not contribute to that number, it'd be bad press for their corporate creators.

Ray watched as Estrella and another limping cop sat at the foot of an opened ambulance. The cop's vest and uniform were stained with blood. Paramedics swarmed the duo, tending to their injuries, before moving onto other matters, like the five body bags.

This was his chance. Ray marched to Estrella and the cop she sat with. The truth wouldn't be blocked from him, and these two, who obviously were at ground zero, were going to give it to him. He was sure of it.

"Excuse me," Ray said to the two, offering his hand in a shake. "My name is Ray Partington, from the Alliance Star."

The cop with Estrella grimaced. "How the fuck did you get here?"

Ray continued to stare at him for the five-second delay he set his glasses. The name of the cop appeared, Marcus Desmond, part of the IW crimes unit of the LAPD. He gave Marcus a smile, despite the fuck off glare he got from the injured cop.

Ray needed something, anything from the two. If he couldn't report anything useful from them then he planned to use them to point him toward a new source.

But first, they had to talk, and Marcus continuing to hold onto his scowl suggested he wasn't in the mood. Ray faced Estrella, the new girl, and kept his face on her emerald glowing synthetic eyes. Arianna would have slapped Ray if she saw him look down at the faux leather bustier Estrella wore.

"I've noticed you're an RW," Ray said to her. "Would you care to comment on what happened moments ago?"

Estrella commented. "Fuck off."

She got up and left, muttering a curse word in Spanish at Ray. Marcus remained, and Ray returned his focus to him. "Are you able to give us any words on what you saw, sir?"

"I'll give you two words. Fuck, and You." Marcus got up, leaving Ray alone. "Someone get this asshole out of my sight!"

Ray left as well, only because he didn't want to get dragged away from the crime scene. The truth was calling to him, pleading for him to discover it and tell the world with his writing. There was an RW that wasn't supposed to be at the scene, and a cop went through hell and back, in an act that saw the need for five body bags, and they were keeping it a secret from him.

Estrella must have botched the job he figured. Was she a faulty unit sent from Buenos Aires because they didn't want her? That could be bad for the city, Yoshida needed to be providing the LAPD with its top of the line RW units, not defective ones. A sense of excitement tickled his thoughts. Ray might have been onto something, something that might cost the lives of innocents unless he blew the whistle. But first, he needed to prove it was the truth. He'd play no role in writing fake news.

He looked to the apartment building ahead. Somewhere inside was the truth, someplace inside was the botched job the RW from Buenos Aires did. It was waiting for his journalistic presence to find it.

The smart glasses guided him to a lone EMT worker, standing idle outside the lobby's entrance, reviewing the information that outputted to the screen of his pad. The data on the tablet wasn't secured in any safe means, and the illegal hacking apps Ray had on his pad confirmed it. Ray held his pad steady, waiting with anticipation as data was quickly siphoned away from the pad the EMT worker held.

Normally, breaking into a device required the use of a botnet to crack the passwords and break through any advanced encryption. Ray had lots of experience in his younger days with those. The pad the EMT worker used, according to the app Ray was looking at, was running an older operating system developed by Yoshida. It had its fair share of security flaws if they applied no update patches.

His screen began to auto-scroll, listing the logs and reports the EMT workers were filing. Ray grinned to himself—easy access. They were asked to remove bodies from a particular room inside the apartment, that part he could guess. The floor and unit number the incident occurred in was part of the in-progress report he read.

The next screen displayed the apartment's network key. They gave it to all first responders in case of an emergency, providing them access to the apartment's lobby, elevators, and directory. Ray downloaded a copy of the key to his tablet and then killed the connection to the EMT's tablet. He walked away as if nothing had happened, hands in pockets, and making no eye contact with the EMTs and police around.

Ray neared the glass sliding door. It was locked as expected. A computer console on the wall played the role of gatekeeper. Ray plugged his tablet into it, and it played the role of an access key card as he transmitted the network key into it. The doors glided open and Ray entered, playing it off as if he lived there and was going home.

He was deep inside when the doors slid shut. He flicked through the new screens populating his tablet. It grabbed a copy of the apartment's directory list next when it was plugged into the entry console. He located the address he came seeking, the unit where the five bodies were pulled out. A family of three lived in that unit, so that ruled out that the RW's AI went nuts and allowed her to kill humans, at least the family.

The five targets were probably IWs that attacked a human low wage-earning family of three. *Perhaps the family would want to comment on this story.*

Ray made it to the elevator, and hit the buttons fifteen times in quick succession, peeking back out, hoping nobody noticed the journalist that didn't live there enter. Cops can't catch what's already in a moving elevator.

The floor where the incident took place had three, perhaps four, he couldn't tell, cops talking, scanning, and taking photos of the white chalk outlines of five IWs that met the wrath of their cyborg counterpart. He kept his face buried in the contents of his pad. He was just a resident trying to get home. He hoped they'd buy it.

Ray didn't like what he was about to do. A true journalist never misrepresents themselves to get to the truth. But nowadays, in the post-world war three world he lived in, with so much corporate and government interference, getting to the truth was damn near impossible. Much easier to say fuck it, and report something fake, and keep your job because you fed your editor something to work with. Ray was okay with breaking the no misrepresentation rule if it meant reporting real news.

Backs were turned when he approached the opened door. He ducked under the holographic police tape carefully, his hacking apps overwriting the intrusion alarm the tape would have transmitted to the cops. Ray was in, and he had very little time to work, as it was clear the family wasn't home. His smart glasses went to work, recording everything, and navel-gazing at the blood and gory chunks that dripped from the walls into the floors.

He made it as far as one bedroom when someone called out. "Hey, you there!"

Sweat trickled down his forehead. Ray faced the cop. "Uh yeah, what's up?"

"Thought you EMTs were done? What the fuck are you still doing here?"

Ray was caught. They also thought he was an EMT, most likely because he could cross the tape without tripping alarms. He knew he couldn't stay around any longer, not according to the frown the cop was giving him. It was a pity, as he was hoping to at least see someone from the family of three, who strangely enough weren't in the room or in the hall outside. He was certain he didn't see them outside too.

Who the fuck attacks a family of three that wasn't home then sticks around long enough for a cop and an RW to show?

With little else to do, Ray kept his sights forward into the bedroom, hoping the five-second delay of his glasses would be long enough for them to auto perform a deep scan. This was his last chance to find something, anything, to guide him to the truth.

"You lost or something?" said the cop as he yanked on Ray's arm from behind. The international sign of get the fuck out.

"Yeah, thought I left something in here, guess I dropped it downstairs." Ray shrugged the cop off, making his way to the exit. "I'll see myself out."

A loud sigh left his lips as he left the unit. Misrepresenting yourself and getting caught was only good when you discovered the truth. When you didn't, that's when you'd regret not opting to make something up that seemed believable.

He strode past the neighboring unit on his way back to the elevator. Then halted when he noticed the door was ajar. Someone within had cracked it open, looking out into the hall, no doubt wondering what all the cops were doing. He wouldn't have thought much of it if it wasn't for the fact he viewed the tenant list prior on his way up.

The unit next to the family of three, where the incident took place, was vacant. Nobody should be inside. Yet, someone was. He faced the ajar door, looking at the person who was looking into the hall, he held their gaze for five seconds, it would have been six, but they slammed the door shut.

Ray's eyes might not have made the connection, but his glasses did. The man at the door matched the profile picture of the owner of the unit belonging to the family of three. He was right there, possibly with his family, hiding in a vacant suite, not talking to the police, and seemingly not present during the attack, and showing little interest in returning to their home. The truth slipped away as quickly as Ray laid eyes on it. He went to take it back, banging his fists on the door. Nobody opened it. He doubted knocking longer would make a difference and gave up.

He selected the basement level for his elevator ride down. Leaving through the lobby might draw some unwanted attention, he was surprised nobody came running up after him, or maybe they were and just using the secondary elevator. He counted his blessings.

The downtime of the long elevator ride gave ample time to review the scans and the recorded video his glasses captured. His lips curled when the footage of the bedroom appeared, the glasses picked up something he did not notice, likely when the cop came from behind, yanking his arm.

The wall in the bedroom was perfect, too perfect. Like someone disassembled a rugged wall with nanites, then put it back together, while not taking into account the nanites would rebuild the wall perfectly.

He reached for his phone, dialing Piper's number, the only RW he could trust at this point. She picked up after three rings.

"Hey Piper, it's Ray."

Piper's kiwi pixie face smiled at him on the phone's screen. "What can I do for you?"

"So, I'm here at the address you told me. I think there was a lot more than just unregistered IWs causing trouble."

"How did you figure?"

"Call it a hunch," he said. "You know anything else about that RW, Estrella Rodriguez?"

"Not much. She's new, the first day on the job in fact."

"She was inside and left covered in blood with five body bags tailing behind. I'd like to know what happened. Anything you can slip me, let me know, okay? I'll make it worth your while."

"I'll see what I can do."

"One last thing," he said, and then uploaded the contents of his glasses to his phone. A screen flashed, asking him if he wanted to share those files with the person he was talking to. He clicked the yes button. "You're an RW Piper, so tell me, what do you think of this wall I scanned. It looks a little suspect; like someone used nanites to melt it then put it back. Would an RW like the new girl be able to do that?"

NINE
ESTRELLA

Estrella had a feeling she wasn't in the clear, not by a long shot. She was asked to return to the police headquarters alongside Marcus when the EMTs finished patching up their wounds, Marcus more than her, nanites were a big help there.

She didn't think much at first, strolling past the desks and computers of the LAPD's staff. After all, her original game plan, after leaving LAX, was to check-in and get started with her new forced reassignment, get all the paperwork finished, make the switch official, and maybe learn what it would take to get the cops to send a commendation to Yoshida. The sooner they liked her, the quicker she could return home to Buenos Aires.

A police captain asked her and Marcus to sit down in his office. He was really firm about the request. She knew right away that her visit to the HQ wasn't for the paperwork stuff; it was about what had happened earlier that day.

She ran a facial scan of the police captain.

Name: Timothy Peters
Age: 43
Species: Human

Occupation: Los Angeles Police Department Officer

Notes: Drinks a glass of whiskey after work

He was a man with slicked-back hair whitening with his age and a pair of reading glasses perched on his face above the thin goatee. A gray mug with steam lifting away from it rested on the top of his desk, as he walked past it, giving the wide floor to ceiling window in his office a quick glimpse at the neon splendor waking up for the evening. Translucent beads rolled off the window from the outside world where rain had fallen upon the city. A wave of his hand forced the window to dim black, and a spin on his heel brought him around to peer at Estrella and Marcus now taking a chair each at his desk.

"Are we going to have problems, Estrella?" Peters asked her, reaching for his mug.

She shrugged playing it dumb. "With what?"

"With you disobeying orders?"

Estrella snorted. "I don't wear a badge."

"You still work for us," Peters said. "You were told to stay put, and you didn't."

"My job is to eliminate or detain all unregistered IWs," Estrella said as Peters sipped his drink. "I knew they were IWs the moment I saw that drone footage."

"Does that include charging them with a shotgun using your overdrive?"

"Gotta do what you gotta do, especially when an electrokinetic barrier is in play."

"The dead can't answer questions. And the way they died is going to get the press asking questions, like why was such excessive force used? I know the LAPD's rep over the last century has been less than ideal, but blasting people's heads away with a shotgun, on purpose, isn't what we do, even in extreme situations."

"People were going to die unless I acted." She shrugged him off. "What can I say?"

Peters lowered his mug from his lips, his face shifting about, searching for the right words to use, she figured. "And where are those people now?"

Another playing it dumb shrug. "Nobody was home when we got in, they probably were out for the day and the gang didn't know."

Peters grimaced at her. "Or, did you let them go?"

"Why would I do that?"

"Because there's a section of the wall that was in prime condition," Peters said, "When compared to the rest of the unit."

She lifted an eyebrow, twisted her lips, and folded her arms over her bustier top. "Show me."

With the mug in one hand and a remote in the other, Peters activated a hologram that floated above his desk like a ghost. It zeroed in exactly on the wall Estrella had melted with her nanites and put back together.

It would appear someone figured it out, Geoffrey commented.

That was fucking quick. She glanced at the hologram longer, hoping her leaning in closer made them suspect she knew nothing of it. "Don't know anything about that," she finally answered.

"RWs are the only people that can command nanites," Peters said. "And unlike IWs, RWs are registered because they're created by Yoshida themselves. It's pretty easy to narrow down who could have done that, you being the only RW in the building."

"Where did those scans come from?" she asked.

A woman leaning in the corner cleared her throat, drawing Marcus and Estrella's attention to her figure in the darkness. The corner she was in was dark, making it hard for Estrella to make out the brief, black, lacy, and gothic outfit she wore, with small rectangular shaped diamonds dangling from her navel. The woman's hair was jet black, cut short into a pixie style. Red highlights added an elegant contrast to her hair and the long bangs that covered her eyebrows.

Her eyes were like emeralds glowing in the dark, locking into the synthetic emerald eyes of Estrella. She held the gaze. Neither of the two could face away. The expression on the woman's face and the cute smile she gave Estrella sent a hidden message. *I know what you are, you're just like me.*

The woman brought her hand up. It was wrapped in the glistening silver of an NC gauntlet. "I provided them." She also spoke with a kiwi accent.

She'd return the smile the pixie kiwi gave her if Estrella wasn't so enraged that someone figured out her secret. "Thought I was the only RW there?"

The woman nodded. "You were."

"Then how the fuck did you get those scans?"

A tilt of her head made the smile fade. "Not important."

Estrella ground her teeth. If they knew she hid an IW family of three from them, then this wasn't a meeting to grill her, this was a meeting to tell her she'd be getting pushed into the RW recycling facility. "It is, important."

"The scans are legit, Rodriguez," Peters cut in. "Whoever it was that took and sent them to her, to verify if RW nanites were in use, did their job. They brought to our attention something you and Marcus failed to do. Someone made a hole in that wall, then sealed it up without taking into account the years of wear and tear the wall originally had when the nanites rebuilt it."

A smug grin stretched across the woman's face. Estrella kept her gaze on it and waited for the results of her facial scan.

Name: Piper Taylor
Age: 35
Species: Real witch/warlock

Occupation: RW unit on lease to the Los Angeles Police Department

Notes: Serial number ... Error

Facial scans weren't able to identify her serial number. Without that, you couldn't search for the product numbers for her synthetic parts and gauntlet.

Is she a newer model? Estrella asked her AI.

Unknown, I am unable to determine further data about this RW.

"I didn't do it," Estrella blurted to fill the silence everyone in the room expected her to do.

Is it wise to lie about this, Estrella? It is our job to bring unregistered IWs to justice.

Bringing a family, struggling to make a living, to justice? Listen to yourself, man.

All my communications with you are logged, there is no reason to for me listen to them should I need to refer—

That was a figure of speech.

Oh, okay, noted.

Look, I didn't sign up to fuck with families, man. Cops would have thrown the book at the parents and then put the kid in a home. I'm not putting that kid through what I went through, even though the circumstances aren't the same.

Anyone could be an unregistered IW.

That's fucked. I'm just here to shoot some IW gangbangers, you know? Was under the impression all unregistered IWs did stupid shit, not live legitimately. I'm not exposing that family for what they really are, period.

Well, Estrella, now you know. IWs can pose as law-abiding humans. It may not be common in Buenos Aires, but in Los Angeles it is quite frequent.

Besides, I want to know why the Bald Skulls gang was after them.

With the aid of the LAPD, we could have gotten that, no?

This is the LAPD bro. I don't fuckin' trust 'em, and it's clear they don't trust us. We're a tool, a product line Yoshida leases out to their clients. We do what we're told and get pushed to the next job. I still wanna know why the gang was there, without the crime scene tainted by dirty cops.

Is learning the truth worth losing your life when Yoshida repurposes you?

I lost my life when I sold my humanity to them, so that I could destroy that fucking gang. Now they're back. Sorry, Geoffrey, I'm not backing away from this, and I'm not putting that family through more stress.

"Marcus?" Peters asked him, snapping Estrella's mind back to the meeting.

"I was out cold when she went in," Marcus shrugged.

Peters winced, placing his mug back into his desk. "So ..."

"She saved my life, sir," Marcus said. "If she was swinging for the other team, I think she would have left me for dead, not sacrifice her limited supply of nanites to heal me."

Peters pushed one of the buttons on the remote, making the hologram above his desk shift into images taken of the unit, the bodies of the five IWs, and the overturned furniture. The gang members were searching for something.

"Why would they attack a small family like that?" Peters asked, staring at the hologram, stroking his graying goatee.

"They weren't wealthy or influential," the kiwi woman, Piper, added. "Better question, Estrella, how did you know they were IWs before you scanned them?"

She shut her eyes, recalling the details. "They took out the drone with accuracy."

"Yeah, because it hit the wall," Marcus said.

"No, they had a telepath with them, and you know that,

Marcus," she snorted. "They sensed the electromagnetic field the drone created."

"You suggested it was because of electrokinesis."

"Doesn't matter, both powers can detect electrical devices. And, there was one warlock that did use those powers." She paused, her face cringing from emotion. "The real giveaway was their tattoos. Skulls painted over their bald heads, it's the insignia of a small IW gang out in Buenos Aires, the Bald Skulls."

"Never heard of them," Peters said.

"They were small-time and got dismantled by me and the mercenary team I was on lease to," Estrella said. "Looks like we missed a few and they moved to the city with me."

Peters' eyes behind his reading glasses focused on her. "Why didn't you tell us?"

"I was their victim," Estrella said, their faces didn't change. She went to show them proof, holding onto the left side of her shorts, pulling them down exposing her bare thighs and the scars. Everyone grimaced. "They take kids, do this to them, then sell the psytrip memory sphere experiences on the black market. That's why I went after them. I couldn't sit back and wait for confirmation since that is exactly what the cops did when the gang came for my family. By the time they confirmed they were IWs, and sent in the RWs, it was too late."

Showing the group her scars pulled Estrella's thoughts back to the bad old days when she got them. When she was held captive by the gang with other children taken in Buenos Aires. She was beaten, cut, raped, or forced to watch others go through the same thing. The experiences were captured by telepaths, transferred into memory spheres. Sick motherfuckers bought them to experience and relive that moment, over and over.

"I see," Peters replied, his voice sounding softer, sympathetic, and less suspecting of Estrella.

She was glad to hear it. "So, am I fired?"

"There's a major shortage of RWs in the city," Peters said. "So, no, as much as you fucked up your first day, we need you."

"Sounds like she's got intel on the gang too," Piper said. "Might be a good idea to keep her on this."

It was the words she was looking to hear, and from the least likely person, that mysterious RW pixie kiwi, Piper. Estrella glanced at her. Piper glanced back with another pleasing smile. Piper liked her, and she couldn't figure out why. She was the one that went to call Estrella out, showing the evidence of the wall and all.

How the fuck did she get those scans?

I am unsure how—

Wasn't talking to you Geoffrey, was thinking to myself.

I can hear your thoughts you know?

Yeah, that's going to take some time to get used to, my old AI didn't.

Peters faced Piper as she remained leaning in the darkened corner. "I want you on this Taylor," he said to her. "Rodriguez's past makes things personal. We can't afford to have another outbreak like that—"

"With all due respect," Estrella interjected, the tone of her voice raised. "But I did fight that gang back in Buenos Aires, and they were a rank above me."

Marcus nodded in agreement. "That's true, she's a rank C, and took them all out."

Peters grinned at Estrella and snorted. "I'm putting you and Desmond where the action is Rodriguez. I want you to patrol the IW populated areas of the city."

"Patrols?!" Estrella spat. "Give me a fucking break!"

"IW terrorists attacked the EU," Peters said. "Nobody knows who they are, why they did it, or where they'll strike next. If there's going to be an attack here in the Alliance then it'd be here, as we have the largest IW community in the world. We need to be ready to act if anything happens here."

Marcus gave Peters a nod. "Understood sir."

"Any questions?" No one said anything, though Estrella wanted to protest her new job, it wasn't going to get her the commendations she needed for Yoshida to reward her with a new post. Then again, she already landed in hot water with her new owners. Best to be the good girl, at this point, and take every chance at digging deeper in the mysterious resurrection of the Bald Skulls gang. And why did they follow her to LA? "Dismissed. And Desmond."

Marcus looked at Peters. "Yes, sir?"

"Keep your RW on a better leash, please? This fuck up is also on you."

Estrella made her way to the exit, stopping before it. She turned and faced Peters at his desk. "Wait. I'm on a leash now?"

"Weren't you sent here to work low-stress assignments anyway?" Peters said to her. "We'll take you off the leash when you get on Piper's level. Until then do your fucking job, or we'll ask Yoshida for a refund. This is the LAPD, not some fucking Buenos Aires mercenary group. Things are different here, Rodriguez."

Estrella didn't wait for Marcus to catch up with her as she stormed out of the office. Piper, the pixie kiwi, called out to her. She faced her and saw the nudge of her head, a nonverbal come-hither look. She did.

"He's trying to protect you," Piper said. "We've lost a lot of good RWs in the last year because of violent IWs. Hotheaded ones like you get put on patrols, where you can't die."

"I didn't sell my humanity to Yoshida, and then move across the Alliance, against my will, to patrol the streets."

"Then step up your game, new girl. And you can start by following orders and not nearly getting yourself and your partner killed."

TEN
RAY

The Alliance Star was the country's most-read news publication and home to some of the nation's most talented investigative journalists. Its office was ninety-seven floors up in one of the most dominant towers in downtown Los Angeles. From that height at night, the cars from the bright urban jungle below looked like pinpricks of white light moving on the purple and pink neon glowing streets.

The newsroom was devoid of people at their desks by the time Ray stepped out of the elevator, marching past a decorative plant or four in the halls. The chair that idled at his cubicle was cold. Ray spent the last few hours writing his article on his tablet pad in his car rather than doing it at his desk.

The events of the apartment attack were too fresh on his mind to wait, that and traffic really sucked. Case in point, he arrived with the article complete, rather than racing to his desk to write it. Self-driving cars were a time saver. He wondered how people a century ago survived without them.

The Alliance Star's editor-in-chief Steven Jarrod was in his office, a glass-enclosed room off in the far end of the newsroom. It had the best view of the downtown LA skyline, and all the air transports zipping back and forth, adding to the city's light pollution nobody gave a fuck about anymore. Rainwater trickled down from the blackened skies, giving the city twenty-five percent of its annual rainfall. Climate change was a bitch.

Steven faced Ray as he entered, shutting the glass door behind. The aging editor ran a hand through his brown receding hair while Ray tossed his report on his pad to him. It spun around across the surface of the desk until Steven caught it and lifted it up to read it. Ten minutes of silence followed as Steven read the report. Ray took a seat and waited for what came next.

Everything in the report was the truth. IWs attacked the apartment unit of a family of three, who were nowhere to be found when the police arrived, the RW Estrella Rodriguez who was acting strange, and the wall that showed hard evidence that a nanite swarm took it apart, then put it back together. Only an RW could do that, and Ray knew damn well who the last and probably only RW that was in the unit. And he found the family of three hiding in the next-door unit, which was supposed to be vacant.

Steven shook his head, sliding Ray's pad back across the desk to him. "I'm not sure about this one, Ray."

"Nobody wanted to comment," Ray said, picking the pad up. "Either I write what every other publication is—that there were IWs killed at the apartment. Or we run this, which dives more into what's going on."

"A story about a hotheaded RW that disobeyed orders, and now the LAPD thinks she allowed the family to escape and avoid a police investigation?"

"It's the truth according to my source," Ray said, thinking back to the recent text message Piper sent him. Apparently, Captain Peters sat down with Estrella, and she tried to lie her way out of it. "And she's been very reliable, as you know."

"I don't doubt that."

"And let's not forget, the police have told no one what

Rodriguez may or may not have done. Why? Because they don't want anyone to know. We can be the whistleblowers with this! Think about it! Us, our publication."

"Ray ..."

"Just trust me on this."

Steven sighed and facepalmed. He sat on his chair ahead of his wide window peering out into the bright light skyline. "Who produces the hardware and nanites for RWs? Hell, who the fuck created the RWs in the first place to combat the growing IW problem?"

It was Ray's turn to sigh. "Yoshida Corp."

"And who's our biggest advertiser?"

"Yoshida Corp."

"And what do you think they'll do when they see us calling out the LAPD that relies on RWs to keep order in the IW populated areas, and call into question the mental state of an RW?"

"Give us a popsicle I hope." Given the heatwave battering the city, Ray could have gone for one.

"They'll fucking pull all their ads, then we can't afford to keep this place running, then I can't afford to pay your salary. I get it, Ray, you're all about this journalistic integrity bullshit from yesteryears. But it's the eighties, nobody cares about that. Half the people that come across our stories on their social media feeds, are too fucking stupid or to fucking busy posting pictures of their dick or tits, to see if its fake or not."

"It's the truth!"

"Yeah, the truth nobody needs to know. Change it or we're not printing it. I can't risk the repercussions if we do."

"Change it into what?"

"I made some suggestions."

Ray looked at his pad and the eight-thousand-word article he wrote and went through a lot of trouble to get, with what little facts were available. He tapped through the screen, noting the brief suggested changes Steven made.

He stopped reading when Estrella was called 'a heroic figure.'

"This doesn't explain the wall," Ray said, waving the pad about. "Or the fact I found the family hiding in the vacant room!"

"Just leave that out for now," Steven spat. "If the cops come clean about that RW, then we can post a follow-up report. Until then, we go with this."

"No, no, no, you don't understand! This is the scoop; what I wrote is fact; facts I verified. Those facts will make our story unique. If you want to increase revenue, this is what we need to do, deliver what you can't find anywhere else."

"Did you forget about Yoshida already?"

"Screw them, we have other advertisers."

"So, you did forget. Okay, let me break it down for you like you're five."

Ray rolled his eyes. "Oh, my fucking god."

"Well, you're acting like a fucking kid, Ray, so I'm gonna talk to you like you're one. Our version of the news makes money; your version of it will make some of us homeless."

"Some?"

"I can't dance, and I don't have tits, so there's no quick backup for me if I lose this job."

Ray spent his entire career as a journalist telling the truth, regardless if it was painful to learn or not. Not once did he lie or make something up to make the editor happy. He did everything by the book, diligently following the nine principles of journalism. His instructor in college drilled those principles into his head over and over every class. By the second month of college, Ray could recite that list, and in order, without thinking.

He flung the pad back to Steven, sending it sliding across the desk. *Steven should be ashamed of himself, hell the whole fucking industry should.* "I refuse to write that!"

"Then get the fuck out of my office! I'll have someone else do it!"

"Fine, just keep my name off it!"

Ray left the office with his tablet in hand, fuming, cursing, and nearly tripping over a pot of decorative plants on his way to the elevator. He asked himself why he gave up the life of a hacker to be a journalist as the slow ride of the elevator plunged to the main floor. At least the juicy news he came across could be posted freely, without asshole bosses working as gatekeepers.

A smile stretched on his face. A new idea came to light.

He reached for his tablet and swiped away the typed article. Somewhere buried within the device was the old username and password to a secret blog he once operated, back before he dropped out of the hacker's scene. The blog was still online, still gathering followers, still getting pages read, despite being inactive for years.

DigiSamurai69 was about to make a comeback.

Out into the rain, Ray walked, moving away from the office tower the Alliance Star newsroom was in. The puddles with dripping water from the heavens reflected the neon allure of the city around him. Ray's drive home was full of thoughts of how the world and the underground hacking scene would react when his rejected news report appears on his soon to be resurrected blog.

———

The rain let up by the time Ray made it back to his apartment in the middle of district three, a humans only area in the city sporting high rent prices, but low crime. It was a fair trade. Motion sensors detected his presence as he strode in, activating the lights. His closet door slid open at a wave of his hand near a black and gold sensor. His dripping raincoat was left to hang and dry beside dark trench coats and business wear.

In the living room, a dark blue hue seeped in from the

window where his personal computer idled on a desk. Long, translucent strains of water dripped down the exterior surface of the glass. Three sky busses buzzed in the empty void between his apartment, and the others across from it. It was the closest thing to a flying car people would see, and for good reason. Car crashes were still one of the leading causes of death in most urban areas, even with the autopilot feature. Giving driver's licenses for flying cars would bring about the end of human and witch life in the city.

He sat at his desk grinning when the dual screens of his computer turned on. One synced with the contents of his tablet pad, and the other displayed his desktop. The desktop picture was a photo of Arianna lying in a garden full of freshly grown, pink and white petalled flowers without a care in the world.

Arianna ...

His phone showed no missed calls or messages from her. The sound of the ringtone ringing over and over when he called her was worrying. A follow-up text message was sent after three unsuccessful attempts at reaching her. News from the EU had yet to reveal the names of those killed in the terrorist attack.

Belly growls took his worrying head off the matter. Ray skipped dinner and was paying the price. A quick type and move of his computer mouse brought up a listing of food available for drone meal deliveries. Options he couldn't afford were grayed out. He placed an order for a cheap half-pound sirloin steak, and fries. The estimated delivery time was twenty minutes, the downside to ordering food during off-peak times. Most drones were in their garages, receiving maintenance and fresh batteries in preparation for breakfast deliveries in the morning.

He wondered how people at the turn of the twenty-first century survived. Having to go to a grocery store, then prepare and cook food in a kitchen inside of your home seemed like such a hassle. Yeah, back in those days you could order a pizza, but you had to pay a delivery fee and tip the driver. Drones don't need tips, and can deliver more than just pizzas—

Ray's phone rang. The name Arianna Kounias appeared on the transparent device as did her number. He felt his heart in his throat and wasted no time accepting the call with a tap of his thumb. Arianna's face appeared, smiling at the man she loved.

"Arianna! Thank God you're all right. How's the EU treating you?"

"I'm fine. I miss the sunny skies of LA, though."

"It wasn't so sunny today."

"Really?"

"Yeah check it out." He pointed the phone at the window, its cameras sending the imagery of the rainwater sliding down its surface. She laughed and he flipped the phone back, making it face him. "It's finally starting to let up now. So, how was your day?"

"Oh, you know, boring stuff, corporate acquisitions and whatnot," she said calmly. Then winced. "Oh, and there was that terrorist attack."

"I heard about that. Were you close to it?"

"It happened in Munich. I'm in London right now, just got in a minute ago. Going to be catching a flight to the Alliance soon, New York, then to Los Angeles."

He couldn't wait, nor could the engagement ring sitting on the desk ahead of him, out of her view of course, with the angle he had the phone at. The purchase of the ring was on the premature side, as he did it before speaking with her father, Norris. But Ray had a good feeling about that act. Arianna was the one. His future wife, and future mother of their children.

"Oh, babe! Check this out." He saw her face look away from the screen, the hotel she was in letting in sunlight from the European morning. When Arianna's face returned to face the screen, she was wearing a crown made of flowers overtop her brown hair full of elegant curls. "Remember these things?"

He smiled, thinking back to that one summer five years ago. "Yeah, you had that on the day we met."

"You said I looked like a hippy."

"You had that white dress, soy ice cream, and that crown on, singing to yourself in the park. What was I supposed to say?"

"I was high too!" Her words produced a light chuckle from Ray, breaking the hypnotic trance her blue eyes always put him in. "What you should have said was, where can I get what you were smoking."

"Would we be having this chat right now if I did?"

She smiled, because in truth, they wouldn't. His hippy comment made her giggle, and it was her giggle that fueled a strange yearning to know more about her, especially what it was that made her smile, so he could use that thing and make her smile all the time.

On the screen, Arianna used her free hand, lifting the flower crown off her head, the other still holding onto her phone. Ray grimaced, his eyes noticing the bandages wrapped around her arm.

"What happened to your arm?" he asked her.

"This?" Arianna looked down at the bandages. Her grin faded, as did the positive mood the two were sharing. After a five-second pause, she said. "Just an accident."

"You okay?"

She remained silent, grimaced, then looked away from the arm, back at him via the screen. "Yeah, I'm good. Hey, I gotta head out."

"Oh—"

A buzzer sounded. To Ray's right, was the hovering delivery drone outside his balcony glass door. Twenty minutes went by fast. Ray's food was awaiting him.

"Sounds like you do as well, Ray," Arianna said. "You got food waiting for you. Soy-based protein I hope?"

He grinned and stood from his chair, walking to the balcony

door, keeping the phone in his hands at his face. "We'll talk again later. I love you, Arianna."

She blew him a kiss. "I love you, Ray."

A call end notification flashed. Ray pocketed his phone, freeing his hands to slide the balcony door open and greet the delivery drone. The robotic device opened, and he felt a rush of warm air hit his face as he reached for the contents within, a small thermal box full of the food he ordered.

The drone spoke with a pre-recorded thank you for your business message, and then flew off into glowing neon and tapering rain. Ray returned inside and prying off the lid of the box, his nostrils twitched with excitement: fresh steak, and fries, grown from the finest selection of stem cells. It was the closest to the real thing you could get, and it wasn't soy-based, his little secret from Arianna as she was away from home.

And he couldn't wait for her to get back home too. If she was here, and knew about the grilling he got from Stevens, she would have rolled a fat blunt and shared it with him. They'd get high watching movies together, munching on snacks, before falling asleep in each other's arms, with a big grin. His heart reminded him how much he missed her.

As he sat and ate, his eyes remained on the engagement ring in its box. His mind drifted for a moment, wondering how she'd react when he put it on her delicate fingers, attached to her slim hand and arm, a bandaged arm at that.

How does a businesswoman like her get a bandage like that on her arm?

ELEVEN
ESTRELLA

Within the bowels of the LAPD HQ a frustrated Estrella stood looking at a glossy map of the city pinned to a wall. Behind her were the desks and computers of various personnel at the station, the blue and white glow from their screens illuminating the back of Estrella's body.

In the background, she heard a few street cops drag in the walking human trash from the city for processing. Cyborg RWs with their silver NC gauntlets carried in the walking IW trash from the IW districts, most of them unregistered IWs, according to her facial scans, though she did spot several registered IWs brought in with cuffs. Even registered IWs had to obey human laws, sometimes.

An RW Estrella couldn't scrub from her thoughts approached her from the side.

"You've been looking at that for a while," said Piper in her kiwi accent.

It made Estrella grin. She needed it after identifying where her new pad was. "Trying to hope this is a joke ..."

Piper moved closer, fixing her stare on the map that had Estrella's attention. She grimaced. "What?"

Estrella handed Piper a torn-off piece of paper. It had a quick handwritten address on it. "They gave me the keys to this place," she said then pointed at the map. "It's right in the middle of the ..."

Piper's synthetic eyes zeroed in on where Estrella pointed on the map. She beamed. "Ha! The IW district!"

"This is a joke." Estrella looked at her. "Right?"

"The IWs there are all registered, so you've got nothing to fear."

"Except for the unregistered ones hanging out there."

"Rent is cheap in the IW district. That's probably why they assigned that place to you."

"Now I know why you guys are understaffed," Estrella said, with arms crossed, facing the wall map of Los Angeles again. "I mean if you make all your new RWs live in the heart of enemy territory."

Piper's elbow playfully nudged Estrella's synthetic arm. "Ah, someone afraid to go home for the night?"

Estrella was silent. Living within the IW district only brought back the feeling of ants crawling at the back of her neck. When the Bald Skulls gang was busy with her as a child, back in Buenos Aires, she was living in an IW district. Those weren't happy times, and she doubted living in LA's IW district would be better, even with her RW powers.

"Why the fuck would they have me live there?"

"They didn't have much of a choice," Piper explained. "The humans living in districts like that are getting fed up with witches, and vice versa. The humans upped and left for less witch-populated areas, meaning rent prices dropped since vacancies skyrocketed. As for elsewhere—"

"Let me guess, the cost of living went up as the availability dropped."

Piper shrugged, lifting her exposed shoulders beneath her lace robe. "Pretty much. Almost daily we had RWs killed when they were called in to detain an unregistered IW, or a registered one acting stupid. Say, how are you getting up there anyway?"

"Was hoping Marcus would give me a ride," Estrella said. "Still haven't gotten my wheels. I got off my flight and came in for work."

"He went home, love."

Estrella sighed loudly, tilting her gaze to the ceiling, facepalming. "Of course he did."

"Do you know the transit system?"

"Not very well. I guess my AI, Geoffrey, will have to guide me."

That I could, Geoffrey offered. *Would you like me to do so?*

Piper's synthetic arm split apart, and she reached for the car keys stored inside it and a pack of cigarettes and a lighter. The arm contorted back to its original state, masquerading as flesh, bone, and blood. It was much better than Estrella's arm. At close range, you could tell Estrella's arm wasn't real. Piper's arm looked like the real deal until it opened. She wondered what it would feel like to run a finger across it.

"I'll give you lift," Piper said. "I'm done here anyway."

"You don't have to."

"But I'm going to, so get in, new girl." Piper smiled again, the Mona Lisa-like one from the meeting. Estrella couldn't say no anymore.

The RW duo left the police HQ with Piper leading the way, her black lace robe waving about in the winds that stopped blowing the rain from earlier. Estrella never realized how much effort RWs went to dress like witches until that moment while looking at Piper's figure, wearing the black leather skirt, bodice, and lace robe. Even the other RWs she saw at the station were dressed like that, not that it mattered, there was no dress code for RWs.

Estrella splashed through the puddles in the parking lot, and Piper's heels clicked through it while she pulled a single cigarette from the pack and lit it, took a puff, and smiled. Piper placed the cigarette pack and lighter back inside her synthetic arm. The sound of water splashing below made the kiwi RW stop and look down.

"Oh blast, I forgot I was wearing these," Piper said. Her NC gauntlet brightened, spraying a small nanite swarm over her high heeled shoes. They turned into gray goo and remodeled into flat shoes. "Much better!"

Piper drove an expensive sports car so eye-catching Estrella had to pause for dramatic effect when she saw it. They lowered themselves into her car, Piper taking the wheel, and Estrella sitting shotgun. The holographic form of a black cat flicked into existence on Estrella's lap as the car's computer powered on, confirming Piper's identity.

Piper set the car to autopilot after inputting the address into its dashboard screen. The car sped off, leaving the parking lot, merging into the wet streets, kicking up fallen rainwater behind it, carving a path to the freeway alongside hundreds of vehicles on the road. The auto-pilot feature gave Piper ample time to indulge on her lit cigarette cradling between her index and middle finger. An overwhelming blast of advertisements floating in the skies kept Estrella's attention, as purple and pink neon glow shined on her face during the Los Angeles night drive.

"I hope you don't mind the smoke," Piper said, then took another puff. "It's been a long day."

Estrella's nose twitched when the smoke neared her face. "Your body might."

"Life support nanites will remove all the cancer-causing shit."

"And drain your battery faster."

When Piper's smoke was finished, she flicked the cigarette butt out the window. The AI cat on Estrella's lap caught her attention when she saw its reflection on the driver's side window. "Cute AI you got there."

Estrella grunted. "So does your AI appear as a black cat?"

"Nope." Piper waved her NC gauntlet right hand. A black raven appeared and perched itself on Piper's shoulder.

The holographic raven spoke to Estrella, its voice played through the car's speakers. "Pleasure to meet you, my name is Akane."

It made her look down at the black cat, then up at the raven. Estrella grimaced. "I wish I had a badass raven."

"They're just holograms," Piper said, "Doesn't matter what they choose to appear as."

She shrugged. "Still, you know, aesthetics."

Piper grinned, and if she wasn't looking at the urban sprawl move past the window, Estrella suspected it would have been directed at her. "You've got all the aesthetics needed for your duo."

Estrella flushed. "Wha'?"

"Don't mind her," the talking holographic raven, Akane, said. "She is always like this with new people she wishes to—" The raven paused while computer code rained down its eyes. "Piper, you have an incoming call, do you wish to pick it up?"

Piper let out a groan and with one hand reached for her vibrating phone. "Hands-free me."

Akane nodded. "As you wish."

Piper's AI remotely accessed her phone, setting it to hands-free mode. There were no video interactions, just audio.

"Ni Hao," Piper said. The woman on the phone replied with the same words. A long conversation in a language Estrella guessed was Chinese ensured.

What are you thinking Estrella?

Estrella let out a soft exhale amidst Piper's phone conversation. Kiwi woman, mid-thirties, limited facial scan data, and speaks Chinese fluently. *Piper's not from around here.*

Indeed, I have been running scans of her—

Why are you scanning her?

I have yet to encounter an RW like her. There is something strange about her I can't quite identify. Her cyberware is vastly different too. I do not believe Yoshida manufactured them.

Who were they made by then?

Unknown. It is possible she is a new RW model, or perhaps a unit in testing. It may explain the errors when running facial scans.

Yoshida doesn't want anyone to identify her.

That could be the case.

If she's a new model, or prototype, then why the fuck is she being leased out to the LAPD?

Unknown.

"Sorry about that," Piper said as she finished the phone call. Her face had turned sour, "that ... that was my ex-wife with some bullshit reason why I can't visit our daughter."

Estrella snorted. "You don't strike me as a family woman."

"Now why's that?"

"Because moving from the Federation to the Alliance isn't easy."

"What makes you think I'm from the Federation?"

"Your kiwi accent, your AI has a Japanese name, and you speak Chinese fluently." The car was on the freeway at that point, driving under raised highway overpasses between the space of monolithic buildings dotted with lights from its windows. "I'm going to assume your ex-wife still lives in the Federation with your daughter?"

Piper smirked, keeping her eyes forward. "You're a smart girl, new girl."

"Meh, I try," Estrella said, shrugging. "Guess you two got a divorce over differences?"

"Maybe."

"Most people from Australia and New Zealand were opposed to the idea of paying taxes to Beijing, especially during the war. I guess you were part of the resistance, and she didn't want any part of it, and kept the kid."

"As I said, you're a smart girl, new girl." Piper's tongue glided across her upper lip. "Except, you got one thing wrong."

"And that is?"

"She kept the kid because we had her egg fertilized. When I lost that rock, paper, scissors match, I didn't just lose the chance to go through the pregnancy, I lost my ..."

Piper never finished those words.

"That would explain why you sold your humanity to Yoshida," Estrella said. "You came across the pacific to the Alliance, broke as fuck like all Federation refugees, and got that offer: sell your body to Yoshida. You remind me of a close personal friend of mine, Yumi. She came from the Federation, Korea. We became room-mates. Taught me a lot about the Federation and what you people have to deal with. She wasn't broke as fuck though, she became an RW because she wanted to." Piper grimaced. Estrella went too far. "Eh, don't tell me your story, it really isn't my business."

"So enough about me, what about you, new girl? What brings you to sunny LA?"

"Take a guess," Estrella grunted. "Let's see how much of a smart girl *you are*."

"You requested a transfer to chase love."

"Guess again."

"You came here for family?"

"All dead, except my aunt and uncle and their kids."

Piper gasped. "Oh, I'm sorry."

"Don't be, I killed the IWs responsible in the end."

"You mean the gang that's back and followed you here?"

"Don't know if they followed me." Estrella shrugged and noticed the signs on the road. They were nearing District 666. *That can't be the fucking name of the place.*

It is, Geoffrey revealed. *They originally called it District 6; someone defaced the sign and added the second and third six. It got both IWs and humans laughing, and so they kept it.*

That's funny as fuck—

A pause made her face become still. She was in the middle of a chat with Piper and then jumped into one with her AI.

Estrella continued. "But it's strange that they suddenly came back from the dead, then came to LA of all places when I get off the fucking plane."

Not to mention targeted an IW family living in secret.

Shut up, Geoffrey!

This is a secure connection. Piper's AI cannot access it.

"Guess I'm not as smart as you," Piper said. "So, what's the reason?"

"I tried putting a bullet in my old boss."

"And so, Yoshida sent you here hoping an IW put a bullet in you. I bet you're regretting becoming an RW now, aren't you?"

"Not really, I needed cash when I signed up," Estrella said, as she reclined on the chair with her hands behind her head. "You know how it is? Got money problems? Depression? Out of work? Scared of losing your job? Sell your humanity to Yoshida; let them jam it with cyberware."

"You'll never have to worry about money, paying taxes, or aging," Piper spoke like she was a salesperson. "Yep, I got that same pamphlet. Now, here we are, getting pimped out like whores."

"How so?"

"Think about it? Yoshida's the pimp. Private security, military, mercenaries, LAPD, and other groups that have problems with rowdy IWs, are the paying clients. You, me, and the other RWs? We're the working girls, gotta make those clients happy so we get whatever cut the pimps, Yoshida, gives us. Makes you wish you'd just become a dancer instead doesn't it?"

"Not really."

"Why not? You got a nice body for it."

Another flush changed the tone of Estrella's face, right when it had returned to normal. She kept it to the passenger side window and then sighed at the signs hanging from the overpass they were poised to drive under. District 666 keep right.

"Remember those scars I got?"

Piper bit her lip. "Oh."

"Who wants to pay top dollar for a lap dance from a cut-up girl? And like I said earlier, I had unfinished business with the IW gang that did this to me. Can't kill them as an eighteen-year-old human girl, I could as an RW."

"You're eighteen?"

"Nineteen now, been at this for a year."

A half-hour later Piper's car drove through what looked like a maze of high-rise apartment units via zigzagging streets. The buildings were like walls keeping the car and others lost, some roads led to dead ends, while others went deeper into the district full of IWs. Every structure around had to have been at least a hundred stories in height. Air conditioning units hung from every other window, lights from the units made the apartment buildings glow yellow, green, and blue colors. Balconies had hanging laundry drying in the warm air, and THC smoke blew away from others. A homeless warlock wearing tattered clothes sat at the sidewalk lifting cupped hands for a change. The two witches walking past kept their eyes forward.

Piper's car came to a stop in front of the address Estrella directed her to, the front entrance to her apartment. Graffiti on pipes raged about RWs not being real witches and that they should all die. They were not comforting words to greet Estrella on her way to her new pad as she got out of the car. Piper joined her.

"Uh, I'm good from here, you know?" she said.

Piper kept walking with her anyway, shrugging. "Thought you might want some company."

Estrella glanced at the apartment building, its dark and gloomy atmosphere, and the empty beer cans littering the sidewalk. Her optical scanners picked up the flashing neon sign of an arcade and pizza hangout further in the distance. It was the only positive thing she saw.

"It's a rough place," Estrella said. "But I'll manage, I've been through worse with the gang."

"Well if you need anything or a lift, give me a call—"

Piper twitched, nearly tripping over the curb. Estrella was quick to run, grab, and hold her steady. Her arm brushed the skin of Piper's synthetic arm, it felt like the real deal.

"You're low, aren't you?" Estrella asked her.

Piper nodded, reaching for a switch at the back of her neck. When she tapped it, out sprung her battery, shaped roughly like a light bulb. Estrella saw the digital screen on the battery flash a low charge warning as Piper pulled it to her face, wincing. "Yep, was supposed to switch that one out when I got home. Guess I shouldn't have had that smoke."

And instead, Piper drove Estrella to her new home. A wave of guilt hit her while she held Piper still, looking up at the apartment.

"My stuff should have been delivered by now, right?"

Piper nodded. "Delivery drones are fast. Everything that belonged in your old place, should be here waiting for you."

"I packed a few extra batteries." Estrella dragged Piper with her beyond the glass sliding doors. "Guess you're following me up after all."

After a long elevator climb and a trek across halls that hadn't been swept in at least a year, Estrella found her unit. Inside was an empty place save for her boxes jam-packed with her belongings. She didn't pack any of it up. People from Yoshida did, probably during that two- or three-day gap she was getting her brains examined and her old AI torn out.

It made searching for the battery frustrating.

She ended up dumping the contents of three boxes on the floor. She hadn't been in her new place for two minutes, and it was already turning into a dump. Piper fell to the floor, leaning her back against the wall next to the exit. The glow from her emerald eyes faded, she was entering power conservation mode. Estrella needed to hurry before Piper's life faded.

The fourth box had two battery cells drop out amongst the contents within it. She swiped one quickly. Piper's eyes were locked into the contents of the box when Estrella approached her. She was probably thinking about what kind of person reads comic books in this day and age, as a bunch of them came folding out to random pages from the box.

Piper lowered her head. The back of her neck was facing Estrella who stood above her. Below the data ports Piper had at the back of her head was the still open slot waiting for a fresh battery. Estrella slipped it in and then folded the hatch covered in flesh shut.

There was a two-minute delay before Piper got to her feet, breathing with relief. The life-support nanites within her resumed their duties, while the cyberware in her had another day or two of juice to operate.

"Thanks," she said.

Estrella nodded. "I was out for two days before I got here. I got two extra cells that went unused."

Piper didn't make her way to the front door as Estrella figured she'd do. She tilted her head about as if she was running scans of the place. Piper patted her leather skirt free of the dust when a satisfied grin spread across her face.

"Well, it was a pleasure to meet you, new girl. See you then."

Piper went reaching for the front door with one hand, waving a flirty goodbye with the other. Estrella flushed as the RW vanished behind the door.

Something about Piper didn't sit right with her. Estrella had doubts she was making a new friend, more like she was about to be used. She held the spent battery, pulled from the back of Piper to her face. It was at thirty percent, low power yes, but not low enough for the act Piper pulled. Piper wanted in Estrella's place. Estrella beat herself up internally for falling for the trick.

What did Piper want? She was, after all, the RW that showed up with the scans of the wall Estrella used to hide the IW family of three. Piper never revealed who slipped her that information. Piper's serial number failed to show on her facial scans, and Piper was clearly from the People's Federation of Pacific Nations. The enemy of the Alliance, even in the post WWIII world.

Was Piper a spy from the Federation? No way, she was an RW, propriety of the Yoshida Corporation after she sold her body to them. If she was a spy, they would have outed her during her augmentation phase. Yoshida wouldn't have been that stupid.

Would they?

Geoffrey.

Yes, Estrella?

Bring up everything you can find on Piper Taylor from the police database and Yoshida.

TWELVE
RAY

Ray pushed his body up from the floor. He had made a miserable attempt at a jumping heel click. He didn't care that everyone in the Alliance Star's newsroom looked at him like he was an idiot for face-planting on the floor. Why? Because he did it. He resurrected his hackers' blog. His old followers were bathing him with more likes than he could count.

He kept his tablet close to his face as he walked to his cubicle. The screen showed the new comments and likes his post generated, the post about the truth of the IW apartment attack, the past day. His followers praised him for calling into question the actions of the RW, Estrella Rodriguez. How she might have covered something up in a crime scene, and then feigned ignorance when her superiors called her out. The truth was out. It made his ego grow, ever so slightly. He'd have to buy Piper coffee sometime for the tip—

"Ray!" The fuming face of the Alliance Star's editor-in-chief peered out from the glass office door. Steven was looking right at Ray. His finger was pointed at his desk. "Get the fuck in my office now!"

Ray shrugged, putting his pad away. "Get the fuck out of my office. Get the fuck in my office, make up your mind!"

"I'm not playing, get in now!"

Ray looked behind at the dozens of reporters as they stood from their desks eying him. Ray's ego was shrinking, as was his happy mood that had followed him up the elevator ride. He walked into the office, ready to face the music, ready to face the editor-in-chief.

More like, emperor-in-chief.

The door shut and locked behind him. No interruptions were allowed.

The glass dimmed to black with a tap of his computer console when Steven got to his desk. By the time Ray sat in front of the desk, Steven had pulled up the webpage of one notorious hacker from the past that came out of retirement last night, DigiSamurai69. He spun the screen around, making it face Ray, shining blue light across his paling face.

Ray grimaced. "Ah."

Steven tapped the computer screen. "What the fuck is this?"

"Heh."

"You think I'm fucking stupid? Like I wouldn't find out?"

"I don't use my real identity on that blog, there's no way it'd come back to us."

"I know who runs the blog though."

"Of course you do. It's why you gave me the job."

"And you're making us look bad! I had Alvin rewrite your story and we printed it." Steven scrolled down the post and into the comment's section, the same comments Ray was reading on this pad. He didn't need to read the comments on the screen, Ray already knew what they said.

Alliance Star is fake news!

DigiSamurai69 is the real hero this world needs.

I'm unsubbing from the Star, tired of this fake news shit. Thank you for giving us the truth!

"It's one thing to put out the news the way we see it," Steven continued. "It's another when people say we are fake news. This will hurt our numbers!"

A soft shrug lifted Ray's shoulders. "At least Yoshida won't pull their ads."

"If people aren't clicking ads, because well, there's nobody reading our stuff to click ... What do you think will happen?" Steven made a good point. Ray fucked up, and his cringing face showed it. "Our views today are already down twenty-three percent because of this ... Give me one reason not to fire you?"

Ray's body wanted to tremble with panic. He got the job because he always got results the publication wanted. A dirty cop was doing bad things? Ray knew which cameras in the city were hackable. A high paying corporate executive was suddenly fired? Ray browsing through hidden emails found out why. Ray was unfireable, he was the best reporter, and the Star needed him. They'd never get rid of him, he'd always thought to himself. It's what gave him the balls to raise his voice to Steven if things didn't go his way, like last night.

And at that moment, he felt his balls and dick shrivel up and want to go inside him.

Ray had to do something and fast. He had to say something to keep his job. This was not the time to be losing it. "Because I still haven't finished making the payments on the ring," he finally spoke.

Steven lifted an eyebrow. "Ring?"

"For Arianna. I wanted to propose to her."

"Well, looks like you're in the shit now."

"Sir, please," Ray said, surprised he didn't fold his hands together in prayer. "It ... it wasn't my intention to fuck you over like that."

"I don't know, after yesterday, you could have fooled me."

"Let me fix this! Please, I need to make payments on the ring!"

Steven sat back, peering into Ray's soul while twirling a pen with his fingers. "Yoshida wants us to run something that will make them look good, assuming we'll have readers left by the end of the month. People thinking RWs like Rodriguez is the norm is going to hurt them. We've been given a damage control assignment."

"Give me the story."

"You? Mister truth, justice and the Alliance way?"

Ray's panic was in the driver's seat now. Gone were Ray's moral code and journalistic integrity. The chat he had with Arianna last night only made him love her more, and that flower crown she picked up, she'd look so elegant with it during their wedding. He had to get that ring paid for. There's no guarantee another job would be available, not in the overpopulated world he lived in with unemployment lines that went on for days. There was a reason people sold their bodies to Yoshida and became RWs.

Fuck that noise.

"Yoshida's hosting a tech convention in New York," Steven said. "We weren't going to cover it originally. But if you get your ass there—"

"I'll cover the show, and do interviews, whatever you need."

Steven pointed the end of the pen at Ray's pale face. "Don't fuck this one up; this is your last chance with me."

There was one other rule of journalism Ray had learned in school but forgot about, only to be reminded of it now. You're only as good as your last article. It didn't matter how many good ones you wrote, if the last one you did was shit, then you are shit. If the last one you wrote was fucking amazing, then you were *fucking* amazing.

Steven was willing to ignore all the good Ray did for the Star, because of the blog post. And he was going to forgive him, if he made Yoshida a happy paying advertising client, one that wouldn't pull ads even though they see a drop in clicks, and sales of their many products and services.

The assignment was Ray's and he left the office in a hurry. He grabbed his phone and tapped through an air flight booking app, booking a flight from Los Angeles to New York. The app reported it withdrew the appropriate funds from his account.

He stopped shy of the elevator doors, thinking back to the conversation he had with Arianna last night.

It happened in Munich, I'm in London right now, just got in a minute ago. Going to be catching a flight to the Alliance soon, New York, then to Los Angeles.

Arianna's layover was in New York.

He dialed her number. He got the voicemail.

"Hey babe, guess what? I'll be in New York very soon, gonna be covering a trade show. Let me know when your flight arrives. Maybe we can hang out for a bit then return to LA together? Call me when you get this message, love ya."

On his way back to his apartment to pack, his tablet pad beeped. A new comment was posted on his blog.

Makes you wonder, why would IWs target a poor family of three like that?

That's a good question, he thought. *Why did that IW gang target them, and nobody else in the building?*

THIRTEEN
ESTRELLA

Piper Taylor, age thirty-five in human years, four in RW. She was originally from Auckland before becoming a refugee in the Alliance, having fled the Federation. There wasn't more to say about her life there. The Federation was pretty big on censorship and keeping foreign eyes out from its network.

If the stories Yumi told Estrella were true, Auckland was home to several underground resistance cells fighting a losing war to liberate the pacific island from Beijing's rule. Piper was likely one of those resistance fighters before the military came down on her hard, forcing her to escape across the big blue pond, landing in Los Angeles.

Falling asleep with Piper's profile open got Estrella dreaming about her. She was back in the car ride to her place, and Piper came into her place from behind. When Estrella turned, the dream Piper transformed into Yumi, her old roommate from Buenos Aires. Yumi was always behind Estrella when she came home. It didn't matter if Estrella had been returning from a mission, or stepped out for a walk, Yumi refused to be alone in their apartment. She was okay with that, Yumi always had a way to dispel Estrella's negative thoughts, especially if they got back from a mission gone wrong.

The dream Yumi sat with Estrella on her bed, commenting on how much more space her new place had compared to the small one-bedroom unit they shared in Buenos Aires. Dream Yumi rested her head and short black hair on Estrella's shoulder. She told Estrella that she missed her, and not to let her absence hold her back from being happy. Estrella groaned in reply.

Yumi offered a backrub, hoping it would make her happy. She accepted, and Yumi went behind Estrella, she felt a synthetic hand on one shoulder, and another made of flesh on the other. The dream was too real. Estrella didn't want to wake up and told herself everything else had been the dream. She wanted the dream she was experiencing to be a reality.

Estrella's phone rang in the dream. Yumi grabbed it, glanced at the screen, and handed it to her. She told Estrella it was an important call.

———

A ringing noise forced Estrella's eyes open. She ignored it, so the noise ignored her nonverbal way of saying fuck off. She wanted to continue sleeping. The noise didn't stop, and neither did the thin rays of sunlight beaming in from her window.

You have an incoming call, Estrella.

She buried her face in her pillow. *You don't say.*

Estrella moved her head to the left and saw the wall. She forgot her new pad had her bed placed inside a large cubbyhole inside the apartment. There was only one way her body could roll out of bed, to the right. She looked in that direction and saw a holographic black cat sitting on a coffee table, gesturing to her phone resting on it. It caused the noise.

The call is from your relative, would you like me to take a message?

"Oh fuck!"

She rolled out of bed swiftly and then cursed once more when her left foot got stuck in the small garbage pail she left next to it. It went flying across her unit, hitting the metal wall with a thud. She'd have to choose a better place for that when she returned to unpacking.

Estrella ran for the phone, slipping it into her right hand, free from the NC gauntlet. That too lay on the table. Her right hand and arm were marked by tiny holes pricked by the gauntlet as it transferred utility nanites to or from it.

Her thumb was seconds away from accepting the call when she looked down and saw the panties she wore and her bare breasts further up from it. She opted for an audio only call. It was probably for the best since the holographic pictures of Piper and her dossier were floating near her bed, near the table, near everywhere. It looked like Estrella was plotting to stalk Piper. Too bad the data Geoffrey found contained nothing Piper didn't already explain.

"Hola como estas!" *Hi how are you.*

Estrella grinned at the sound of the voice. "Hola como estas tía Anna." *Hi how are you Aunt Anna?*

"¿Has llegado a salvo a Los Angeles?" *Have you arrived safely to Los Angeles?*

"Si estoy bien." *Yes, I am fine.*

She continued to speak with her aunt, the woman that helped raise Estrella after she was rescued from the Bald Skulls gang's captivity. She never had the chance to say goodbye to Anna, or give her the heads up of her transfer to LA. Anna heard of the transfer from some rep in Yoshida, spitting a bullshit story that Estrella needed stress relief, grieving over the loss of Yumi, and sought to do it right away.

Anna calmed Estrella's thoughts as she walked around her unit during the call, informing her she received the money transfer Estrella sent before confronting Ricardo. She gave the air-conditioner a firm strike with her synthetic fist which left a fist-sized dent on it. It shut off at least three times during the night. There was a reason Estrella ended up stripping down to her panties, and why she was in no hurry to cover her sweat-drenched body, while beads of sweat formed at the tips of her nipples.

She appreciated the call when the chat was coming to an end. The warm feeling in Estrella's chest was proof that somewhere, out in the fucked-up world that humans continue to ruin every year, there was a person who still cared for her wellbeing, and supported her choice of becoming an RW, going in for the operation that turned her body into a network of wires, cyberware, and a colony of nanites, working around the clock to maintain the genetic manipulation done to her body.

A voice told her that attacking Ricardo might have been a mistake. She'd still be in Buenos Aires if she hadn't, close to family and friends, with the ability to mourn the loss of another correctly. On the other hand, Ricardo was going to keep telling lies to Yoshida that Estrella wasn't worth the fees he was paying for service. He always viewed RWs as trash, untalented and uneducated people that couldn't make it as anything else in life, not even as a sex worker.

With the call over, Estrella flicked away the screens with Piper's flawless smile, the last images she saw before nodding off. She knelt before the pile of her stuff dumped from the moving boxes, still a mess all over the floor, ignoring the heat from the sunlight shining on her bare back, and long black hair sticking to it. She had Geoffrey remotely activate the radio. It was the only form of entertainment until she found a place to put her TV.

Sifting through the comic books, she looked for several items of importance. She couldn't start the day without them. The first item was found after a minute, her toothbrush and paste. The second item was found in the fourth box she dumped out for Piper, an unused battery.

Standing up, Estrella reached behind, parting her long dark hair, searching for the set of data ports above the small hatch for her battery. She pulled out the old battery, throwing it no place in particular, and replacing it with a fresh one. She felt the life-support nanites swimming in her blood move up to the back of her head, like hungry fish in a tank during feeding time. The battery sent jolts of energy to nanites that linked up with it inside her, recharging their internal cells. RWs that couldn't supply energy to their life-support nanites didn't live very long, cyberware also needed power too, and the battery gave it that.

The cyberware in her body produced harmful toxins as a byproduct, the nanites worked to cleanse the body of that. They also prevented cells from making the body age, conducted mainte-nance, and prevented what little humanity RWs had left from rejecting the implants and genetic enhancements.

Some argued it was a gimmick Yoshida developed to keep RWs loyal. Only Yoshida provided the replacement batteries. If an RW went rogue, they'd be dead in a day or two without a new battery, and no RW would risk sharing theirs. Yoshida made sure to only deliver enough to last a week at best, further reminding RWs who was truly their lord and savior. Throw in utility nanites, which also sapped energy life from the battery when injected into the body, and RWs during combat situations could find themselves burning through battery power faster, pleading to Yoshida for more.

It was a drug made of technology to control and prevent RWs from rebelling as IWs did, and Estrella was addicted, and had been the day she sold her humanity for the almighty Alliance dollar. She couldn't get agitated about it, that's what the rule book said, and she knew it when signing up for this life. There was another reason she couldn't get agitated about it; she was focused on brushing her teeth.

She was in front of the bathroom mirror at that point, still half-naked in front eyeing the augmentation done to her body, and the scars left on it from her past, her breasts shook slightly with each stroke of her toothbrush. The bullet holes in her body were long gone, and not a mark was left on her tanned skin. The existing scars would never be healed, however as she received those during her days as a human. The nanites could only heal new wounds received as an RW.

A holographic black cat leaped on the countertop as she finished spitting out the mint-flavored foam from her mouth.

You seem ill, yet I detect no signs of viral or bacterial infections, nor any allergic reactions.

She cupped a stream of running water in her hands from the tap, splashing it upward, washing away the lingering toothpaste foam from her lips. *Just not looking forward to patrolling jobs. Thought we'd be doing what we do best, keeping IWs in their place.*

There is a strategic value to this. We can now gain a better lay of the land and the population. Such data and experiences may become valuable when we are finally able to, as you put it, keep IWs in their place.

My aunt thinks I'm already doing that. Every day that we do patrols, I'm lying to her and my family back home.

I'm sure they will be proud of what you've achieved regardless.

No, they wanted me to move on up. They were all cheering me on when I became what I am. And now I fucked up and ruined it, I couldn't protect Yumi when she needed me to, and then I ended up socking Ricardo for it. And so far, it looks I'm on a train to fuck this last chance Yoshida's giving me.

It is my understanding that you were made a victim to the Bald Skulls, correct?

Yeah.

So, isn't this a move up? Isn't this something your family could be proud of? They took you in after you were rescued from the gang and raised you the best they could given the physical and psychological trauma you were forced to endure.

With her teeth brushed came a much-needed shower. It was easy enough to do that, just slip out of the panties and leap in. It was her first time showering alone since she met Yumi. The thought made her chest hurt. When she was finished washing away the survivor's guilt and sticky sweat from her body, and cooling it down with chilly water, she left the washroom and didn't bother to dress up. There was a reason for that. She motioned joyfully, looking down at the pile of her belongings on the floor near the fourth box she emptied.

Oh, hey, Geoffrey?

Yes, Estrella?

Possible I could get, uh, some privacy?

I'm part of you. You know there is no true privacy. Furthermore, I am simply an AI.

Just, drop the cat image for a bit.

As you wish. May I ask why?

She found the reason why, a pink tubular-shaped object. *I got a hot date with my vibrator.*

Estrella didn't get far with the toy, the radio playing the news distracted her thoughts, and killed the desire to relieve stress, the real way, not the forced relocation way. Upping the volume on the radio allowed her to take in the words of the news broadcaster. They talked about the aftermath of the Bald Skulls assault on the apartment. She wasn't happy to hear her name get dragged through the mud.

Some hacker named DigiSamurai69 posted proof on their blog that the Alliance Star's report on the attack was fake news. She had no idea where her vibrator had tumbled off to. A fit of rage clouded her thoughts when she learned the hacker posted proof that an RW, her, melted the wall away, and then later the family of three was found hiding in the vacant neighboring room.

There was no mention that the family of three were unregistered IWs. She was in the clear for that. Still, learning that this hacker had all the intel Piper shared, had Estrella fuming enough to smash her hand on the table ahead of her.

That's how Piper got the intel.

Hmm?

Didn't you listen to the news?

You asked for privacy, so I went to idle mode.

Well, you can get out of it because I'm not getting off anytime soon, not after hearing that shit.

Piper wasn't at the scene, therefore the hacker was, physically. Estrella thought back to that night, thinking of every face she saw on her way out. One of those faces shouldn't have been there. It wasn't Marcus, he got shot with her. The EMTs? The other cops? They didn't look suspect. Who could it be?

Estrella gritted her teeth. *Ray Partington.*

The Alliance Star reporter?

Yeah, he was snooping around and then left.

I believe it was you and Marcus that left him.

The Star was also the first publication to report on the attack too. Fucking Partington must be the hacker.

And, therefore, he knows that the family was indeed at home at the time of the attack, unlike what the Star is reporting.

The radio report continued. "A bald warlock bearing a similar description to the gang that was slain by Rodriguez yesterday, was reported to have been seen taking part in an armed kidnapping early this morning—"

"Fuck off!" Estrella blurted, drowning the address the kidnapping took place at as the radio reporter continued to talk.

"... police are asking any witnesses to the attack to come forward with information."

She ran her fingers through her hair, frustrated, and fearful.

The gang's return wasn't an isolated incident. More were back, and operating in LA, still kidnapping people.

Did you catch that address?

I did. Geoffrey revealed. She exhaled with relief. *It is not far from here.*

As in, it happened in the IW district?

That is correct.

The gang was targeting IWs, no questions asked, something that worked against their MO. Why? Estrella didn't know, but she had to find out. She had to prevent others from going through what she experienced, witch or not. She went searching for clothes, having realized she was still naked.

Estrella went for something light as it was only going to get hotter when the afternoon rolled by. Black tank top and shorts for the time being, after that, she slipped her right hand into her NC gauntlet, stored a pistol inside her synthetic arm with spare mags and a fresh batch of nanotubes.

Geoffrey, call me a taxi, she asked while moving to the exit.

I presume you're taking it upon yourself to follow up on the kidnapping?

There's no fucking way I'm sitting around knowing someone else out there is about to experience the pain I did. We're tracking that motherfucker down, and we're doing it now.

She stopped before the door, her hand hovering just above the handle. Looking back, she saw where the pink vibrator had fallen. She blew it a kiss goodbye. "Sorry, maybe tonight."

Estrella left her pad. She hoped to have the answers why the men that murdered her parents, then raped and cut her weren't in the ground where she put them, by the time she returned.

FOURTEEN
RAY

A taxicab brought Ray from JFK International Airport to his hotel across wet roads reflecting neon. Looking back, he smiled warmly knowing that the love of his life would be flying in from the EU soon, landing at the airport he'd just left. Ray sent her a message informing her he switched phones. He kept multiple phones on him, one for each area code. Being a seeker of the truth with hacking skills carried risks. Piss off the wrong person, or enter places you weren't meant to be in, and they'll come searching for you via tracking your phone. Having six different phones kept people guessing where Ray was. Few people knew about his New York only phone.

After checking into the hotel, Ray got ready for the trade show Yoshida was hosting. They gave him a media pass which he proudly clipped to his business suit and entered the show. Any media kits Ray wanted, he got, if he needed to cut ahead in line to an exhibit, the staff made it happen, no questions asked. The media pass was godlike.

High-tech robots were on display, showing off their abilities to create items out of thin air with nanites. Other robots were part of a line of automated construction equipment. Yoshida showed off their next generation of assault rifles and pistols the military contacted them to produce, along with new TEK suits for infantry soldiers.

The updated TEK suits had multiple jets slapped to the back, hands, and feet, enabling users to fly or hover for prolonged periods of time. It was going to be a game-changer in the theater of war. It made him cringe, bringing in weaponized IWs was supposed to be a game-changer in war. All it did was change the world and not for the better.

A new update to IW tracking devices had crowds of onlookers swarming the Yoshida sales representatives. Everyone loved tech that kept a firm leash on IWs, almost as much as RW tech, which was on display at the adjacent booth. Two RWs stood like fashion models, one male, one female, flaunting off the new designs of the NC gauntlet, and several other new nanotechnology abilities that could be deployed to combat high ranking IWs refusing to cooperate with the police.

Ray had enough of the show floor. He had an article to write, a bias one that went against everything believed, in order to keep his job. Most men that lost their jobs ended up as RWs. There wasn't much demand for male dancers or escorts.

He came to sit in a crowded presentation theater. The lights and murmurs of the crowd dimmed when Yoshida's CEO took the stage, a woman the world only knew as Lady M. Nobody was ever able to get her actual name out of her, not even facial scans, they were all edited to display what she wanted them to show. Yoshida, after all, was the company that developed the back-end technology behind it.

Some argued Lady M wasn't even a real person as she rarely appeared in public, and when she did, it was a holographic projection, just like the one on stage giving a presentation to the media. This led to speculation and rumors Lady M might be an AI or just a clever ploy developed by the corporation. It'd explain her flaw-lessly smooth skin that never seemed to age, and her long dark shiny hair that seemed to remain the same length year after year, same style too, long and loose with strands of it covering the top of her shoulders from the strapless gown she wore.

Between her fingers was a long, vintage cigarette holder, the same kind women back in the 1920s used, white smoke rising away from its red glowing tip. With M being a projection, nobody could smell it.

Lady M delivered a touching speech about Yoshida's rise to power over the years since the Great War ended, complete with holograms illustrating the words she spoke. She praised the humans that donated their bodies to become RWs, which had led to fewer crimes committed by those that wield IW powers, as they captured or killed IWs that went living for years unregistered and untracked with the GPS devices the company developed.

People with IW powers were a threat to the survival of humans, she argued. It generated loud applause from the audience full of members of the press and suits. Ray's hands remained idle. Only the advance nanites and cyberware found within RWs could provide an effective and safe counter to deal with that problem, and Yoshida was the corporation that would see to the preservation of humanity and the new challenges it faces.

Ray cringed at the statement as he noted it in his pad. He'd have to write a news report on this soon and make Lady M look like the savior of human society when, in reality, it was corporations like Yoshida that created IWs. Ray knew better than to call them out on that. His job depended on it, same with his humanity.

When the show was over, they moved Ray to the back press-only area. He had a scheduled one-on-one interview with Lady M, inside one of the rear rooms. What he saw when he arrived were suits, way too many of them standing around. Some had finished interviews with members of the press, and others were flipping through notes on handheld tablets. Ray found one suit who didn't appear busy, with dark shades covering his eyes. Strange considering they were indoors. They must have been smart glasses with the tint setting on maximum, turning them into shades, and hiding the holographic overlays that would have been made visible to those watching.

Ray approached the suited man, grabbing his attention with a wave. The man's face remained neutral, and the tint on his glasses never changed. He couldn't read him at all.

"Hello, uh I ..." Ray said.

"Yes?" The corporate man said." May I help you?"

"My name is Ray Partington, Alliance Star news." Ray flashed his press badge. "I'm here for the interview with Lady M."

"Ah, Mr. Partington," the corporate man drawled. "I should have recognized you. We've been waiting for you."

"Recognized me? I don't even know you."

"Victor Ashford, Yoshida CFO," he said with a half-smile. "Arianna speaks highly of you Mr. Partington, she's even registered you as a significant other in the corporate database." Ray couldn't tell if there was more Ashford wanted to say but opted not to. "Lady M's interview you said?"

Ray nodded. "Yes."

"Right this way, Mr. Partington. I'll take you to it."

Ashford escorted him to one of the private interview rooms. Ray took a seat ahead of the enigmatic owner of Yoshida. He saw her body flicker three times as she adjusted her gown to sit. It was still the projection he was going to talk with. A pity, if he had met with the real Lady M, if she even existed at all, it would have been quite the news exclusive.

He put his glasses on, tapped the side panel on them, setting them to record and auto transcribe the words the two would speak. Tiny displays appeared showing the transcribed text in the left lenses of the glasses. A record icon flashed on the top right corner.

"Fantastic presentation your company has put together tonight," Ray said.

"Why, thank you," she said with a smile. She puffed her long cigarette stick elegantly, holding it between her index and middle finger, exhaling the mist at him from her red glossy lips shaped into an 'o'. Every sense in his body told him to brace for cigarette smoke, smoke that wasn't really there.

Ray glanced at his pad and asked the first question he noted on it. "I wasn't aware that there we so many RWs in active service around the world. Exactly how many are there currently?"

"We've produced approximately forty-four thousand units which provide IW suppression services throughout the Alliance, EU, and African Dominion. While we don't provide RWs for the New Soviet Union or Pacific Federation, we have sold cyberware needed for those nations to create their own."

"Is it really necessary to have this much power over IWs?"

"Yes," she said firmly, then puffed her stick and elegantly released the smoke, this time upward. "World War III saw the rise of the first imaginary witches and warlocks, or IWs as we all like to call them. Nobody knows which side created them first. All we know is after a few months of fighting, the New Soviets, China, before it controlled the Pacific, and the former United States and its allies had weaponized IW soldiers on the frontlines."

"Right." Ray vividly remembered those details from his history lessons in school. "Humans with magical powers from old legends."

"Only they weren't legends." Her voice became condescending. "And I wouldn't call them humans, nobody would."

Ray saw an opportunity. He smirked at M, and then took it. "Some people would take offense to that, don't you think?"

"No." The 'no' was firm and direct. "IWs have been genetically proven to be a different subclass of humanity that went extinct thanks to the witch hunts in Europe during the fifteenth century. Someone, during WWIII, again, we don't know who, found the lost witch gene and placed it in a dozen test subjects. Those subjects developed their powers quickly and went on to become the first generation of resurrected witches and were forced to join the military, and fight in the war. Fast-forward to today and we now have the problem we face today, a weapon that can walk, talk, kill 'n' destroy when it wants to. We were powerless to stop it until the RWs came online."

This wasn't Lady M's first interview. Ray continued, treading carefully. "To my understanding of history, we created, rather, re-created witches and warlocks correct?"

She nodded. "That is correct."

"We weaponized and sent them to fight for our countries, and now they're a 'pest' in our cities. What are your thoughts on that and how it came to be?"

"Using witches and warlocks as walking weapons of mass destruction was a mistake." She took another puff on her long smoking stick, then quickly crossed her legs. "War makes people desperate for a victory, especially if you're losing. Just look at the atom bomb, it was created because the Americans wanted a win button. When using nuclear missiles during the war wasn't enough, humans went to search for a new win button, witches. Days after they were first used in combat, we saw the death toll and destruction of the war increase tenfold. It wasn't nukes doing that, it was witches 'n warlocks and their uncontrollable desire to destroy everything around them. When generals and admirals told them to hold back, they disobeyed orders, and who could stop them? Would you place a soldier under arrest for insubordination if they had the power to melt a tank with the snap of their fingers, or cast hexes and curses on you and your family? IWs were the worst weapons humanity created; you can control nuclear weapons by not launching them. You can't control IWs if they want to sink an aircraft carrier because they don't like how it looked, and they'll do it too."

"I see."

"So, to answer your question, it came to be because we made a mistake in bringing them back, but we can't dismantle them like we can with nuclear weapons. We can't wipe IWs out, we tried that toward the end of the war when they rebelled, and things got nasty quick. IWs back then were too powerful and could easily wipe out humanity. We can't stop them from having children in secret either, so their population only grew. The only option was to limit their power, ban all training, and prevent the weaponization of a new generation IWs as per the IW accords. After that, we in Yoshida created the real witch program and tracking devices for registered IWs. It's the perfect counter to the growing IW population, and our only means of controlling the first, and hopefully only, sentient WMD."

"Some would argue that the plan Yoshida has in motion isn't a viable long-term solution for the future."

"It took a world war to resurrect witches. That same war pushed the Brits back into the EU. World War III paved the way for the impossible to become possible."

Lady M was as good as her sultry looks. "But," Ray said while twisting his lips, searching for the right words to use. "But ... aren't we just repeating the past, by creating a new breed of witches and warlocks, being the RWs? One that uses nanotech to deal with our problems?"

"I don't believe so." Her projection reached for a glass of wine that lay off-screen. It looked like her hand reaching for it vanished for a moment, only for it to reappear with the drink. She sipped it, puffed her smoke, sent the glass back down off-screen, and continued. "IWs are more likely to commit crimes because they know their powers can let them get away with it. If you give evil tools to someone, they'll use it for evil. There's a reason the witch hunts hundreds of years ago existed. The people back then knew the danger they were facing from those that possessed the witch gene and knew if they didn't act first, then the witches would wipe out or enslave humans. Those witch hunts were in some way a warning to us, don't trust witches, sadly, we didn't listen to it until now. This is why the registration of IWs is important, and with our tracking technology, we can not only monitor IWs but keep tabs of how many new ones are being born."

"In the years since Yoshida has created this technology and provided it to the world, has anyone ever questioned if it's right and ethical to do?"

"No. Many religions praise us, firmly believing that IWs are the work of the devil, and many surveys have shown that the human population feels much safer knowing that our technology and RWs are keeping them safe at night. The alternative is, we go back to the witch hunts of the past, but again, that's a deadly option now. Even though weaponized IWs don't exist anymore, in great numbers, IWs are still extremely powerful. The safest and less violent path is this, mandatory registration and tracking of IWs, with RWs working to enforce the laws that prevent IWs from learning how to grow and harness their more destructive abilities. Lives of humans and IWs are better preserved with our technology in the end."

Not in the last week ... he thought back to the recent news in the EU, the terrorist attack Arianna avoided, and it involved IWs. *Come to think of it, those IWs were strong ... more so than normal.* "What about the IW terrorist attack in Munich?"

He sat back, eagerly awaiting her reply. Ray had enough info to make Yoshida look good. It was time to get some dirt. The truth was always something unclean.

"To my knowledge those IWs were unregistered. If they had been tagged with our tracking tech and registered, the authorities in the EU with their RWs could have seen the attack coming. Even if they had failed to do that, the devices display the estimated rank of IWs."

"I wasn't aware of that feature."

"It was part of a new update. IW tracking devices now allow us to measure their power growth and predict what their rank is. If an IW goes from rank D to A quickly, then there's a good chance they were training, which is illegal. Authorities from there can dispatch the RWs they have on a lease from us to detain the IW threat should they deem it necessary—"

Ashford entered the room, cleared his throat while adjusting his expensive suit and tie. "I'm sorry to interrupt, but Mr. Partington's time is up."

Ray checked the time on his phone. "I still have another sixteen minutes."

"That was changed early this morning," Ashford said, his expression hidden behind his shades. "We accidentally overbooked on the interviews. Other news organizations are waiting time with Lady M."

"Couldn't you have told me earlier?"

"Our PR did, Mr. Partington, check your email." Ray received no message. He checked his messages every five minutes. There's no way he missed it. "Now, if you will."

Ray nodded, bidding farewell to the projection, still debating if she was real and just sitting in front of a camera from her home. He made a long face as he walked away from the room, angry thoughts eating him up at the lackluster questions he asked. Ray was losing his touch as a seeker of truth. In his younger days, he could have come up with better questions, and probably stumped her too. Then again, in his younger days, he just hacked what cameras, computers, and emails he wanted for news, then asked questions based on what he saw. Losing sixteen minutes of time was the icing on the cake of failure.

Ashford's face had been directed to a barrage of text messages that came in suddenly on his phone. Ray took notice and discreetly reached for his phone, flipping on his data packet sniffer app. He had a feeling the true reason his interview getting cut early lay in

Ashford's text messages. Whatever signals Ashford had been receiving, Ray's app might pick up on them, and being in close range of Ashford's phone only made the process easier.

His sniffer app revealed the ass end of Ashford's text messages.

Wilcox: Package from EU arriving at JFK soon.

Ashford: Keep me posted when she arrives.

'She,' Ray thought to himself. *Since when were packages, referred to as a person?*

———

Ray was back in his hotel room when the night fell upon the city, bringing out the light show of signs, and white and red dots from cars. He loosened his tie after shedding the business jacket from his body. Sitting on the bed, he went to kick off his shoes when his phone vibrated. Arianna's name appeared on the screen. It made him smile, filling his chest with blissful waves. She should be landing soon. He glanced to the engagement ring resting on the nightstand. It'll be on her finger in less than twenty-four hours.

Less than twenty-four hours, he couldn't wait.

"Hey babe," Ray said, picking up the video call.

Arianna's face looked disturbed as she sat on her chair in the plane. "Where are you right now?" She also sounded disturbed.

He grimaced. Something was wrong. And her being in the middle of the flight didn't help his growing concerns. "In my hotel, here in New York—"

"Okay, good." She peered cautiously to the side, then the other like she was expecting someone to be listening. "Stay there for now."

"Uh, is everything okay?"

The connection went dead. He hoped she was the one that cut it. If it was someone else, or something else ... He shook his head clear of those thoughts. It had to have been her that did it, and she didn't seem happy to see him either or even ask how his day went. True, he didn't ask her either, though if the conversation didn't go the way it did, he would have.

All will be answered when she arrives, he thought. *When is that?*

Ray fiddled with his phone, accessing a tracking app capable of pinpointing where an incoming call arrived from in the world. He used it to locate the origin of Arianna's last call, hoping to see how far away her plane was over the Atlantic.

What he got instead was static, like she was trying to mask where the call came from. Odd for a businesswoman like her, working for Yoshida, not wanting to be traced, especially by the man she loved.

He spent the next hour decrypting the signal, drawing upon long-dormant hacking skills and the illegal apps he had on his phone and tablet pad. A red blip over the Atlantic Ocean appeared on his tablet's screen. It was the location of Arianna's last call and it was approaching New York City, which was to be expected.

The blip was a lot closer to New York than expected.

Bringing up a list of all flights from the EU, planning to land in New York, unveiled a new chilling fact. There was one flight inbound from London, the one she should be on, and it wasn't due to land just yet, as expected. The next flight scheduled to land was from Munich, and its arrival time matched with the arrival time of the flight where Arianna's last message came from.

Arianna was on the plane that left Munich. She said she was leaving London.

She lied to Ray, she also insisted he stay put. He didn't listen and got up from the bed, racing to the exit of his hotel suite. Ray's concern for Arianna's safety and wellbeing was too much.

Munich was the location of the IW terrorist attack as he recalled. If those IW terrorists wanted to use their abilities to take over a plane, then the one Arianna was on could have been one of them.

He called for a taxi on his way down to the lobby. The flight from Munich was set to land soon. Ray had to be there at the airport when it did, against Arianna's request. If something bad was about to go down, he needed to be there for her.

If this was to be the day she died, then they'd die together.

Wilcox: Package from EU arriving at JFK soon.

Ashford: Keep me posted when she arrives.

The image of Ashford's text message wouldn't leave his head. Especially the usage of the word 'she' for a package.

FIFTEEN
ESTRELLA

An aura of purple, blue, and green neon light awaited Estrella when she arose from the self-driving taxi. She blew a large pink bubble from the gum she chewed and stood alone in the heart of District 666, where the IWs of Los Angeles made their home, close to Santa Monica boulevard. The few palm trees that were present rustled their leaves above the traffic and pedestrians going about their business.

Several hateful glares hit her from all angles. It was hard for Estrella to hide the silver NC gauntlet she wore on her right hand, reflecting what little sunlight the wall-like high-rise structures let in. A warlock spat at her feet and commented that his cousin was killed by an RW nanite swarm. She spat her gum at him. It was losing its flavor anyway. A witch with pentagram tattoos on her arms and forehead called Estrella a whore, then flipped her the finger. Estrella flipped one back.

It didn't help to know that these people were her neighbors, or at least lived in her neighborhood. She made plans to buy an extra batch of locks for her pad.

A police patrol car drove past slowly, it was the only thing that drew attention away from Estrella. She felt safer until it turned the corner at the next set of lights. Two blocks up, she spotted the location the kidnapping took place at, a bus stop close to a dark alley, most likely where the Bald Skull member had been hiding.

She entered the bus shelter, moving her head about, searching for a surveillance camera. She found it; a black orb-like object nestled in the top corner. She turned around, peering at what was behind her, then to the left, and right. Nobody was looking. Estrella reached for the hidden surveillance camera with her NC gauntlet hand, touching it.

Can you connect us to this? she asked her AI.

Yes, I can. Would you like me to do it?

Please, Geoffrey.

She felt a single swarm of utility nanites within her pool into her arm, into the gauntlet, then spray onto the camera. The nanites entered the camera, locating its stored memory within its electronics and formed a bridge, transferring control of the camera to Geoffrey, a control which he shared with Estrella so long as she remained touching it with her gauntlet.

When the link became stable, her eyesight changed. It showed what the camera was showing, and what it showed was Estrella's NC gauntlet obscuring its vision. She needed something else to look at, its past recordings. She had Geoffrey review it, her eyes replayed the morning scene from the bus shelter's camera in reverse.

A gathering of witches and warlocks exited a bus walking backward, stood in the shelter, and then left walking backward. The similar sights repeated until the police and an RW walked backward into view, taking witness statements in reverse. When they vanished from her sight, the Bald Skull tattooed gang member came out from a car, holding a young man, no younger than seventeen.

He put the young man down, then raced away backward into the alley.

Estrella replayed the video, this time moving forward. The Bald Skull member was alone and stood looking at the young man waiting for the bus. He made a quick call on his phone, most likely verifying something. When the call was done, he went into the bus stop, and flicked his wrist as his hands glowed white. The young man froze still with a psychokinetic stun. She was impressed that he could stun him quickly.

With the young man frozen in time for three seconds, the gang member grabbed him, just as a black car pulled up while its passenger side door slid open. The two disappeared into the vehicle as it sped off. Three witches stood pointing fingers, their faces flabbergasted at the event taking place.

The video played back once more, and this time Estrella ran facial scans on the gang member and a young man. Nothing turned up for the gang member, as expected, they were all unregistered IWs, even back in Buenos Aires. The young man, however, the scans weren't able to get a proper read on his face, as he didn't face the camera.

Geoffrey, is there anything you can do with the scan of that kid?

I can take what little data we have on his face and compare it to faces of a similar look, and body size.

Do it.

Be advised, this will take some time.

She released her grip of the camera, commanding the nanite swarm in it to return to her gauntlet. It looked like a mist of flying microscopic machines. She verified that nobody saw her meld with the electronic device and left, allowing Geoffrey to use his processing power.

She stopped.

The car the gang member, and the kidnapped young man, went

in, moved northbound. Estrella traveled in that same direction, hoping to discover something to work with, prepared to not turn up anything at all. There were at least three intersections on the roads going north, and that car could have turned on any of them.

Melding with other cameras was a no go as they were too high for her to reach. She needed to touch the cameras since it'd reduce the communication lag between the nanites and Geoffrey, not to mention save what little battery power they'd have left once released. She'd have ten seconds of access before the nanites lose battery strength and die while using a remote nanite hack—

"Thank the Goddess you're here!" A soft-spoken voice called to her.

Turning around, she saw a warlock wave a skinny bronze hand at her ahead of his bleached blond hair. The warlock's clothing was jet black with a white necktie loosely wrapped around his neck and hung over his chest. She glared at the warlock in confusion then pointed a finger at herself. There were at least four other pedestrians walking next to her, and one of them had the nerve to shove her to the side when she stopped to face the warlock.

The bronze warlock nodded. "Yes, you, honey! I see that RW glove."

Estrella stepped to him. "What's up?"

"Huh? Aren't you here to help?"

"With?" Her confused glare remained.

"With a kidnapping. Some bald dick head went into my bar, and snatched one of my customers, darling! Called the cops on that fool a minute ago. Was surprised to see they sent you so quickly."

The LAPD didn't send her, today was Estrella's day off. But, commendations to Yoshida would get her back in Buenos Aires in no time. Working on your day off was a good way to earn those commendations. She smiled and followed the bronze warlock into his bar, a place where a neon sign flashed the words 'The Witches Brew' above its entrance.

A kidnapping by a bald man ...

The attack on the family of three was no doubt a botched attempt by the Bald Skulls. The young man, at the bus stop, and now someone from the bar, wasn't. The Bald Skulls were stepping up their game, and fast. Not bad for a group of dead IWs.

Thumping luststep music came blasting at Estrella as she entered the bar, full of life, following behind the bronze warlock. It was hard to tell what the natural color of the walls, ceiling, and tables were, as the flashing lights made everything, and everyone, look purple and pink. Two IWs flashed her an expression of hate. Estrella's kind was not welcomed. The bronze warlock leading her in didn't seem to care.

"So ..."

"The name's Robbie," he said.

She nodded. "What happened exactly?"

He guided her to a circular table with two women sitting around it. Their faces looked depressed. One of them wiped tears away with the back of their wrist. Robbie gestured to them.

"Those girls will know," he said. "All I know was, I was at the bar, serving some drinks to a couple of hot guys, then that baldy had to come in and start a commotion. He left holding one lady these two girls came with."

"Shit."

"He also didn't tip! I expect that from humans, but not fellow IWs. Ya feel?"

At the table, Estrella stood looking at the two women. They looked up at her. It was the first time she saw IWs happy to see her presence. That was the funny thing about being an RW. Everyone hated her until an IW started trouble, and then they came begging the RW to make the bad IW go away. Then promptly went back to hating her.

"I'll fetch the surveillance footage for you too," Robbie said while taking his leave.

She nodded then ran facial scans of the two women, and analyzed the results, starting with the one on the left.

Name: Helen Pillar

Age: 19

Species: Imaginary witch/warlock

Occupation: Dancer

Notes: Rank D Telepath

Next up was the one on the right.

Name: Vina Blanchard

Age: 20

Species: Human

Occupation: Dancer

Notes: Error, please try again later

Estrella twisted her lips. Vina didn't strike her as a human, not by the black lace she wore, pentagram necklace, and eye shadow darker than Estrella's. Then there was that familiar error message. It was time to ask questions before the real cop and RW that was called to the scene showed up.

"Word has it you ladies had an interesting day," Estrella asked.

A loud sigh from Vina followed as she looked at her friend Helen. "Does that *thing* need to be here?"

"Yes, it's protocol." Estrella cut in, not knowing if it really was LAPD protocol. But it got them listening to her. "Don't worry ladies, I don't bite. So, what happened?"

"Well." Vina hesitated. "Helen, and my sister, Portia, and I came here thinking there was a gig waiting for us."

Estrella crossed her arms, looking at their makeup, hair, and clothing barely covering their curves and girly bits. She factored in a Bald Skulls gang member was targeting women dressed like that, with the promise of a gig. Estrella knew what was up.

"Was that a psytrip gig?" she asked them.

The two women shared a grimace, still hesitant to talk about the matter. "Eh? What?"

"You heard me, was it a psytrip gig?" No answer. "Okay so, there were three of you originally, right?"

"Yes."

"The third being Vina's sister, Portia, right?"

She nodded. "Yes ... he, he grabbed her and ran out the door."

"White glowing hands then a quick stun?"

"I think. It happened so fast." Vina looked to the table, her eyes filling with tears again. "I thought stun takes at least five seconds to use?"

Estrella's shoulders came up shrugging. "Thought so too ..." She studied their appearances again. "Was Portia dressed like the two of you?"

"Well, yeah."

"You three were dancers looking to make the switch to psytrip adult actresses?" No answer, just hesitating faces. "Look, I can't help you if you don't tell me everything."

Helen broke her silence. "Yes ..." She looked up at Estrella with her dark shadowed eyes. "He told us he was an agent and had some work for us. Dancing isn't consistent money, you know? He showed up using a fake telepathic projection."

"Being a telepath, you must have seen through his mental manipulation."

Helen eventually and hesitantly nodded. Estrella knew why. Helen was a rank D telepath, there's no way she'd be strong enough to tell the difference. Someone else of the three did. Thing was, Vina's profile listed her as human therefore her sister, Portia, should be as well. Estrella had doubts Vina was a registered IW, her sister too. And it'd fit the puzzle, the Bald Skulls were targeting IWs since their return, not humans.

"He was pushy before I, uh, called him out," Helen lied, but Estrella knew the truth. "He wanted us to come with him and get started right away. We told him the deal was off, and things got fucking stupid from there."

"We tried to get away," Vina said. "But Portia, she wasn't fast enough, and then got hit with his stun."

"You girls did the best you could," Estrella said. "I was one of their victims." Vina broke down with somber weeping. "Trust me, I'll find your sister." *And that kid from the bus stop ... she finished internally. Geoffrey, did you get anything on that kid?*

I narrowed it down to six different males.

Six ID profiles obscured Estrella's view of Helen and Vina. She briefly skimmed them and grimaced. *The fuck? They're all human.*

That is correct. Perhaps the gang isn't targeting IWs as you suspected—

No, they are. Look at the addresses to these names? It's all here in the district, didn't Piper say the most of the humans living here packed up and left?

Correct, that is why rent prices in the IW district are low.

Then there's a good chance anyone living here, especially with kids, isn't human. That kid was a fucking warlock.

Yes, the probability of a human family living in the IW district is extremely low. And it is unlikely a minor like the one kidnapped lived alone.

That family of three all had their profiles listing them as human. But you and I know the truth, they were unregistered IWs. Vina and her sister, those two had to have been telepaths, and it's pretty fucking obvious they were looking to get their adult psytrip careers started. You need to be a telepath for that. So, what does that tell you, Geoffrey?

The Bald Skulls gang is targeting unregistered IWs, telepathic ones to be precise if your hypothesis is correct.

And if you're going to kidnap any IW, you'd go for the unregistered ones. They don't have tracking devices and live in secret—

Alert Estrella.

She grimaced and bid farewell to the two women. Looking ahead to the entrance stood Marcus and Piper, the cop and RW that was originally called to the scene. The situation was about to get awkward. Estrella kept her face to the floor and moved to the bar, vanishing beyond the sea of drunken IWs as Marcus and Piper entered, and spoke with Robbie.

Robbie's gasp made her chuckle softly to herself. Probably confused why Marcus and Piper were responding to the call, when Estrella had shown up, posing as the responder. Estrella took a seat at the bar, keeping her back to them, trying to blend in. She waited for Marcus and Piper to pass by, and speak to the soon to be confused duo sitting at the round table—

"You!"

It was Robbie. He was standing behind the bar now, facing down Estrella at her stool, his hands clasping his hips.

"Hey, listen, Robbie—"

"You've been a bit of naughty girl."

"So, they went and told you, huh?"

"I figured it out."

"I'm assigned to the LAPD, so it's not like I lied or anything."

"But you weren't on duty."

"My duty to them right now is patrols. But I need to be investigating this. I know who this gang is."

"The guy that took the girl is a gangbanger?"

"Supposed to be dead, I killed them all when I was in Buenos Aires. Now they're here in LA, every single one of them, alive and kidnapping ..." She stopped herself from saying unregistered IWs, best to wait and see how things play out before revealing those details.

"So why not ask your LAPD masters to help with the case?"

"'cause I'm on probation."

Robbie smiled. "Oh? Please, do tell, honey."

"Assaulted one of Yoshida's clients back in Buenos Aires."

"Thought you RWs couldn't hurt humans?"

"I hacked my old AI and turned off the safety." He laughed. She laughed. They both laughed some more. "It got sent me here as punishment, and then I immediately disobeyed orders when I found out the gang was attacking a family of three."

"You're Estrella Rodriguez, aren't you?"

She nodded. "Yeah."

"Girl, your face has been on the news, everywhere! The RW that might be defective, and the LAPD doesn't care."

"I'm not a fuck-up, just made a few bad choices that landed me here, stuck to patrol work. They don't want me helping with the investigation, because they don't trust me to handle it right."

"So, behind their backs, you're working on it anyway."

"I need to know what the fuck is going on, and I don't trust the LAPD to do it right. I can't and won't able to sleep at night knowing the men that killed my parents, did sick shit to me, and others, are alive and free after I sold my fucking soul to Yoshida, so I could get the powers needed to fucking kill them. All that work, just for someone to hit the undo button."

"Your secret's safe with me, girl, don't you worry."

"Thanks—"

"Well, well, well." A firm and familiar human hand patted her shoulder. "Why am I not surprised to see you?"

Turning in her barstool, she saw Marcus and Piper behind. Neither looked thrilled to look at her. "Just slipped in for a drink."

Marcus crossed his arms across his police uniform. "Sure you did, Rodriguez."

"It's true," Robbie interjected in her defense. "She, uh, heard about my new happy hour prices on drinks. That other RW I mentioned? She's long gone! This is totally not her."

Marcus and Piper weren't buying.

Piper beamed. "Strange, since those two girls claimed an RW that looked like you Rodriguez spoke with them before we arrived."

Robbie shot Estrella a wink, then stepped away, taking orders from a fresh arrival of pentagram tattooed warlocks. She appreciated Robbie trying to cover for her regardless. Marcus was going to say more, adding to the grilling of Estrella when his radio interrupted.

"All units, we got a twenty-fifty, in progress."

Marcus' lips twisted. "Twenty-fifty, shit." He reached for his radio, stepping back and away from Estrella and Piper. "Hold on, let me take this."

Estrella watched as Marcus backed away, locating a quiet spot to speak into the communication device. She looked up at Piper; she too held the same concerned look Marcus had. "What's a twenty-fifty?" Estrella asked her.

"Violent IWs committing a crime," Piper said. "I hope you're packing heat, new girl, because that usually means all RWs get your ass in gear."

Piper's synthetic eyes, glowing with an emerald hue, shut like she was trying to focus. A silent conversation with the holographic raven sitting on her shoulder, Estrella figured.

Marcus came back fast. Piper backed away, giving him space to approach Estrella. "We got to go now," he said. "IWs are ripping up shit up downtown, and in Beverly Hills."

"Looks like you were right, Piper," Estrella said and waited for Piper's snarky response. There wasn't one. Both Marcus and Estrella looked to where Piper was last standing. It was just an empty spot. "Where did she go?"

A quick three-minute search for Piper turned up no results, and neither did calling her number. She was gone, left to get a head start on the call, they concluded. Something they needed to do.

Marcus and Estrella leaped into his police car, parked outside the bar, with haste. Its computer screen turned on, as he powered the vehicle. The screen had comprehensive details listed of the twenty-fifty call, and its critical nature.

There were three red-shaded areas on the map of the city high-lighted, indicating the location of the violent IW crime in progress. Two were downtown and one was in Beverly Hills. Estrella glanced closer at the screen, noting the red highlight in Beverly Hills was a residential home.

It belonged to the Kounias family.

SIXTEEN
RAY

Another call to Arianna. Another voicemail reply.

Ray stood near the arrivals atrium at New York City's JFK airport. He lowered his phone into his pocket after getting the voicemail sound for the third time. Cold sweat dampened his body, heavy breathing made his chest move rapidly, and trembling in his arms made his fingers twitch.

Flight information screens showed no delays for all incoming flights to New York, especially those coming from across the Atlantic. The flight arriving from London, which Arianna was supposed to be on, was a minute out. The flight he traced her phone signal from should have landed already, and that flight came from Munich.

There were no panicking faces, or explosions, so that ruled out that terrorist IWs were aboard her flight. It helped slow the twitching in his hands, clearing his thoughts enough to possibly accept that fact that maybe, just maybe, he was just being extremely paranoid brought on by the desire to propose to her.

Arianna not answering her phone however was odd, especially when he tried calling her after the attacks in the EU. Gone were the days where you couldn't use phones mid-flight. There was no reason for her to cut the call earlier, and no reason for her not to reply to his last message.

Two men dressed in black hooked his attention. One man was tall with pale skin, and short brown hair, his hands were stuck in his pockets all times. The other was a large African male, a body-builder by the looks, with muscles on his arms, legs, and a chest that wanted to burst out from his black attire. Both men wore dark shades and kept to themselves. Ray did the same and hung behind the crowds leaving the airport, his eyes remained fixed on the two strange men.

Another group of men entered the airport, dressed in plain clothing. Was it five men? Or Seven? Ray couldn't tell, they were walking so close to each other. He thought nothing at first, until he noticed they all wore shades. It was a little late in the day to be wearing those, especially indoors.

The two shady men trailed behind the newly arrived group of men in shades, like stalkers. Something told Ray he should do the same. Something else told him he should have listened to Arianna and avoided the airport. But he was already in deep now, and his journalistic mind wanted the truth. Who were these men? It didn't look like they were there to pick up someone.

Ray made it as far as the check-in area, having followed the two men to the departures terminal. Looking ahead, he saw the large group of men walk past security robots, personnel, and scanners. No questions were asked, not even by the massive line up of passengers, who should have protested that the men jumped the line.

He made another call to Arianna, and his sweaty palms left their mark on his phone. She didn't reply. The suspicious men were out of sight when Ray drew his eyes away his phone. He stood still to collect his thoughts from his panicking mind. It wouldn't stop flashing images of Arianna dead or kidnapped as she got off her flight. The flight she wasn't supposed to be on.

Passengers and security personnel stood idle at the security check-in area. He thought there was a hold-up at the end of the line. He looked to the front, examining the teams of security staff manning the body scanners they required everyone to enter. The passengers and security remained still, like idle mannequins in a store. The feeling was eerie.

Ray tried asking what was wrong, but nobody replied. He cut in line, and nobody objected. The security personnel didn't mind that Ray walked away from the body scanner, then ignored the genetic screening robot, whose job was to confirm that all people passing through the checkpoint was human. IWs were banned from flights in the Alliance, they were considered to be weapons.

He walked backward, leaving the security checkpoint, crossing the point of no return. Ray kept an eye on the security checkpoint and the lineup of passengers that remained suspended in time during his backward walk. Two minutes later, life returned to it. The security teams resumed their jobs, the passengers waiting in line continued to complain about the wait. Nobody realized they were frozen for five minutes, or that Ray slipped in without getting cleared by security, or the two groups of shaded men.

Crowds of passengers scurrying to or from their flights with carry-on luggage in hand moved ahead or around Ray. They knew where they needed to be, and he didn't. Ray felt lost. He reached for his tablet pad and located the men's washroom. Once inside, he locked himself in a toilet stall for privacy. He brought up his hacking apps, searching for the opened data ports the airport used for its security personnel. Lines of computer code slithered across his pad's screen. He typed away on the virtual keyboard, hopping from node to node, bypassing several firewalls and security encryptions.

The surveillance cameras of the airport belonged to him now, their contents visible from his pad's screen. Ray had hundreds of cameras to check, and only one of them would have footage of the two groups of strange men, or Arianna.

Two cameras got his attention, their video feeds were set to pause, and it wasn't by him. They automatically restarted a moment later, only for cameras in the next connecting area of the airport to pause. Once again, it wasn't by Ray's hand. Someone was deliberately pausing the recording like they were trying to hide the path of someone that shouldn't be seen.

Ray took control of the camera in the main security room. A uniformed airport security man lay motionless next to his station when the live feed displayed on his pad. Ahead of the lifeless man was a wall of monitors, displaying footage from the hundreds of surveillance cameras at the airport. He zoomed in. The motionless security guard's chest wasn't moving. Tilting the camera up, he saw the equipment pause and restart cameras throughout the airport, on its own.

There were IWs in the airport. It had to be. Ray was the only hacker inside the network, he would have detected another if that were the case. IWs here would explain the strange idling of the passengers and security teams at the checkpoint. What it didn't explain was how the IWs did it. They weren't powerful enough for that level of control. The answers to Ray's questions lay with the two groups of strange men. He found their location with the cameras. They were moving to a flight from the EU that just arrived.

Ray grabbed his phone, frantically dialing Arianna's number, hoping she'd pick up, but expecting the same voicemail sound. If she was still at the airport, she had to leave right away. Something bad was going down, and unregistered IWs were behind it. No way would registered ones have made it this far without their tracking devices sending out an alert.

The ringback tone stopped. Arianna's voicemail didn't activate that time.

He exhaled deeply. "Arianna, where are you?"

"My flight just landed."

"Okay great, I'm coming to get you."

"What? No! Stay in the fucking hotel like I asked!"

The tone of her voice was fierce, sharp, and direct. It wasn't the calm hippy girl he fell in love with. It was like someone else was in control of her.

"I'm already here," he said, cradling the phone with his shoulder, it freed his hands to continue operating his pad.

"Jesus fuck, why?!" Once again, it didn't sound like the Arianna he knew. "You need to get out now!"

"I'm not fucking leaving without you!" That and he just stumbled upon a major news scoop. The free people of the Alliance needed to know. "Listen, I have reason to believe there's unregistered IWs moving to your location, and they aren't here to kiss and greet someone."

"How do you know that?"

"Trust me on this." He leaned his face closer to the hacked security feeds on the pad. "Take a left then move north. Don't look behind."

He watched her move following his directions. She stepped out of view from one camera and into the next, while he shifted about looking at the cameras that continued to pause when a particular target entered its view. It was his guide, a heads up where the shady men where. It was his only means of guiding her away from them and into safety, and it wasn't working. The shady men changed directions when Arianna did. They knew where she was at all times.

They must be telepaths. Of course, they would. "Fuck. It looks like they're on to you."

"I'm cutting this call. I'll get back to you later, please stay safe!"

"Arianna! No, wait—"

She cut the call without saying goodbye. It didn't seem like the Arianna he knew at all. Calling her again seemed like a waste of time. After making note of her location in the airport, he power-walked out from the washroom, turned a corner briskly, nearly knocking over an elderly man, and kept walking. There was no time to stop and say sorry. He had to get to Arianna before they did.

He checked his pad two minutes into his walk through the busy and buzzing airport. Arianna was near. So were the two groups of shady men—

Ray was flung through the air.

He heard the rumble of a market kiosk blowing apart. Scream-ing, and panicking sounds filled the air. Three claps of a gun. Make that five, then seven. The world went black for a moment.

By the time Ray came to, pushing his body up, he saw people running and shouting, from a warlock with jets of flames gushing from his red glowing hands. The warlock burned everything he pointed at, namely the airport security RWs. Three men hunkered behind a pillar, the pistols they fired curved around the corner, keeping three RWs pinned down. The three men were IWs.

A swarm of nanites entered the air and caught one of the three men cowering behind the pillar, and his body burst into flames. His friends didn't seem to care. Behind, Ray heard the thumping foot-steps of men, shouting various military jargon into their headsets, back up for the RWs perhaps. He'd retreat behind them if Arianna wasn't still within the messy RW and IW exchange.

Ray leaped to his feet, moving closer to ground zero. He told himself over and over there wasn't anything he could do for the people on the floor he had to step over. The floor rumbled, the aftermath of an explosive pyrokinetic ability. It shattered the windows peering out to the runway. It didn't stop Ray from pushing forward, hoping Arianna wasn't one of the several unmoving bodies on the ground.

Keeping prone, he crawled forward and saw the first two shady men, the tall brown-haired man, and the brawny African. The brawny man stepped into the fray, cracked his fists, and then roared. Fangs had sprouted made visible from his majestically roaring open mouth. A soft, golden mane grew around his head, while a tail of similar color emerged behind him. His hands became claws and the appearance of fur covered his body. By the time he got on all fours, he had taken on the appearance of a lion. Biokinesis was at work, the man had altered his genes to a lion, making him a shifter, a werelion, an angry one that bolted in, leaping, and mauling someone, Ray couldn't see who. Might have been one of the RWs, might have been someone else.

The tall man went to assist his werelion partner. His body went flying out the now shattered window. A thump on the tarmac below followed. An Asian man with long black hair tied into a ponytail stood at the edge where the tall man fell. In the ponytailed man's hand was a sword, like a Japanese katana shimmering with indigo color. He snapped his fingers, and his body vanished. The IWs before Ray weren't your ordinary ones.

There was an opening because of that. It gave him the chance to push deeper into the fray, searching the debris for Arianna, ducking his head from the bolts of electrokinetic shocks and pyrokinetic flame jets the IWs unleashed. He hoped the werelion didn't smell his presence.

Arianna wasn't among the bodies he found. By the time he stood up, ready to give up, he laid eyes on her, golden curly hair blowing in the winds let in from the shattered windows. She ducked behind an information terminal, its screen flicked on and off as sparks sprayed from it. She saw him. He saw her. Ray went running for her, half expecting to eat a stray bullet or devastating IW ability.

"Arianna!" His hand held onto her, she was warm and breathing. She also looked at him strangely, like she had never seen him with her hypnotic eyes.

Ray tried to leave while holding her hand. Arianna remained still, forcing him to look back at her. Now he had a confused look.

"What's wrong?"

The armed RW and security backup arrived behind the two. The battle he sought to run from only grew in intensity. Arianna embraced him, resting her forehead against his. He loved feeling her body close to his, and he'd love it even more if they got the fuck out, ideally alive.

"Give me more time please," she whispered.

"We can have all of that and more once we get out of here—"

"Another minute, please."

"Arianna?"

Was she talking to him, or someone else? Ray couldn't answer that question. Arianna's embrace tightened, and Ray felt the temperature of his head, skull, and brain increase. A sharp pain stabbed his frontal lobes, and high-pitched ringing sounds muted the surrounding chaos. He wanted to scream but forgot how.

He was on his knees before Arianna, his hands holding his head in agony. When the ringing noises ended, he mustered the strength to look up at her. She ran her palms across the side of his head, gently, slowly. Arianna beamed.

"Thank you," she said. "The future is now in your hands Ray. Don't fuck it up."

Her finger gliding across his head stopped near his ear. Ray's vision turned to mathematical equations, long strings of scientific formulas, diagrams of molecules, atoms, and DNA strands. A facility in a tropical jungle erupted with flames, a woman wearing a guest badge butchering humans by the hundreds. The woman was a witch.

The vision ended with a man putting a gun in his mouth and was asked to pull the trigger. When Ray looked at his palms, he saw the white glowing hands of a witch covered in blood.

Ray wasn't himself anymore.

SEVENTEEN
ESTRELLA

Estrella couldn't shake the suspicion. The suspicion that the world was about to enter a turning point it might not recover from. The police car Marcus drove swerved around dozens of cars, as its sirens and red, blue, flashing lights told the world to step back. The tall skyscrapers of various geometric shapes and lights from the city, moved past in rapid succession.

A computer screen on his dashboard populated with updated data about the three separate IW attacks in the city, most of the first responders reporting heavy casualties, and at least two RWs killed. Marcus plowed into the wealthy suburban neighborhood of Beverly Hills. She and he were the first car at the scene, everyone else had been called to quell the two downtown IW calls.

Estrella and Marcus stood side-by-side holding a pistol each after they exited the car, its blue and red lights still flashing. The Kounias residence looked silent upon first glance, no signs of violence, or raging IWs. They walked to the front gate with weapons ready for action.

The gardening robots lay in pieces on the front lawn. Sprays of sparks flared up periodically. She felt the crunch of broken glass beneath her footsteps, shattered bedroom windows were the providers of that. Bullet holes ruined the front door which was left wide open. Marcus pushed in first, the flashlight mounted to the top of his weapon switched on automatically when they crossed into the darkened home. Estrella's eyes switched to night vision mode, clearing the path before her.

Holes in the walls punched in by bullets were commonplace. Computer screens flicked, furniture that wasn't covered in bullet holes was flipped over, and flowerpots laid in a mess of ceramic fragments, mixed with the black soil and the remains of plants. Upon closer inspection, the shattered pots lay next to a wall, and above on the wall, were massive dents dusted with soil.

Estrella lowered herself, rubbing her fingers across blackened burn marks on the floor. They smeared her fingertips with soot, just enough for her nanites to come up and take quick scans, relaying the data to Geoffrey when they returned inside her.

These marks are consistent with IW attacks, Geoffrey said.

She cringed looking at the shattered flowerpots. Someone threw the pots as a weapon and missed their target. That's why the mess on the walls. An IW threw them with a psychokinetic push.

Any idea of their rank? Estrella asked her AI.

Rank A possibly, or rank S.

"Fuck me sideways," she said out loud and faced Marcus. "We got possible rank A or S IWs here."

He snorted. "Guess this would be a bad time to ask if you've graduated to rank B or not."

She stood, aiming her pistol forward, ready to keep investigating. "Yeah, not really." *Wait, Geoffrey, rank A or S you said?*

That is correct.

What the fuck is a rank S?

Any IWs ranked as an S are considered to be weaponized.

She entered the living room with her optical scanner enhanced by night vision searching for anything of suspicion. She saw only bullet holes, burns marks on the ceiling, and shattered pictures. The thought of Rank S IWs had her worried.

Weaponized ... Isn't that, like, the shit they used in world war three? I thought training up to that rank was banned?

It is and is considered impossible. The only facility that could provide that level of training has long been demolished and its instructors have grown far too old to pass on their knowledge.

"Might wanna wait for the cavalry for this one," she snorted.

"Huh? Why?"

A figure on the couch stopped her from replying. They didn't look hostile. Estrella ran to them. "Hold up, got someone here ..."

It was a woman, lying back first on the couch. She lowered herself to the woman and gave her wake-up shake. The woman didn't wake up.

Estrella ...

What?

Look down ...

She did.

"Fuck!" Estrella leaped back and away from the woman on the couch.

The woman had a grisly bullet hole between her still wide-open eyes, and an expression of shock on her face and opened mouth. The woman didn't know the attackers, nor was expecting them to charge in shooting.

Marcus came in running behind her, the light from his pistol shined upon the woman's face. "Shit."

Blood drenched the couch where the woman's head had been resting. The single gunshot that ended her life went right through.

Marcus groaned. "What a way to go. She must have been lying down watching TV when they came in shooting."

Estrella stood up, shaking off the memories of how her parents went out. Her hatred for the Bald Skulls grew. "They shot her in the head without thinking twice."

White light from Marcus's flashlight shined upon the walls and the makeover the bullets gave it. "Then why the fuck did they go trigger happy here?"

Marcus had a point. It made Estrella look longer at the bullet holes making her optical scanners work in overtime, its data outputted over her vision. The woman got one slug in the head, it's all they needed, and she was wide open for the assault as it started. There was another target in the living room.

"Someone else survived," she said and moved out into the halls, following the path of round holes punched into the walls. It led them up to the staircase to the second floor.

Marcus' flashlight shined, brightening the walls, and identifying bullet holes in it on second floor. "Whoever they were shooting at, must have been really good dodging bullets."

Geoffrey, I forgot to run a facial scan. Does her face ring a bell?

Processing, please standby. A three-second pause followed. *Yes.*

An ID photo of the woman killed, and her profile appeared over Estrella's vision.

Name: Maria Kounias

Age: 57

Species: Human

Occupation: Liquor warehouse manager

Notes: Daughter is an employee of Yoshida

The woman was Maria Kounias, a resident of this household and wife of Norris Kounias, whom she shared this house with.

Anything that would suggest they might be unregistered IWs?

Please standby. A ten-second pause. *No, they are not and—*

"Rodriguez," Marcus cut in. "You got all silent there."

She grinned, looking down at the holographic black cat

following her while the two searched room after room in the upscale house turned into a warzone. "Just having a talk with my AI." *You were saying, Geoffrey? You got more, right?*

Yes, it is unlikely Norris and Maria are unregistered as they have a daughter named Arianna. She is an employee of Yoshida Corp and is the reason they were given this house to live in.

I can't see the daughter of unregistered IWs, working for the corporation that spends its money to keep IWs in their place.

That is correct; furthermore, genetic screening is a requirement for seeking employment in Yoshida. Her IW nature would have been discovered long ago.

They shot Maria dead at the start, Norris most likely saw it happen and ran, and somehow managed to dodge every single bullet shot at him by a user of IW abilities from the main level floor. The thoughts made Estrella grimace. She and Marcus kept searching the bedrooms of the house. She wasn't sure if this was the work of the Bald Skulls, especially when factoring in weaponized IWs might have been present.

Fascinating, Geoffrey's voice echoed in her head. *Their daughter Arianna is currently in a long-term relationship with this man.*

A photograph of Arianna and her boyfriend loaded, taken while the two were seated in the kitchen of the home they were searching. Their smiling faces were gushing with pure happiness.

"What a cute couple—" Estrella zoomed in on the face of Arianna's boyfriend in her vision. She recognized him. Ray Partington. "That's the fucking journalist!"

You are correct. Ray was also the last registered visitor to this residence prior to the break-in.

"Hey, Marcus!" He stopped and turned to face her. "What are the chances you can get someone to search the address of Ray Partington?"

His eyebrow rose. "There a reason for that?"

She gave him her reason. Ray Partington was the journalist the two of them told to fuck off, after the apartment attack by the Bald Skulls. She had reason to believe he was the one that tipped Piper off and was the hacker known as DigiSamurai69. Ray was the last person to visit the house, into which the IWs stormed in an unknown time later.

What was the connection? Ray. He must have been the target the IWs were hunting for, and when they couldn't find him, they went searching for his last known locations, then killed the Kounias family as they were witnesses. If she was right, then Ray's place should be getting ransacked.

The only question that remained was who were the IWs? If it wasn't the Bald Skulls, then who? The terrorist IWs from the EU? Or did the gang upgrade to terrorists?

The two stood in front of a door to the last unsearched bedroom. Marcus pushed the door open and entered, Estrella followed behind.

There was sunshine, bright enough to make her night vision go haywire. She had to switch it off as she shielded her eyes, processing how the hell the sunlight was so intense during the early evening. She looked to see Marcus' reaction since he entered first yet remained silent at the surprise.

Marcus wasn't there. Neither was the house.

Estrella stepped into her bedroom, the one she had as a kid back in Buenos Aires. The sunlight beaming into the 109th floor suite was the same too; so were the hand-drawn crayon pictures scattered across the floor. A young Estrella looked up at her, smiling.

"Marcus ..." Estrella said, looking for the cop that was supposed to be with her. *Geoffrey?* Her AI was as silent as was Marcus.

Voices in Spanish erupted behind her, terrified ones at that, ones she hadn't heard in ages. It was her parents. The thundering sound of a door getting kicked in came next, Estrella and her younger self leaped up, startled by the crash.

No, no, no! She panicked internally, drawing her weapon, aiming it forward as she went into the main hall. That too changed. Estrella was back in the past, back in her old home from yesteryear.

Four members of the Bald Skulls stormed into the small apartment unit, all of them warlocks holding various types of shotguns. None of them heard the pleas of Estrella's mother, begging for mercy as one member of the gang backed her into the corner. The event played out just like Estrella remembered, her mother getting blasted away first with a single shotgun shot to the chest. She looked away from the spatter of red that re-colored the kitchen counters and plates.

Estrella was screaming now, shooting her pistol at the gang members, something she wished her younger self watching in horror had the power to do. The bullets didn't seem to do anything, just traveled through the four warlocks, like they weren't there. She was incapable of saving her parents then and incapable of doing it now.

Her father roared at the loss of his wife. He kicked and screamed as two gang members held him still, one on each side. A telepathic gang member silenced her father's lips. He was driven to scream internally. The gang forced him to look up at the barrel that would end his life. A cock of the weapon primed it for another blast. A pull of its triggered turned her father's head into gore, plastering the wall behind him in half a second.

Young Estrella watched that too, the newly drawn picture she held floated away from her tiny hands. It landed next to her bare feet.

She looked back at her younger self, and the tears welling up in her eyes, human eyes at that. Estrella missed having those in her head. The weeping noise young Estrella made drew the stares of the four warlocks, their faces brightened with perverse grins.

She saw her younger self turn and run, just like she remembered. She didn't get far, the door to her bedroom shut on its own, the blinds around the windows clattered. Her body became still, numb, cold, vision distorted. Young Estrella had no means to fend off the abilities of the four warlocks and telepaths.

That was the day they took her. The day they laughed all the way to their hideout within the slums of Buenos Aires. Young Estrella became the gang's newest pleasure and memory sphere girl to be peddled on the black market. Everything the gang did to her as the years passed on was recorded and transferred to memory spheres for underground psytrip experiences. Even the memory spheres of her parents' ends were sold. Sick motherfuckers loved to experience the thrill and bloodlust gangsters like the Bald Skulls went through. She really hoped the later years that followed didn't replay next. Estrella spent years trying to forget the number of X-rated and snuff psytrips she was forced to produce.

She collapsed to her knees, her hands holding onto her head, screaming. This was the past, it was done. Why was she back? Why couldn't she return to the present? Was it all a dream? Had her life going forward been a fantasy this whole time? She didn't know anymore.

Estrella took a deep breath and then held her right hand to her face. She was wearing an NC gauntlet. There's no way she would have dreamed about having that, same goes for her left synthetic arm and hand. She touched her body, top to bottom, she had womanly curves. There's no way her younger self would have fantasized about living long enough to become a woman.

A telepath was fucking with her mind. She continued to ground her thoughts back into reality, while holding back the urge to find the telepath that accessed her memories without her permission and create the illusionary vision of the past.

I'm not a girl anymore. I got free. I traded my humanity for witchhood. This isn't real!

When Estrella returned to the present, she was looking down at the floor. Darkness surrounded her as did the expensive bedroom furniture belonging to the Kounias family. Ahead was her pistol, separated from the grip of her hands. She reached for it and winced. The pistol moved to the side, on its own.

Someone laughed at her because of that.

EIGHTEEN
RAY

There wasn't much of a difference between dreams and psytrip sessions. Both had you placed in situations you had no control over, forcing you to watch and experience the events play out. In some cases, you could find yourself in the body of a different individual, lost and wandering around. So, when Ray opened his eyes and saw himself walking through the overcrowded streets of Munich, he had to ask himself, what was going on? Was this a dream? Or a psytrip session he forgot he paid for?

His body felt lighter than he last remembered, and his hair was long, curly if he were to guess. He'd touch it to confirm but had no control of the hand that reached for their phone. They were Arianna's hands, and the more he thought about it, this was her body. He'd explored every inch of it in the bedroom over the years the two had been together. He was in Arianna's body, experiencing what she saw in the EU.

The phone she held had his caller ID, her thumb tapped the ignore button. This wasn't the Arianna he knew, nor were the thoughts going through her head. She was paranoid, worried if anyone caught sight of her fleeing. Arianna was repeatedly looking behind her, expecting either the police or men from the Federation to be tailing her.

Arianna mused to herself about making a mistake and that it might catch up. Her avatar was in danger as was the package she had. She needed to get back to the Alliance and fast. Once there, she'll be protected from the Federation, clear from the EU authorities aggressively searching for all those involved with the attack. The further she got away from the hotel, the less likely anyone would suspect her of any wrongdoing.

———

Ray opened his eyes again. *His* eyes.

He sat up swiftly, lying on an emergency room bed with vital monitor equipment displaying his current condition. His heartbeats translated into the sounds of beeps. To his left was a wide window peering out into the nighttime New York skyline. The rain from earlier had transformed into white flakes powdering the city. The mixture of the snow and neon glow turned the darkened skies into a majestic magenta. Some of that aura shone into his hospital room, making the white blankets and a hospital gown he wore the same color.

It took him another minute, after looking away from the window, to remember why he was there. When he last checked, he went to the airport, against Arianna's request, and then came the attack. It came back to him, though the details of it were fuzzy. He remembered the assault, and two groups of shady men moving to intercept Arianna as she got off her flight. They were IWs, unusually strong ones too. He'd say they were weaponized, but that was impossible and highly illegal worldwide.

What happened next?

Ray knew he found Arianna, at least he thought it was her. It looked like her, felt like her, had the same voice as her, but that's where things stopped. Her personality wasn't right. It was like the Arianna he just finished dreaming about. He couldn't remember anything else but looking at his body lying on the bed it was clear he blacked out and was rescued. And if he was recovered Arianna should have been as well. There's no way she would have escaped without him.

That's not your Arianna, man. She would have left your ass there. He shook his head free of that thought.

It had to have been her. She probably was having a bad day. He would too if he knew IWs were stalking him.

A doctor dressed in a medical coat entered. He smiled at Ray when their eyes met. Ray was sitting up and awake. The doctor typed a quick note on the tablet pad he carried. When he was done, he stood next to Ray's bed, running a small handheld scanner around his head. The device hummed softly, outputting its results on a narrow screen attached to it.

"I was starting to worry about you," the doctor said.

Ray gave him a worried look. "What happened?"

"Was hoping you'd tell me. Airport security and an RW team pulled you out from that mess."

"Just me?"

"No, there were survivors. The other bodies recovered are in the morgue."

"Shit." He ground his teeth as the scanner was drawn away from his head. "Did you see my girlfriend?"

The doctor shook his head. "I don't know who she is."

"Her name is—" His body tensed up, thoughts of Arianna not making it clouded his thoughts. He told the trembling in his hands to leave him alone. "Arianna Kounias, uh."

Ray went searching for his smart glasses, patting down his frame, finding nothing but wires and tubes stuck to him, all plugged into the medical monitoring equipment. His face cringed when he came up empty-handed.

"Everything you had is still in your clothes."

Ray was left with one option, describing Arianna's appearance verbally. It was much easier to show a hologram of the individual. But without his phone or glasses, that wasn't happening. It was weird.

His head lay back on the soft pillow and looked up at the ceiling sighing. "She has long thin curly hair," he said, recalling Arianna's features.

Ray was thinking about the dream, being stuck in her body, walking through Munich, searching for men following her. It felt like he left the hospital instantly. His brain struggled to make sense of it all—

"And...?

The doctor's voice pulled his head back to the hospital bed. Ray continued. "Uh, brown hair ... beautiful blue eyes."

The look the doctor's face wasn't a promising one. "Sorry, I haven't seen anyone like that here."

"She was with me when I blacked out."

"From what they told me you were found alone, passed out with no signs of trauma."

Ray faced the doctor, his head still lying on the pillow. "You mean I fainted?"

The doctor shrugged. Ray wanted to as well. Blacking out because of the trauma he could see happening. Fainting because of stress? That wasn't him, and he didn't care what medical scans said.

"We're not sure what happened honestly," the doctor said. "Your brainwave patterns look like you had a run-in with a high-ranked telepath. Other than that, you're perfectly fine, it's like you went for a nap."

"There were telepaths with the IWs?"

Another flashback sent his head traveling back to the airport. An Asian man with long black hair tied in a ponytail, telepathic powers, and a nanite infused katana. Ray couldn't remember what became of him. He was there, and then gone like he performed a magic trick. Then again, these were IWs, witches, warlocks, telepaths, and shapeshifters. They were performing weird tricks in the womb.

"Usually telepaths play mind games, or read your thoughts," the doctor explained. "Making someone blackout is new unless they spooked you good with a frightening dream."

Ray shook his head. "No, nothing like that," he said. "I was with her, we were talking, and then I was here." There was the dream too, but it was just that, a dream. Then he remembered the doctor's last words. A frightening dream. *Did that dream cause me to blackout?*

The doctor made a note of what Ray said, typing it into his pad. Ray wondered if omitting the dream's details was the right thing.

"That's an interesting story—"

Two men dressed in black suits and ties entered the room. Ray and the doctor gave cocked glares at the interruption. One of them used their phone to project a large holographic ID card. It read Special Agent Miguel Cortez, Alliance Investigation Team. The second newcomer flashed his holographic ID, Special Agent John Reynolds. Alliance Investigators, top-level Alliance G-men who should be at the airport searching for clues about the attack but were now standing in Ray's hospital room. They came to have a chat with him, and he doubted it was about football.

"Mr. Partington," Miguel said to him when his ID faded after putting his phone away. "We have a few questions for you about what happened earlier today."

John nodded. "Mind telling us exactly what you told the doctor before we entered?"

The doctor stood still with his arms crossed. He let out a deep sigh. "Can this wait a bit, guys? He's still my patient."

"No, it can't," Miguel said. "You even said so yourself, he's fine."

The doctor left the room at the request of the men, leaving Ray alone with the two government agents. The door shut behind him as he passed through. Ray couldn't find a panic button to mash. He had a feeling he would need it, given the emotionless looks the two suited agents gave him. He hoped someone on the outside was monitoring his vitals, still hooked up to the machines.

Miguel stood to his left, John to his right. Their large imposing bodies caused the trembling in his hands to return. He made sure to keep them hidden under the blankets. Ray was asked to tell them what he experienced, so he complied. He explained to them he went to check-in early for his flight and described the battle that broke out, leading to him blacking out when he made contact with Arianna. All incriminating details, such as the fact he hacked the airport's security systems were left out, he wasn't in the mood for getting charged with cybercrimes.

John pulled out his tablet, keying the details onto it. Something big happened if the AIT were here, bigger than the attack being a bunch of rowdy IWs trying to bring harm to humans.

"What was your girlfriend's name again?" Miguel asked.

"Arianna Kounias," he said, and hoped there was some good news waiting for him. "She was on a flight from the EU to New York. She arrived moments before the attack."

"And you said she was coming from London?"

That was what she told him, but he had reason to believe she was on a different flight. He nodded. "Yeah."

The two agents looked away from Ray, making eye contact with each other. John typed and tapped on his pad, bringing up, something Ray couldn't see. When the agent was done reading the contents, he faced Miguel, shaking his head. "There's no record of anyone on that flight by that name."

Feelings of devastation punched him in the gut. "What about the flight inbound from Munich?"

John looked down, checking his pad and the new screens that

flashed, his face changed to blue and white colors from the pad's backlight. He shook his head again. "Nothing. Honestly, there's no record of anyone of that name on any of the flights that were coming in. The best we got was that she was booked to take a flight from New York to Los Angeles."

Which made sense as Arianna was to transfer to a connecting flight in New York, heading to Los Angeles. Arianna not being a registered passenger on any flight arriving from the EU into the Alliance for that day, however, did not.

"We'll let you know if we find anything new, sir," Miguel said to Ray. "The surveillance equipment in the airport was not only tampered with during the attack but hacked by a third party."

Little did the two agents know that Ray was that third party. He smiled once he remembered the blankets had covered his hands. Now wasn't the time for the AIT to point fingers at him for committing cybercrimes moments before IWs launched an attack, not while Arianna was missing, and a pile of mysteries about her floated to the surface.

The two agents left him alone. It helped with the jittering nerves. And with that came the ability to think straight and brain-storm several theories regarding the disappearance of the woman he loved.

Ray was glad he had five years as a journalist on his resume, and many more as a hacker. He would need those skills going forward.

NINETEEN
ESTRELLA

Estrella saw the man that laughed at her. He stood next to the bedroom door, an Asian man, with long black hair tied into a ponytail dangling behind him, a katana remained idle at his side with its sheath. His well-chiseled body enjoyed the protection of a suit of combat armor hugging the muscular ridges of his arms, and chest, while his hands were wrapped within black leather gloves. Faint traces of white light escaped from the ends of the gloves near his wrists.

It was the telepath that got into her mind. Estrella debated if she'd kill him fast or make him suffer slowly first.

"Hello, Estrella," said the ponytailed telepath. His voice had a touch of charm in it. "Forgive the memory intrusion; I merely wanted to get to you know you better."

She was on all fours when she looked up at him, frowning fiercely. Her returning strength and mental will to live made her crawl to the dropped pistol. "Fuck you, pendejo," she added on her journey.

"Fuck me?" He snickered. "I'm trying to be nice, saying hello, and this is how you greet me?" She neared the fallen pistol, reaching for it. It faded when she held it. It wasn't real. Neither were the six others that appeared around her. He was still in her brain. "Now, now. I want to chat, not fight."

Geoffrey ...

There was silence in her mind.

Then, there wasn't.

Please standby, I am attempting to match the frequency of his telepathic mind. I should be able to block it, but I will need him to continue to use it.

Fuck that.

If I cannot learn his brainwave pattern, then he will maintain his assault on us with his thoughts. This is the only counter I can provide.

She took her chances, leaping for one of the six pistols. That one too wasn't real. She wondered if the sudden migraine that erupted was real, or just mental manipulation thanks to the telepath. Not that it mattered, real pain, imaginary pain, it was all the same and all very debilitating.

Geoffrey being back online, however, was a good thing. Her nanite swarm should be ready for battle. She faced the telepath again, extending her NC gauntlet hand to him, and requested her nanites spin every partical in his body until he ignited and inciner-ated. Geoffrey denied her request, multiple error windows flashing over her eyes.

I have temporarily disabled your utility nanites. He may try to use mind control on you.

Geoffrey, you're not helping me.

Believe me, I am doing my best. You will die if I cannot help you, and so, I will cease to function. I am programmed to prevent that from happening.

The ponytailed telepath crouched, and his eyes met Estrella's. "Where are the Bald Skulls?"

She snorted. "Asking the wrong person."

"Really?" A light chuckle followed. "Last I checked, you were investing a lot of time tracking them today. So, I ask again, where are they? How many did you confirm are still alive? How many people have they taken? Answer these questions, and you'll be free to go. You have my word."

The pain of the migraine was like having her brain placed in the jaws of a lion. "I ... take it you're not with the ... gang."

"Does it look like it?" He tapped his armor, then his katana and pistol. "Does the damage down below look like the gang's work? Come now, Estrella, you know this family has very little value to the gang. They weren't here, though I wish they were."

The chaos she saw coming up to the second floor, the death of Maria, bullet holes in the walls, and the flowerpots. It was him. He attacked the Kounias family, not the gang. Whoever the fuck he was. Estrella was looking at a secondary threat, or the gang's activities were a smokescreen.

"Who are you?"

"If I tell you, will you cooperate?"

She snorted. "Maybe."

"Let's go with the name Nobuo, for now." Nobuo spoke again. "Answer me now—"

Something changed, and she saw it on his face. Rising to his feet, Nobuo reached for his pistol and took aim out into the hallway. His pistol clapped three times, someone else clapped back.

"Rodriguez!" It was Marcus' voice. He just picked a fight with Nobuo a telepath, one that sensed him coming without having to look or hear.

Marcus was a dead man unless she got to her feet.

Estrella went rolling across the floor below the hail of bullets as the exchange continued. She nearly passed out from the pain in her aching head. She stood with her back against the surface of a desk. The computer screen above had turned into shards of plastic and flickering, sparking wires.

I'm almost finished Estrella, please prepare yourself. And that she did, clenching her fists within the NC gauntlet.

Marcus was hunkered outside the door when she peeked around her cover. It was the last time she saw him alive. Two bullets through his forehead put him down. Nobuo didn't need to aim, he simply pointed his gun exactly where he predicted Marcus would peek out, then fired.

"Don't bother wasting nanites on him," Nobuo said. "Don't think they can repair his brains leaking out the back of his head."

Ten seconds, Estrella.

Little fucking late for that!

Nobuo stepped toward the desk she was behind. A katana now replaced the pistol he held.

Five seconds.

"Your partner's actions, and your unwillingness to answer my questions carries a penalty."

Three seconds.

He glanced at the sharpness of his blade. It lit up with indigo light, brightening his face in the darkness. It was a nanite infused katana. Estrella watched videos of those cut through reinforced steel doors with one swing.

"Please come out and make this easier for us both."

Now.

The excruciating pain of the migraine lifted. It made Nobuo's footsteps come to a stop. He knew his mental powers were being resisted. Impressive, considering even the most adept IW telepaths weren't able to sense that. She pushed those thoughts aside. Nobuo didn't need his telepathic abilities to kill her.

Geoffrey released the restriction of her utility nanites. With clenched fists, she stood up fast and confirmed the command she sent to the swarm.

Disable firearm

Nanites sabotage the interior of firearms, preventing their use in combat.
Min. nanite swarm(s) required: 1
Nanite swarm(s) remaining: 2

The first swarm sprayed from her gauntlet and flew into the pistol Nobuo held. It took two seconds for all vital components that made a gun work to get taken apart at the subatomic level.

Estrella didn't bother to wait for the confirmation signals from the swarm. She was too busy reaching for a spare nanotube, pulled out from the inside of her synthetic arm. She plugged the syringe of the device into her leg, the pain was brief, and so was the feeling of a new swarm of nanites entering her body, syncing with her and Geoffrey.

Her combat HUD flashed an update.

Nanite swarm(s) remaining: 2

Nobuo was running at her now, his nanite enhanced katana held steady to make a clean cut aimed at her neck. He must have known his pistol was useless, thanks to his powers. The desk she covered behind slid across the floor, crashing into the wall. He could still move objects with psychokinesis. Overdrive was her next trick of choice, and the world slowed down to bullet time, not that any of those were coming at her.

Nanite swarm(s) remaining: 1

Estrella sidestepped, watching the swing of his shimmering blade cut through the air. From her point of view, it took ten seconds for the blade to reach where she was once standing, Nobuo, moving in slow motion, was none the wiser about what was happening. His disabled pistol dangled slowly at his side during his attack. She reached for it while signaling the nanite swarm still within it and ordered them to repair the damage with what little battery power they had left. The pistol was now in her hands, and she took three steps back, aimed it at the back of his head, and went for the trigger.

The nanites committed to powering her overdrive were losing power. She'd have to send another swarm to keep the ability active. Estrella opted to save the remaining nanite swarm and put an end to overdrive. When the overdrive effect wore off, her world and its speed returned to normal. Nobuo's running left to right cleave that was meant to end her finished, cutting nothing but the air. He stood, looking shocked at an empty spot before him. Estrella's trigger finger moved multiple times. She emptied what remained in the clip.

Every bullet floated in the air. Nobuo's black-gloved white glowing hands extended toward her and the floating bullets, his back still turned to her. The bullets clattered to the floor with a single snap of his fingers. Nobuo had precognition in combination with advanced psychokinesis, a combination of gifts that was impossible for IWs to use in this day and age.

He spun, sizing her up with the katana. Estrella ordered the remaining nanites within her into firearm. A weapon selection screen appeared over her eyes, she browsed through a selection of melee weapons. The screen confirmed the pistol contained enough raw materials. The weapon she held liquefied, turning into gray goo. In three seconds, she nano printed a short sword using the metal from the pistol. The tip of its newly forged blade pointed at Nobuo. It was faster than reaching for a new nanotube, one his precognition might have predicted.

He grinned at her then faced the door to the room which her back was turned to. Something caught his attention, something that made him wince, nod, and then slash empty air ahead of him. In the wake of his shimmering blade was a rift, a temporal doorway for his escape. He slipped through it. That too was impossible last time she checked. The rift vanished in a flash as she ran, charging him with the short sword in hand seeking his blood.

Estrella spun and went for the door. Something there got Nobuo running from the fight. Was it Marcus? Did he survive the attack? Perhaps watching him get shot was part of the illusionary vision the telepath had conjured. She sure hoped so.

She saw a pair of emerald synthetic eyes glowing in the darkness near the door. The owner of those eyes moved into the room. Out from the shadows of the hallway entered Piper, lowering her pistol. Neither of them looked away from each other.

Estrella grimaced. "Piper?"

Piper holstered her weapon to the leather skirt she wore. The holographic raven of her AI perched on her left shoulder. "You're welcome."

"What are you doing here?"

"Saving your ass?"

The two stood above Marcus' body. His chest wasn't moving, and nearly all the blood in his head had seeped out into the floor, growing into a large puddle. Estrella stopped herself from driving her synthetic fist through the wall. Instead, she pointed a finger at Piper.

"You got the worst fucking timing!" Estrella roared. "You and Geoffrey should make a club."

"Give me a fucking break! I just got here!"

"You left before us, didn't you?"

Piper answered with a grimace, pushed past Estrella, and walked to the area of the bedroom Nobuo vanished from. It reminded her of his actions before running away. Nobuo looked at the door, he made eye contact with Piper, and she did the same with him. He knew Piper was standing and watching as Estrella's back was turned.

Piper didn't just get there. She'd been there the whole time.

Geoffrey, did you pick up Piper's signal at all?

I'm not receiving it now, or when we discovered she was here.

Didn't think so. Estrella's lips twisted. She looked at the figure of the mysterious RW wrapped in the tight leather skirt, and lace robe rustling as she moved, searching the room with the optical scanners in her glowing emerald eyes.

"Hey Piper, how come I can't pick up your transponder?"

"Get your AI looked at," she said, her radiating eyes not looking into hers. "My systems are operating fine on my end."

Geoffrey?

I did not receive any damage during the confrontation. I am operating at normal parameters.

Three police cars and their wailing sirens echoed in the skies outside, nearing the Kounias residence. Estrella pondered how she would explain what happened and where Norris Kounias ended up. There's no way an aged man like him escaped from the katana-wielding psychopath.

TWENTY
RAY

The cold air of winter hit Ray on his exit from the emergency room. He missed Los Angeles already and the normalcy of his life. He grimaced, looking back at the hospital that was vanishing in the distance behind. Arianna wasn't with him and neither the AIT nor the police knew where she was.

The only saving grace he had was that her body was not among the bodies getting dragged out from the airport, which were mostly the IWs, security, and RWs that went to fight them. That was also the reason he was discharged so quickly. Doctors determined Ray had blacked out, probably from a run-in with an unregistered IW with telepathic powers. No need to take up the limited hospital beds for the critically wounded that needed it.

He was glad to see nobody accessed his phone or tablet pad, at least not from what he could gather. Even if they did, the illegal hacking apps he had on them were well hidden and required biometric access. That's when he noticed the unmarked vehicle parked near to the hospital. The AIT was still there, probing for answers about the IW attack. Answers his devices had. His speed increased, and he was constantly glancing back, ensuring nobody was following him.

Ray felt exactly like Arianna in the dream he had, leaving the hotel, always looking back, searching for men from the Federation. He wouldn't have been surprised if the IWs involved in the attack came from the Federation. He physically felt like Arianna during the walk, as if someone swapped his male body out with a woman's. Panic and confusion hit, and it caused him to stagger slightly in the snow below him.

He reached for his phone, switching on its selfie camera. His face flashed back on the screen, and it was the man he knew he was. Nothing physically changed about him. Mentally, well, that was another story.

Ray tapped through several windows on his phone, bringing up a taxi summoning app. The onscreen notification informed him one would be at his location in two minutes. He stood next to the road, and waited, watching cars, snow removal drones, and occupied yellow cabs zoom past in the busy New York streets. The falling snow took on the colors of the neon and holographic ad spectacle.

Making calls to Arianna's phone helped pass the time, though, he wondered why he even bothered. Even his phone flashed a prompt, informing him the recent calls he made to her number had gone unanswered such as the one he just made. It gave him a sick feeling. This was the day he was to propose to her. Now, Ray might be facing a dark moment in life where the woman he loved was taken before he could ask. And his last memories of her? Was a woman that didn't act like the one he knew—

New York's busy, loud, and colorful streets were gone.

Ray stood watching a computer screen and it wasn't his eyes looking at it. It was Arianna's; he was in her body again. Diagrams were on the screen, and they looked like blueprints. To what? He couldn't make it out: a device, robotic parts, cyberware implants?

Scientific equations upstaged everything he saw, numbers, letters, mathematical symbols, and none of it could he make any sense of.

New York came back with the honk of a taxicab as it pulled up to him. His ride had arrived. Three onlookers from the sidewalk shot him odd glances as he moved across the snow into the cab. He was afraid to ask what he was doing when the vision hit.

His body felt the soothing feeling of warmness once he sat inside the cab. So did his mind when he saw Arianna sitting in the cab with him.

"Arianna!" he shouted gleefully.

She didn't reply, she was also dressed differently from when he looked at her at the airport. Arianna wore a lab coat with a guest visitor badge clipped to her top, listing a name that wasn't her. She faded away when he reached to touch her. Upon a closer look, Arianna was never there to start with. It was another vision. Ray's sense of reality and dreaming meshed. He shuddered at the thought of him driving in his current condition.

His ride back to his hotel went on without incident, the images were lingering after-effects of that ponytailed telepath he figured. The access keycard in his hands unlocked his suite door, but he didn't enter his hotel room. He entered a laboratory when he walked through the door. The visions returned, and backtracking into the hotel's hallway wasn't an option, as the door he stepped through was gone.

Arianna walked away from him like she had been a ghostly figure inside. He followed her into the vision of the lab. Glass chambers holding naked test subjects in stasis pods lined the walls. At the end of the lab was a computer station, the same one from his last vision. Arianna led him right to it, and she ordered a man wearing a lab coat to give her access to it. The red and yellow flag of the People's Federation of Pacific Nations hung on the wall above the station.

The vision turned into more equations, numbers, diagrams, and blueprints. None of it made sense, and none of it would go away, not even when he shut his eyes, in fact, that made things worse. He felt himself thrown into a woman's body again, breasts, long hair, his penis and balls vaporized and replaced with a vagina, the works. He was Arianna.

And she was asking the man with a lab coat to put a gun in his mouth.

The world of the normal returned. Ray was in his hotel suite. He placed his hands down his pants, searching for his junk, making sure they were there. They were. He was overjoyed to have them back and glad to be back in his original form. The experience had him checking his body every five minutes when he saw equations and numbers flash before his eyes.

His tablet played the news as he sat at the edge of the bed, his head buried in his twin facepalming hands. There was very little mentioned about the airport attack, most journalists were only now getting the word about it. Violent IWs used their powers to bypass security and cause trouble, that's all the world knew, and had no idea how or why it happened. IWs weren't strong enough for that level of power.

He went to read news from Los Angeles, hoping to learn of something on the positive side since he'd been gone. There was a missing person report filed for a woman named Portia Blanchard. She was abducted by force from the IW district in Los Angeles, along with another young man earlier that same day. So much for the world being a positive place.

The news went on, rambling about attacks happening in Los Angeles, right around the same time as the airport attack in New York. He lowered his hands from his face, leaning his head closer to his pad next to him on the bed when the mention of IWs in Beverly Hills was made, and the name of the two RWs that were called to the scene. Estrella Rodriguez, and Piper Taylor, while a cop named Marcus Desmond, assigned to work with Rodriguez was found dead with two of Estrella's bullets in his brain. No addresses were given, or any other names dropped of the victims as the police were searching for the next of kin—

His phone beeping took his attention away from the news.

Ray went racing to grab the phone, his heart pounding rapidly, hoping it was Arianna reaching out to him. When he picked up the phone, looking down at the display, he cringed. It wasn't Arianna shooting a text message. It was Steven, his editor, sending him an email.

Steven asked why he couldn't reach Ray via phone. He grinned. Ray left his Los Angeles only phone at home. Also in the email, Steven asked if Ray had any knowledge of the airport attack.

He did. He was there, and he had the scoop no other journalist in the world had. Ray replied, explaining he left his Los Angeles phone and was using a secret New York one. Steven wanted to talk, rather than send messages back and forth. Ray called him, using the hotel room's phone. He still wasn't going to risk exposing his phone's number to anyone, not even Steven.

"Hey," Ray said when he saw Steven's face flash on the phone display screen.

"Do you seriously have an exclusive about the attack?"

He nodded to the screen. "That and more, I saw the whole thing unfold."

Steven's jaw dropped like a teenage boy after experiencing his first adult psytrip. "Holy fucking shit you just renewed yourself." Steven's roaring laughter made the phone he carried on his end shake. It looked like Steven had been caught in an earthquake. When the laugh stopped, Steven's face returned to the screen, his smile was bright and wide. "Ray! Give us everything you fucking got on it!"

"What about the expo—"

"Fuck the expo! I want this exclusive!"

"Wow." Ray scratched the back of his head. "Didn't know you were okay with real journalism."

"I'm okay with whatever the fuck will pay the fucking bills. And your exclusive scoop, my friend, is going to pay a lot of them, so long as you don't shit all over our sponsors. You won't do that right?"

He reflected back to the attack and thought back to the dreams and visions. He saw too many fingers pointed at the Federation. "I think the Federation might have been involved."

"Those commies aren't paying us, so fuck 'em. Tell the world what you saw."

Fake news when it makes money, real news when it could make even more money. Publications were no better than corporations; the almighty Alliance dollar governed how they operate. If people wanted news stories about funny unicorns seen during an acid trip, and it paid the Alliance Star well, they'd run that too.

Ray was a journalist born in the wrong year.

"I'll get you your story," he said, to Steven's delighted face. "Hey off-topic, did my girlfriend Arianna contact you recently by chance?"

"No, is she supposed to?"

"She's ... missing sir."

"Sorry to hear that bud."

Yeah, bull-fucking-shit.

"Please, don't go all sour on me because of that. Need you to focus."

Steven didn't care.

"She was also at the airport when the attack happened," Ray added.

"Oh, really?"

"That's why I'm worried; she might be involved in it."

"Shit man that sucks, like, really it does. If you're cool with it though, try to say something about her too. Readers are going to dig the emotional side to the report."

Now Steven cared, but only because he saw it as another means to squeeze the story for more money. The call ended, and Ray went to gaze out the window, looking at the same New York skyline shining its glow of neon up into the white dust from the skies. He was looking to collect his thoughts, hoping the article he planned to write might shed light on Arianna's disappearance, and maybe her change of attitude.

Instead, reality melted away and the dreamlike world of Arianna's journey overseas replayed. None of it showed like she was abroad on business, hell; none of it looked like she worked for Yoshida at all. He saw Arianna get chased throughout the Federation by IWs. He watched her do the same to them, then saw their mangled and twisted blood-soaked bodies fall to the floor. Arianna was the sole survivor of whatever battle she found herself in.

It felt like Arianna had stolen something, and she was killing to prevent it from returning to the owner.

There was more going on, and the visions were more than just weird dreams. Someone with telepathic powers forced them in his head, which made what he had seen in them a fact. It was going to be hard to compose a news article based on the visions. Why? Because he couldn't prove it without hard evidence or real sources. It was just him and a claim that a telepath put the visions in his mind.

He sat at his hotel room desk and began outlining what he was going to draft. And what he outlined was only what he saw personally from the airport attack. As for the strange visions? He made plans to post that on his blog. But first he had to make sense of it, and he needed someone with telepathic powers to do that.

When he was finished writing the article, Ray brought up a search on his pad, looking for the nearest Pause, Play, Rewind center in New York's IW district. A memory sphere from a psytrip experience was the only thing he could think of that would extract the facts from the weird visions making a mess of his head. He placed a reminder on his phone to visit them the next day.

The rest of the night was spent staring out the window, as the snow continued to fall. He hoped that if Arianna was out there, lost, that she was making her way back to him.

Together, they could find a solution.

TWENTY-ONE
ESTRELLA

Goodbye Buenos Aires ...

Thoughts like that repeated in Estrella's head. They didn't stop, not even during the debriefing she had with Timothy Peters. She hadn't been with the LAPD for a full week, and she was getting her second grilling for a botched job. Peters had little reason to send positive commendations of her work to Yoshida, and she knew it. She could tell by his eyes and various optical scans of his face, all of them showing displeasure when he looked at her, sitting across from his desk.

Piper stood at Estrella's side with arms folded over her elegant black lace top. The two RWs took turns explaining their part of the story, and how Marcus ended up with Estrella's bullets through his head. Turns out the pistol Nobuo held during the confrontation was hers. There was no way to sugarcoat what happened to him. Further proof she was stuck in LA for good or going to be sent off for recycling.

Goodbye Buenos Aires ...

Peters adjusted his glasses, pushing two of his fingers up against its central rim. "Sounds to me, like you brought your problems from Buenos Aires into our city, Estrella."

"I'm telling you, we killed them all back home," Estrella said. "The Bald Skulls, we fucked that whole gang over."

"Yet, they're here, alive and well, and now we have this new fuckwit turning my city into a warzone looking for them."

Piper made a face at the words warzone. "How bad was it?"

Estrella thought back to the original call. It wasn't just the Kounias residence that was attacked by IWs, but two other locations in the city, simultaneously, all of them with IWs a lot stronger than your usual rowdy ones.

Peters laid out the bad news. "IWs hit three targets, the Kounias residence as you know, an armory used by the SWAT, and some apartment complex downtown. They left six officers, and eight RW dead, and five more fighting for their lives."

Piper's eyes widened. "Fuck."

"Oh, there's more," he added. "We lost a gunship."

Her eyes still widened. "They blew up a gunship?"

"No, it's just gone. Not stolen, or destroyed, simply vanished in thin air."

Estrella grimaced. "Civvies?"

More bad news, courtesy of Peters. "Eleven dead, including five children," he revealed. "That's a lot of lives thrown away by this IW, Nobuo, looking for the Bald Skulls if your report is right Estrella."

She shook her head and then joined Piper in the arms crossed game. "I don't know what the fuck to tell you."

"And I don't know what to tell Marcus' soon to be grieving family, why his RW partner double-tapped him."

Estrella shooting her gun off at imaginary gang members her mind told her were there, when lost in the illusion Nobuo made, wasn't helping her image. While none of those shots hit Marcus, anyone could argue that they did. Only she and Nobuo knew who shot Marcus dead, and she doubted he'd come forward and take credit.

"That wasn't my doing," was all she could say.

Peters reached for his, probably now cold, coffee on his desk. "I know. You and your medical scans prove it, a telepath got in your head. Still, your bullets are in his body, and the IW attacks in the city are a result of a new threat looking for the gang that followed you here. People are going to question if Yoshida giving you a second chance at life was the correct move."

"If I may, sir." Piper stepped forward with a brisk wave of her hand like she was painting an image on thin air. A holographic screen appeared, and its light helped brighten the slightly dark office. Piper directed their attention to the screen's contents. "Estrella's right about the gang. According to this, several gang members died in the hospital after an RW raid in Buenos Aires."

Estrella eyed the report written in Spanish, grinning at the photos of the dead Bald Skulls members. She wasn't sure how she should feel about the fact she officially killed some of those members twice now.

Regardless, Piper's reveal was promising news. She liked her a bit more. "You see? I'm not fucking making this up."

Peters gleamed at the report, lines of words moved across the lenses of his glasses, automatically translating Spanish to English in the hologram for him. He sat back in his chair when done, folding his hands together. "How does a gang come back to life and then make their way to Los Angeles right as Rodriguez does?"

A question Estrella had been asking since her first day in the city. She was glad to see others were finally as well. "I'd like to know why Nobuo went on a mission to find the Bald Skulls only to end up attacking the Kounias, murdering Maria Kounias, then struggling to get her husband Norris. Did we locate his body?"

"I don't think there's a body to be found," Piper said with a shake of her head. "One of the rear bedroom windows was smashed, he must have escaped."

That got Estrella facing Piper. Marcus and Estrella where the first to the scene, and she knew it. If he was alive, he'd confirm it too. There were no other vehicles parked near the house and no other signs that Piper entered before them.

Piper showed up when Nobuo got into Estrella's mind. Yet Piper spoke as if she had been there, conducting a lengthy search. She'd say something on that, but what was the point? Piper's official report stated she arrived before them and they missed each other. Piper also left Marcus and Estrella behind at the bar, meaning she had a head start.

Still doesn't explain how she got there before us without a vehicle.

Peters looked up at Estrella, her face still lost in thought. "Rodriguez, you said Ray Partington from the Alliance Star was dating the daughter of Norris and Maria Kounias correct?"

Estrella nodded quickly. "That's right, and he was their last visitor before the attacks."

"I think we should pay him a visit," Piper added. "Arianna too, she'll want to know what happened to her family."

Peters concurred, and then grimly added. "Assuming nobody got to them already."

Estrella stepped forward. They made no mention of her getting the defective stamp on her head. She was still part of the team. This was her chance to make things right and get that commendation. "I'll get on it," she said with brimming confidence.

"No," Peters shot her down hard and fast. "I need you to take it easy—"

"Oh, come on!"

"If these gangsters are here in the city for you, then you need to stay low. If they're sighted, this new IW group Nobuo is working with will make their move and we'll require more body bags to clean up the mess."

"Both you and I know the Bald Skulls have their own plans," Estrella asserted. "Remember? The kidnappings?"

"Kidnappings you conveniently were near, Estrella," he said. "They're probably trying to bait you to come after them."

By targeting unregistered IWs? No, that's no coincidence.

"What about the other two attacks? I wasn't near them!"

"Still a mystery we're investigating," Peters replied. "For all we know, the gang was in the area, and this new IW group found out."

She'd argue her point more, but the words that came out of Piper's mouth next sealed the deal. "I'll handle this sir," Piper offered. "I know Ray personally anyway."

Peters nodded. "Do it. Rodriguez, sit this one out for the time being. Let's see what happens."

———

"Need a lift again?"

Estrella snapped out of her ominous gaze into the city outside. She was sitting on the front steps leading into the police station. Originally, she sat to collect her thoughts, calm her nerves, and recover mentally from what transpired during the evening. Instead, her mind had wandered off, daydreaming, and fantasizing about Yumi, and a funeral that may or may not happen thanks to Yoshida claiming ownership over a part of Yumi's body. Estrella's family wasn't far from her thoughts too, and she'd never be able to see them unless they showed up for a visit. RWs don't get vacations. Yoshida still viewed her as a product rather than a person.

She had no means of getting home, other than calling for a taxi or using a train. That was the second reason she came to sit at the steps. Estrella had a lot to think about. She imagined dream Yumi sitting beside her in those cute tight shorts she'd wear, telling

Estrella things would work out because Estrella's a great person. Dream Yumi put her hand on Estrella's shoulder.

"Estrella?"

She looked behind and saw Piper. Her synthetic hand came to rest on Estrella's shoulder in a comforting manner. It felt nice. It made her smile. Dream Yumi faded when Estrella realized who had been really touching her.

"Yeah, didn't get my wheels yet."

Piper returned the smile, twirling her keys with her other hand. "Come along then!"

She was in Piper's sports car again, strapping herself in as her rival RW powered the car on. The same car Estrella was positive wasn't anywhere near the Kounias residence, contrary to what Piper told everyone.

The same nighttime neon sights graced Estrella's vision, reminiscent of the last drive home Piper offered. She briefly wondered if Piper would come up with another life or death reason to enter her unit. There was more to the pixie kiwi woman than she was letting others know, including the LAPD.

"Talk to me, new girl."

Estrella faced Piper and was instantly charmed by her Mona Lisa-like smile. She felt obligated to speak. "Meh, wasn't expecting my debut in the city to be so fucking stupid."

"Well, you're almost home and got a few days off by the sounds of it."

"Yeah ..."

"Unpack your stuff. It's making a mess of your place."

An eyebrow raised on Estrella's face. "What makes you think I haven't done that already?"

Estrella hadn't finished unpacking but had more than enough time to do so. Reading up on Piper was an excellent distraction that night. How did Piper know she didn't finish unpacking? Or that her place was a mess with her belongings scattered.

"Just a guess is all," Piper said, her synthetic eyes returning to the road ahead. "When you get to my age, you learn to read young people like you."

"You're thirty-five, you're not that old."

"Been reading up on me, have we?"

Estrella pursed her lips, and she felt her face flush. It made Piper smile again when she took notice. "Take the downtime to hang out with whoever you came here with, Estrella, and start again."

"I came alone."

"Oh, that's right, sorry I forgot." An awkward silence fell. "So ... you alone, huh? No friends or anything like that?"

"Everyone I knew is back in Buenos Aires." *And the only friend I had is dead ...*

"Holy shit."

Piper set the car to manual control, took the wheel, and made a sudden turn with it as it drove amongst the cars on the freeway. It slipped under an overpass, driving away from the signs guiding those to district 666. The path to Estrella's home was drifting away rather than closer.

She twisted her lips, watching the unfamiliar portion of the freeway move past. "Going the wrong way, Piper."

"No, we're going the right way," she replied. "You need some friends. Fuck, I think you need some pick-me-up food."

"I can order drone food like everyone else."

"Fuck that. What you need, is some ice cream."

"Yeah, can get that too, you know."

"But you prefer the real shit, no?"

"The real shit isn't all that real."

"Then you're going to love this place, I guarantee it, sweetie. It's expensive but worth it. I'll buy; it will be my treat, okay?"

TWENTY-TWO

RAY

Ray didn't need to wake up when his hotel alarm told him to, blaring its screeching sounds. His eyes had been open, lying on his bed, and staring at the ceiling. The same ceiling he'd been looking at for the last eight hours. Or was it twelve? He lost the willpower to keep count.

If life hadn't been so fucking brutal this past two days, then he and Arianna would have been officially engaged by now. The two would be on a flight to LA, dreaming up plans for the big wedding day. Now, Ray spent his time writing an article on the JFK airport attack, which could have potentially ripped Arianna out from his world for good. At least the hotel was kind enough to extend his stay until the airport reopened.

With JFK being down, no flights had entered or left the city since the attack. The only way out or into other local airports was on the ground and police and AIT had been conducting vigorous searches of all vehicles and trains since the incident, none of them reporting Arianna's presence. It gave him hope he'd reconnect with Arianna. She was alive, his journalist mind told him so, and there wasn't enough evidence to suggest otherwise. She was in the city, somewhere, hiding from the IWs. Why else would her name not be on the flight? She knew someone from the EU was following her. She was trying to throw them off, and it backfired. He really hoped it wasn't because of him.

None of the cameras in the airport could get a glimpse of what happened to her or him when he blacked out. The IWs that had been pausing and unpausing recording did it to the area he found Arianna. His visions were the only proof that Arianna or at least a woman looking like her arrived in New York. The visions were also a mess of weird stuff he couldn't shake off. Like the feeling of becoming Arianna, complete with all the heightened sense of awareness, like she was doing things she shouldn't be doing, against her will.

Pause, Play, Rewind. He remembered he made plans to visit them and set out to do so after a quick shower. He grabbed his phone off the nightstand, thumbing in the number to the owner of the local Pause, Play, Rewind location in New York. An old news source of Ray's.

The call was answered after two rings. The bearded face of a man with receding hair, wearing a jean jacket and tattoos all over his face and arms projected on Ray's phone's screen. There was a lit cigarette in his mouth he pulled away with his fingers to speak.

"Hello?"

Ray smiled at the sound of the voice. "Joel, hey long time no see."

"Fucking, Partington, that you?" Joel exhaled smoke.

"Yeah man, how you've been holding up?"

"I should ask you that after that article you wrote last year. You fucking made me, my business, and fellow IWs look bad!"

"It's the truth; you guys had some illegal psytrip stuff for sale."

"We didn't know they were part of our stock! If I had, then I would have trashed them."

"Whatever, I'm not calling about that."

"What are you calling for then?"

"I need your help."

"Oh, big fucking surprise," Joel puffed his cigarette. "What's up now? Need a new source for a smear job story?"

"I need a telepath to poke around in my head," Ray said. "There's some material there I'd like verified."

"What kind of stuff?"

He shrugged slightly. "I don't know, was hoping you could tell me."

"Does it have to do with the recent attack?"

"Maybe."

"Swing by in an hour and I'll see what I can do," Joel said after a long pause. "This is gonna cost you know?"

"Whatever it takes, man."

A 'message ended' flashed on his phone's screen. He slipped his phone into his pocket and got ready to leave.

———

The New York Pause, Play, Rewind establishment was in the city's IW district, much like its LA counterpart, dead center of lower Manhattan. Coming off the high-speed train that took Ray from his hotel to the district brought him two blocks away from the establishment. The streets were devoid of the snow that fell the previous night, self-driving snowplows made their rounds hours earlier by the looks.

New York's IW district wasn't like LA's, there were fewer IWs and a lot more humans. A bit of anxiety nipped at Ray's head as he pushed past a wall of men and women with spiked hair, mohawks dyed pink or purple, with way too many piercings in their tattooed bodies. Ripped jeans and leather jackets were the attire of choice.

One IW man with a phone in hand and a ghetto blaster in the

other glared at Ray when he caught him looking at him. "The fuck you lookin' at human?!"

Ray raised his hands in a please, I'm sorry motion, and moved away fast before the IW's friend put a hex on him. Assuming one hadn't been put on him already, it'd explain the shitty luck that had hit Ray recently.

Loud dark synthwave music pulsed through the air when Ray got to Pause, Play, Rewind. Warlock bouncers gave him a nod, allowing him to venture deeper in. Like the LA version, the establishment doubled as a brothel. It was the perfect place to record new memories and then sell the memory spheres to those looking for a hot psytrip. He avoided the halls leading to those rooms.

Being there brought back memories of the last time Ray had visited, and the research he was conducting on the illegal memory sphere trade. Selling telepathically recorded memory spheres to be used in psytrip encounters wasn't illegal of course, provided the source giver gave their consent. The New York Pause, Play, Rewind had every experience you could think of, it was one of the biggest in the country, and its telepathic staff was more than willing to make you experience what other people did in the past.

Adult playtime in the bed? First dates? Amazing adventures? They had something for everyone. And if there wasn't, then they paid money to those that had those memories, witch or human, to come in and have a telepath record and create the memory sphere. Ever wanted to climb a mountain? Just buy a memory sphere with that encounter, and then have the telepath give you the psytrip experience and relive the experience of someone else doing that. The sights, smells, feelings, you temporarily become that person during that moment.

It was a good business until people secretly sold under aged sex memory spheres and the like. The New York location Ray stood in was home to the biggest distribution point of that thanks to one of their employees that collected them behind the management's back. Ray's investigative report got those memory spheres destroyed, and the men and women behind it hunted down by local RWs.

Ray found Joel in the dark halls standing next to a woman with short brunette hair sitting on a lounge chair. The sides of her head were shaved and decorated with pentagrams.

"Punctual, as usual," Joel glanced at the time on his phone and grinned. "You must be serious about this."

"I'd rather not be here, and you know that," Ray said drily.

Joel nodded to the woman beside him. "This is Celia; she's one of our best." Celia smirked, sitting back in the lounge chair, arching her back to make her breasts, wrapped in a fishnet top, stick up enticingly. Ray kept his eyes averted. He still had high hopes of reuniting with Arianna. "She'll get what you need, Partington."

Ray grimaced. "Of course, shall we?"

"Payment bro."

Joel informed him of the cost, one thousand Alliance dollars. It was way overpriced. Joel was striking back at Ray for the exposé he wrote. As he recalled, Joel lost a lot of business for the first half of '81.

With a nod, Joel had Celia stand and guide Ray to the rear rooms, the non-brothel one he hoped although Celia wasn't dressed for that kind of service. She wore mesh stockings, and a micro skirt so short you could see half the shape of her thong and it was completely transparent. He wondered what the point was of wearing it in the first place.

Closed doors and translucent walls lined the corridor in the hall Celia guided Ray through. He could see the shadows of people fucking, some were even bold enough to fuck next to the translucent windows, like the woman squashing her high breasts against the glass, while her partner gave it to her from behind. She winked at Ray, and then licked the glass with lust in her eyes, a ribbon of witch saliva smeared across the glass. Ray was regretting coming here. Celia had the wrong idea, he still loved Arianna.

"Uh," he went to speak up. "I think we're in the wrong place."

"Naw," Celia replied. "There's only one room available, and it's down here, hun."

The only free room in question slid open with a wave of Celia's hand near a biometric scanner. Ray peeked inside. A bed, nightstand, and mirrors were all he could see. He wanted to turn around.

Celia pushed her slender fingers against his back, preventing that. "Right this way," she whispered.

The door closed and she locked it. Ray was alone with Celia. She mischievously held him by the hands and pulled him to the bed where he sat on its edge. Ray yanked his hands away after she sat, keeping them to himself. This is not where he should be. Joel's idea of revenge was cheeky.

She sat beside him, smiling, playfully stroking her fingers across his shoulders. Blood filled his penis and stiffened it.

Ray shut his eyes, hoping the weird mathematical numbers would appear. That'd take his mind off the situation. It did nothing but make Celia's hands, now running a finger down the middle of his shirt, stop. One good thing came of it.

"You need to relax a little," she purred.

"I just need what's in my head out."

"I can't do that when you're like this." He felt the bed move; Celia had stood up. He was quick to open his eyes, fearful of what she might pull next. She stood ahead of him, hands on her hips. "You gotta be calm, mellow, or the memories won't come out clear."

"Sorry, I thought Joel would be doing this."

A twist and lick of her lips. "You prefer men?"

"Oh, no, it's just—"

A hopeful smile spread across her face. "So, you like girls then?"

"I have a girlfriend."

"Is that so?"

"So please stay away from my memories of sleeping with her?"

Her left hand touched the side of his head while she lowered her head, it glowed white. With Celia's eyes shut, Ray felt a surge of mind-tingling waves tickle his brain. His vision became a blur. When it recovered Celia wasn't standing ahead touching him. It was Arianna.

He jerked his head backward, his confused face wondering if it was the real Arianna, the imaginary one he'd been seeing since the hospital discharge, or Celia.

"What the fuck?" he spat.

"I'm still here," the Arianna ahead of him said with a voice that sounded like Celia. "It's just a mental projection. You're seeing what I want you to see." Celia looking like Arianna took a step backward, running her hands up along her body, still dressed in the fishnet and micro skirt grab, only it was Arianna's body. "So how do I look? This is how your girlfriend looks, right?"

More blood hardened his penis. "Spot on."

"Like Joel said, I'm good." She quickly leaped back to the bed, sitting to his right, and ran a hand down his arm. "Good, you're getting relaxed." The same hand that grabbed his arm pulled him to the bed with her. "Lay with me, it should make the connection better."

Part of Ray wanted to panic. The other part told him Arianna was back and kept his nerves in check. It's all part of the process to find the real Arianna and get his life back to normal. He convinced himself that over and over as she climbed over his body, breasts that looked like Arianna's dangling over his face from the fishnet top.

His penis wanted to break out from his trousers. Celia's hand grabbing the lump that formed on his pants confirmed that. She giggled. "You're so cute."

Ray looked to the locked door, wondering what would happen

if the real Arianna bolted through. He sighed. "Can we just skip this part and get this over with?"

Celia cocked her head to the side, making a disappointing glare he figured. "Sure you don't wanna?"

"No."

"She'll never know, and neither will your brain. And you know Joel ripped you off right?"

"I'm aware of that, he knows I'm desperate."

"Get your money's worth then." Her head lowered enough to feel the heat of her breath on his neck. "You could fuck me. I don't mind, you've paid more than my usual clients do."

He felt the moisture from her lips next, press against the side of his neck. She was on top of him, her technique was good, he couldn't feel her enhanced breasts squashing against him. It felt like Arianna's chest, as did her skinny hips, and hands forcing his head to face her. Another kiss met him, an open-mouthed one on his lips. His penis was in pain, being crushed against the fabric of his clothing. He only knew of one approach to stop the torment. He didn't reach for that idea.

This wasn't Arianna. He was not a cheater. He overpaid for a memory extraction and got this, a dancer and telepath that wasn't taking no for an answer as she dry fucked him to the sound of the synthwave music.

All part of the process. Joel's process to get new memory spheres to sell. Ray could see it now, new memory sphere for sale, reluctant journalist forced to fuck a hot witch. If Ray wanted it gone, he'd have to pay more.

He got swindled.

Ray had to resist Celia, but how he couldn't figure out. She was every bit like the real Arianna. She got into his head and pulled out everything he loved about her, applying it to the mental veil. Arianna's smell, her looks, her touch, his strong need to be with her, reality and fantasy became a blur. It's no wonder witches put most human sex workers and the porn industry out of business. Who could compete with powers like that?

Celia pulled her lips away from his, wincing. "No dice, huh?"

His sleeve removed a layer of excitement sweat from his forehead "I'm sorry, you're great and all, but my heart belongs to her, not the projection of her."

"All right fine," Celia said, climbing off him. "Where do you wanna start?"

Ray sat up. "Yesterday evening at JFK airport."

She stared at him astonished. "You mean when the attack went down?" He nodded. She sounded astonished. "You were there?"

"Yep."

Eyes shut, head looking down, both white glowing hands holding the sides of Ray's head. Celia went into a trance, reaching into Ray's memories, the service he overpaid for.

His world turned into a flash of light. When it came back, he was standing with Celia, back in her normal form. They stood in the airport, hours before the attack, when Ray first arrived, watching the flight status screens.

He grinned. Progress at last. "Okay perfect, capture everything. I need to review everything in more detail."

JFK airport appeared just how he remembered it. Ray and Celia were invisible forces to those around them. They watched Ray from that time scope out the two shadowy men, the African guy, and the tall pale lanky man, and then later, the other group of shadowy men. Men who were all unregistered IWs.

Ray in the past checked in and passed the security checkpoint when the IWs used whatever powers they had to bypass it. He watched as he went into the washroom stall, hacked the cameras, and made a call to Arianna. The whole thing played out like a movie, right down to the attack.

An Asian man with a nanite infused katana and ponytail stood next to a shattered window looking out to the runway where the tall IW was pushed out of. His katana glowed indigo as he snapped his fingers, stepped through a blurry rift and vanished. Ray in the memory playback found Arianna seeking cover. The two were embracing moments later as she murmured strange words.

Celia stepped ahead, studying Arianna and Ray intensely from the recollection. "You know she's a witch, right?"

TWENTY-THREE
ESTRELLA

Piper found parking in an overcrowded eight-story parking lot, right at the top level. It gave a nice view of holographic advertisements lined up along the buildings ahead, mostly advertising new fashion trends, smartwatches, and some new flavor Coca-Cola had been pushing for the last two months.

A glass-covered walking bridge carried the two across the drop between the eight-story parking garage and another building. That too had a few ads on it. Down below were the streets, traffic lights, and cars zooming back and forth, as pedestrians on the sidewalks walked to or from the various establishments. Nobody seemed affected by the IW attacks, not even when a news broadcast played from one of the larger screens in the brightly lit commercialized jungle.

The block was crammed with the new smart hologram advertisements Yoshida rolled out. They were ads that spoke to people as they walked past, telling them what they should buy and where to get it. Every ad was customized as they pulled up your personal profile, accessing your everyday activities in the world. One facial scan and a dip into Yoshida's database, and the holograms knew exactly what you came out to shop for or how to use fear to make you spend money on stuff you don't need.

Men were informed where to find those perfect shoes that would make any woman fall for them. Women were advised how their bodies should look, and how much better looking they'd be with a particular fashion trend, hair spray, and breast augmentations.

When Estrella faced an ad, they informed her that the Alliance Star was offering a subscription discount. That data harvested likely from her recent searches. Piper's custom ads directed her to a new lesbian witch nightclub that had opened.

The corporations of the world worked hard to harvest data on people's personal lives, sell it to the highest bidders, and then use that data to exploit them. True freedom and privacy were a myth.

The NC gauntlets the two wore caught the stares of three women with shopping bags in their hands in the orange and yellow neon glow. A man and a woman, no older than seventeen, sat at the edge of a bench, their lips locked in a wet make-out session. The woman's arms were around his body, and the man's hands were inching down her leather shorts. Estrella envied the girl. She never had anyone kiss her like that. She wondered what it would feel like.

Following Piper's lead, Estrella arrived at an ice cream parlor. The scent of fresh dairy hit her the second she entered. She didn't need to run an environment scan to know it was the real deal, regardless of what the screens above the order table said.

Piper approached to order. "Two rocky road bowls please."

The clerk nodded, keying in her request on the computer. "Soy or synthetic?"

A half-smile spread on Piper's face. "The real shit."

The clerk returned the gesture.

As promised, Piper paid for the two bowls of rocky road ice

cream. One heaping spoonful of the desert told Estrella's tongue that what she ate was against the law. Not that she cared, she hadn't had real ice cream since childhood, and it was a one-time deal. The two came to sit on the hood of Piper's car together, legs crossed, a bowl of ice cream in hand, and eyes gawking at the big cityscape touched and brightened by never-ending hologram signs and neon colors.

Estrella looked at her bowl of ice cream, now half-finished. "You know this is illegal, right?"

Piper snorted. "No shit," then did that smile that made Estrella flush. "My body getting leased out to the LAPD has its benefits. The original ice cream place got shut down for serving ice cream produced from milk, harvested from a real cow. So, the people that ran this place bought the space out, rebranded it under a new name, and kept the real ice cream a close secret."

"Hard to imagine police raiding an ice cream shop."

"Real cream requires a farm and cows. All of that banned in order to reduce our carbon footprint in the world."

Curious, Estrella.

Estrella spooned another mouth full of ice cream before the humidity finished it for her. *What is it?*

Reviewing your recent conversation with Piper.

She continued spooning the delicious dessert into her mouth as the silent AI chat went on. *You invading my privacy now?*

She knew your dietary preferences.

Yeah, didn't I tell everyone that?

You did not mention it to Piper. How did she realize it?

Estrella's next spoon of ice cream stopped shy of her opened mouth.

Geoffrey made an excellent point. How did Piper know Estrella preferred real ice cream over soy or synthetic? It was two things Piper knew about Estrella that she never told her. The more she looked at the pixie kiwi RW sitting beside her, the more she wondered if she was a spy from the Federation, having snuck into the Alliance with a sappy story that she was looking to trade the life there, for the freedom here.

The synthetic arm on Piper felt like a real one, her NC gauntlet, even her eyes, the longer she peered into them, weren't standard cyberware. She doubted Piper was a new unit. Why would Yoshida give a woman from the Federation experimental parts? Somewhere, deep inside Piper's head and AI were the secrets. Secrets that wouldn't reveal themselves, no matter how long Estrella stared at her as they ate ice cream.

Piper caught her staring. The look on her face suggested she liked it, same with that damn Mona Lisa smile. Sitting close to each other didn't help. Neither of the two spooned new scoops of ice cream into their mouths, instead Estrella and Piper gazed into each other's emerald glowing synthetic eyes. Estrella wondering what Piper's endgame was, and Piper wondering, whatever went through her head when she looked at Estrella like that.

Let's ask her.

I would advise against that, Geoffrey said. *Piper appears to be calm right now. Bringing this to her attention may cause her to worry and become reclusive.*

I don't like the idea of someone spying on me.

Perhaps we should take this chance to build rapport with her, and then, when the time is right, make an inquiry to your questions.

He was right. Then again, Geoffrey was an AI, so he was always right. Sitting together with Piper on the hood of her car put the mysterious and captivating RW in a state of bliss. This was Estrella's chance to learn more about Piper that her files didn't reveal.

Estrella returned to what remained of her bowl, her eyes turned to the neon and hologram filled skyline. "So, what made you want to go under the knife and become an RW?"

Piper shrugged and watched the skyline too. "It was important for me, and the people I care for."

"You did it because you wanted to protect your daughter, and wife, at the time?"

Piper held the bowl with her synthetic hand, bringing her other hand wearing the NC gauntlet to her face. She examined it up and down, so did Estrella. "Got sick of seeing the world turn their backs on people that didn't deserve it."

It was a typical response of those that fled the Federation, and an understandable one. China had annexed various Pacific nations into a super nation, similar to the Alliance during the third world war. Most of its citizens, to this day, weren't happy to see Chinese forces refusing to leave, and not pleased to discover the rest of the world refuse to do anything out of fear of triggering another war.

Einstein didn't know World War III would be fought with weaponized witches, but with the way the world was going, sticks and stones might be the weapon of choice in the next world war.

"So, you became an RW not to fight IWs, but to use your powers to resist another force." *Like those that ruled over New Zealand.* "But that plan backfired, so you came running into the arms of the Alliance, and then offered your body, already jammed with cyberware, to Yoshida."

Estrella felt a soft nudge of Piper's elbow. "You're a smart girl, new girl."

"You know, one day, you're not going to be able to call me that."

"What? Smart girl?"

"New girl!"

"You'll be the new girl until another one shows up." Hearty kiwi laugher followed. "And they got to be a girl! If it's a guy, then you'll still be the new girl."

This time the two shared laughs. It ended with Piper eyes magnetized to Estrella's when she faced her.

"But, being smart and new is a good thing," Piper said. "Usually, the new people are foolish and get killed during their second or third fight with an IW. You've survived two so far. You're off to a decent start."

"Thanks."

"Just, don't go running your mouth off about this ice cream place. It's the only one in the city that has this secret. Getting these folks busted again, would be dumb."

"I won't."

"It'll be our secret, okay?"

"Got any other secrets to share?"

Piper raised an eyebrow. "Wouldn't you like to know?" her voice had a touch of fascination in it.

"Well, that's why I asked."

Estrella was worried she might have been too firm. But she couldn't think of any other way to put it. Leaning back on the hood, with elbows supporting her body, Piper asked. "What are you trying to get at?"

"Why did you give up your fight and come to LA?"

"What was I supposed to do?"

"Keep at it," Estrella's gaze returned to the neon and hologram ad skyline ahead. "I mean, look at this. The world's fucked, even here in the Alliance. We get up to please our corporate masters every day, working jobs we don't like, using our money the way they tell us to, believing the media when they start flapping their lips. All this stuff? It's just an illusion to keep us blind, happy, and spending."

"Could be worse."

"After three fucking world wars, it should be better." Estrella paused when she heard Piper snort. "You think I'm just some kid ranting, huh?"

Piper chucked. "Yep, and it's pretty cute honestly."

"Sorry. When someone important to you dies because of greed, well, it tends to open your eyes."

"The world isn't all that bad. Some folks are working and living their dreams."

"Dreams have a habit of turning into nightmares," Estrella said with a grimace. "Just ask my old roommate, Yumi. She wanted to be an RW, and now she's dead."

"That the close friend you mentioned?"

Estrella nodded, holding back the wave of sorrow that appeared in her chest. "Yeah, it is. Eighteen is too young to die in combat."

"No offense, but it sounds like she didn't understand the risks and jumped into this. Our line of work is dangerous."

"Yumi understood the risks. What she didn't realize was that her boss could try and have her killed, to take advantage of an insurance loop-hole."

"What are you going to do then? All I hear is ranting, love."

Estrella grinned at the dark city that was in a dire need of change. "First, I need to get my shit sorted," she said, the grin held. "And then? I'll find a way to tell people they need to wake up and smell the bullshit the media and corporations are shoving us."

A gust of humid wind blew past the two. It made Estrella's long black hair tickle the side of Piper's face while Piper's lace black robe skirt fluttered. Droplets of water, reflecting the neon glow fell from the skies shortly afterward. It was time for the two to be on their way.

The news played on the radio as Piper drove Estrella home, deep within the IW district. The broadcaster spoke of an update to the report that'd been making headlines across the Alliance. In addition to the mysterious IWs attacks in Los Angeles, a group of IWs attacked JFK International Airport in New York. Estrella's head went racing searching for the connections.

Piper's charming face melted into one of despair and concern. Something about the news gave her anguish. She placed her car on autopilot, reaching for her phone and dialed several numbers. None of them responded to Piper's calls.

Piper threw the phone, her immaculate white teeth visible from her frown. "Fuck!"

TWENTY-FOUR
RAY

"No, she's not."

The vision came to a standstill. Arianna, pulled from Ray's memories of the airport attack, held him, perpetually frozen in time. Celia's white glowing hand pointed an index finger at Arianna's head. "Your girlfriend's syncing with your mind, telepathically."

Ray shook his head in denial. "Arianna's human, she works for Yoshida. They wouldn't hire an IW, registered or not."

"I don't know what to tell you." Celia shrugged. "But at this point, your mind was getting opened up with telepathy. If it wasn't her, and I really doubt that, then it was someone else."

"There were other IWs there, maybe it was them?"

"Yeah, and none of them were telepaths, except for ..."

Ray and Celia approached the fall to the runway. They saw nothing but a blur of colors. Ray at the time wasn't looking at the drop, and therefore wouldn't know what was going on regarding the ponytailed man, who had been standing near it before he vanished.

Celia crossed her arms. "Thing is, it feels like it was coming

from her, and no one else. That guy that stepped through that
portal thingy is a telepath, yeah, but he ain't here anymore."

"You're sure of that?"

"Positive. Don't forget, we're both in your head. I can experience what you did. The only difference is I'm a telepath. I can
sense telepathic power coming from your girl, Arianna. I was able
to sense it from that guy with the ponytail, right up until he
vanished."

"Where did he go?"

"The fuck if I know. Never seen a telepath just vanish into thin
air like that."

They both returned to the still visage of Arianna holding Ray.
Celia was convinced Arianna was a witch. Ray was convinced it
was a trick, mental manipulation, like the one Celia used. It'd
explain the change of character in Arianna's personality. She went
to the EU, and someone else came back in her place, a telepath that
made people around them see Arianna, and not the real IW they
were.

The AIT agents also claimed Arianna's name wasn't on any of
the flights. She was still in the EU as far as he was concerned, and
her business trip took a turn for the worst. An IW chose her, of all
women, to impersonate. That had to be it. There's no way Ray had
been putting his penis in a witch for the past five years and then
want to marry her. And what of her parents, Norris and Maria?
They weren't witches.

Nothing was changing Ray's mind on that.

Ray looked at himself in the vision. It was the version of himself
that was seconds away from blacking out, only to awake with weird
shit in his brain. "What's happening to my head exactly? Because
as I recalled I blacked out a second later."

Celia motioned to the frozen image. "Let's see."

Ray's memories of the airport incident continued like someone
hit the play button. He saw Arianna hold him and mutter words

that made little sense, acting out of character as he remembered. The airport turned black, leaving Ray and Celia standing, hovering in space without stars. He floated, watching Celia lost in a deep trance, her hands waving about to focus, then they glowed white. The blackness of the void dissolved. New memories played, none of them belonged to Ray.

Celia verbalized her personal thoughts on the matter. "What the fuck?"

They were in Arianna's head, or the IW impersonating her. Looking about, Ray quickly recognized the room the memories transported them to. It was a hotel in Munich, where Arianna had been staying. He remembered it from the video call he had with her when she first arrived, back before the terrorist attack in Munich. The Arianna he spoke to that night was the woman he loved, no questions asked.

Now he wasn't sure if an IW had been impersonating her.

"Looks like we got another set of memories," Celia said. "I can't get all of it though. I ain't a high enough rank for that."

He grunted. "What rank would you need to be?"

"That's the 'what the fuck' part," she said, her voice carrying a little uncertainness to it. "An S ranked witch did this."

"What the fuck indeed." Ray briefly thought back to his basic knowledge of IW ranks, his fingers stroking his chin in a sage-like way. "I thought rank A was the strongest?"

"It is." She nodded, and the white glow of her hands remained. Celia was using all her energy. "Rank S is a weaponized IW. You need some serious military training to get on that level."

"Weaponized IWs haven't existed since the war," Ray said. "Every country agreed to disband and outlaw IW training programs to prevent them from achieving that power."

"Looks like someone out there lied and kept training. Whoever put this shit in your head was a weaponized IW. Highly illegal internationally and fucking dangerous."

Celia waved her white glowing hands again, attempting to focus her abilities and play the new memories. Nothing replayed in order. One moment Ray saw the hotel, the next a jungle burning, an idle structure in the middle of the cause of it, then a science lab, then the hotel, then the jungles of a tropical forest.

The science lab appeared again; it was the same as he'd seen in his weird dreams. A man dressed in a lab coat put a gun into his mouth and then blew his brains out, spattering it up against the ceiling, walls and glass stasis tubes behind him. The crimson and pink remains of his head slowly moved down on the smooth glass surface of the tube leaving behind grisly lines, obscuring whatever it was, whoever it was, inside.

The reflection of Arianna's hypnotic blue eyes shot back on the glass not yet coated with the dripping blood.

Another flash of memories. Ray saw the hotel again in Munich. Arianna was there, along with men and women, shades covered their eyes. Some had chunks of metal in their limbs, cyberware by the looks, what manufacturer, he couldn't tell. Everyone's lips were moving, but no sound came out, not even from Arianna.

The memories distorted. When it returned, the room had turned into a warzone. The curtains were stained red, and bullet holes shattered the windows behind them. Rays of sunshine touched the bodies on the floor with expanding pools of sticky crimson leaking away. Arianna was in the washroom, red droplets raining from her, painting the bandages on her arm when they fell upon it. She plunged her hands into the bathtub full of water, turning it murky with blood.

When she brought her hand up, a man's head followed, splashing the murky water in every direction. Upon closer inspection she was holding a man under the water, drowning him. No, she was torturing him. How did Ray know? Because the two exchanged words before she forced his head under again, the water roared when the man was denied the air needed to breathe.

After the fifth time of her yanking his head out from the bathtub, she raged, yelling something. She pulled on his hair, exposing his neck, holding a dagger with her other hand. Arianna put the blade to his neck and cut. A three-inch deep gash across the man's neck squirted arterial blood, four times in three different directions, maybe more. Ray was too sick in his belly at that point to keep count.

The murky bathtub water turned red when she kicked his body in. Arianna's dagger sank into the back of the deceased man's arm, sawing back and forth, cutting down to the bone, so Ray had thought. She cut down to a cyberware augmentation, pulling the flesh and muscles off it like a butcher deboning a cut of meat, back when butchery was a legal profession. Arianna read something on the metal jammed inside the man, a serial code, a manufacture number perhaps.

Ray's eyes narrowed when he saw the Chinese letters and the corporate logo of the cyberware's manufacturer. "Zhang Industries."

The Arianna in the vision stormed out in a rush, stripped naked, whipping the red sticky juice off her curves and face. She looked like an occultist that finished having a blood orgy. He was certain Norris and Maria didn't raise Arianna to act like that.

"Okay," Celia stepped forward. Her face had grown pale from the horror. "I'm shutting this the fuck down."

"No wait—"

"Fuck that! I didn't sign up for conspiracy shit."

A bright flash put an end to the vision.

Ray opened his eyes. He was still sitting on the bed, the sheets below him drenched with the sweat that trickled off his body. He was shaking internally at the secret they unlocked, unsure what to do. The erection that wanted to rip a hole in his trousers went away at least.

Celia stood ahead of him, dragging her hands away from the

left and right of his head with a look of terror on her face. Her hands came together and then pulled apart. A memory sphere appeared after a three-second burst of white light. She looked at the shiny orb in her hands, winced, then handed it off to Ray.

"This is everything I got," she said.

The memory sphere joined his phone in his pocket. "Thanks."

"There's more in there, but like I said, I'm not high enough rank to get it. And honestly? I don't want to know what it is."

"I understand. Thank you."

"Want my advice? Destroy it and break up with your girl-friend." Ray said nothing as he went for the door. "Seriously," Celia called out to him. "If you miss her that much, you could just fuck me with the projection. I know a lot more about her now that I've been in your head."

He replied with more silence.

On his way out, Ray grabbed his phone, thumbing in a quick internet search on the name of the corporation stamped on the cyberware part Arianna discovered. Zhang Industries was it?

The first site listed was Zhang Industries, the exclusive provider of weapons tech and cyberware to the People's Federation of Pacific Nations military. No one else, not even Yoshida sold tech to the Federation's military. Anyone with Zhang developed tech were trained members of the Federation's military.

The men Arianna killed in the hotel were Federation soldiers. The hotel was most likely the one talked about in the news, the one IW terrorists attacked in the EU. They must have come for Arianna because of what she did, and torched the place, before chasing her out of the EU. The story of her going to London must have been a cover to trick those following her. Arianna never left Munich before catching a flight to New York.

Terrorist attacks. Ray didn't like that label. It wasn't the correct one to use. These weren't terrorists they were dealing with. They were Federation black ops operatives. And they had IWs supporting them, weaponized ones.

The Federation was planning a war, and just like with the third world war, witches and warlocks would be the weapon of choice. Too bad the Alliance, along with the rest of the world, sought to oppress and ban IW training.

That was all speculation of course. Ray needed proof. He went seeking it by bringing up directions to the morgue where the dead IWs from the airport attack should be.

TWENTY-FIVE
ESTRELLA

Traversing through the streets of LA during the day was akin to walking through a forest. The most common thing one would find in a forest? Trees, and they were usually taller than everything else and did a good job blocking out most of the sunlight. Here in Los Angeles, however, it was the skyscrapers, and they too used their height to tell the sun to fuck off and brighten someone else's day.

Estrella was beginning to understand why Los Angeles was home to the largest IW community in the world, because it was home to some of the tallest freestanding structures darkening the streets twenty-four seven. Witches and warlocks loved the darkness.

She was in the human district by midday, stepping out of a taxicab, hopefully for the last time. It was time Estrella got wheels of her own. Following Piper's advice, after she dropped her home, Estrella tracked down a vehicle shop off in the less than fantastic areas of the city.

The architecture of the buildings there kept their prewar look. Brick and concrete formed walls, rust touched fences forged barriers between different properties, and old tires from cars that used fuel lay in the corner of some structures. It was as if Estrella walked back in time, and if it wasn't for the high towers in the background, built after the war, she'd believe it.

It was a snapshot of the early twenty-first century when witches and warlocks were just imaginary beings told of in stories, and allegedly hunted to extinction during the medieval witch prosecutions, hence I in IW, imaginary.

There was no door to the shop she found, just a transparent plastic tarp nailed to the top door frame. Knocking wasn't an option, neither was ringing a bell. She walked in, announcing herself, no need to eat a shotgun blast to the face because someone got the wrong idea.

A weapons rack on the wall caught her attention. It hung above a convertible with the insides of its front hood torn out. She counted at least five different shotguns, six assault rifles, and seven pistols on the rack. There was even a fucking rocket launcher off to the side. Past that, and the guts of a car manufactured back in the 20s, was the man she came seeking. So she hoped.

He looked like him though, mid to late fifties, tank top and jeans, with grease stains spattered across it in no particular direction. His hands and arms were synthetic and clearly looked like it even from afar. They looked like silver-colored skeletal hands typing away on a computer. At least Estrella's arm looked natural until you got up close.

"Hey," she called out to the man. His eyes remained forward at the computer. She grimaced at that. "Yo! Ese, you there?!"

The man pulled aside that time, facing Estrella. She narrowed her synthetic eyes. Its emerald glow was more prominent in the low lighting of the garage. The man's profile appeared in her left eye when the facial scan completed.

Name: Tyler Thompson
Age: 53
Species: Real witch/warlock

Occupation: Mechanic
Notes: Retired RW unit

He offered his metallic hand to shake, it felt like shaking hands with a metal spatula. "Hey, nice to meet you ...?"

"Estrella Rodriguez."

"Ah yes, Piper said something about you swinging by. Just call me—"

"Tyler?"

"Fuck that noise," he laughed. "TT, that's what people in these parts call me."

He stepped away, walking deeper into the garage. She followed, eying the various parts on the floor and shelves. Some of them weren't vehicle parts at all. Her optical scans highlighted at least three AI cores, like the one in her head, circuit boards, microchips, and synthetic arms and legs.

"You deal with more than wheels I see."

He chuckled, lifting his metal arm up. "I fix all things broken, even RW parts."

"Really?"

"It's all I'm good for these days. Was one of the first RW models. Got retired when they rolled out your kind."

"Sorry, not sorry."

"Ain't your fault, they built your models to be upgradeable. Mine? Fuck, they didn't even know if we'd live beyond the two-year mark."

He stopped at a black tarp protecting the vehicle for Estrella. His metal hands came to hold on to the tarp. "Well, here it is!"

He pulled it away, unveiling a slick red motorcycle. Estrella neared the bike, running her fingers across its polished and reflective surface, free of dust, dents, and the signs of aging. And what an aged bike it was, she looked down at its computer screen.

"Is this a Tesla?"

"Yep, super fucking rare too. Not many of these were made after Musk retired."

"This is fucking great."

"Well then, there it is, ready to kick some ass when you need it."

"How much?"

"I owe Piper, so four grand, and it's yours."

Estrella grimaced. She had the money now that she received her first paycheck since coming to LA. She also needed to send some of it back to her family in Buenos Aires. A part of her wanted to say fuck it and stick with taxis. But it was a real nice bike and a nice price.

TT grinned at the hesitation plastered over her face. "Too much, eh?"

"Well ..."

"Tell you what, I'll sweeten the deal." His voice was like an old school street hustler. "We can do installment payments. And, what the fuck, I'll throw in some upgrades."

"Upgrades? For the bike?"

"Naw girl, for you." He tapped her synthetic arm. "Remember, I'm one of the first RWs. Had plenty of time to learn what makes us tick, especially you newer models."

"Can't Yoshida update me?"

"They can, but will they? The best upgrades go to the RWs that perform since those are the ones that tend not to die when getting in a scrap with an IW."

"Meaning they don't want to waste money upgrading someone that's going to die the next day."

"Exactly, but me? I don't give a fuck." He waved his metal hand at the shelves ahead of them, all full of RW cyberware and software disks. "Most of this stuff I got secondhand from Yoshida. I fixed it up, rewrote some software codes, and sell them back to folk like you."

Folk like you, as in RWs like Estrella who isn't anywhere near the top and would never see free upgrades from Yoshida. Estrella stood at the shelf, her eyes bright with excitement. "What kinda upgrades you got?"

"Buy the bike, and I shall reveal all."

She crossed her arms while running her tongue on the inside of her cheek, lost in thought. Secondhand cyberware and software upgrades from some wrench out in some rundown shop didn't seem like a wise choice. Getting killed trying to earn that commendation to return home to Buenos Aires seemed like a worse one. Secondhand upgrades could prevent that.

She faced him, grinning. "I'm sold."

"Fuckin' right you are."

Estrella grabbed her phone, logged into her bank account, and frowned when she saw the balance plummet after sending the wire transfer funds into TTs. He tossed her keys to the bike when his phone beeped, confirming the money transfer. After that, he waved for her to follow him once again, into the basement.

It was dark, save for the six computer monitors shining their light. She could make out a small operating table with three machine arms mounted to its side. He patted the table, instructing her to take a seat. She did and really hoped she would not regret it.

TT grabbed a large tablet pad and keyed in a password. "I'll give you that free update now, a little sample of my work. If you want more though, you'll have to pay."

He plugged a data transfer cable into the pad, and then with the other end, found Estrella's data port at the side of her head, jacking her into it. Her vision turned into a series of menus listing various pre-programmed abilities her nanites could perform. TT selected one ability for her, and she read the screen that appeared.

Scan Copy

Scans objects, storing its patterns into your AI for nano printing usage.

Min. nanite swarm(s) required: 1
Nanite swarm(s) remaining: 1

"With this upgrade," TT explained. "You can use your NC gauntlet to scan any object and store its patterns in your AI. If you ever come across the right materials, you can nano print one on the spot."

"I can already nano print stuff."

"Yeah, only objects Yoshida programmed into your AI, which I'm going to guess is limited to a few weapons, right?"

She snorted and twisted her lips. "Yeah."

"That's Yoshida trying to control us RWs, limiting us to nano printing what they want you to use. You know what I say? Fuck that shit, print what you like, but first, you got to scan it to build a profile of it."

A confirmation prompt flashed, asking her if she wished to receive the files from the pad.

Geoffrey?

I am not detecting any computer viruses or malicious properties. The update is safe to use.

She accepted the update. A blue progress bar moving from left to right finished in three seconds. She found the upgrade after browsing through her nanite abilities menu via screens in her vision, confirming the update was successful.

TT handed her a biker helmet and a leather suit. Both were red like her new bike. He gave her a nod. "Try it out."

She grasped the helmet first with her NC gauntlet, and selected Scan Copy. The single swarm of utility nanites in her body sprayed from her glove into the helmet scanning every inch, every molecule, and atom, analyzing everything that made it whole. When the nanite swarm returned to her gauntlet, they relayed that data to Geoffrey, before entering back inside her veins, idling until she called for them to act again. And that she did, when she held the suit, scanning that.

The patterns for both the helmet and suit flashed in her left eye. If she ever lost or had the items damaged, she could synthesize a new one provided the right materials were on hand. A wide smile spread across her face.

TT shared the same gestured. "Want more?"

Estrella looked at him, eyes wide open in shock. "Fuck yeah I do!"

She browsed through his catalog of upgrades with the pad's data cable still jacked into her head. Most of the upgrades carried a four-figure price tag much to her disappointment. She ran a search for two and three-figure items, a small list appeared, most of the items were things she already had, like a pattern for a 12-gauge shotgun. Three items caught her attention. She had their detail screens appear in her vision.

Disable Vehicle

Nanites disassemble wheels to small vehicles, preventing usage.

Min. nanite swarm(s) required: 1

Nanite swarm(s) remaining: 1

And the other.

Induce Muscle Spasms

Nanites disrupt motor skills of the selected target by attacking muscle tissue.

Min. nanite swarm(s) required: 1

Nanite swarm(s) remaining: 1

Both programs cost one hundred dollars each. It was a bit out of her price range. The last thing on the list caught her attention. She read the screen that materialized.

Defense Matrix

Nanites hardens body and attire prior to taking physical trauma. Duration and effectiveness diminish with each hit you take.

Min. Nanoswarm(s) required: 4
Nanoswarms remaining: 1

The cost? Twenty bucks. "I'll take it."

"Nice choice kid. Keep in mind that one's still in beta."

"Was going to say, why doesn't Yoshida at least have Defense Matrix pre-installed with us all?"

"Yoshida's still developing it." He tapped commands on his pad. "I got my hands on their latest build and made some changes. It should be good for an RW of your size."

Her synthetic hand pulled one twenty Alliance dollar bill from her pocket, handing it to TT. He sent her the software update, and another blue progress bar moved across her vision. Once completed, she jacked out from the pad and sat up. That was enough spending for the day. She made her way to the stairs.

"Come back any time if you need more upgrades."

She looked back, stopping shy of the stairs, one hand on the banister. "I will when I get the chance. Thanks again."

"Of course, physical upgrades will cost more," he said. "So, if you're thinking about those, you'll want to save up the cash and make an appointment. It takes a few hours to install cyberware. Though, I'm sure a model like you knows that already."

Back on the main floor in the repair shop, she slipped into the tight, red leather, biker suit. She pulled the zipper up, from the midsection to her collar. The helmet came on next, a holographic HUD appeared over the visor and synched with the bike as she approached.

TT lifted the garage door open as she sat on the bike. She held its handles, her smile, covered by the helmet projected her excitement. She felt the vehicle vibrate as she powered it on and heard a little noise as it accelerated forward, out of the shop, turning into the streets, driving at speeds higher than the speed limit. Her long black hair waved about in her wake with the air rushing past her.

For the first time in days, Estrella felt free. Los Angeles was free for her to traverse. And with her new abilities, that commendation was going to come her way.

Returning to Buenos Aires wasn't a dream. It was a goal that would be achieved.

―――――

Estrella let out a relieved moan.

Three things brought her pleasure, at once. Looking at her apartment now set up, belongings unpacked, and furniture laid out the way she liked it. A cold can of beer in her hands was the second thing and the third? A fresh new battery she finished slotting into the back of her head, swapping out the battery that had dropped to twenty percent. It granted the life support nanites inside her extended time to live, work and recharge when needed.

She lay down on the couch, resting her legs across its arm. In her hand was a tablet pad, its screen listing various news publications and their latest feeds. She pulled a data cable from the storage compartment of her synthetic arm and used it to jack her head into the pad.

A confirmation screen flashed over her left eye, asking if she wanted to connect to the pad. She selected yes, and the pad's screen became what her eyes saw, her thoughts controlling the scrolling and clicking abilities.

She read a news article from the Alliance Star first as it caught her attention, written by none other than Ray Partington. The article gave a chilling description of an IW terrorist attack at JFK International in New York City. Ray was there when it went down, so was his girlfriend Arianna Kounias, who according to his statement went missing because of the attack.

Arianna Kounias.

Kounias.

Why was that family so important?

Geoffrey, are you seeing this?

I am. Quite the coincidence, don't you agree?

Were the Bald Skulls gang reported in New York?

Scanning NYPD database, please standby. Five seconds later. *Negative, it would appear the attackers of the airport were of a different group of IWs. Hmm ... Interesting.*

What's up?

Geoffrey took control of the pad. She watched as he typed in the internet address to a blog the two became familiar with since arriving in Los Angeles. The blog belonged to DigiSamurai69.

You may be correct in your suspicions that the hacker of this blog, DigiSamurai69, is Ray Partington.

The latest post on the blog rambled on about the disappearance of Arianna Kounias, the blue-eyed, and brown, curly-haired hippy girl who worked for Yoshida. She went to the EU on business and hadn't returned home because of the airport attack. DigiSamurai69 made a plea to the public, asking them to email him tips so he can help Ray and the police locate her.

A secondary blog update, made minutes after, informed readers that DigiSamurai69 was working on a big leak that would expose those involved in the attacks. He asked those reading to keep their eyes on the Alliance Star news when he sends them the news tip.

Right ... Estrella snorted. *Let me get this straight. LA gets rocked with three IW attacks at once, one of them being Arianna's parent's home where we found that Nobuo guy. IWs attack New York, as Arianna gets off her flight. Now she's missing, yet nobody else in the airport at the time of the attack went missing.*

There is no doubt a connection here.

Piper too ... Estrella's head briefly flashed back to the image of Piper's face, her perfect smile, and hypnotizing emerald eyes.

It made her heart quiver. She wasn't sure what to make of the feeling, jealousy perhaps. Piper got put on the mission, and Estrella got told to stay home, and home was a word she really didn't want to use to describe her apartment. It implied she'd never get back to Buenos Aires, and never be able to visit Yumi's grave, if Yumi's family came up with the money to bury her. She'd tear up if the eyes in her head were real.

Estrella was getting off-topic.

Okay, connection. Estrella sat up, the image of the pad's screen still part of her eyesight. She blinked, forcing it to switch to windowed mode, and with a thought of her mind minimized the screen. She could see her apartment again. *IWs strike a hotel in Munich.*

That is correct.

And then, days later, hit New York as Arianna gets off her flight, along with three attacks throughout LA.

Yes.

As for the attacks here, they were Arianna's parent's home, the SWAT armory where a gunship just magically vanished, and ... Where else?

Geoffrey sent her the answers, the address to an apartment tower downtown in the human-only district. A slideshow of photos of the place moved from left to right across her eyes. *This is the address, the third location the IWs assaulted.*

And they saw none of the Bald Skulls?

Police are still investigating as are AIT, but currently, they were not. The last reported Bald Skulls incident was the Witches Brew bar.

Where they snatched that unregistered telepath, Portia. She thought about that for a moment. *Okay, so. The Bald Skulls want unregistered IW telepaths, and Nobuo who's working with the IW terrorists, want the skulls.*

That is the correct theory.

Then why hit New York, the Kounias residence, the SWAT armory, and some random apartment, when none of the skulls were there? And what about Munich? There's a secondary aim we're missing.

Perhaps I found it.

She beamed. *Hit me.* Ray Partington's ID profile appeared in her left eye. It listed his address at the bottom. It was the same address as the apartment the IWs hit. Estrella grinned at the exact match. *Bin-fucking-go, I was right.*

Nobuo and the IW terrorists may have been searching for Ray as well. Though, according to his report, he was in New York.

Then they hit the Kounias' knowing he was the last person to visit them, put a bullet in Maria, tried and failed to get Norris, who's missing. Meanwhile, they had a team hit the airport to get Arianna and missed Ray. Now Arianna and her father are missing.

According to Yoshida, Arianna was away on business in the EU. Let me guess, Munich?

That is correct.

Now ... where does Ray fit into all this?

Perhaps—

Wait.

Estrella stood from the couch and jacked out from the pad. A connection lost prompt flashed, and the minimized screen on the pad vanished. She went for her phone that lay idle on her bed, dialing the number of her rival.

The pixie kiwi picked up the call, her face on the screen was delighted to see Estrella's. "Hey, Piper you home?"

"Not for long, I'll be heading out in a few."

"Ah, so you'll be on duty?"

"Yes, still need to search Partington's place."

Not if I get there first!

Get where first?

Shush! Let me finish this call!

Piper's head slanted to the side. "Why do you ask?"

"Uh, well."

Estrella tripped over her words. She got what she wanted from the call and didn't plan how to end it without giving herself away.

Piper's warm smile made it hard to think. "You wanted to hang out, didn't you?"

And so, Estrella said the first thing that came to mind. "Uh, yeah."

"You're such a bashful little thing, new girl. Well then, what are you doing tonight?"

"Not much. All finished unpacking 'n' shit."

"Do you want to grab some drinks when I'm free?"

"Uh, sure."

Assuming they weren't enemies by the end of the day.

After the expected goodbyes, the call ended. Estrella sighed. The last part of the call wasn't supposed to happen, but it got her out of the situation she jumped into with no exit plan. She hoped Piper wasn't thinking what Estrella was plotting.

Is it really necessary to do this? Geoffrey asked.

Yes. Estrella went for her keys, biker helmet, and suit. *She's supposed to be searching Ray's place today, right? And according to that call, she hasn't left home yet.*

That is correct.

We got a head start on this. I don't trust her to reveal any evidence she collects if she's really a Federation RW spy. This is our chance to see if the IWs left behind something we could use at Ray's place. Or if Ray did.

TWENTY-SIX
RAY

New York City. It was the Yoshida Corporation's poster child, the city that was ravaged during the third world war, when the New Soviet Union invaded it and the east coast of what was once known as the United States. You couldn't see just by looking, but Yoshida constructed every arching high building after the war ended, and you certainly couldn't tell that the statue of liberty wasn't the original one that got toppled over by Soviet forces during the war. Yoshida came in and restored the city with its army of drones, robots, and nanotechnology.

The scars of the third world war were washed away and replaced with a city that was ten times more beautiful than it was before the war, winning the respect and hearts of everyone in the Alliance. Except for the street market strip Ray walked through. That place was a shithole before the war and remained that way after it.

He maintained a low-key appearance. Shades, coat, baseball cap, and his face down when walking. Nobody gave him a second look during his stroll through the busy street markets of New York. Merchants chirped their ultra-low prices for goods, stem cell grown protein, and tofu so tasty you'd think you're eating the real thing. It tempted him to grab a beyond meat made hotdog, but the sound of his phone beeping took his mind off his gut.

A notification informed him a third party had hacked and accessed his email account recently. It didn't look like they sent messages or did anything malicious. Hell, they didn't even bother to change the password or security settings. Amateur shit, probably a bunch of script kiddies. Or the Alliance digging up dirt on him. He wasn't worried, though, a change of the password was in order. He'd track the origin of that third party too if his source wasn't waving to him off in the distance.

It was Jax, well, that was his screen name at least. Jax was young, probably sixteen or seventeen. He reminded Ray of when he was that age, hacking his way to good grades, and exposing dirty secrets high school teachers had, well, the ones that gave him low marks. Jax sat at the steps to a building with a radiant sign flashing the words 'Girls, girls, girls!' next to a pink neon figure of a bare-breasted pole dancing woman.

Ray was curious why the bouncers didn't tell Jax to fuck off. It takes more than a leather jacket, torn blue jeans, and chains dangling around his neck to look eighteen plus. He sighed. Ray knew damn well what systems Jax manipulated to change his facial scan profile.

"Hey, D'sam!" Jax exclaimed with arms open for a greeting. "Back in the hacker realm, I see?"

Ray shook his head, keeping his hands in his pockets. "Not really."

"A shame. Heard you were something else before you went legit."

"I've grown up and moved on."

"Yeah, fucking right." Ray stepped forward, past the club, through the markets, past people that paid the two no mind. Jax followed. "Look, if you need back in, just say so and we'll forget about how you left us."

"Don't. I just need access to—"

"Hold up." Jax held his hands ahead of Ray, stopping him in place. "First, let's eat. Want anything to eat? It's on me."

Ray's eyes narrowed. "Seriously?"

Jax led him to a merchant selling street food. Two women with purple and green hair walked away with bowls full of rice and sushi.

"This dude's got a fancy new food printer," Jax said, pointing at the street food vendor. "Been meaning to try food made with one, that and, my empty stomach's killin' me bro."

"Speaking of killing," Ray said and looked at the device sitting on the back counter behind the vendor. "I need to kill something with my teeth and then swallow it."

The two met as the vendor gave them a nod. Electronic beats boomed from his radio off to the side. "What you like?"

Ray ordered first. "Cheeseburger."

"Tofu hotdog please," Jax ordered next.

The vendor approached the food printer. It looked like an over-sized coffee maker with six needles full of goo. The food printer responded, adjusted its nozzles, and built the required items out of thin air. After five seconds, a steaming cheeseburger was ready, sitting next to a juicy tofu hotdog sitting in a golden-brown bun.

He was presented both items. Ray was impressed at the fact they were goo and protein seconds earlier. Jax forked over fifteen Alliance dollars for the food. With their lunch in hand, the two ate and walked. Ray indulged in his food, the first meal he had all day. His belly stopped making noise, and he didn't even realize it had been doing that. The fear of death was distracting his appetite. Jax looked at him disgusted.

"How can you eat that?" Jax asked Ray.

Ray patted his mouth clean, focusing on the burger's aftertaste. "It's delicious."

"It's not real ..."

"Could have fooled me ... and my taste buds, and stomach."

"When was the last time you saw a real cow?"

"Stem cell grown meat isn't any different from slaughtered meat."

"Doesn't make it real or natural." Jax bit into his tofu meal. "At least tofu and soy, you know what you're getting and where it came from."

"Still tastes and feels like the real thing."

"I'd rather the real thing."

"Nobody raises livestock anymore. Doing that will send you straight to jail."

"Yeah," Jax said after taking another bite. "And that's the problem."

Their food was devoured, and its paper-wrappers tossed in the recyclers. It was time to get down to business. Jax spoke up first. "So, what's up?"

"As I was going to say, I need access to your botnet." Ray kept his face forward and the tone of his voice soft and neutral.

Jax did the complete opposite. "What's in it for me, man?"

"You won't have to worry about getting drafted into a war."

"What war?"

"The one that might start, unless you lend me access."

"You dug up some shit?"

Ray came to a stop, looking about. Nothing but hustlers shouting to potential shoppers below the neon glow. He regretted not glancing back earlier and more frequently. His editor Steven knew of the secret phone Ray held, just not the number. If someone from the Federation got to Steven, they'd learn why they couldn't trace Ray further.

"If you can't or won't give it to me," Ray said, facing down at

Jax. "I'll just brute force my way in."

"With what botnet, D'sam? You'll just wake up every fucking government spook monitoring the network in the process." They continued walking, keeping their voices a notch lower.

"Yeah, so don't put me in the position."

"Okay, I'll give you access, five minutes. After that, I'm changing the passwords."

He patted Jax's shoulder. "That's all I need, thanks."

Ray went to leave, looking for a path to the main streets in the maze of alley markets.

Jax had more to say. "By the way." Ray turned to face him, Jax gestured for him to come closer. So, he did. "Rumor has it you're fucking a corporate bitch."

"Fuck off man!" There was a bite in Ray's voice. It drew several hustler stares.

"That's some bad shit bro," Jax said. "Worse than putting your dick all up inside a witch's pussy. She's gonna light your balls on fire if you stick with her. So, if this is her putting you up to it, just walk away now, man. No corporate pussy is worth whatever it is you plan on doing with my botnet."

A loud grunt and an about-face to the market's exit, and Ray was gone, leaving Jax behind. Who was Arianna to him he wondered? Days ago, that answer was easy, the woman he loved and planned to marry. Now? He wasn't sure. Arianna could still be that, she could also be a witch running secret covert ops in the Federation. Or maybe she was just corporate pussy, and he was about to make a grave mistake in pushing forward to learn the truth, thanks to the botnet access Jax was about to give him.

Scratch that, Jax just gave it to him. Ray pulled out his phone and saw the new notification from Jax. It was time to get back to the hotel. Ray whistled for a taxicab, using an app on his phone.

He stood waiting for the cab, and changed the password to his email account, wondering who accessed it.

The city of Los Angeles sped past Estrella like someone had been watching a movie on fast-forward. High office towers, condos, apartments, hologram ads, neon signs, all moved past her in a dazzling and mind-blowing blur as she raced cars and trucks on the road. Her long hair escaping from the back of her helmet was like the rapidly flapping wings of a giant crow behind her.

She was jacked into her helmet's primary computer. She never liked the holo displays it had over its visor. Much easier to have that data relayed into her head, then projected across her synthetic eyes. The speed of her bike appeared in the bottom right corner of her right eye, the estimated battery charge in her left, 87 percent. The top right corner of her eye had a mini-map of the city, a red dot represented her, a blue line was the path she needed to take, and the navi-point at the end? That's the apartment Ray made his home.

Estrella had to get there before Piper did. Failure to do so would risk evidence vanishing faster than Arianna and her father Norris did. Piper was all sweet kiwi accent talk, and Mona Lisa smiles for a reason. Piper was a woman whose loyalties might have lain with the Federation, who knew what she wanted, and got it with her enthralling appeal. And what did she want? Well, Estrella hoped to find that out by the end of the day.

I never understood the need for humans to operate vehicles at unsafe velocities.

Estrella smirked, her white teeth obscured behind the helmet. *I'm not human, Geoffrey.*

You were born human and operate their vehicles. And currently, we are traveling 22.6 percent over the recommended speed limit for these roads.

Just keep scanning for cops.

And Piper?

Yeah, her car too.

Though, as Estrella recalled, she had a head start on the race to Ray's apartment. She should be good. She just needed to get in and out before Piper arrived.

When Estrella was two minutes out. *Alert, I have detected Piper's car.*

Location? Geoffrey updated the mini-map. Piper was traveling on the parallel street which had slightly less traffic than the one Estrella was on. *Fuck sakes!*

She will arrive before us.

No, the fuck she won't.

Estrella increased speed, swerving around cars like they were obstacles on an obstacle course. A four-way intersection neared, but she didn't wait for the lights to change. She plowed through and then made a hard turn to the right. Her body and the bike leaned forty-five degrees to the side. Her knees lightly grazed the streets during the tilt turn. Cars honked their horns in disapproval. She didn't give a fuck, especially after she leveled off and sped up between multiple buses and cars. The nice thing about riding a bike, one could fit it in tight spaces that cars on the road couldn't.

She was on the final stretch, meaning Piper wasn't far off.

Sweet drenched her brows. She had to get there first. The adrenaline mixing with her life support nanites pushed her to continue. Estrella's bike came to a screeching halt outside the apartment. Fluttering palm trees rustled their leaves above her as she rushed to the entrance, looking back for signs of Piper's car. There were none, yet.

The NC gauntlet flashed blue, spraying nanites across her suit and helmet. They melted into gray goo, unwrapping Estrella's form in her black skirt and black lace halter top that lay under it. The gray goo that was once her helmet and leather suit pooled up inside the storage compartment of her synthetic arm that split open, then closed shut when the goo entered.

Gone was the biker girl look. In was the cyber witch look.

The lobby's glass door entrance was locked. Only a biometric scanner let tenants in or buzzer computer screen. Estrella placed her gauntleted hand on the scanner.

Geoffrey, will you do the honors?

Of course, Estrella.

A small swarm of nanites left the gauntlet, entering the scanner, and accessing its core operational systems. They worked as a bridge, linking Geoffrey and the scanner together. Computer code rained across Estrella's eyes, when the rain finished, the hand scanner flashed green. The glass sliding doors opened.

Access granted, Estrella.

Estrella entered, escaping from the daytime heat. The air-conditioned breeze hit her, slowly removing the sweat buildup on her forehead. She pushed forward to the elevator, summoning it with a push of a button on the wall. The mini-map in her right eye updated, Piper's car decelerated near the apartment. Estrella was running out of time.

She vanished beyond the elevator doors as it opened, pushing the floor number to Ray's unit. They slid shut, blocking out the lobby's view. She imagined Piper would move in to speak with the landlord first, making it look like she was here on official LAPD work. That meant Estrella had at best five minutes before Piper made her way up.

In and out, nothing more.

I would recommend that as well.

Wasn't talking to you, Geoffrey.

Oh.

She was on his floor when the elevator stopped and went sprinting out of it when the doors opened. The hallway was long, possibly the longest apartment hall she'd ever seen. There were intersections linking it to other parts of the building, and halls leading to overhanging walk bridges, those too connected to adjacent buildings. She was in a maze where the walls were closed doors with biometric scanners and keycard panels.

Geoffrey pulled up a list of the tenants, collected during the hack earlier. Her mini-map changed to a floor plan of the current floor, and Ray's unit was highlighted green. She found the door after a long run down the halls, and her NC gauntlet hand rested upon the door. Once again, the nanite hack ability was selected from her menu.

This will take much longer, Geoffrey revealed.

Her face contorted, looking down at her gauntlet. *Why?*

Ray changed the security encryption. It will take me at least ten minutes to break it.

We don't have that time. She rested the palm of her gauntlet on the door's smooth surface. *Let's get rid of this door, shall we?*

The nanite swarm turned the door into gray goo, forcing it to pool on the floor below. It was faster than hacking but left signs that an RW like her changed it, just like her first day in LA. She had to take the chance. Time wasn't something on her side. When she stepped through into Ray's unit, the gray goo on the floor rose, took shape of the door that was there before, and rebuilt it. Geoffrey's black cat holographic appearance appeared next to her, leaping up onto the coat rack, standing watch.

In and out.

She ran from cabinet to cabinet carefully pulling items out, then putting them back. It only made the anxiety tingling in her chest worse. Searching quickly was easy, doing that plus making it look like you were never there while on the clock? She wanted to scream in frustration and pull on her hair. It was too much. She underestimated how fast the task needed to be.

A minute was left, so she guessed. She ran for Ray's computer, idling ahead of a window that wanted to let in the sunlight, but couldn't thanks to the adjacent buildings, forming a wall of metal and windows across the sky. The computer powered on with a spray of nanites from her gauntlet, its password was a lot easier to hack than the front door.

Time was limited, so she had Geoffrey copy as much of its hard drive to her head as was possible, before quickly logging out and walking away as if it had never been on. She browsed briskly through the downloaded computer files now in her head, their contents appearing in her left eye, her right eye remained on the sights of Ray's apartment, as she continued searching.

She grinned when document files appeared. They were rough drafts of articles that eventually ended up on DigiSamurai69's blog. *Ray and the hacker,* she thought. *They're the same. This confirms it.*

It may be wise to keep this information to ourselves to protect him.

Estrella found coding programs and various hacking apps in the next batch of downloaded files. *Looks like he was a bit of a trouble-maker before he hung up his coding jersey.*

And might still be one. Geoffrey brought up a new screen— newly compiled phone and tablet pad apps. *According to this, Ray programmed custom made hacking apps and installed them to his phone and pad for ease of use while away from his home.*

You're telling me that pendejo doesn't need his computer to crack stuff?

That is correct Estrella.

Shit.

It might be best if we did not cross him. Should he plug his tablet into you, he may compromise my systems.

Estrella believed it too. Ray was dating Arianna, an employee of Yoshida. Who knows what corporate secrets she shared with her lover in private? Yoshida manufactured most high-end tech. Ray learning how to crack their codes gave him unlimited access to everything that made the Alliance function on the technology side.

As impressive as Ray's abilities were, she had doubts that this was the reason the IWs tried to attack his place of dwelling. They backtracked when they realized nobody was home. And what a backtrack they made. Estrella looked around, and she saw very few signs the place was broken into. Upon finishing a quick optical scan of the unit, she learned the front door wasn't forced open, and probably wasn't hacked.

How the fuck did the IWs get in?

Perhaps the same way Nobuo escaped from the Kounias residence?

What? Cut a hole through the air and jump in?

It would explain things. If he had the power to create micro-singularities connecting two points of space together, then yes, that would be possible.

Wanna dumb it down for the witch?

If Nobuo was an S ranked weaponized telepath, then it is conceivable he made a portal to escape from us. Therefore, he might have used that same portal to enter this apartment unit.

And the SWAT armory. Estrella sighed when she put things

together. *And the New York airport ... That asshole had the power to be in four places at once.*

You might want to take a look at this, Estrella.

Geoffrey showed her a new screen containing contents downloaded from Ray's computer. Emails, and lots of them. Ray's most recent messages were confirmation messages from an autoresponder. He booked a flight from Los Angeles to New York, the itinerary on the flight listed his return flight, and it should have landed in Los Angeles. Only, it didn't, not with JFK temporarily shut down.

Ray's still in New York, she thought, her eyes still skimming through his hacked email account.

It is most likely he discovered something of importance, which required him to stay.

How do you figure?

The airport is now allowing some flights to land and depart. Yet, Ray did not get a new ticket for his return to Los Angeles.

You're right. She scrolled through the messages. Ray was taking his time booking a different return flight home. *And he's not dead if he's still posting as DigiSamurai69.*

Further proof Ray was alive and not missing, was a recent message sent to the editor-in-chief of the Alliance Star. Attached were drafts to his report on the airport attack. There were other email messages Ray and the editor, Steven Jarred, sent. Most of it was Jarred rambling that he couldn't call or send text messages to Ray's number. Ray replied, claiming he was using a different phone with a local New York number. It makes it harder to track him if people don't know he swapped phones. Ray was glad to do it too, as he felt like he was being watched. He came across something big, really big, something that could start the fourth world war. Ray just needed proof—

A phone rang. Its charming ringtone directed Estrella to it. It was the local Los Angeles phone Ray left behind intentionally. She wouldn't be surprised if the IWs that attacked traced its signal to his place.

She held the transparent phone in her hand, and its screen displayed the caller ID of the person calling, Piper Taylor. Piper had left several unread text messages.

It made Estrella gasp. *Piper is reaching out to him.*

It also reminded her that Piper was probably seconds away from entering.

She hit the ignore button and looked at the phone longer. *Piper and Ray know each other.* She held the device tightly in the grasp of her NC gauntlet. *Same deal with the computer, Geoffrey. Nanite hack this phone, download, and analyze everything on it.*

This phone's data is heavily encrypted. It will take some time to break.

Do it.

Processing please stand by—

The front door unlocked and slowly opened. Geoffrey's holographic form standing watch vanished. *Piper is here now, please take cover.*

Estrella had that to do and more. Looking to the computer and phone in her grip, she realized Piper would get what she was seeking. Estrella couldn't allow that. She dispatched a swarm of nanites to the computer and watched as they turned it to gray goo on the floor. A flick of her gauntlet hand sent orders to the swarm, making the goo retreat under the couch. The sudden discharge of all utility bots in her body halted the hack of Ray's phone. She was thinking on her feet from that point.

Piper and the apartment's landlord entered. Estrella darted into Ray's bedroom, out of sight for the time being. She snickered at the white lingerie in the corner, probably belonging to Arianna during her last visit. Arianna had a killer body, despite wearing a bra size smaller than Estrella's.

She pulled a nanotube from her opened arm. It swam in the

gray goo that used to be her helmet and leather suit. A quick injection sent a replacement swarm into her body. She had Geoffrey perform a Scan Copy of Ray's phone, before turning it into goo. The newly injected nanites carried the goo, formally Ray's phone, into her arm, before it shut. She made plans to hack it later. Preventing the evidence from getting into Piper's hands was all that mattered.

Estrella needed an exit plan. *Geoffrey, suggestions for escape?*

We must make it back into the hallway. However, every unit on this floor is occupied with tenants.

I take it, repeating my trick isn't going to work?

Disassembling the wall as a means to flee is not advisable. You risk being detected by tenants in the unit you will pass into.

Estrella had to find the wall that separated the unit from the hall.

The footsteps and chatter between Piper and the landlord grew closer to Estrella while she remained hidden in Ray's bedroom. She ran an optical scan of the apartment. It flooded her vision with numbers and a three-dimensional floor plan layout of the interior and exterior of the building. Ray, as did all tenants, had a balcony. It'd make for the perfect escape, just slip out on it, then scale down to the streets, leaping to the balconies below. And if Piper and the landlord weren't lounging around in the living room, then Estrella would have done that.

She found her best bet, Ray's bedroom window.

Piper and the landlord drew closer. Estrella had to make her move now.

Silently, she power walked to the window, tiny hairs on the back of her neck wanted to rise and keep watch for what she couldn't see behind. She placed her NC gauntleted palm against the window and ordered a swarm of nanites to deconstruct it bit-by-bit. Rippling circles flowed across the glass from where her palm touched it. The glass looked as if it had turned to a clear liquid, and the rippling waves were like a rock that got tossed into a pond. The window was melting.

By the time her nanites were done and returned to her, the glass turned goo beneath her heels. She crawled up and through the glassless window, while winds from the high altitude rustled her hair. Vertigo kicked in when she glanced down, her heart thumping. The streets looked like black lines with specks of dots moving across, gigantic shadows cast from the apartment and others close by darkened everything below. Delivery drones zipped back and forth, delivering meals and goods to those that ordered them in the high-rise neon jungle.

To her left was the line of balconies hanging off the exterior of the building. She positioned herself carefully while perched up on the windowsill, wondering if she was out of her mind. Then she leaped.

As she fell, she waved her blue glowing gauntlet hand, ordering a spray of nanites to fly back into Ray's bedroom and find the gray goo on the floor, restoring the window to its original state. She continued falling for five seconds holding her hand forward, waiting for the return of her swarm back into the gauntlet and then to re-inject inside her after the job was done.

She was still falling, her black hair rippling like she was caught in a wind tunnel. Balcony after balcony lifted out of her vision. The surface got closer, real fast. Estrella was out of arm's reach to grab a balcony. Maybe she really was crazy.

At fifteen seconds into her drop, her synthetic arm grasped the corner of one balcony, breaking her tumble down the urban well. She released her grip and fell, catching the edge of the next balcony, and then she did it again. And again, and again. Her cyborg body and speed felt no stress on the way down to the street and her parked motorcycle.

Estrella marched away from the apartment after coming to a landing. A triumphant smile brightened her face as she made her approach to her idle bike. Her synthetic arm opened once again while she browsed through the saved patterns on her screens. She selected the red helmet and red leather suit, and Ray's phone.

The gray goo pooled inside her arm spilled out, most of it falling to her feet. It covered them, slowly spreading up her legs, covering her skirt, midriff, halter top, then head. It took the shape of her helmet and biker suit and solidified from the gray goo. The last of the goo spilled into her hands and became Ray's phone. She placed it in her pocket and got on the bike, powering it on.

Leaving already? Geoffrey asked.

She drove away from the apartment with her hair flapping in the winds. *I think I got exactly what Piper wanted to get.* She patted her suit's pocket, feeling the solid object in it. *Access to Ray's phone, email, and network. Now we need to find out why she needed to get a hold of him so badly after the attacks.*

Back in the hotel, out of the cold, with feet up on the desk. Ray sat back, holding his pad fingering it rapidly, making the keystrokes needed to instruct Jax's botnet to hack the network grid in question. What's in the network? The morgue.

His pad relayed live surveillance camera footage from the morgue's front parking lot. There were two black cars parked that caught his attention. He enhanced the view of the plates with an imaging scan. Two new windows formed and ran a database check. He wasn't surprised to learn the plates were registered with the AIT. Alliance government agents were in the morgue, searching for clues on the IW bodies pulled from the airport attack. At least he assumed that was the case, since it was the reason he was there hacking the cameras.

Oh yeah, they're here for that all right.

After six camera hops, Ray found the one camera overlooking the cold storage area, where all the dead were kept. IWs included. He recognized the neutral faces of Miguel and John from the AIT. They ordered one lab tech to the computer console, where he typed in some codes, and placed his hand on a biometric scanner.

A beep or two sounded, and then a section of the wall pulled open like a storage drawer. When the mist was waved away, the three stood looking down at a naked body trapped within a stasis tube. The body's lips were blue and above that, if you looked closely, you could see a gory hole through his head, two fingers wide.

Miguel gestured to the lingering morgue workers in the background. "Do they need to be here?"

"Not really," said the lab tech to him.

"Then get them out of here."

The tech moved forward, instructing his team to leave. They all left without asking questions, vanishing from the view of the camera. Ray sat up straight, pulling his pad closer to his face.

John stopped at the recently released body while the lone lab tech pulled more bodies out from their stasis slots in the walls.

"I've never seen IWs like this," he pointed at the carcass. Ray zoomed in. He saw cyberware joints on the arm of the body. "IWs don't get cyberware like this. IW genes and their abilities don't work well with cyberware tech. Only RWs get them, and that's because they were born human."

A secondary window popped up, obscuring Ray's view showing the footage from the parking lot camera. He'd minimize and ignore it if it wasn't for the red letters flashing, stating new movement had been detected. A new car showed up and parked in the lot outside the morgue, four men exited wearing large coats. Large enough to hold weapons inside. He ordered window one to remain on the agents examining the bodies. Window two was to follow the four newly arrived men.

He focused eyes and ears on window one.

"Have you identified them?"

"No, their facial scans don't show up anywhere. These IWs never stepped foot into the Alliance until today."

"So, they are from overseas."

Window two's view switched to the main entrance of the morgue. A member of the staff went to speak with the four men and ate a psychokinesis stun to the face. Their body crashed to the floor, rolling and convulsing. It caught the attention of three AIT agents who were standing watch. The agents drew their pistols. Four pairs of white glowing hands rose, and a psychokinesis stun locked the agents down. The four glowing hands reached for pistols with silencers attached. Six or seven flashes of muzzle fire sent curving bullets ripping holes through the AIT agents. A splash of red and exiting gore made the walls sticky and gross.

Nobody in window one heard how the dead met their ends. Ray had no way to warn them that theirs was coming.

"You have no idea." It was Miguel's voice. Or was it John? Panic made Ray forget how they sounded.

The four men continued moving through the morgue on window two. On window one, Ray saw the lab tech with gloved hands pull the flesh back on the arm of the second body. A gunshot had torn right through it, but not the cyberware under it. Ray zoomed in.

"These parts?" The tech said pointing. "Zhang Industries made them. This is triple-A Federation tech, only used by their military. Last time I checked, recruiting IWs to any military was banned internationally."

With crossed arms, John asked. "So, you're saying the Federation is weaponizing their IWs with cyberware?"

"Not just any cyberware, high-end shit," said the tech. "I think these implants were enhancing their powers, bringing them to an S rank, maybe beyond."

Miguel mumbled. "No fucking way. What would be beyond S rank?"

"I don't know." The tech shook his head as he moved about, showing the two agents the cyberware the recovered IW bodies had. "I saw pictures of the attack at JFK. Hard to imagine regular

IWs did that. And it's troublesome to imagine that a group of terrorists got their hands on these parts. Someone figured out a way to put cyberware in IWs, make it work without problems, and then trained them."

"How did you see that?" Miguel's voice was firm and to the point, directed at the lab tech.

"Eh? See what?"

"Footage from the airport attack."

The tech shrugged. "Well—"

"Never mind, you shouldn't know that. Fuck, nobody should."

"The video of the attack was leaked to me since I was working on these bodies."

On window two, the four men were drawing closer with their silenced weapons in hand. Men ... they were IWs, probably friends of the dead ones in window one. Ray rubbed his palms together. The reality that he might be forced to watch more lives end had hit. He stood as the only person to save them.

His heart was pumping. *Think, man, think!*

Ray still had access to the network. He could work with that, hack a computer, send a message, and hope they'd believe it. He went searching for network nodes linking to the computer console the tech used.

"Does anyone else know?"

"No."

Window two, the four IWs turned the corner laying eyes on the lab workers who were asked to leave. The bullets moved faster than their mouths that wanted to call for help. Bodies fell on the crimson floor.

Ray still couldn't find that console.

"What about this shit?"

He had no idea who was talking, his eyes locked into the computer in a third window.

"Just me and my team you sent away."

He found the console. He began typing a warning.

"Keep it that way. We can't have this getting out, not yet—"

His hands weren't fast enough.

The door ripped open like a tin can, four IWs with four silenced pistols raised running in. They didn't need to aim. Curving bullets always hit their targets, especially those twitching from a psychokinetic stun. Miguel, John, and the lab tech lay in a sea of red, and it expanded enough that you couldn't tell whose blood belonged to whom when it mixed.

Ray remained in his chair, the feeling of defeat, and failure prevented him from doing anything else. He sat there looking at the pad's screen, his punishment for not moving quick enough and losing focus in his search for the truth.

Flames erupted with a snap of red glowing fingers. They spread fast. Way too fast to be natural fires. One of the IW stopped and looked directly at the camera. He made eye contact with Ray like he was there in person watching.

"I see you." The IW said, seemingly to Ray.

All cameras went black after that. He disconnected from the network in a hurry, just in case. Ray flicked off his pad, and it shrouded him in darkness. He sat in his chair for an hour, maybe longer. He was too frightened to move, too frightened to call the police, too frightened to think of a way to deal with a threat that was literally a walking WMD that moved with no one knowing.

He had the truth recorded on this pad. And if he remained silent, he was sure he'd die along with it. But if he got it out now, while he was still breathing, the world might fight back and defend itself from IWs seeking revenge against humanity.

Ray went for the hotel suite's phone, dialing his editor's number. He spoke when his face appeared on the screen.

"I got more on the airport attack," Ray said.

"Shut the fuck up." Steven grinned. "You're the man right now."

"It wasn't a terrorist attack. It was the Federation. They've been weaponizing their IWs in secret."

"That's a big scoop ... and a little hard to believe."

"I got the proof and a lot more with a psytrip memory sphere. And get this; the Alliance was trying to keep a lid on it."

"I don't know about this one."

He raised an eyebrow. "Why not?"

"Federation IWs killing Alliance people on Alliance soil? This could start some shit."

"It's the truth and the people have a right to know."

Deep sighing on Steven's end. "Let me think about it—"

"Don't think, do it," Ray cut in. "My last article ... hasn't it driven up traffic and revenue?"

Steven nodded stroking his chin. "It has. That's true."

"I have a lot of shit, breaking news stuff that nobody else knows. They will know soon, however. We can beat every news organization to the punch right now if we run this story. Think of the revenue it'll bring."

A five-second pause on Steven's part. He finally answered. "Send me what you got ASAP."

Ray's pad powered on again when the call ended, illuminating his dark room with the screen's backlight. He loaded his word processing software and began typing away the first draft of a new article. The article that would be read around the world once printed. It was up to the people in the Alliance and Federation to do their jobs and prevent a war with the knowledge Ray had to feed them.

If someone had Arianna, then they'd need to release her, because the gig would be up. And if she's gone into hiding because of this, then she can come out soon.

Everyone would be exposed the next morning.

TWENTY-NINE
ESTRELLA

Federation this, Federation that.

It's all Estrella heard and read about after she awoke the next morning. She regretted jacking into her pad. The images and words from the news were forever burned into her system logs.

Sometime, early in the morning, the Alliance Star released an exclusive front-page story, with additional details about the JFK International Airport attack. IWs with cyberware, manufactured by the Federation's largest corporation, a bunch of AIT agents, and morgue workers dead. Their charred bodies were pulled out from the morgue after a team of IWs moved in to silence them.

The news was picked up fast in the media across the Alliance, and soon afterward, the EU and probably the African Dominion by now. Doubtful the New Soviet Union or Federation ran anything on it as censorship was all the rage out in those parts of the world. Though, Estrella had doubts they'd censor the story about a fleet of Alliance warships in the Pacific prepping to move out.

And who was the reporter? Ray fucking Partington, of course.

Estrella groaned, sitting up quickly from her bed, her breasts shifted about in the process. It was another humid night with the AC burning out.

It's like every time I look, there's a big fucking finger pointed at the Federation. She reached for a long tank top, pulling it over her head. Its ends barely covered her panties. *Geoffrey, how's that decryption of Ray's phone coming?*

Almost complete, however, accessing Ray's contact number directory will take longer.

Shit, and that's the one we need the most. His New York phone number should be stored there.

You can pass the time by reviewing the data I have decrypted so far.

Such as?

Piper and Ray sent many messages back and forth and made a number of calls.

Geoffrey's black cat hologram sat next to Ray's phone on her desk. She approached the device, sliding it in her hand, viewing its screen. Estrella made a face at the decrypted text messages and call logs. *Piper was his source.*

That would be the correct assumption. The Alliance Star was known for being the first to get breaking news regarding IW crimes committed in the city.

Piper was giving Ray the heads up before everyone else clued in. The two ran a side-by-side comparison of the dates Piper contacted Ray and the news articles he wrote. Most were twenty-four to forty-eight hours apart. *She did it a lot.*

Piper was also the one that knew of your actions when you first arrived in the city.

The wall incident. Estrella licked her lips, thinking back to the grilling she got. Piper mysteriously had that information, and Estrella saw Ray in the area. After that, he posted a report on his blog, using his hacker screen name. *That's how Piper found out.*

Ray most likely entered secretly, made the scans, then forwarded his findings to Piper, hoping she'd follow up with more information. She put the phone back on the desk. *That means Piper has something to gain for helping him. The question is what?*

According to his phone logs, Piper reached out to Ray first.

And no one else I'm guessing. Estrella brought up Ray's file photos in her left eye. She looked at his beaming face on the photo which had Arianna hugging him from behind. Estrella's twisted lips remained still. *What makes you so special, Ray?*

His hacking blog, perhaps? Geoffrey suggested.

Which he's trying to keep a secret. She sat down and rested her legs and bare feet on top of her desk, not caring her panties were exposed. Not that anyone could see her. *Admittedly, he did a bad job of that. But I doubt Piper made the connection that he's the hacker too.*

She focused again on Ray's photo on the phone, zooming in on the blue-eyed hippy girl hugging him with a smile brighter than his. Estrella was asking the wrong question. *Arianna, it has to be Arianna.*

Perhaps. Ray has mentioned in a text sent to Piper that he and Arianna were in an intimate relationship.

Piper gets word he's close to Arianna. Estrella snapped the fingers on her right hand. It was a weird feeling since the NC gauntlet was off. *She feeds him news tips to keep Ray happy and talking to her. Then Arianna travels overseas on business, and on the day she's returning ...*

I see. Geoffrey clued in. *Her family is attacked by Nobuo and weaponized IWs.*

And at the same time, JFK gets hit, supposedly by weaponized IWs from the Federation, and the SWAT armory, Ray's home. Arianna goes missing, along with her father. She clapped her hands firmly. *That's it!*

That's what?

The Bald Skulls. What were they trying to do when we first got here? Kidnapping that family. What did they do the next time we heard about them?

They abducted an unregistered IW in public, followed by an adult psytrip actress.

Right, all were unregistered IW telepaths, same with that family. Piper's working for the Federation, I'm sure of it. She's a spy sent here to scout out targets for whatever it is the Federation is plotting. Piper must have been using Ray to learn about Arianna and her family, and when she'd be traveling away to the EU. The skulls were just hired guns going after targets she pointed them to.

Then why did Nobuo want to know where the gang was?

Because of me. Think about it? I'm not supposed to be here. Nobody was expecting me to bring to the LAPD's attention that they were dealing with a Buenos Aires IW gang that was personally put down by me. Me opening my mouth fucked up their plans, and the skulls became a liability to the Federation IW's plot. They needed to get rid of them and do things themselves.

She was still uncertain how the Bald Skulls were chosen for this. Her best guess was Federation agents revived them in the hospital, reported them dead, and then shipped them out of Buenos Aires to work for them. And that work? Locate and capture all unregistered IWs with telepathic powers.

It was a slick plan. Nobody in Buenos Aires would ask what happened to the bodies of the Bald Skull members after they were disposed of, and nobody in LA would recognize who they were, not with the high IW population, and new gangs spawning daily in the city.

That's quite the accusation, Geoffrey commented.

Estrella nodded in agreement. *We'll need to find proof to make sure I'm right. That shouldn't be hard now that we know what to look for.* Her thoughts went back to the breaking news. Zhang Industries were the manufacturers of the cyberware the Federation

IWs in New York had. *Yo, Geoffrey, is there a way we can learn who made Piper's RW cyberware?*

Not without removing them from her body.

Fat chance of that happening without killing her.

Actually, there is one method we could attempt.

Shoot.

Your nanites. If we can inject them into Piper's body, I could remotely command them to run a scan of her internal cyberware.

She grimaced and crossed her arms. *Sounds way too simple. What's the catch?*

Piper's life support nanites will see it as an intrusion and seek to remove them. You will have to directly administer the nanites into Piper's body. From there I will have a matter of seconds to conduct a scan before her AI eradicates them.

And how do we do that? Doubt she'll let me inject her with my nanotube or NC gauntlet.

I will have to synthesize a small concealable delivery device. From there it will be up to you to make contact with Piper physically, inject her, and hold it long enough for the nanite swarm to enter her system.

Geoffrey began a search through his database, looking for an item that could give the results. Estrella reached for her phone, sat up straight, making sure only her face would show up in the video call. The tank top she wore and everything below would reveal too much.

She dialed the number and waited for the caller to pick up.

They did.

"Hey, Piper, it's me, Estrella," she said waving to the pixie kiwi's smiling face. "You free for those drinks you talked about earlier?"

THIRTY
RAY

Ray had that dream again. He was in Arianna's body, and this time he was facing his own. It was the last night the two were together, only the memories played from the perspective of Arianna. He went through what she did, felt the emotions she felt, and saw how he looked through her eyes.

It was weird, especially when he felt a pair of hands caress Arianna's breasts. They were his hands. He felt himself touch Arianna. And now that they were naked on the bed, he was about to feel his own penis penetrate her. He felt her become wet as they fucked, her breasts shaking with each thrust. Women experiencing sex was a lot different from how he imagined it to be, especially the orgasm that hit seven minutes into the thrusting. His mind wasn't sure how to process the feeling of female orgasms, and the fact he didn't have to ejaculate semen. That, too, was weird.

———

The dream ended. It sent Ray sitting up from his bed in the hotel he stayed at. His deep breathing was the only sound heard, his penis hard from the dream. Don't get him started on that. The glow from New York's neon and hologram ads bled into the suite's window, the sun was still hours away from rising.

He sat at the edge of the bed, still confused about the memories that weren't his stuck in his brain. Still emotionally scarred at the grim reality that he may never see Arianna again, and she'd never know of the ring he bought her that was resting on the nightstand.

The door made an electric whistling chime. His body jolted at the sudden shock of the unexpected sound. Someone in the hall was requesting entry. Ray's phone flashed the time when he gave the screen a tap, 3:34 a.m. *Who could that be?* Ray mused.

Ray remained silent, even when he approached the door, tiptoeing to it barefoot. A screen near the door control panel listed the visitor outside as room service, a secondary typed message had an apology for the early call, claiming the room service team had a long day ahead and needed to start now.

He didn't buy the story. They would have posted a memo about this if that were the case. Ray said nothing more and tiptoed back to his bed where he would have been had it not been for the dream. A lingering sense of paranoia told him to be on edge. He wasn't out of this yet. That paranoid voice was right.

The person outside the door opened it and entered. Ray rolled off the bed, then under it. He saw a pair of boots meander within the darkness of the suite, the neon glow of New York gave it an eerie feeling.

"I don't see him," said the owner of the boots walking about, who was clearly not room service as promised. He was glad he didn't open the door and meet them face to face. He probably wouldn't have a face anymore. "Understood."

The intruder was one person and was communicating with another. If Ray had his gear, he might have been able to hack into their device and listen in to the conversation. He watched from under the bed as the boots went for the closet, slowly making their rounds in the room. The intruder was hunting him.

Ray was panicking. The only place left to search was his bed and the washroom. His options for continual survival shrank with each second. He saw the back heel of the boots. The intruder was searching the desk. They turned their back to the bed. Ray dragged himself across the floor like he was a ninja. He heard his heartbeat, and a part of his brain told him the intruder would too unless he calmed down. He remained prone in the darkness after he left the protective cover of the bed. Still crawling across the floor, Ray made his way into the washroom. He was too scared to see if the intruder was looking at his phone and tablet.

Inside the washroom, he got to his feet and eyed a fire extinguisher resting in its storage alcove. He reached for the small wall panel next to it, tapping the only button. The glass covering the alcove pulled up inside the walls. Ray's confidence grew slightly when he held the heavy red object in his hands.

Backtracking was no longer an option. Moving forward was, and what was forward was the bathtub. Ray strode briskly to it, his shoulders brushing against the towel holder in the darkness. By the time he climbed inside the damp tub, he noticed the towels had shifted. He really hoped they didn't plop to the floor. It was silent enough that even a bath towel falling would be heard.

His eyes remained locked on the darkened towels slowly slipping from their rest on the wall. Sweat moistened every inch of his body, and his heart felt like it had engaged in a boxing match with his chest.

He heard the intruder speak to whoever they were communicating with. "Found his phone and tablet."

Just take it and leave. Ray didn't care at that point. He just wanted tonight to not be the last day he was alive.

The towels fell from their rest on the wall. Ray screamed internally as they dropped in slow motion, making a soft plop sound on the ceramic tiles of the washroom floor. Footsteps came next and neared the washroom door, following the source of the soft plop, and echoing their terror throughout the suite. The lights turned on, and the intruder was inside the washroom. Fear pulled the hairs on the back of Ray's neck. He kept his body within the tub as low as possible.

More echoing footsteps mixed within the thumps of his heart and rapidly breathing chest. The washroom wasn't very large, it would be seconds before the intruder neared the tub and pulled the shower curtains away to see the cowering Ray holding a fire extinguisher.

The footsteps stopped, and if he were to guess, the boots that made them were next to the tub. Now or never. Ray waited for the sound of a hand pulling back the shower curtains and then let self-preservation and animal instinct thoughts take over.

They pulled the curtains back.

Ray leaped up, swinging the fire extinguisher, screaming, and panicking. He shut his eyes. It was a bad idea considering he needed his hand and eye coordination working at top performance to make the extinguisher hit something. Fear was the biggest motivator to do stupid things.

He felt the fire extinguisher swing through the air. He missed, he figured. The ball would be in the intruder's court if that were the case. He had very little doubt that their next move wouldn't miss, especially if they were an IW.

The extinguisher's movement came to a sudden stop. It hit something solid, something meaty. A thudding sound followed up seconds later. When he opened his eyes, he saw the intruder lying face-first on the floor. The man was dressed in black, had a pistol in one hand, phone in the other, and a trickle of red leaking from the side of his head. Ray hit him good.

Standing over the body of the intruder, Ray took notice of his chest. It was still moving, and he was certain he heard something that sounded like a groan of pain. The intruder could be a threat when he came to, and he realized the weak hacker-turned-journalist got the jump on the man, who was clearly some black op operative.

Ray grabbed the fire extinguisher tightly and imagined the intruder's head was a nail, and the fire extinguisher was a hammer. Two deep breaths and three blunt strikes to the intruder's head silenced his groaning. He wanted to leave after that, as he felt his stomach do something he'd rather it not do.

But what if he gets up after that? Or worse, is faking it?

The fire extinguisher came down on the intruder's head, and then again, and again. Fear made you do stupid things, with the promise that if you listened to its instructions, you'd live to see tomorrow. And that's all that Ray wanted; a guarantee he'd walk out alive. Fear told him if he continued hammering the intruder's head, he'd be able to do that. So, even when blood started to splash and spray-up, covering Ray, the walls, and ceiling, he kept on smashing. When the intruder's skull was caved in, forcing out all sorts of red and pink gore onto the floor, Ray's fear told him he was safe to leave.

The intruder wasn't breathing. He killed him. Dead threats can't hurt you.

He dropped the fire extinguisher. The impact cracked a ceramic tile. Ray killed a man. He was a murderer now.

But it was in self-defense. Though, he had doubts that would hold up in court. He could argue the first strike as self-defense, everything after that was questionable.

You're a murderer.

But he was going to kill him.

With what proof?

Ray fell to his knees. The trembling in his body wouldn't stop. *You're a murderer.*

His eyes remained locked on the body, convinced it would get up and look for revenge. When it didn't, he was convinced the police would haul him away in cuffs and charge him with murder. And with those IWs on the loose, what would stop them from attacking the jail cell he'd end up in?

The intruder's phone had partially slipped out from his hands after the bludgeoning. Ray scooped it up, flicking through its recent activity logs. He found a series of back-and-forth text messages. He read them.

You: We tracked where the second hacker is staying.

Nobuo: Excellent.

You: And get this, it's fucking Partington.

Nobuo: Really?

You: Yeah, so two birds with one stone here. Witnesses gone and we get Arianna's package. We can call off the hunt for her after I'm done with him.

Nobuo: Good, we're stretched thin as it is with the search for the Bald Skulls.

Nobuo, who was he? Someone of importance he figured, after taking a double look at the messages. There were more messages, but he dropped the phone, kicking it away. Further usage would only leave behind more digital evidence that it was in use, and the mention of a 'second' hacker had him worried. Jax had given Ray access to his botnet which he used to hack the morgue's cameras, and then tell the world what he saw. Nobuo, and whoever it was he was working with knew he was involved.

Ray had to escape, and it had to be now.

Changing his clothes was a hard task. His hands never stopped shaking, not even after he washed the murder blood down the drain. His shirt went on backward at first. It took him two minutes to get it on correctly. Getting his pants on took longer.

You're a murderer.

Only his phone, tablet, memory sphere, and engagement ring went with him when left the suite. It was debatable if that was wise given the gear the intruder left behind, like his pistol, which would have been nice to have for protection, but walking around with Federation black ops gear was a good way to draw attention to you, especially if there were tracking devices on them.

Cold wind bit at his cheeks as he walked away from the hotel hastily. He was alone now, just the weather, flickering neon, and the odd pedestrian on the surrounding streets, and none of them knew of the new murderer that was secretly on the run. And why? Because he witnessed the airport attack, and then later the hit on the morgue.

Ray reached for his phone, his hands ignoring the numbing winds biting at them as the transparent object flashed to life with a dial pad. He called Jax, and he replied quickly.

"Where are you?" Ray asked, relieved to see Jax's face on the phone's screen.

"Play, Pause, Rewind joint—" Static cut off his next words.

"What the fuck are you doing there?" No reply, the static continued. Someone was interfering with the call. Ray asked again.

"You asked me—" Static.

"Say that again? You're breaking up."

Static. "... meet you here ..."

"I didn't."

An error message blinked a connection lost sign. Re-dialing Jax's number yielded other error messages and dinging noises he'd rather not see or hear.

Ray wasn't in contact with him after the morgue went up in smoke. It proved his previous suspicions right. Jax was a target that wasn't allowed to contact anyone. He wasn't sure what to do. Leave

Jax and go into hiding? Going for Jax meant returning to Pause, Play, Rewind, now that he had no other means of reaching Jax.

Stay or take off, both options carried an uncertain future for Ray and Jax. Ray chose to find Jax. Get in and get Jax out without forcing any hands prematurely.

He hoped he made the right choice.

THIRTY-ONE
ESTRELLA

The Witch's Brew bar Robbie ran was bustling with life, significantly more than the last time Estrella remembered. What was once a straightforward bar out in the middle of Los Angeles IW district quickly became a crowded dance floor. Piper was dressed for the night, sporting a black faux leather skirt, matching strapless crop top, and transparent heeled boots. Estrella wished she could say the same, but she was never one to participate heavily in nightlife and lacked the attire. A simple black skater dress had to make do.

Piper flashed her wallet when she got to the bar, alerting Robbie to her siren-like appearance. The first and second round of drinks was on her, tequila shots. Piper mumbled something to her. The booming luststep music blasting from the speakers covered in strobe lights rendered her words mute. Estrella had to sit closer which was fine by her. The newly nano printed ring on her finger required Estrella to make physical contact with Piper, long enough to inject her with the nanites.

Piper smiled intoxicatingly at Estrella as she neared. She paid no mind to Estrella's touch with her hand equipped with the nanite ring.

"I said, you wanna dance?!" Piper repeated now that Estrella was in hearing range.

"Well—"

"That's a yes!"

Piper stood from the barstool pulling on Estrella's arm. She dragged her to the middle of the lively dance floor, past the waving arms of IWs and their alcohol-powered dance moves. Estrella released an internal sigh. Dancing wasn't on the menu; extracting Piper's secrets was. She played along, she had to. The two were drinking and now dancing. Estrella needed to keep up the happy emotions and hide the malicious act brewing on her finger.

Great, we're wasting time.

Actually, Estrella, this may be the perfect chance to remain in physical contact with her.

By dancing?

The ring must come in contact with Piper for a prolonged period of time. Consider using a stance that forces you to hold her.

How long? Because I held her with the ring already, but it didn't activate.

I need the ring to be in contact for a minimum of five seconds to release the nanites and bypass her AI.

Dancing next to a friend was one thing, having a dance partner that'd you hold on to for over five seconds, was awkward. Estrella had to wait for the liquid courage to take hold and throw that awkwardness in the trash. Piper swayed hips and hands in sync with the music, her skin turning to a myriad colors from the light show of the dance floor. It forced Estrella to pause, gazing deeply at Piper's hips in the black leather skirt. She grinned. Piper's exposed midriff would be the perfect place for her palms to touch, according to a quick optical scan.

When Piper's back was to Estrella, she made her move. She

held Piper from behind and felt her fingers press into the flesh of her exposed waist, syncing her body's movement with Piper's. Estrella's head was overloading. Never had she danced this close to someone. She could smell the scent of Piper's lavender fragrance, feel the heat of her body, and had the movement of Piper's ass shaking against Estrella's front. Estrella's face turned red, and it wasn't because of the booze.

Establishing a connection, Geoffrey reported, and it made dancing and close grinding with Piper hard.

You're supposed to enjoy the company of a dance partner, not wonder if the nanites you were secretly injecting them with would make it in undetected. Estrella's hands trembled.

Connection lost. She was panicking.

Geoffrey, what happened?

You must keep the ring still. Please try again.

She tried to steady her grips, keeping them still as she continued holding onto Piper's dancing body. When she did, Geoffrey updated her status, the five-second countdown to breach Piper begun. It made it as far as three seconds.

Connection lost.

Piper enjoyed having Estrella hold her from behind. She lowered her hands resting over top of Estrella's, grabbing hold of them. Synthetic hand held synthetic hand, fleshy hand held the other. Piper twirled, holding onto Estrella's hands. She wanted to dance face to face, the emerald glow of her eyes met Estrella's. Estrella was experiencing life on the dance floor with a partner for the first time, with a woman who was a decade and a half older than her.

Estrella's screen continued to flash connection established and disconnected messages for the next fifteen minutes. It made her wonder if Piper knew what she was trying to pull. Piper's moves were fast and were strangely erotic, yet pleasant. She was a wild, moving, feisty woman, drawing a variety of ogles as the dancing went on. Estrella felt the tips of Piper's fingers stroke her hip pressing the fabric of her dress against it. She didn't want her to stop. So, Piper didn't and lowered her hand fondle to Estrella's thigh. The sensation increased the rate of her heartbeat. Estrella had to shake it off. She had a mission to finish and was failing to get it done.

Two minutes and a lot of jealous glares came and went. Piper was yearning for another drink and a break. Estrella was glad to hear it; an idle Piper would be easier to touch and hold. The two left the dance floor, navigating past the mass of dancing strobe light flashing bodies. Piper took a seat at the bar, and this time, Estrella pulled a seat close to her. Close enough for their shoulders to brush. It made a smile grow on Piper's flushed face.

Estrella braced herself, this was it. The window of opportunity would open soon. She would get this right. Just reach over and hold Piper's arm or hand when the time was appropriate, without it looking awkward or suspect. Inject the nanites, then come up with a new plan if her AI detects the intrusion and reports the source— her—to Piper. She'd have to deal with that later.

Piper turned away from the bar, facing Estrella. Her face had shifted from pink to purple with the lights. "You look exhausted, Estrella."

"Yeah, I think—" I overdid it on the dance floor, is what Estrella wanted to say.

"I need another drink?" Piper put words into Estrella's mouth.

Estrella shrugged. Her thoughts pondering how to spin this into getting the scan done, the reason she showed up in the first place. "Well—"

"Robbie!" Piper's intoxicated voice was loud, making Robbie jerk his head away from a patron sitting at the bar. He looked over, smiling at Piper and Estrella. "More drinks for the two of us!"

"Eh ..." Estrella mumbled, not that either of them heard her over the music.

A smile and a lean forward by Piper, her chin was practically resting on Estrella's shoulder. "This one's on me too, love."

Another drink might not hurt. Geoffrey suggested. *It will make Piper more intoxicated. I've already detected a 4 percent drop in her reaction and movement speed.*

"Fine," Estrella said with a beaming smile.

"Another tequila shot?" Robbie offered.

Piper faced him nodding. "Please."

He faced her back, glanced at Estrella, then back at Piper. Robbie's eyebrow lifted with fascination. "Piper, darling, you sure you can handle this one?" Roaring laughter came next from them both.

"Please," Piper said after the laugh, waving a tipsy index finger at Robbie. "I can do this all night, until *six* in the morning—"

"*Sex* in the morning?" Estrella cut in, unsure of if the music made her misunderstand Piper's words, or the booze.

Piper repeated, her gaze shifting back to Estrella. "Six!"

"I heard sex ..." Snickered Estrella.

"You making fun of my kiwi accent?"

"Oh no, it's just."

"Six!"

"Sex."

"Six, six, six."

"What's this about sex?" Robbie said, having returned with the two lime wedge tequila shots in hand. He offered one to Piper and the other to Estrella.

Piper rolled her eyes. "Oh, my fucking god."

"Oh, someone's blushing!" There was silence as the two knocked back the shots. "You might be in over your head there, Estrella."

Two empty shot glasses hit the bar in sync. Estrella's courage was replenished. "I'm good."

"Piper's a cougar," Robbie said. "She likes the younger girls—"

"Robbie!" Piper winced.

He giggled in response, pointing a finger at Piper, then Estrella. "Oh wait." Robbie looked confused. "You two ain't?"

"Just hanging out, man," a defensive-sounding Piper muttered.

"Oh, I'm sorry, didn't mean to—" Embarrassment hit Robbie. He backed away from the two slowly, his hands out delivering a nonverbal apology. "Ah, shit, I'll just mosey myself out of this talk."

Estrella watched Piper's legs as they moved to cross. Piper leaned closer to Robbie. "What made you think I was here to seduce Estrella?"

"The way you two were dancing? And the talk about sex—"

"Six!"

Robbie copied Piper's kiwi accent. "Sex!" He laughed. "Right, moving on!" And backed away, this time for real.

Piper was gazing at Estrella now as Robbie left the two alone at the bar. "Don't mind him."

"He's cool for an IW." Estrella said, making Piper wince again. She wondered why. "I'm surprised none of the IWs here had me lynched since I arrived, given the reception I got. It's fucking breathtaking."

"You're breathtaking."

Intoxicated giggles were exchanged. Piper was drunk, and so was Estrella. She was right where she needed her.

Piper gestured to the exit. "I think I'm gonna head out."

"So soon?"

"Yeah, not much going on here."

Estrella had to change her mind. She couldn't let Piper walk out with all her secrets. She had to come up with something, anything, that'll keep Piper's interest locked onto her.

"I was just getting to know you better, Piper." It was the first thing that came to Estrella's head. The tequila shots were working.

Piper ran her index fingertip around the rim of her empty shot glass. Estrella piqued her interests. Piper's emerald eyes opening wide as her smile sent the message that she wanted something more.

"Oh?" Piper purred. A soft smile accompanied it.

What am I doing? Estrella thought as an enticing gaze from Piper remained locked on her figure. She saw Piper's eyes stare and gave Estrella a top to bottom gawk. Piper paused for three seconds when her gaze halted around Estrella's cleavage.

Pipers eyes found Estrella's eyes again. "What about me has you so interested?" Piper asked.

"Oh, well, uh—"

Piper's flirty hand stroked the flesh of Estrella's real arm. Estrella flushed. The tips of her fingers leisurely inched toward her hand with the ring. This was it. A chance to nanite scan her, and they were still at the bar. She wasn't sure what to do. Take the shot? Or let Piper take her home with her. There'd definitely be more opportunities to touch and hold her then.

Her stroke of Estrella's arm stopped at the wrist. "Don't tell me," Piper said. She bit her lip before continuing. "Come back to my place, and then you can ask me anything." Her face was closer, the tone of her voice changed to a whisper. "Or do anything."

Estrella was holding Piper's hand, and she had no memory of how that happened. Piper didn't let go. The grin Piper had on her face suggested she was enjoying the small embrace too much to do otherwise. The ring came in contact with Piper's flesh again, and the countdown resumed, its numbers working from five to zero. The booze killed all nervous twitching in her hands. Estrella was calm, and relaxed.

Attempting to gain access, Estrella. Please standby and keep the ring still.

Two pairs of emerald synthetic eyes remained fixed on each other. Estrella wasn't sure what was going through Piper's head, but Estrella's gaze at her was to scan for any sudden changes in her facial expression. A crawl of text and numbers covered the upper left corner of her vision. Geoffrey gained access to Piper's cyber-ware, and the data was coming through.

Piper's face leaned closer to Estrella, her lips leading the charge. Piper shut her eyes. A sensual rush surged through Estrella. It reminded her of Yumi, and she couldn't figure out why. She sensed the texture and heat of Piper's lips on hers, Piper was trying to kiss her. And had Estrella remained still she would have experienced her first kiss. Instead, she jerked her body away.

The awkward stance flashed a connection loss error message when their holding hands parted.

A soft sigh left Piper's lips, lips that touched Estrella's for half a second. "Oh, I'm sorry."

Shaking her head, Estrella said. "No, it's uh."

"I thought you, well, you know."

"Eh?"

"Thought, you were lonely." Piper looked away, her face drenched with moisture. "There was a vibrator on your nightstand."

How the fuck did she know? Estrella thought though Geoffrey was silent in his explanation. She thought back briefly to the call she made to Piper. She had left the vibrator on the table in the background. *Ah shit.* "Ah," Estrella said to Piper still facing away. "So, Robbie was right?"

"Well, it wasn't my intention at first, but ..." She sighed again. "Sorry."

"It's the drinks."

"Yeah, that was some powerful shit."

"Yep."

Data analysis complete, Geoffrey revealed. She was happy to hear his words, having become worried that the sudden broken link might have corrupted the download. *However, we have been scanned by a telepath—*

What, where? Nothing. *Geoffrey, talk to me.*

New status screens opened. Geoffrey was taken offline, somehow. With Geoffrey offline Estrella lost control of all utility nanites. Even if Piper let her touch her again, she wouldn't be able to conduct the scan. And if Estrella were to come under attack now, she wouldn't be prepared to defend herself with her nanite's sorcery. The feeling was foreboding.

The giggling and happiness Piper was projecting were gone. A cringing face replaced it as her eyes went searching for the exit. "I should go."

She stood from her seat, leaving Estrella alone at the bar. Piper bolted to the exit in a hurry.

Estrella reached for her not that it did any good. "Piper!"

She got up immediately to follow Piper, perhaps too quickly. One second she saw the sight of the pixie kiwi making a move for the exit, and the next Estrella could only see the floor with her hands holding her up. She was too drunk to chase.

Robbie was at the bar again when Estrella pulled herself back up using the edge of the bar. "Oh, where did Piper go?"

Her tipsy body swayed from left to right as she eyed the exit. The kiwi pixie flew away from Estrella's net. She'd ask for Geoffrey's assistance, but her status screen still had him listed as offline.

"She split," Estrella's dejected voice revealed

"Didn't seal the deal, huh?" Robbie snorted. "Tisk, tisk, you gotta be more confident than that if you want an older woman, girl!" Robbie joined Estrella, watching the exit as three witches entered showing more skin than Piper was. "I shouldn't talk; I should have been keeping my eye on her too. Piper's been known to split without paying her tab."

Estrella reached for her purse. "I'll handle it—"

"Oh, no, you keep that, honey," Robbie snorted. "Piper'll be back, she does this all the time when she realizes a cutie like you ain't coming home with her for the night."

The night went from something strange and magical to pure

apprehension after Piper upped and left fast. Geoffrey's last words said something about a telepath invading her mind. Her instincts compelled her to run facial scans, searching for an IW. Except this was an IW establishment, there had to have been dozens of people with telepathic abilities. And with Geoffrey offline, she lacked the ability to detect who exactly would be strong enough to enter her thoughts, and possibly Piper's too. Why else would she have left in hurry?

Piper sensed danger and ran before it involved her. Estrella had a feeling she should do the same and called for a taxi.

Ray looked to the neon logo of Pause, Play, Rewind which was brightening his face. He then faced the streets behind him. Ray came alone as far as he could see with nothing but IW hookers offering their after-midnight special deals, and himself a wandering journalist though the holographic advertisement urban jungle.

He entered, keeping things low key. Only when he made it past the reception desk was when he lifted his gaze forward, searching for troublemakers. Ray saw none. He kept moving through the sparsely lit halls and found a long faux leather seat where Jax sat waiting.

He looked to the left, to the right, and behind. There was nothing else threatening, just IW telepaths escorting clients to the various private rooms for a psytrip. Though Ray striding into the establishment alive, when he should be dead, might change that soon. He had to be quick and get Jax to leave with him.

Jax remained sitting when Ray approached, his arms opened in greeting. "Ray, what's up?"

"You tell me," Ray said, gesturing to the exit. "Let's go."

"No, you tell me," Jax spat, his ass remaining where he sat. "You asked me to come here to this fucking witch brothel."

"I didn't, but let's talk about this outside."

"You contacted me ..." Jax pulled out his phone, shoving the screen to Ray's face. "See?"

Ray leaned forward eying the communication log the two had. There was no mention of the message. "See what?"

Jax was now the one carefully viewing the phone's screen. He made a face. It was a face Ray didn't want to look at.

"What the fuck?" Jax roared and bashed the edge of the phone against his leg. Not that it would make it work better.

Kids these days.

"It was right there a second ago," Jax panicked. "I fucking swear man. You sent me a text message today, asking to meet up here."

"You got hacked." Ray grabbed Jax's sleeve, yanking him up.

Jax's gaze remained on the phone's screen. "No fucking way! I ain't no lamer, and you know that."

He was right. Jax was a hacker who broke into devices, not the other way around. Ray froze suddenly when it all came together. The men that attacked the airport and morgue were powerful IWs, and most likely lured Jax here. You don't hack a hacker's phone with fake messages, as they'd be able to figure out they were fake. Telepathic mental manipulation was a different story, until the fake veil wore off.

Jax saw the messages because a telepath wanted him to see something fake. Ray couldn't maintain the phone connection with Jax because an IW with electrokinesis most likely disrupted Jax's phone temporarily. IWs targeted Jax specifically, and the two stood in a building full of IWs behind the dozens of private rooms around them.

Ray looked at all the closed doors, wondering what was really going on behind them. They needed to leave—

"Yo, fuck this shit." Jax got antsy, yanking his sleeve free from Ray's grip. "I'm out!"

In a panic, Jax dropped his phone and raced for the exit. His loud voice drew the glares of those still in the hall as he pushed past.

"Jax," Ray said to him, keeping cool and calm. "We'll figure a way out of this, but you really got to stay with me right now and keep your voice down."

A middle finger was the reply from Jax, and he went for the exit. Two doors one left and one right opened. A hole exploded through Jax's head before he made it to the front reception desk. Ray heard the blood splatter on the floor as Jax's body went limp and fell. He was sick of death and destruction following him everywhere he ran.

The IWs and their clients in the hall erupted with panic and flailing arms after watching Jax's end. The warlock bouncers heard the gunshots and came running forward. The shooters that remained hidden in the two private rooms made their presence visible amidst the screams and fleeing footsteps. Three bullets that curved around corners and a splash of crimson brought the bouncers to the floor.

The sound of boots marching from the two opened doors came next. Ray didn't stick around to count how many of them were holding rifles, or how many flaunted their pyrokinetic abilities when he heard fires take shape around him. Escaping through the front door was no longer an option. He'd have to get past the new choke point the ambushers set up.

Ray backtracked instead, rushing past the chair Jax had been sitting on, moving in the opposite direction of those fleeing in terror. His feet kicked something during his retreat, it was Jax's phone. He grabbed it and kept running, hoping its contents might provide some answers to his questions.

"There!" A rugged voice yelled louder than the screams. "Don't let him escape!"

Ray braced himself for his death. It didn't come, only the chaotic stampede behind now comprising bouncing bare breasts and dangling erect penises as the back rooms started emptying out. The black-dressed IWs were selective with their targets. Those fleeing behind Ray inadvertently created a shield for his escape. These were the IWs from the airport and morgue. They were here to finish the job. Ray's unexpected protection wasn't going to last long.

The black-dressed IWs with pyrokinesis powers turned the floors and walls into raging fires near Ray. Psychokinetic IWs tossed tables, chairs, and those fleeing, through the air. Bullet curving rounds would be fired soon. Ray ran. He didn't know where he was running to just that he needed to be far away from the exit.

Two turns in the halls later and he saw an open vent up on the walls. Its grille was inches below the ceiling. He stood on top of the chair and climbed into the air vent before the IWs turned the corner. He was grateful fear wasn't working against him that time.

The vents were dark except for the orange glowing light seeping in from one grille. The flames from the IWs were spreading, as was the smell of smoke and flesh. He watched from the vents as the black-dressed IWs fanned out, red laser light from their weapons went searching for their mission objective, Ray. He had no plans to make their job easy and crawled deeper into the vent.

What the hell was the Federation doing that was so important that they had to send these men here to chase Arianna and Ray? Thoughts like that and more ran rampant in his head as he continued venturing through the vents, trying his best to not alert the black-dressed IWs searching for him below. It didn't appear any of the IWs below heard him. Ray looked behind in the darkened spaces he crept through every two minutes just to make sure he was still alone.

The air vents overhanging in the main halls approached. He made the turns and slithered through them. Below was light shining up through the grille, and the exit should be further up. Footsteps echoed past the sounds of expanding fires. Ray chose to look before he leaped out of the vent. Peeking through the grille, he saw two black-dressed IWs brandishing heavy assault pistols. One of them looked up and took aim at the vent, making direct eye contact with Ray.

Telepathy alerted them to his presence, he figured. How else would he have known to glance up the second Ray put his face to the grille to peek? Ray pulled his face away from the grille as fast as he could. Two loud bangs and the appearance of bullet holes piercing through the vent's grille came next. Ray made a hasty retreat, back into the dark maze of the vents, amidst the gunshots.

"Stop!" He heard one of the IWs yell. "You might shoot him in the head!"

The gunfire ceased. He heard his own deep breathing now. They wanted him alive he figured. Ray took another deep breath once he realized the bullets shot at him didn't curve to hit him. That IW hit his cooldown phase, maybe the others too. Ray's window to act had opened.

"He's right, no headshots," a second voice from below the vents said. "Shoot him anywhere but in the head. If you can't guarantee that then don't shoot."

"What if we cut his head off?"

"That's acceptable so long as there's no trauma to his brain."

Ray backed away slowly. He was wrong, so very wrong. They wanted him dead, just not headshot dead.

"He's moving."

"Smoke him out."

There was a telepath below tracking his movements, telling the other IWs where in the vents Ray might be. He had to get ahead of them and break the link. That meant crawling faster regardless of the noises he'd make. Crackling noises of new flames breaking out echoed and the temperature within the vents increased, drenching his body in sweat right down to his boxers and socks.

"Come on out, Ray!" The telepath taunted and followed him from below. "I promise I won't shoot you … in the head."

Breathing became difficult. The flames laced every gasp of air with smoke and heat. It felt like his lungs were roasting. The number of paths within the vent crawl became limited. Some connecting vents seared the palms of his hands when he tried crawling through. Others forced him to turn away when he saw the bright glow of flames at the end.

"This her?"

That was a new voice to him.

Curiosity made him crawl to its source. Peeking out the vent grille, Ray saw the room he had his psytrip experience. Celia stood, looking frightened in the corner.

"Yes, she operated on him."

He saw two black-dressed IWs corner Celia. Red laser sights on their weapons aimed at her chest. She was on the floor now, still wearing that skimpy outfit. It looked like she was begging them to spare her, tears streaming down her cheeks, her IW powers useless against them.

"Is this really necessary?" said one IW to the other.

Celia pleaded with her sobbing voice. "Let me go!"

Neither of the two listened to her and neither of them was aware Ray was above watching. It meant he escaped the mind of the telepath or forced them to enter their cooldown stage like the others. Ray was free to do something other than run. Jax was dead because he offered to help Ray. And if Ray continued to lie watching, Celia was going to join Jax. He had to do something. But what?

Ray went searching for his pockets. He needed to distract the

IWs. The first item he found was Jax's phone. It brought a smile to his face when he swiped the screen, gaining access to it, and the number of hacking apps, passwords, and botnets, Jax had. This was the advantage Ray was seeking.

"She knows who we are," said the IW. "We can't take the risk."

He looked away from the phone's screen briefly. The red laser light of the pistol moved between Celia's eyes. She freaked out in a fit of psychokinetic panic. The bed hovered an inch off the floor and then got hurled into the IWs. A clock floated off the wall and went flying at the IWs like a Frisbee. They shook off Celia's abilities as if nothing happened. She tried running for the door, but a bullet through her leg stopped her from going through it.

Celia was down on the ground, screaming. Ray looked away, accessing the botnet Jax's phone gave him access to. Access to the city's network grid was moments away, provided the botnet could brute force its way past the firewalls and passwords.

He glanced back at Celia, one of the IWs stood above her aiming his weapon at her. He didn't pull the trigger. Ray needed him to keep that pose. He was eight seconds away from gaining access. The two IWs spoke again, he listened.

"She's a telepath, we could use her."

"She's registered. The tracking device would compromise us."

He heard a sigh when he broke through the first firewall, only two more to go. "Anyone else?"

"With her gone? No, it's just Ray, find him or that psytrip memory sphere, ideally both." Two firewalls down, and no gunshots. It was promising. "Finish her, we don't have time left."

"I don't wanna waste good pussy, though."

Third firewall down. A new screen appeared on the phone, a map of New York, its power grid to be exact with green and white lines crisscrossing at every intersection of the map. He zoomed in on their location and located the power distribution nodes providing power to the Pause, Play, Rewind.

The app displayed a window that required his attention.

Hack power disruption node.

This will disable or enable power for a city block of a targeted area.

Ray executed the program and sent the botnet to work. One whole city block went dark, including the lights in Celia's pleasure room.

"What the fuck?"

He heard a struggle and then some gunshots and shouts. Red lights from the laser sights crossed about, as random muzzle flashes brightened the pitch-black room. Was Celia alive or dead? Ray couldn't tell in the darkness.

"Don't let her leave!"

"For fuck sakes! What the fuck happened to the power?"

Thumping footsteps sounded, and then there was silence with the exception of a commotion in the halls outside her room. He hoped she got out alive because as of that moment, he was left with no other choice but to continue crawling through more vents, lost and meandering through the maze of pitch-black metal, with only the glow on his phone to light the way.

People are dying because of me ... he mused. Ray brought the memory sphere out from his pocket, giving it a hard look, pondering about the memories recorded on it that weren't his. *Arianna, what are you? What did you put in my head that's worth the lives of so many?*

His phone rang. His phone, and not Jax's. He was in no position to silence it fast as he held the memory sphere in one hand, and Jax's phone in the other. He moved quickly, trying to rectify the issue, reaching for his phone while putting everything else aside.

"You hear that?!" mumbled an IW.

"Fuck yeah, I do!" He heard running footsteps. They were getting closer to the vent Ray was in. "This way!"

Shaking hands held his ringing phone, giving his position away. He went to hit the ignore call option and then stopped when he noted the name and caller ID.

Piper Taylor.

How did she get this number?

Ignore the call? Or pick it up and risk giving himself away?

Ray thumbed the answer button and continued crawling through the vents with one hand holding the phone to his face.

"Piper, this better be good."

"Make a left and then go north."

"What?"

"Do it now!"

Following her instructions brought him to a new set of vents to crawl through. None of them headed toward the outside world. He grimaced. Ray needed an escape, not to move in circles.

"Has anyone called you on this number?" she asked.

"No, this is a secret number I use when I'm in New York."

"Have you been in contact with an RW named Estrella Rodriguez?"

"Name rings a bell, but no."

"Good. I'm the only RW you can trust right now. If Rodriguez tries to contact you, ignore her."

"What the hell's going on, Piper?"

"Arianna's family was attacked."

"Fucking hell, when?"

"Shortly after her arrival back in the Alliance."

"Why is it only now I'm hearing about this?"

"Next of kin needs to be notified, being Arianna."

And nobody can get a hold of her. "What about the rest of her family?"

"That's complicated right now."

The air vent crawl came to a dead-end. And somehow, Piper knew that. "Look down." He did. "What do you see?"

"The washroom," Ray said as he peered down through the grille, his eyes spotting the movement of two men below in the darkness. The backlight from their weapon's ammo count screen made it easy to see both were armed with rifles. "I see two IWs ... I think they're from the airport attack."

"That's because they are," Piper revealed. "Say hello to them."

A beep sounded. Ray cut the call and blocked her number. She led him into a trap as the two men faced up, making eye contact with Ray looking down at them through the grille. One of them smiled and waved to him. He tried to backtrack and escape before the guns went off. The grille he was viewing the two men through came apart and crashed to the floor like someone ripped it off and chucked it down. One of the IWs had used an electrokinetic blast on it, destroying the bolts keeping it together.

Backtracking was pointless. Ray was on top of the grille when he was looking down at them. His body fell out of the vent, crashing to the washroom's floor below. He saw the boots of the two men in the darkness, the light on Ray's phone worked as a flashlight. They took a step closer. He backed away in dismay, Ray's flailing legs made it hard to get to his feet, and the wall he backed into didn't aid in his escape.

He recognized the two IW men ahead of him from the airport fiasco. One was the IW that used biokinesis and transformed into a lion, and the other was the tall lanky warlock accompanying him. None of them pointed their weapons at him.

"Sup, malaka," the tall warlock said waving to Ray.

His partner pulled out his phone, dialed a number, and spoke into it. "We got him, Piper." He spoke with a heavy African accent. A pause came, Piper responding to him he figured. "Okay, understood."

"What's our move Bashiir?" said the warlock.

Bashiir grinned. "We are to take care of Ray, Theo."

Bashiir gave the washroom exit a big boot, the warlock Theo

stood behind him, his pistol held high and ready for action. Outside in the hall was the extent of the chaos Ray had fled from, black smoke and glow from the flames slowly consuming the now out of power building. Three black-dressed IWs took notice of the three in the washroom, their weapons rose to the occasion.

A roar surged from Bashiir's mouth, and in a matter of four seconds, his biokinesis abilities altered his DNA, changing his body into that of a lion once again. His majestic form charged out into the chaos, mauling the first IW that failed to escape from his jaws. The darkness and smoke made it hard to see what happened next but judging by the screams, Ray figured that IW met a painful end from Bashiir's jaws.

Theo went out into the hall next, his gun blazing briefly lighting things up. Electrokinetic sparks rained from his hands, glowing purple. An arch of electrical bolts made the two hostile bodies twitch violently. Theo followed by finishing one twitching target off with three bullets to the face, Bashiir mauled and ripped out the throat of the other.

"Partington," Theo called out to him. "Follow behind and keep your fucking head low."

Ray did as they two told him, not that he trusted the two men. They were part of the airport attack, and now they were aiding in his escape, blasting away the black-dressed IWs that had been pursuing Ray. There were two groups of IWs that had an interest in him, most likely for the strange visions he'd been having, and the knowledge that existed in the memory sphere that jingled in his pockets with every step.

Nobody could be trusted, not until Ray sorted out who had bad intentions and who had good. Assuming good people existed in this bloodshed to capture him. Probably not. Ray kept his eyes open for an opportunity.

Bashiir and Theo ran into heavy resistance by the time the three neared the main exit. The two were focused on three IWs covering behind the reception desk, exchanging curving bullets, and dazzling pyrokinetic or electrokinetic abilities until their abilities were forced into cooldown, dimming the glow of their hands. Guns and keeping them loaded became the weapon of choice until their powers recharged.

Those engaged in combat weren't keeping their eyes on the exit, Ray however was. When the IWs behind the desk ducked to reload, Ray sprinted to freedom. The cooldown period was still in effect. IW powers couldn't stop him now.

"Ray!" Theo called out to him, not that Ray had any plans on listening. "Malaka, come back!"

Bullets clapped again, their thundering sounds coming from behind. Ray had left the madness behind, fleeing out into the cold streets of the city. His lungs thanked him for getting free of the smoke. A large flock of onlookers stood in awe, watching as Ray emerged from the burning building. Some of them were survivors from the attack. Once again, those survivors worked as the perfect shield to cover Ray. He slipped into the stream of terrified bodies and disappeared past the traffic and the glimmering neon.

As much as he appreciated Bashiir and Theo, he couldn't trust them or Piper for that matter, not until he had more facts. Ray was onto something big, something the world needed to know before someone silenced him. Or the police arrested him after learning of the body in his hotel room.

He pulled out his phone as he power-walked through the crowded streets and went to access his news blog. He was ready to make a quick post about what he discovered. An error message greeted him; his blog had been deleted. A sigh of frustration left his mouth along with the white mist.

Ray flagged down a self-driving taxi, got in, and ordered it to drive him to the airport. On his way there he purchased a last-minute ticket to Los Angeles on the next available flight. If he was lucky, the flight should be in the air before the hotel's staff found the body in his suite. And if he was very lucky, he should be free from any shady IW operatives until his flight came to land back in LA.

Part of him wondered if this was what Arianna was feeling before she boarded her flight back to the Alliance. Like her, Ray was about to flee on a plane from violent IWs from the Federation, carrying in his head something of great value.

And Piper knew all about it.

THIRTY-THREE
ESTRELLA

Drunken footsteps carried Estrella back to her apartment. The taxi's AI charged her extra for vomiting in the backseat. Her life support nanites did a poor job at preventing that, so her battery must be low she figured. She couldn't tell as her HUD turned to distorted pixels. She'd hate herself in the morning when she looked at her bank account.

During the taxi ride, she dialed Piper's number several times, but there was no reply. It was like she had gone off the grid or was just embarrassed at what happened.

Geoffrey never came back online, which was concerning. She sat at the end of her bed and jacked into her tablet pad, accessing its diagnostic software. It took her drunken hand three minutes to locate the network jack on her head. A lengthy scan of the computer electronics in her brain began, attempting to detect the problem with Geoffrey, and hopefully fix the issue.

If it didn't work, then it would force Estrella to give Yoshida tech support a call and have them take a look, and most of the time, that required her to be put out, while some guy pulled the AI electronics out from her brain. Some of those guys fondled female RWs when they were deactivated. It wasn't a pleasant thing to look forward to.

A crawl of text and numbers covered her vision as the diagnostic scan of her AI continued. She tried calling Piper one last time, but the phone rang and rang. The stress was getting to her, and she tossed her phone across the room in response. She lay back with her hands behind her head, but her mind wouldn't let her escape the fact she was moments away from her first kiss in life. Seconds away. If she had hesitated longer, Piper would have been her first kiss, ever. Blissful vibes warmed her chest. It made her smile. It reminded her of Yumi.

Yumi had tried to kiss Estrella once after they showered together. Estrella pulled away at the last second. She regretted doing that as Yumi ended up dead the next day. Estrella had a chance to experience the last gift Yumi wanted to give her and threw it away.

Regardless of whose side Piper was on, she had shown interest in Estrella. What Robbie said only reinforced it. The dancing, the drinks, holding her warm waist, and then later her hand, Piper enjoyed it. If she had gotten her way, she would have carried Estrella home with her. What would have happened then?

She put the diagnostic on hold and jacked out from the device. It was time for a shower. Estrella stood from her bed, her head lost in thought and struggling to cope with the newfound silence of her AI being gone. She felt trapped, disabled, bogged down by the restrictions humans normally had to deal with. There was nobody Estrella could chat with internally, no means of interacting with her nanites, and limited use of her cyberware. She didn't do much in the shower as the water poured over her naked body, the typical signs Estrella was in emotional distress.

Estrella missed the days when Yumi would shower with her. Yumi knew when Estrella had long showers, she wasn't feeling good. Yumi had made it a habit to join her and then console her from behind when the distress floated to the surface. She groaned softly, Yumi was a great person, someone she really needed in life, especially now. She needed a hug from her. Estrella hugged herself instead, imagining it was Yumi showering with her from behind, resting her chin on her shoulder. She'd cry if her synthetic eyes would let it.

"Yumi, I miss you so fucking much ..."

When the shower was over, Estrella made her way back to her bed, sans clothing. Her AC unit was unsurprisingly silent. She reached for her tablet, ready to continue the diagnostic. Her hand stopped when she noted her vibrator next to it, the thing that she should have put away when she called Piper.

The thing she delayed having that date with. With a grin, she grabbed the vibrator instead. The diagnostic can wait. She was already dressed for her date too. She fell backward, smiling onto her bed, flicked it on, and listened to the buzzing noise it made. She lowered it to the small patch of fuzz between her legs.

She never really thought of other people when doing this. Men had a tendency to make her have flashbacks to her younger days when the Bald Skulls enslaved her for years. It was just the way things were for her. She thought back to Piper's lips and the kiss she almost had. The kiss she didn't have. Questions clouded her head. What would have taken place tonight if she didn't jerk her head back? What would have happened if Piper took Estrella home with her?

Her guess was they would have had sex, something else she'd never done, not willfully at least. It was odd the more she thought about it. Estrella had seen Yumi naked many times as they showered together, felt her breasts press against her when she hugged her in the shower too. Technically, those showers were the closest to intimacy Estrella had gotten in life. She began to wonder what could have happened between her and Yumi. She liked her company, a lot, and so did Yumi.

She moaned briefly as the vibrator pleasured her, speeding up her heart rate. Thinking of other women while using it felt nice, nicer than not thinking of anyone. Never in her life did she visualize women when pleasuring herself. She beamed brightly. Tonight, she would try something new.

Thoughts of Piper came first. She imagined her hand, massaging her right breast and hardened nipples, was the hand of Piper. It made her wet. She licked her lips, imagining that was Piper's work too, that made her moist below too. She thought about Yumi holding her with her comforting embrace in the sprinkle of shower water, her wet breasts squishing against the square of Estrella's back, her chin resting on her shoulder. Estrella entered a fantasy world where she and Yumi kissed and held each other's waists as the drenching water rained upon their body and soaked black hair.

An orgasm hit, and it made her drop the vibrator. She was surprised it happened so fast. It felt incredible. Deep breathing sounds echoed throughout. After a two-minute break, she lowered the vibrator again, finding her intimate spot. An imaginary Piper lay next to her, making eye contact with her. She wished she could touch the fantasy Piper, as she already had a very good idea what it felt like to hold her bare waist.

Estrella wasn't sure how to feel about this. She was pleasuring herself while thinking about a woman that could be the enemy. That was a level of thinking that could get you killed when bullets started flying.

She grimaced and shut the vibrator off, sat up and went for her tablet and network cable, plugging it into her head. The rest of Estrella's night was spent looking up at the darkened ceiling while a crawl of numbers and computer code scrolled. Hopefully, Geoffrey would be back online in the morning.

———

I'm sorry to wake you, Estrella.

Her eyes shot wide open, almost as if she wasn't asleep at all. Ahead of her view of the ceiling were the results of the diagnostic scan and the report that it rebooted Geoffrey in her sleep. The news had her sitting up with the biggest grin she felt on her face in days.

Geoffrey was back at last. The rush of excitement had her fired up and ready to reconnect with the AI that had been gone longer than she would have liked. Her smile transformed into a grimace. There was a time in Estrella's life when she didn't have an AI that was constantly connected to the net, back when she was human. And now, when that AI was taken offline for less than twenty-four hours, she was about ready to murder someone.

Technology was like a drug. Naturally, you don't need it. But once it was introduced into your way of life, you love it, and you'll never give it up for anything. You become dependent on it, and then suddenly when you can't use it, you lose your fucking mind, and ability to reconnect with that past life when you didn't rely on tech to start with.

Estrella yanked the cable from her head, jacking out of her tablet. She was still naked, thanks to the heat in her unit that wouldn't have it any other way. *What the fuck happened, Geoffrey?*

Piper's AI detected our intrusion and launched countermeasures. It took me offline with malware.

Fuck.

She knows what we did and gained several files, including the pattern for Ray's phone. If she has the correct raw materials, she can use her nanites to nano print a copy of Ray's phone for herself and have her AI hack it.

She slapped the edge of her desk hard. It was still in one piece. Had she done that with her synthetic hand, then she'd be picking up its remains. *You said something about a telepath before you went offline, any idea who it was?*

They have corrupted most of that data.

An out-loud groan broke the silence. *Of course.*

It was a target nearby, however.

The night at the bar replayed in her head. It surprised Estrella she could remember anything at all thanks to the drinks. But it was there, clear as mud, including the first kiss she could have felt. She flushed.

Only Piper and Robbie were close to me when you went offline. Lips curled as she tried to paint a mental image of the telepath. Was it Robbie? Maybe, then again with the drinks she and Piper had, there could have been another standing close and neither of the two realized it. *Piper left right away and hasn't been returning my calls. Pretty sure the telepath made her run.*

It's possible the telepath did. But more than likely however Piper left after getting what she had been seeking. There was a pause in the silent chat. Then there was a notification in the right half of her vision. *Alert, there is new activity with Ray's email account.* She inspected the screen, Ray had new mail, and he read it. *A confirmation message was recently sent to his account. Ray just purchased a one-way ticket from New York to Los Angeles.*

Estrella's smile returned, just not as powerful as before. *He's coming back.*

Indeed. I have the flight number and estimated time of arrival saved. It is likely Piper may try to intercept him once he arrives since we cannot reach her.

And if Piper did nano print her own copy of his phone, complete with its stored passwords and accounts, then she too would have gained access to his email. Maybe even Ray's secret New York number saved on the phone. Geoffrey never got around to finishing its decryption, but Piper's AI could have with the hours that passed. The thought eliminated Estrella's desire to go back to sleep.

Piper was ahead, and it was her fault for allowing it. The

Alliance and Federation were beating war drums, and the Federation had louder beats. Piper and whatever it was she was cooking up for the Federation had to be stopped.

Put me through to the LAPD.

Establishing a commlink, Estrella. Please standby.

———

Estrella's commute from her apartment to downtown LA was a brisk one. She did a solid thirty over the speed limit on her bike, receiving an onslaught of middle fingers from various morning rush-hour commuters. All she gave them in return was her long black hair rippling and waving behind as she drove dangerously close between, ahead, or behind cars.

At the police station, she sat in on a meeting with Timothy Peters and a couple of other officers whose names she couldn't be bothered to read with the facial scanning software's windows that populated her vision. She gave everyone a quick recap of the previous night's events and how she felt they were all connected to the mayhem that hit the city since her arrival.

It had Peters running his hands through his hair. He had to take a seat before the frustration got to him. "How the fuck did we miss that?"

"Piper's an RW," Estrella said. "Paperwork and all says she's the property of Yoshida, like the rest of us RWs. But it's probably faked, like her refugee status. My AI has confirmed none of her cyberware was developed by Yoshida."

She gave Geoffrey the cue to show them what little data he could gain from Piper before the malware corrupted him. A holographic screen rotated in the office; it was an image of Piper's internal cyber bones taken from the nanites Estrella's ring injected into her. The tiny red and yellow flag of the People's Federation of Pacific Nations was visible.

"Piper's cyberware was manufactured in the Federation," Estrella continued.

"The Federation must have been planning this for years," Peters said. "All of it leading to the incidents in the EU, spilling into New York."

"Ray was correct in his report," Geoffrey's hologram black cat spoke, his voice audible from small speakers Estrella had her network cable jacked into. "It would appear the Federation has been secretly weaponizing their IWs. There is a high chance Piper is affiliated with them, and quite possibly the IW telepath that scanned Estrella last night."

"And Ray is connected to it all," Peters said, his voice was heavy with worry. "He's the hacker behind the now dysfunctional blog."

"JFK's surveillance systems were also hacked, shortly after Ray arrived," Estrella said. "And a morgue holding the cadavers of the suspected Federation IWs was also hacked before they attacked it."

"You think Ray was behind that as well?"

"It seems to be. Geoffrey picked this up from New York," she said and had Geoffrey change the projection in the room. She pointed at it. "Ray met with this man prior to the hack." Peters glared at the projection of the young man Ray met with, a hacker that went by the name 'Jax', its light illumining his face in the dark office. "Then after IWs attacked the morgue, Ray and that same man went to meet in a telepath memory club." The projection switched to recent news reports from New York. A body found in Ray's hotel, a Pause, Play, Rewind caught fire after a shootout, and a hacker that broke into its systems during the violence, knocking out power for the block it was in. "Now that place went up in smoke, with Ray seen fleeing from it. And hours ago, hotel staff found a bludgeoned to death body in the suite Ray was staying in. Seems everywhere Ray goes, people die, and stuff gets hacked."

Peters grimaced, facing her. "Why?"

"He's concerned for a woman named Arianna Kounias."

"Right, the daughter of Norris and Maria Kounias," he said.

"She still missing I take it?"

"Yes, and I'm thinking Arianna going missing, and Nobuo coming after her family wasn't random. Some kind of Federation black ops operation is being conducted on Alliance soil. Whose side Ray and Arianna are on isn't quite clear—"

"Isn't clear?" Peters injected, his voice raised. "He's probably working with them as a hired hacker. His news reports are just there to make him look innocent."

"Once we chat with Ray, we'll know for sure," Estrella said. "He's in the air now. He got on the flight before the NYPD clued in on what he'd been up to. Thankfully, he's got no place to run. Once he lands at LAX, we'll grab him. We just need to do it before Piper gets to him."

Voices in the meeting expressed worry if Ray was even on the plane. Given everything that happened with his name, they called into question how he could get a flight to start with. Estrella had wondered that, and then remembered Ray's hacking abilities were far beyond your typical hacker. Knocking out a whole city block during the middle of a shootout in a burning building was no easy act. Buying plane tickets, then editing the details of them shouldn't have been hard for someone with his skill and access to whatever the fuck it was hackers these days used.

"Grab Ray when he lands at LAX," grunted a concerned officer. "That's assuming LAX doesn't end up like JFK."

"Which brings us to the second part of this briefing," Peters said and tapped a console on his desk. The hologram changed. "LAPD and the Alliance investigators will set up shop around the airport. Nobody gets in or out. Estrella, I want you in on this."

The hologram was an attack plan.

A top-down view of LAX with various dots and lines represented the various teams, their patrol duties, checkpoints, enhanced security. The works. Estrella felt uneasy.

"Can't we shut down the airport for the day?" she asked. "There's gotta be like what? Fucking thousands of people moving to and from it? Not to mention the staff working there."

"All the more reason we can't shut it down," Peters explained. "There are too many people that need to catch or leave on flights, and at least half of them work for the corporations. We shut LAX down, even for a few hours, and there'll be at least six corporations with Yoshida being one of them, making sure none of us have a job by the end of the month."

Estrella shook her head facing the hologram. "There's gotta be another way to do this ..."

"There is," Peters said, standing from his desk, "It's called you use that expensive corporate tech in you, so we don't have a repeat of New York when Ray lands and brings his problems to us."

"Fine," Estrella said, crossing her arms. "Let me borrow two hundred bucks?"

Peters gave her a cockeyed stare. "What? Why?"

She smiled. "Trust me on this."

He reached for his wallet.

Estrella pulled out her phone and began typing a text message to TT. The four fifty-dollar bills, Peters lent her was just enough for two small updates. After that, the meeting ended. Everyone received their orders, their weapons, armor, and game plan: capture or kill Ray and Piper. Estrella was to lead the charge.

She was the top RW in the LAPD's pocket now.

THIRTY-FOUR
RAY

The city of Los Angeles approached, made visible from the small window to Ray's left side. It forced his anxiety to return. Soon, the flight would land at LAX, and Ray's feet would be on the ground, vulnerable to the shadowy forces he hoped were left behind in New York. He failed eight times in a row to tell himself that was the case. Arianna's parents were attacked, so were other locations simultaneously in Los Angeles. Whatever he ran from in New York, was waiting for him in Los Angeles, and had been before he bought the tickets and doctored them to fit his new fake ID.

He regretted not taking a flight somewhere else. Fear makes you do stupid things.

Ray spent the last hour of his flight copying the contents of Jax's phone into his, including the trove of hacking apps Ray didn't own. Jax's botnets were now his, and the eye-raising code cracking power that came with it. He linked his phone, tablet, and glasses together. All three devices shared the same modified code and data. When Ray put his glasses on, superimposed lines of text, icons, and labels appeared over the lenses.

He looked at a passenger on the flight that had fallen asleep beside him and held the stare for two seconds. A small window displayed over his glasses' lenses.

Name: Alan Nyn

Age: 32

Species: Human

Occupation: Software engineer

Notes: Married with one child

Ray now had access to RW facial scanning software. He smiled. A secondary window appeared below that, listing all electronic devices the man had, namely his phone, smartwatch, and the IP address for those devices. They were vulnerable to hacks.

He looked above and saw superimposed labels hovering ahead of the overhead storage compartments of the flight. The labels told him carryon bags were inside, and the IP addresses to their digital locks. If Ray wanted to, he could use the botnet to crack the passwords and open them. Passengers with phones in hand had their text chat screens hover above them when he looked at them with the glasses. Those on social media had what they were viewing or liking displayed on his lenses as well.

Ray's world changed. His glasses, linked with his phone and tablet showed him the technology buried everywhere, and personal data the corporate world harvested from consumers. He felt a bit safer leaving the plane once it landed.

With thirty minutes left before landing, Ray sat back and issued a command to his glasses, forcing the lenses to darken. They turned to a pair of shades instantly. No need for a curious person to look at his face and see the labels floating on them.

His flight made a smooth landing, taxied to the arrivals terminal of LAX, and began the usual procedure exiting a plane. The large crowd of passengers left the plane, and Ray made sure he was within the middle of the group, keeping his face low as he pushed deeper into the airport, hurrying.

There was no trek to the baggage claim area for him, not that he brought much to start with. The two phones, tablet, glasses, the ring for Arianna, and the memory sphere. He'd forgotten about the sphere. Ray placed his hands into his pocket, the memory sphere was still there, and within the sphere was a glance at the truth, something Arianna saw which got her in trouble, and now him.

That thought had him sweating as he looked about at the buzzing airport with people moving from their flights. The last time he saw Arianna, she was leaving a flight, after being chased out of the EU. Now he was in the same position as her, backing away from the flight, hoping the black ops IWs from a far-off nation weren't in pursuit. And like Arianna, Ray boarded the trip under a false ID.

Every two minutes Ray touched the memory sphere in his pocket, ensuring it was still on him. He was more concerned about someone pickpocketing that than his wallet. You can't start a war with the contents of Ray's wallet. The other item next to it, you could.

Two men armed with assault rifles, combat armor, and helmets, stopped a traveling couple for questions. The journalist in Ray wanted to stay and watch why that was the case. The paranoid hacker in Ray told him to keep moving and not make eye contact. Assault rifles and combat gear was a little excessive for airport security.

Four minutes later, he spotted three men, armed like the last two. The three geared-up men huddled around each other, speaking like they were giving each other an update. One of them spoke into a headset communicator. Ray made sure to walk away from them. Two police officers left a coffee shop with their sidearm's dangling at their sides. Both were wearing a vest as if they were expecting trouble. Ray made sure to walk away from them too.

Security was not this insane when he left for New York days

ago. Was it in response to the New York attacks? Or were they looking for a person of interest? They did all seem to be extremely close to the general area his flight delivered its passengers.

They also made it impossible for Ray to make it to the exit. It didn't matter how many turns he made, there were cops or heavily armed commandos at every corner. He caved in, and tried to mosey past, his arms dug into his pockets, and his eyes looking forward like the hundreds of other men, women, and children with their parents around him.

Two men with assault rifles over their shoulders held a hand out to Ray. They wanted to talk with him, demanding he stepped aside to the wall. Ray was caught. He slowly went searching in his pocket for his phone as his glasses darkened again. He hoped the two men had vulnerable and networked devices on them.

While he waited for the app to load, Ray shot the armed men a smile, and asked. "Uh, can I help you?"

One of the armed men handed Ray a phone. He raised an eyebrow to it and faced the two. They look dazed and confused upon a closer look. "Piper said to give this to you ..."

Ray took the phone. "Thanks?"

"She said to move while the window is still open."

The two armed men stood still like they were store mannequins. They didn't object to Ray walking away from them, with the newly gifted phone in hand. A police officer had called out to Ray, demanding he stop. So, he did. Then the police officer froze still, no words left his face, just like the two armored men that gave him the phone. Something wasn't right. It was as if they were mind-controlled by a telepath.

Facial scans turned up no signs of IWs in the area when his hacking app booted up. Everyone was as human as they came. Then again, they'd probably be using fake profiles, though he saw nothing that showed the usual signs of a doctored profile. Whoever the telepath was, they had range or got to those men with pre-programmed suggestions beforehand.

The phone they gave him vibrated. There was an incoming call.

He picked it up with nervous hands and winced. The phone he was offered was his Los Angeles one. A soothing kiwi accent greeted ray's ears. "Ray."

"Piper."

"Listen, LAPD and federal agents are combing through the airport looking for you."

"I've noticed."

"Follow my directions, and I'll get you out of this."

"Just like in New York?"

"You're in this mess because you didn't follow my instructions." Her voice grew bitter. "If you keep running when you want to, you'll end up dead. Run when I tell you to and you might get out of this alive."

He saw four armored men with rifles, and none of them looked dazed and confused.

Deep breath buried the growing terror that wanted to take hold of his body. The appearance of multiple labels and icons, on his glasses, directed Ray to vulnerable objects in range. Ray's confidence went up a notch.

"Okay," he said, "what do I do, right now?"

"Look up."

So, he did. A large black raven was perched on top of a souvenir kiosk, hidden behind the kiosk holographic sign. The raven's eyes peered down at him. "Follow the raven."

The raven took flight, its wings flapping as it flew down the halls. The raven was a hologram, an RW AI. He followed it and at one point had to run to keep up. The raven's flight path led him through droves of people moving about in the busy airport terminal. Some were taking a break while they waited for delayed flights, and others were like Ray, looking for the exit to get outside. None of them were armed with weapons. This was the path through the airport he wanted to seek, one devoid of the increased security.

Daylight was in sight. Ray made it to the foyer, its glass walls and doors were a welcomed sight. An RW woman with long black hair standing with three armed police officers, however, wasn't. His glasses relayed the facial scan results from the RW.

Name: Estrella Rodriguez

Age: 19

Species: Real witch/warlock

Occupation: RW unit on lease to the Los Angeles Police Department

Notes: Serial number 78392

Ray put the phone back to his head. "I see Rodriguez."

"Stay away from her," Piper's voice spoke. "She's spearheading this. You need to avoid her at all costs."

He grimaced while walking away from Estrella. She was the one that pushed him into this mess, indirectly of course. Had she not been here, he wouldn't have written that article, and then he wouldn't have taken the assignment in New York. He wondered what would have happened to Arianna if he wasn't in New York. She instructed him, originally, not to come to the airport. His presence probably triggered the attack.

"Noted," he said, as his head returned to the present. *Estrella is the bad RW, Piper is the good one. I hope.*

The gap between Ray and Estrella widened. Nobody had seen Ray follow the holographic raven flying high above the heads of those seeking him out, and those looking to leave the airport. There was a sprawl of passengers with luggage in hand ahead of Ray. He sought to blend in, use their bodies to block the line of sight of Estrella and her police partners.

The crowd parted aside, as if on cue, just for Ray. An eerie feeling swept through him as he walked further, the faces of those in the crowd all appeared to be in a daze. Nobody spoke, and nobody called into question why a large gathering of people had suddenly spread out when Ray approached, then closed back around him, blocking him from sight. He tilted his face up, the raven's flight continued, and he continued to follow it.

When he cleared the crowd, their lips had sound once again. The crowd continued walking for the exit or standing around waiting for a ride away from the airport. Ahead of Ray stood an RW woman with a cute black pixie haircut, red highlights on her bangs. Her synthetic arm was extended, providing a spot for the hologram raven to land on.

In her other hand was a phone placed to her ear. She spoke into it. "That's me. Move quickly."

The raven was Piper's AI. Ray and Piper both ended the call, no point speaking when they were two meters away from having a face-to-face conversation. He scurried to Piper, hoping to not draw attention from whatever threats were behind him and the crowd that had parted and closed around him for some spaced-out reason—

"Freeze!"

Ray heard two sets of heavy feet march toward him from behind. Piper standing ahead of him didn't look happy. She stepped closer as the owners of heavy marching feet aggressively asked Ray to raise his hands and spin around. Whispers in the surrounding crowd followed. Two men had their assault rifles pointed at Ray when he turned, their faces hidden behind the blackened visor of their combat helmets.

His glasses projected three different vulnerable objects on the men, their weapons, headset, and phone. A warning on his glasses flashed and informed him the three vulnerable objects were encrypted and locked down with passwords. His botnet reported it would take ten seconds to hack and crack.

He didn't have that much time, let alone hands free to reach for his phone to select the right app. He had doubted his hands racing back down to his pockets, and grabbing the phone, would be faster than the barrage of bullets that'd likely happen in response.

Piper stood next to him. Her hands were glowing with white luminance. She placed her left and right index fingers on the sides of her head, then shut her eyes, focusing deeply. The two armed men lowered their rifles. One of them reached up tapping their communication headset.

"He's here, everyone to my location!" a voice over the headset yelled.

Ray's face turned pale. Piper opened her eyes, grinning. He saw why moments later. The two men spun around and went sprinting back into the arrivals terminal. They left Piper and Ray alone. Several police officers and armed security personnel did the opposite, silencing the crowd with more whispers of worry and concern.

He turned to face her, wincing at the glow of her hands that slowly faded. It was a glow that RWs shouldn't be able to wield. It had him debating if he made the right choice.

"Piper," Ray said. "You're a telepath."

THIRTY-FIVE
ESTRELLA

"Okay, get these people back now!"

Members of the LAPD were quick to respond to Estrella's request. She along with Peters and another cop rushed into the chaos slowly brewing in LAX's arrivals terminal. Estrella's pistol was out and kept low as she advanced with the murmur of concerns leaving the lips of the surrounding crowd.

Her nanite abilities menu was still open as she moved out. The menu listed the two new programs she grabbed from TT with the cash Peter's lent her, Disable Vehicle, and Induce Muscle Spasms. She had no regrets about the quick detour to TT prior to coming to LAX. Especially after learning Ray was allowed to leave his flight. She had to snarl internally about that.

"There a reason the flight crew let everyone from Ray's flight leave?" Estrella asked Peters. "I thought they were gonna keep the doors locked until we grabbed him?"

Peters shook his head. "I wish I had an answer. We contacted the pilots before they landed to do that, and they ignored us."

Two men wearing full body armor, helmet, and tactical visors stood like they were zombies close to where Ray's flight delivered its passengers. She, the AIT, and LAPD arrived a minute too late. Estrella glanced at the men, surprised they knew how to hold their assault rifle in the current state, and gave them a top-to-bottom stare.

Her optical scans of the spaced-out men finished, its results displaying over her narrowing eyes as she read it. "Mind control," she said. "There's a telepath nearby!"

"Guess that answers your question," Peter's said to her. "The passengers on his flight left because the pilots might have been manipulated into ignoring our request."

Estrella grimaced. "A telepath affecting pilots in the air? That IW has some impressive range then."

"Shit, you're right," Peters said, while reaching for his radio with one hand, the other still grasping his pistol. "We got an IW on the loose, they compromised unit six with mind control and possibly the pilots of Partington's flight."

"Understood," the voice on the radio replied. "Look sharp everyone."

"Okay, guys no more fucking up!" Estrella stepped forward, her head looking for the telepath. "Let's not turn this into another New York!"

The dazed and confused armed men ahead of her shook their heads and groaned, snapping out of the trance. She waved a hand at them, watching closely with her synthetic eyes. Geoffrey scanned them, and the report scrolled over her vision.

It would appear that the mind control has broken, Estrella.
Noted.

Both were released at the precise same time. This would indicate the telepath IW that did this, has moved out of range. With the layout of the airport, I may be able to extrapolate their approximate location with this data.

Do it.

Peters looked concerned. "Talk to me, Rodriguez."

"They're not mind controlled anymore. The telepath controlling them stepped out of range." She faced the newly freed minds. "Hey, you guys all right?"

One man stomped his foot. "We had him! We fucking had him."

Estrella's eyebrows rose. "Had who? Ray?"

The second man nodded and pointed to the hall leading to the rest of the huge terminal. "He just got off! We went to move in and ..." Hesitation silenced him as he looked to the floor.

"And?" Estrella's synthetic hand moved in a tell-me-more fashion.

"Taylor," he grunted softly. "Man, she was fast."

"Piper Taylor did this?" Peters asked.

"I've been mind-controlled before, but this was something else," said the man. "She had total control over us."

"Fuck sakes!" Estrella exploded. *Geoffrey put me through to the LAPD's channel.*

You are connected.

Estrella spoke, the internal communication cyberware in her head sent the broadcast out. "Piper Taylor's here and is an IW!"

A rough cop voice replied. "Say again?"

She sighed while putting together the previous night's events, and what the two armed men said. "Piper's a fucking IW! She's the telepath that scanned me last night and probably got Ray."

Estrella and Peters sprinted forward. "Give us a few," the armed man said from behind. "We'll catch up."

Assertive chatter was on the comm line. The LAPD was tightening the noose around the entire airport, narrowing their manhunt for Piper and Ray. Cops and AIT men and women slinging assault rifles with full-body armor put people on edge. Passengers eyed those involved in the search with concerned looks, Estrella getting the brunt of the attention and whispers. An RW with a gun drawn and pumped full of nanites, waiting for action, damn near made some folks have a heart attack.

Estrella roared over the comm as the search continued. "Anyone spot them?!"

"Nothing."

"Remember guys, Piper's a telepath," she said. "She can, and will, make you see what she wants you to see."

Stores were checked, kiosks were searched, and restaurants grew silent when Estrella wandered in, running quick facial scans of its patrons. A few voices yelled out over the comms, they found Ray. Estrella and Peters came rushing over, only to see a spaced-out cop or AIT member, battling the lingering effects of mind control. Piper was playing them all for fools.

Peters shook his head, looking away from the mind control cop. "We can't resist her." He looked to Estrella. "It's all you, Rodriguez, unless one of us can remain out of her range."

And her range is quite large for an IW telepath, Geoffrey chimed in. *If I were to guess she might be an S ranked IW.*

Weaponized?

It would appear so and would explain why she was able to control the minds of the pilots. Piper is a weaponized IW and deceived us all, including my scans.

Federation refugee my ass.

Piper was the enemy from the east, and had infiltrated the Alliance, and was seconds away from snatching Ray, whatever his involvement in the chaos that'd gripped the nation was. If Ray wasn't working with the Federation, she was probably here to extract intel from him, then kill him for what he knew and experienced in New York. Estrella went running, not stopping to let the others keep up with her. The cyborg bones in her legs gave her speeds that'd put Olympic runners to shame. She had to stop this.

Estrella was in the foyer when she came to a stop. Her head moved left to right searching and saw nothing but a crowd of passengers leaving to catch taxis, or head to the parking lot. From the corner of her eye, she spotted a lone figure with no baggage. It might have been Ray, if only she could get a glance at his face for a scan. The best Geoffrey could do was a body scan, the data displayed over her eyes. It was a perfect height match for Ray.

Her lips opened to make the call. No words came out. She saw the crowd ahead of him part as if they were the Red Sea. It was like the crowd was ordered to stop where they were and give the man, which could be Ray, safe passage.

A telepath got into their heads and gave the order.

Estrella sprinted to the anomaly then stopped when the crowd closed in tight, swallowing up the lone man that stepped through. Piper's powers were something else. She continued anyway, pushing past the hordes of men and women almost standing shoulder to shoulder, forming a human barricade.

"I think I found Ray!" she yelled, not surprised the crowd didn't react to her voice.

She broke through the crowd and gave the man she'd been chasing a second look. Half his face had tilted to the side, watching two armed AIT members stand idle. Whispers of concerns echoed from the crowd with their minds now free. The half face of the man was just enough for her to get a facial scan. The results populated her vision.

Name: Ray Partington
Age: 25
Species: Human
Occupation: Alliance Star journalist
Notes: Suspect in JFK International attack

The profile had changed to a fake one half a second later, likely a result of some hack Ray was using. Most humans wouldn't have noticed the quick change. Good thing Estrella wasn't human and had an AI that captured the original loaded profile.

"He's here, everyone to my location!"

The armed AIT men backed away, letting him escape.

Geoffrey updated the mini-map at the top right corner of her vision, a top-down map of the terminal. Numerous red dots appeared at its edges, sprinting to the yellow dot that was her. Two new dots appeared ahead of hers on the map, Ray was one, and the other was an RW woman he was approaching, Piper.

"Get roadblocks set up," Estrella added as she ran forward. "I think they're making a break for it."

Piper grabbed Ray using her synthetic arm. There was no way he could break free from the cyborg grip. The reluctance in his body language suggested he was about to receive something he didn't sign up for. Estrella kept running, shoving the crowd of curious onlookers aside.

Piper and Ray vanished beyond the glass doors and sunshine. Estrella didn't wait for backup that was coming in according to the mini-map. Then again, what was the point? Only Estrella had the power to resist mind control now that Geoffrey knew of Piper's brainwave patterns.

She joined Ray and Piper outside. The wanted duo had two cops walking closely with them as an escort. Neither of the cops had mentioned anything on the comm lines. She thought about asking them why they were escorting Piper and Ray. She also knew asking a stupid question during a time like this wasn't helping anyone.

Estrella checked the status of her weapon, an SS Foldable 67 as her combat HUD loaded. Its bullet count and spare ammo status flashed at the bottom left of her vision. It wasn't the best weapon, but it'd get the job done. That and she lacked raw material for something with better range.

Geoffrey, activate Defense Matrix.

Understood.

She felt the utility nanites within her swarm about, creating a physical barrier, hardening her body to prepare for physical trauma. Her bones became unbreakable, the fabric in her clothing toughened like it was Kevlar as the NC gauntlet glowed and hissed. She quickly pulled two nanotubes from her arm that split open, injecting herself with them, her HUD automatically informed her of the current count.

Nanite swarm(s) remaining: 2

Technically she had six utility swarms inside her, but four were committed to Defense Matrix. Estrella was in combat mode now. A targeting reticle appeared over her eyes as she drew her gun and reluctantly aimed it at the back of Piper's head.

Her heart wasn't sure how to react. Her lips, however, were. "Piper!"

She stood, holding her pistol steady, wincing as the red laser sight put a dot on Piper's face as she spun. Piper took aim back with her drawn weapon, as did the two mind-controlled cops. Ray's body language became uneasy.

Estrella snarled. "Drop it." Piper's weapon remained her in grasp. Fury made Estrella's lips curl. "I said drop it! Step away from Ray!"

"You first." Piper's free hand began to glow white. She waved it a circular motion.

Incoming mind control, Estrella.

You can block it, right?

I already have. You are safe to proceed.

Her mind was free from Piper's control. Piper didn't look pleased to see that. Estrella tapped her head and added. "I know what you are, Piper."

"Well, that's a pity." Piper's glowing fingers snapped. The two mind-controlled cops rushed forward. "I really wished this could have ended better between us. I really, really do."

Hostile humans detected, Estrella. Temporarily disabling human protection protocols.

Geoffrey predicted the cops were reaching for their trigger. So, Estrella went for hers, aiming for limbs and hands. Triggers from both sides got pulled at once. Echoing gun claps sent civilians running, and cars speeding away. She glimpsed Ray run for a taxi-cab. For some reason, the cab had backed up into the fight, rather than away from it. Ray leaped up and slid over the hood and took cover behind the vehicle.

He was safe for now, Estrella, not so much. She was standing out in the open with no cover in sight. Every bullet fired at her, hit.

THIRTY-SIX
RAY

Minutes earlier ...

Piper said nothing at first. She turned away from the crowd and security forces while marching for the exit. Ray remained still, second-guessing every action.

"Let's go," Piper called.

He shook his head fiercely. "No, wait! How the fuck does an RW pack a trick like that—"

She sighed, ran, and grabbed his arm, forcibly dragging him outside with her. He tried to break free, but it was Piper's synthetic hand that held him. Her cyborg grip was like handcuffs.

"Long story," she finally spoke.

Radiating sunlight made his eyes squint, increasing the buildup of moisture on his forehead, and raising the temperature of his body, no longer embraced by the air-conditioned airport. He saw various LAPD and AIT vehicles idle in the parking lot, setting up checkpoints, and searching cars that were leaving. This was all for him and the memory sphere in his pocket.

Arianna ... what did you do?

Two policemen approached the duo. Piper's white glowing

hands tapped her head. The two policemen lowered their pistols and walked with Ray and Piper, shoulder to shoulder as if they were bodyguards. Their mind-controlled faces asked no questions. Ray locked his eyes into Piper, his glasses linked with his phone and tablet did the rest, conducting a facial scan of her. The data sent back wasn't useful at all, though the detection of her RW cyberware implants was confirmed, just not the serial number, oddly enough.

Piper was like the IWs that attacked New York, and her powers had been hidden behind her veil of RW cyberware. She was an IW with cyberware, further proof that somewhere across the ocean, someone created the ultimate cyber witch. And the personnel at the morgue in New York were hours away from figuring out who and why, until the Federation IW black operatives silenced them. Federation ... Piper was from New Zealand, Federation territory.

Ray, Piper, and their mind-controlled police escort made it to the bottom of the stairs. The parking lot was less than a minute away according to Ray's glasses. Somewhere out there was Piper's high-powered sports car. He hoped he'd be in the passenger's seat and not the trunk. Ray was minutes away from finding out.

"Piper!"

They stopped when the sound of a weapon drawing and cocking came. Estrella Rodriguez stood behind with both her hands wrapped around her pistol taking aim at Piper. Estrella's NC gauntlet was primed, its lights flashing, and ready to release nanite swarms.

Piper drew a weapon of her own. Its red laser light pointed at Estrella's chest. She didn't move an inch, neither did Piper.

"Drop it," Estrella demanded. Piper continued aiming. "I said drop it! Step away from Ray!"

Piper sneered. "You first." Then waved her glowing hands at Estrella. Nothing happened. Piper's smirk turned to a cringe.

Estrella chuckled. "I know what you are, Piper."

"Well, that's a pity." Piper snapped her fingers. The two mind-control police escorts sprung to action like puppets. Their weapons became the second and then third guns pointed at Estrella. "I really wished this could have ended better between us. I really, really do."

There was some shouting from Estrella, and then Piper. Ray wasn't sure who had fired first, he was too busy looking for a means to survive the bullet barrage. There wasn't any cover he could see, other than an idle taxicab that his glasses informed him was a vulnerable target. It was too far for him to run to, however. Then he remembered his botnet access.

Ray ran in a straight line, keeping his head low when his eardrums picked up the crackling sounds of bullets. The taxi was an automated vehicle with a vulnerable icon hovering next to it, seen from his glasses when he faced it. His phone came into his hands, flicking through to a vehicle hacking app.

Remote Vehicle Hack

Take control of vehicles or small aircraft with an autopilot mode.

Access to the taxi's AI was granted when his botnet kicked down the security lockouts. A push of a button on the screen sent the taxi in reverse, right to where he was running. Ray's cover from stray bullets had arrived.

He leaped and slid across the rear hood of the taxi, landing perfectly on his feet when he reached the other side. Ray ducked immediately as the gunfight, between Estrella and Piper with her mind-controlled policemen continued. His eyes caught the end of the fight. Estrella was on her back, arms, and legs, laid out across the ground. Screaming onlookers fled in every direction, cars with humans at the wheel mashed the gas.

Piper remained standing, lowering her smoking pistol. A dejected cringe stuck to her face full of regretful emotions. It looked as if she had to put down her beloved pet. Ray wasn't sure what connection Piper and Estrella had, but whatever it was, it was officially broken, and she wasn't happy about it.

The two mind-controlled cops went running off with a wave of Piper's white glowing hand, as she raced to Ray, collecting him from the cover of the taxi. Her car wasn't parked far away from the terminal. Whatever it was she told the mind-controlled cops got the rest of the armed men and other cops to swarm Estrella's body. They were too distracted to see Piper and Ray as they strapped on their seat belts.

Piper's foot mashed the gas pedal, hard, not that cars used gas anymore. Her high-powered sports car went speeding through the parking lot, breaking through the barricades. Piper waving her hand from left to right and sent a psychokinetic push, flinging larger barricades, and cops, with their weapons drawn away from the escaping car.

She was on her way to the freeway, moving at speeds so fast, Ray's back felt like it was glued to the seat of his chair.

"Ray," Piper spat, as she kept her eyes on the roads that turned to a blur of colors. "Do you still have the memory sphere?"

He hoped he did. He hadn't been patting his pockets down recently to ensure it was still there. His nervous hands dipped into them, searching. The memory sphere was there. He held the sphere in his hand for her to look at.

"Yes."

Piper half-smiled. "Those memories will make or prevent a war. Hold onto it."

"Make or prevent a war." Ray grimaced. "Which of those two options is the good one?"

"That depends," she said. "Do you think it's a great thing to see all IWs have free will?"

"Heh."

"The answer to that question will be the answer to if a war starting is good or bad."

The rearview computer screen on the dashboard picked up three cars following, and none of them were there a second ago. Their size was expanding the longer Ray looked at the screen. Piper briefly looked at the screen. It made her scowl and display her immaculate white teeth.

"Shit!"

"You used mind control back there," Ray said, facing her. "Can't you, like make them turn around?"

"Doesn't work like that," she said, her hands making the wheel turn and her car pass another one ahead. "The range is limited, and the effect's duration isn't consistent. I'm surprised I made it this far without problems." Once clear of that car, Piper adjusted the stick. Their speed increased. "And RWs can resist it if their AI is on point."

Like Estrella, who Piper and her mind-controlled policemen gunned down. And if Ray were to understand Piper correctly, the cops she had under her control should be snapping out of it now, and calling for help, like the cars in pursuit of them.

There was one problem he realized after double-checking the rearview screen's projection.

"Those don't look like police cars."

Piper winced. "I know ..."

They were being followed by a third party. Ray pulled out his phone. Its hacking tool kit app was still active while his glass labeled all vulnerable objects in range. He checked the status of his botnet. It was good for more action.

"Keep driving," he said as their speeding car neared a traffic light. The lights had a vulnerable icon hovering beside it. "I'll take care of everything else."

The lights were yellow when Piper sped past several cars ahead. Ray's glasses locked into the traffic lights vulnerable label. His phone did the rest, listing all the actions he could take against it.

Hack traffic lights

Force traffic lights to change to the desired signal or disable entirely. Select light signal. Green, Yellow, Red.

The botnet went to work, giving him access in less than a second. The lights turned green suddenly when all cars ahead of them were slowing in preparation for the red. Piper drove past them. Once clear, Ray sealed the deal, making all lights at the four-way intersection turn green. None of the cars knew who was supposed to drive forward. The crashes that came in the aftermath slowed their pursuing cars as they twisted to avoid it.

Piper laughed. "Nice, what else can you do?"

Ray thumbed his phone and browsed through the list of apps at his disposal. He looked ahead to the various vulnerable icons hovering around traffic lights, streetlights, and cars with their IP addresses on display for him.

"Oh, just you wait."

THIRTY-SEVEN
ESTRELLA

Estrella felt like she got nailed by a speeding car, only for it to back up and hit her again.

The Defense Matrix held, but it wasn't doing much to steady her body, or keep her from falling over. Her aim with her pistol, as a result, was all over the place. If she didn't let up, she risked hitting a passerby or fatally shooting the mind-controlled cops, or Piper. Defense Matrix ate four swarms of nanites to keep her alive, forcing Estrella to use her two remaining swarms to keep Defense Matrix active. She needed a new plan.

Disable their weapons.

Warning: That will greatly diminish Defense Matrix's power.

I know, sacrifice one swarm for the job.

Understood, please standby.

Geoffrey made the swap, ordering one swarm of nanites to cease contributing to what remained of her Defense Matrix. Estrella felt pain flare-up instantly from the new bullets that crashed against her body, the force from those shots knocked her back. She made a note not to run into a gunfight with so few nanites on Defense Matrix duty.

Estrella pushed her NC gauntleted hand forward, and her palms opened for the wide spray of nanites. The single swarm took to the skies like microscopic bees, seeking the three weapons Geoffrey instructed them to. The swarm split up into thirds, one entering the pistol of a mind-controlled cop, another entered the second cop's, and the third for Piper's pistol. The internal components to the three guns fell apart while in their hands, preventing future usage—

The final fired round hit Estrella square in the chest. Its force sent her to the ground, back first, and face up. A message flashed over her eyesight; Defense Matrix had failed. The remaining utility nanites in her ran out of power. The pain hurt, a lot. She opted to remain on the ground a moment longer to collect herself.

Damage detected, returning the swarm.

What remained of the swarm she sent to dismantle the weapons returned, swarming around her gauntlet, before vanishing inside. Geoffrey ordered a first-aid repair of the minor injuries she received from the bullet and administered painkillers.

She heard a car speeding away in the distance. Piper and Ray were escaping. She got to her feet when the pain faded enough for her to do so. Members of the LAPD, AIT, and Peters surrounded her, all of them concerned for her. She shoved their helping hands off and went running into the parking lot. Her eyes glimpsed Piper's sports car, using psychokinesis to remotely move police barricades, and with one checkpoint, the police themselves.

Status …

Piper has fled with Ray—

I mean my body.

She vaulted over car hoods, and pushed people out of the way, before Geoffrey replied, populating her status window. Estrella's idle red motorcycle came into view, getting closer while her cyborg run continued.

I have healed you back to 8 3; I recommend you wait until—

No waiting, they're getting away.

She jumped into place on her bike, ordering her arm to split open. Her last six spare nanotubes swam in a pool of gray goo and waited for her right hand to take them. She grabbed the tubes one after another and injected herself with them.

Nanite swarm(s) remaining: 6

Tell everyone that isn't mind-controlled we're in pursuit.

The red motorcycle powered on with its electric engine. She pulled out and away from her parking space and selected her red biker outfit and helmet patterns from her nano printable items menu. The raw materials for it, stored in her synthetic arm, poured out, covering her body and head with gray goo, materializing into the selected gear.

With a beaming grin, Estrella sped away in pursuit, following the path of destruction left behind in Piper's wake. There were a lot more broken police barricades than she thought. The first intersection Estrella approached had a multicar pileup, the traffic lights were green for all sides, and it looked like it remained that way as she sped toward it. She swerved her bike gracefully around the mangled vehicles, barely letting up on the acceleration, keeping her speed and momentum moving, her hair rippling behind.

The lights remained green as she zoomed away. Someone hacked them. She pulled a network cable from her synthetic arm, slipped it under and into her helmet, and jacked into the bike's control console. Connection established screens appeared.

Geoffrey, buff up cybersecurity on this bike. Someone's out there hacking shit left and right.

Affirmative.

I just fucking got this bike, and I don't need a hacker taking it for a joyride!

She increased speed, hoping to shrink the gap. A rush of wind blew past her, shaking the network cable plugged into her head and the bike. A car neared, so she moved to the left. Two others were ahead, taking up both lanes, so she moved the bike between them and accelerated forward. A crescendo of honks followed. An intersection approached, and it too was a mess of cars, its lights green on all sides. It was an obstacle course to traverse. She zigged and zagged around the overturned and smoking wreckage of cars.

If you spot Piper's car, keep track of it. More roadblocks in the form of mangled cars at an intersection neared. The lights were all wonky. *And tell the fucking LAPD to get their cybercrimes unit on this. We need these fucking lights working for us, not them.*

That would not be possible, Estrella. The hacker has blocked all users from connecting with the traffic network.

The hacker? You mean Ray? She grimaced beneath her helmet. *Why is Ray helping her escape? It's pretty clear now he's not working for her.*

He is most likely being forced to help her or was manipulated into believing Piper is here to protect him.

In the distance was the familiar sight of Piper's sports car, driving recklessly. There were other vehicles behind it, and none of them seemed like they were on the LAPD's payroll. Back up for Piper, she figured. Geoffrey highlighted Piper's car with a red outline in her vision, a floating arrow appeared above it. The estimated distance in meters between Estrella and Piper's car showed below as numbers moving up or down.

Piper's car made a hard turn onto the freeway onramp. The three cars behind it did the same. Not one of them signaled. Estrella pushed her bike to match their course. Up and onto the onramp she went, merging into the lively freeway. The race continued. Now they were surrounded by hundreds of cars, many of them mashing their brakes when the reckless driving of Piper and her three tailing cars sped past.

Estrella closed the distance by the time the racing vehicles made it to the top overpass; there were six or seven overpasses below. She watched the navigational marker on the right highlighted car intently. One car of the three behind Piper's, mashed their brakes, its screeches echoing through the air. It turned, its front facing the left guardrail of the freeway, spun out and flipped over three times, four times, five times. It was airborne too.

What the fuck?

That was no accident, Estrella.

There were two choices, brake, or go faster. Estrella went faster. She ducked her head as the spinning airborne car was poised to crush her, its shadow loomed over her. She kept going and didn't stop to count any blessings when she cleared the falling vehicle. A loud crashing noise blasted from her behind.

Let's get Defense Matrix back up ...

Understood, Estrella.

She felt four swarms of nanites swim throughout her body, hardening her biker suit, bones, and flesh.

Nanite swarm(s) remaining: 2

She made a mental note that four swarms were still in her, dedicated to Defense Matrix duty. The count for that would drop as time passes, or with every bullet she got hit with. There was no more room for error.

Her speeding bike remained in pursuit, and she checked her current speed displayed on her HUD.

186 mph (297 kph)

Two vehicles were behind Piper's sports car, and it looked like their windows were rolled down. Estrella had a feeling it wasn't to let in nice daytime air. She focused, ordering her synthetic eyes to zoom in and enhance the opened passenger windows of both cars. A man dressed in black combat gear leaned out, grasping an SMG. Its muzzle flashed, and bullets started flying. They required no aiming since the bullets curved and went seeking the nineteen-year-old RW on her motorcycle behind.

She felt the impact of three bullets, but her Defense Matrix soaked up the blows. Estrella was still alive, but the feeling of someone taking a sledgehammer to her face and chest, while riding a speeding motorcycle, threw her off balance. Lucky for her she was still jacked into the bike's console. Geoffrey took control of the bike, averting what would have turned into a complete slide and wipe-out. Crashing your speeding bike on the freeway with cars and trucks around you was hazardous to your health.

Geoffrey returned control as she gripped the handlebars again. Cars ahead hit their brakes, their drivers paralyzed with fear when they clued in that there was a gunfight brewing in the high-speed chase. She made a hard turn to the right and hoped to not crash. She almost did.

Estrella brought the two cars back into sight. One man faced her, his purple glowing hands sparking with electrokinesis. They quickly gathered up flickering, white-hot sparks of electricity and flung a ball of it at her. Defense Matrix was useless against IW abilities. Estrella had to let up on the acceleration to escape from that.

Her vision zoomed onto the men facing her, in between the spray of curving bullets and balls of electrokinesis. Her optical scans did the rest.

I'm detecting multiple IWs within those vehicles, Geoffrey said. *IW tracking shows, no registered IWs should be in the area.*

Meaning they aren't registered.

My guess would be these are the Federation IW black ops teams. They must be here to assist Piper.

Federation IW black op teams were everywhere. Not a hard thing to pull off if you had powerful telepaths at your disposal. Wave your hand and you were never there to the masses. Toss in an IW adept at DNA altering biokinesis, and you could infiltrate any nation on the planet, carry out any assassination, or conjure a deadly plague to wipe out the local population. There was a reason weaponized IWs were banned worldwide. It was only a matter of time before someone said fuck the rules and created their own IW black ops teams—

Estrella.

She neared the trailer of a truck while her random thoughts were distracting her. A shift to the left put the trailer to her right. A honk of its loud horn roared when she swerved directly ahead of it, putting the red highlighted sports car and its two speeding wingmen back in her view, their occupants still clapping their curving bullets in between shooting electrokinetic lightning. All she could do was duck her head and hope for the best.

She lifted her head to view them. *Lock onto everyone that's hostile.*

Now the two cars and their passengers wielding deadly electrokinesis and SMGs got highlighted red in her vision. Geoffrey also took the time to split Estrella's vision. Her left eye displayed what was ahead, her right eye showed what was behind, according to her bike's rear camera feed. There was one car approaching from behind, and like the others ahead, it too was highlighted red.

Geoffrey gave his report. *We have one hostile vehicle on approach from behind.*

How do you know they're hostile?

She got shot in the back six times.

That's how.

The impact of the rounds nearly threw her off the bike. Once again Geoffrey took control, returning it back to Estrella when she recovered. She asked Geoffrey for a status update to Defense Matrix. Two out of the four nanite swarms committed to it remained. She opted to not commit any more nanites to Defense Matrix for the time being. Her right eye saw a man in the car from behind, gathering a charge of electrokinesis energy with his purple glowing hands.

Random turns to the left and right were her only defense, outside of using the other cars in the lanes as cover. But then, she'd be putting innocents at risk, more so than they already were. That was unacceptable.

A beam of electricity struck the road to her right. It left blackened marks on the pavement. Another to the left, then right, cyborg reflexes were a lifesaver. And then, there was nothing. Like the IWs ahead, there was cooldown period where they couldn't use their powers. They entered that cooldown phase. They only had their guns with straight traveling bullets until the cooldown phase ended. This was her chance.

Estrella focused. She had two cars ahead and one behind. All were preventing her from catching Piper's sports car. Geoffrey took control of the bike again when she let go of the handlebars. It looked like she was riding a self-driving motorcycle with no hands. With her pistol in both hands, she looked and aimed behind while getting rid of the split-screen view.

Targeting data populated her HUD as she faced the solo car from behind. She had her vision zoom in as far as it could on the driver, placed the targeting reticle over his head, then pulled the trigger six times. No good, six bullets stopped and floated in midair. Psychokinesis was a bitch. It also meant the driver might have been a telepath with precognition. He also wasn't on cooldown.

She gave him a smile, not that he could see it with her helmet on. She holstered her pistol, and readied her NC gauntleted hand, pointing at the lone car behind. She browsed through the menu of utility nanite abilities. Incinerate was selected.

I would advise against that, Estrella. We will have to drop Defense Matrix to gain enough nanites to use that. It will render us vulnerable.

She checked her nanite swarm numbers and grimaced.

Nanite swarm(s) remaining: 2

She had another two dedicated to Defense Matrix. Pulling one swarm to gain the three needed for Incinerate would reduce Defense Matrix's effectiveness. The bullets that hit her almost threw her off the bike. She didn't want to know what would happen with a single swarm powering Defense Matrix.

Got no fucking choice, man!

One nanite swarm was left to defend her body, the rest sprayed from her gauntlet into the air. She watched her HUD as her nanite count dropped to zero and hoped all three cars had no bullets. The three nanite swarms flew into the rear pursuing car via its opened windows, swarming the passenger, entering the orifices on his face. He flailed his arms in terror, making futile attempts at swatting them away is if they were hornets stinging them. The telepathic driver panicked. Even the most powerful adept telepath couldn't psychokinetically push the nanites away. There were just too many and too small.

The passenger's eye sockets and mouth exploded into flames and erupted like a volcano. Black smoke filled up the interior of their car and floated from the windows. The remains of the nanite swarms spread to the driver. His flesh combusted and melted from the flames seconds after the nanites entered him. He lost control of the car, and it spun around and landed upside down. The truck behind them mashed its brakes. The upside-down burning car shifted forward once more from the impact.

Return as many nanites as you can!

Estrella kept her gauntleted hand out as the surviving nanite swarms returned. She faced the two cars, plus Piper's ahead. No bullets had been fired recently, nor electrokinesis used. Her window of opportunity was about to shut. Geoffrey updated her status screens.

Nanite swarm(s) remaining: 1.5

I have a gift for you. Geoffrey snickered. An alert appeared as her synthetic arm opened, receiving said gifts, gray goo and lots of it from the returning nanites. *I obtained raw materials from the car and one of their weapons stored in the backseat. I believe this weapon would be more effective than the rest.*

A new weapon pattern was acquired, an MX-57 sawed-off shotgun. Following Geoffrey's recommendation, her NC gauntlet released a new swarm, deconstructing her pistol, and using the newfound gray goo, fusing the two together, and then returned it to her. Once completed, Estrella held the MX-57 shotgun in her hands. It was lightweight, quick to maneuver, and fully loaded. She lacked the materials to nano print extra shells to reload it. This was her last chance to end this.

Estrella had the one and a half swarms reinforce Defense Matrix, bringing it to two and half swarms defending her, leaving Estrella with zero to use for other abilities. She saw a break in the traffic ahead, most likely people pulling off to the side having realized something was afoot. It was Estrella, Piper, and the two wingman's cars. She pushed the bike to its maximum speed. No fear.

Two SMGs discharged. She had to ignore the pain, hope the force didn't throw her off the bike, while letting Geoffrey take control again. The two wingman's cars sandwiched Estrella between each other, one car to the left, and the other to the right. Her single swarm of nanites powering Defense Matrix was losing strength with each hit. Hands glowing purple with electrokinesis flared, the cooldown was over. She took aim at the right car, and her enhanced zoom and optical scanner scanned the hands of the wheelman. Geoffrey predicted he would ram her based on his motions, and they were close enough to do that.

She selected overdrive, after canceling the Defense Matrix, storing her last remaining nanite swarm for new use. Estrella's world slowed down enough to see bullets leave the barrel of their weapons in slow motion. The head of the driver in the right-side car was perfectly lined up with her barrel. A single pull of the trigger turned it into a canoe shape. The blood, gore, and spread of the shotgun shell splashed slowly, smacking the passenger in the face. Both bodies, little-by-little tilted to the right side of their car.

Of course, while that was happening, Estrella had cocked the barrel, lined up another shot against the car to her left, and the electrokinetic IW seconds away from blasting her with a thunder ball.

She pulled the trigger. Her weapon boomed in slow motion. The shell ejected and went for the head. Four seconds later, from her point of view, it was gone. She cocked the barrel, zoomed into the driver before the veil of spattering gore plastering him. It wasn't a headshot. It was a head-is-gone shot.

Both cars were no longer a threat as they no longer had someone alive at the wheel. A loud screech, boom, and crash erupted behind Estrella. Her speeding bike was now directly behind Piper's sports car. Her world returned to normal with the cancellation of overdrive.

One swarm remaining, Estrella.

Estrella grinned. She didn't use overdrive long enough to eat through the single nanite swarm. *Stand by. I wanna take out their back wheels when in range.*

Estrella selected Disable Vehicle from her menu and went to maneuver to the perfect spot to spray disassembling nanites at Piper's rear tires. She had to rethink that when a van ahead made a sudden turn crossing Estrella's intended path. Two other cars and a pickup truck did the same, and then another car. Ray was back to hacking, using the cars around as obstacles to slow Estrella. It wasn't enough to stop her. Estrella remained in pursuit and eagerly watched as the distance between her and Piper's sports car counted down. Her NC gauntlet charged, in preparation to release her last remaining swarm. She needed another five seconds to be in effective range.

At three seconds, a truck further up jackknifed and flipped ahead of Piper. Ray must have made a mistake with that hack. Piper braked and skidded across the freeway's surface, leaving black lines from its tires behind. Her sports car crashed into the trailer ahead. Smoke lifted away from both vehicles. Traffic crawled to a standstill after that. Too bad Estrella was still at maximum speed. She was poised to crash into the trailer as Piper did.

She braked, but it wasn't enough to stop her momentum. She

turned the bike, forcing it to make a sharp and sudden ninety-degree spin. The freeway ahead, the crash of Piper's car, and trailer came out of view, replaced with the left guardrail of the freeway while her back faced the right. Estrella's bike continued to slide forward, she lowered her left foot and dragged against the pavement. She braced for impact. No such thing happened. A deep exhale was her response.

Multiple cars were mashing their brakes and stopped before Estrella's idle bike, Piper's crashed car, and the jackknifed trailer holding up traffic. Nobody was going anywhere, not in a car at least. She double-checked her ammo count—six shots left. Good enough. Slowly, Estrella walked forward with her shotgun leading the way. Her optical scanner assessed the chaos ahead, relaying its data over her vision via a crawl of numbers and text. Her targeting reticle remained active, searching for any sudden movement.

Sirens wailed in the distance, up in the sky to be exact. Medivac air ambulances were flying in, and probably the rest of the LAPD now the chase had come to a standstill.

Piper's car was a burning mess by the time Estrella neared it. The crash shattered every window, its front hood a mangled mess of twisted metal, sparks, fires, and smoke. Her scans detected the presence of the airbag, what remained of it thanks to the flames. Did they survive? She couldn't tell, she needed a closer scan.

Estrella peered into the passenger side window, but her scans found no signs of bodies amidst the smoke. It picked up something else. A small passage had been melted right down the middle of the forward end of the car. Nanites did it. Piper literally dissembled the wreckage of her car to create an escape route. Estrella's eyes followed the path. It led into the trailer of the truck—

Click. Someone loaded a gun, and it wasn't Estrella. She had done that long ago.

A turn to the left, and Estrella saw the buildup of traffic. A spin again put the pixie kiwi into her view. She went for the trigger.

Piper's white glowing hand flicked in response. Estrella felt her body lift off the ground and get flung through the air. A blur of stuff clouded Estrella's vision, cars, flames, the sky, the road, all while Piper stood still, and shrank in size.

Gravity took hold of Estrella's body. It was pulling her down, way down off the overpass. Piper pushed Estrella off with a psychokinetic shove. She was falling to the lower freeway roads below which were full of speeding cars, oblivious to her plummeting body.

Estrella was spiraling to her death.

THIRTY-EIGHT

RAY

Heart monitors beeped and beeped. An engine roared in the back, it sounded like an AC unit, but Ray could tell the difference. It was the engine that propelled and powered small aircraft. It hurt to open his eyes, so he kept them shut, and hoped that the countless hands touching and prodding his sore body were the medical professionals in a medivac air ambulance.

Why the hell am I in an airborne ambulance? he thought.

He didn't remember much from the crash. One moment Piper was in a panic trying to escape from the cars pursuing her. Then Estrella, in a bizarre twist became the main threat. Ray hacked as many cars as he could, forcing them to move and block Estrella. Then came that truck, he wanted to hack it, but someone else had plans for it. It looked like it got picked up by an invisible giant and tossed at them. Everything was black after that. Then, he was here, wherever the fuck here was. His eyes were still too sore to open.

It had him worried about the future. Piper's powers, the IWs in the pursuing cars, and the one that most likely forced the truck to crash with their powers. How do you defeat S ranked IWs that could do that? Hell, how did humanity live through WWIII with

IWs and the subsequent uprising? How do you stop a force that could snap an aircraft carrier in two by snapping their fingers? Not even RWs had that level of power, and they were supposed to be the counter to hostile IWs.

There were more IWs in the world today than there were during the war. The only difference being they weren't weaponized and lacked the skills and training. If someone changed that and provided the guidance and development necessary, and then IWs decided that humanity should be exterminated, they could do it, pretty easily.

Is this what he stumbled upon he wondered? A secret plot to remove humans from Earth? Or was it a means for the Federation to continue the war, while the rest of the world kept their IW populations untrained, and on a leash as per international laws.

Ray opened his eyes fifteen minutes later. The painkillers were working. He saw paramedics with deep blue gloves on, tending to his bruised and bashed body. No words were spoken, not even when one of them looked at him. Next to Ray, on a tray, were his phones and tablet pad. Their screens were cracked, but operational judging by the flashing light. He grimaced. Someone searched his body. How else would they have gotten his devices? He didn't see the memory sphere anywhere. He didn't feel it in his pockets either.

"Excuse me," Ray said. "Has ... has anyone of you—" They ignored him and continued working. "Anyone? Hey, listen, there was a memory sphere on me. Did you see ... it?"

Nothing. He was almost invisible to them, odd. Paramedics should at least be willing to speak to and comfort their patients and maybe ask how they feel. The scanning equipment can only give them so much data on what's going on with Ray.

"There was a woman with me," Ray continued. "Is she okay?" Nothing. His fists clenched. "Are any of you fuckers listening to me?!"

Nothing.

———

The medivac circled above downtown Los Angeles, as the city's towers caused perpetual darkness from its shadows to dull the streets and smaller structures below. The medivac lowered and landed on top of a building. Which one Ray wasn't sure, probably the hospital rooftop, though he could still see the sky. Last time he checked, no hospitals were tall enough to get a good view of the sky at this height. Worry stirred in his chest.

The paramedics gave him an injection of some strange medication he couldn't pronounce if his life depended on it, it was eighteen letters long. Whatever it was, it got him back on his feet and stopped his head from spinning like a top. He was escorted outside as the medivac's doors lowered and turned into a loading ramp. The paramedics continued to ignore the many questions he had, pushing him out into the sunlight.

They landed on a rooftop all right, and it wasn't the hospital.

Elevator doors swung open, and three men holding rifles with zero emotion in their faces stepped out, grabbing Ray by force, and dragging him into the elevator. The three men weren't fond of answering Ray's questions either. The elevator doors slid shut, casting out the sunshine. He felt it lower for a few minutes, then ding.

The armed escort pushed Ray through a series of halls, with black pristine tiles, and flickering holograms of decorative flowers. Real flowers were too expensive to maintain. Sleek black chairs were lined up against the white walls, in between each batch of chairs, were a bunch of shut and locked doors, and above that were zigzagging light fixtures.

The holographic logo of the Yoshida Corporation and its Japanese translation prominently floated above the set of doors he was guided through. He thought about asking what was up with that but had a feeling the reply would have been silence.

Ray was offered a seat in a waiting room. It was a big comfortable couch placed next to the wall. The room too was decorated with green leafy plants, all fake holograms. The three armed men stood silently, shoulder to shoulder ahead of the glass door they entered.

"You guys know this isn't the hospital, right?" Ray got the expected response. "Right you don't want to chat. How fucking silly of me for trying."

A door to the side opened. A man dressed in a dark gray business suit and tie entered through it. His head was cut and styled like a typical corporate yes man, with a clean-shaven face. His eyes were red but didn't look synthetic like an RW. It was a haunting sight.

The corporate man was joined by another, a woman, provocatively dressed in a black and red outfit, sporting cleavage that made Ray's face turn red. Arianna would have slapped him had she seen his reaction. The woman had long white hair spread across her shoulders, the rest of it running down her back. Her red lipstick was almost as red as the man's eyes. The duo faced the armed guards and gave a silent nod. Ray was left alone with the two newcomers. Correction: that was a haunting sight.

"Mr. Partington," the corporate man spoke, his voice sounded familiar. "Or do you prefer the name DigiSamurai69, your hacker codename?"

Ray was taken from Piper, patched up and brought here, alive for a reason. Someone in Yoshida had a use for him. He gave the corporate man a second glare. It took Ray a few moments, but eventually, he recognized him.

Ray sneered. "Victor Ashford, right? I remember you from the convention in New York, I didn't recognize you without your shades. You here to offer me a job for my skills?"

"Not looking for people with your skillset at the moment," Ashford said, pulling up a chair ahead of Ray. The white-haired woman remained standing at his side, her eyes never moving away from Ray.

"That's a shame," Ray said and pointed at his head. "I've learned a lot over the years with computers, all of that's up here."

"You're right about that," Ashford replied. "You have something of benefit in there. Just, it has nothing to do with your skills."

"This is about New York isn't it?"

Ashford nodded while leaning back on the chair, steepling his fingers together. "You have something that's of great value to my employers. Something Arianna gave you."

"She gave me a hug. And no, you can't have it."

"She gave you more than that, and you know it, so does Piper and her associates. Look, let me ask you something. What happened earlier today on the freeway, and in New York. Do you want that to be a normal occurrence in your life, Mr. Partington?"

"Not really."

"Good." Ashford adjusted his tie. "So, I offer you this. Explain to me what Arianna gave you, everything you can. And we will make all the bad things go away."

"I want Arianna back in my life."

"I can't give you that."

"Why the fuck not?" Ray leaned forward, upping the volume of his voice by three. "If you can make the bad things go away, you can give her back to me. Don't give me this it's out of your power bullshit." Ashford laughed, so did the mysterious woman next to him. "Seriously, what's the big deal about Arianna?"

"Arianna's our valued employee," Ashford said. "And if she was here with us, we wouldn't be having this talk."

That confirms they brought me to Yoshida's LA headquarters. Those men and paramedics were probably private contractors, on the company's payroll.

"So, I say again, Mr. Partington," Ashford's voice grew firm. "What, did, you, see?"

"I don't know man, just some trippy shit some telepath put in my brain."

"And you made sense of it?"

Ray shook his head. "No, I didn't."

"Your blog post says otherwise. You saw what was put in your head. There's more to that data dump. Tell us about it."

"You mean my blog that got deleted without my consent?" Ray barked a laugh. "I get it now; you corporate fuckers used your influence, and had it removed."

"You're about to start a war using intel you shouldn't have in the first place."

The silent and mysterious white-haired woman touched Ashford's shoulder. Her red fingernails brought Ray's attention to the length of them. She could probably kill someone if she eye-gouged them. Ashford faced her, she faced him. He gave her a nod. She smiled and stepped to Ray. Her heels echoed in the silence that fell.

Ashford reiterated his stance. "The data Arianna gave you, Mr. Partington. What is it?"

"What data?" Ray lied, trying his best not to panic as the woman drew near. "She's just a sales rep. I don't know fuck all about Yoshida sales numbers if that's what you're asking for."

Ashford tapped his watch, summoning a small hologram. He pushed to float in between Ray and the mysterious woman. The hologram played recorded footage of Arianna assaulting men and women in a hotel in Munich. It switched to fuzzy surveillance footage of Arianna in a lab, along with a man dressed in a lab coat. She asked the man to put the gun, in his hands, into his mouth. He begged her not to do it. She asked him to pull the trigger, so he did. It reminded him of Piper's actions hours ago. Arianna possessed mind control abilities.

"Arianna, as you can see," Ashford said as the hologram replayed. "Is more than a sales rep for our company."

Now Ray was the one giving the silent treatment, though his reason was the visual reminder that Arianna lived a double life, one that caught up with her upon her arrival in New York, and then made Ray a part of it before she vanished.

"Avatar 33," he called out to the mysterious woman. "Scan Mr. Partington."

She nodded. "Understood, sir."

The mysterious woman invaded his personal space. Two things happened because of that. He got a better glance at her face and he recognized her. She was in the news, a kidnapped woman snatched from a bar in the IW district of Los Angeles by some gang. It happened hours before the New York attack. Portia Blanchard was her name. He wanted to ponder more about the connection, but then the second thing happened. Ray lost his mind.

A buzzing noise rang in his ears first. It was so loud Ray couldn't hear his own words or Ashford's. His head exploded with pain. Images flashed. Arianna. The EU. A Federation lab in the middle of an Indonesian jungle. Blueprints. A weapon. Arianna again. Arianna with blood on her hands. Arianna with glowing hands. Arianna spreading fires onto people with psychokinesis winds, their charred bodies curled in a fetal position.

He saw the mysterious woman's face when the pain and images faded. Her eyes fixed into his eyes and their foreheads were nearly touching. Avatar 33 was what Ashford called her, but this was the missing girl Portia, there was no doubt about it.

She shook her head disappointingly. "It's too far in his head. Someone buried it deep in. A deep scan can do it, but that'll take hours and will kill him."

Ashford winced, his fingers still steepled together. "Do it."

She sighed, facing away from Ray, back at Ashford. The scent of her perfume tickled Ray's nostrils. "I'm—"

"You're what?" Ashford cut in.

Her white glowing fists clenched slowly, she brought them to her face. "Not strong enough. This body doesn't have the mental discipline to do it. Most telepaths aren't."

"Try away."

So, she did, turning back to face Ray. The pain and ringing in his ears returned. New images flashed. Pause, Play, Rewind, the one in New York. Guns busting, IWs everywhere. Celia was smiling, tempting Ray with sex. Celia got into his head, pulling out what Arianna left in it, then gift wrapped part of it in the memory sphere.

"Hold on," Portia said having broken the telepathic scan with Ray. "He had a psytrip session in New York. Some telepathic whore made partial sense of it and then suppressed the memories. That's why I can't get it."

Ashford was intrigued. "Find them."

She continued. "He had a memory sphere of the experience. He brought it with him to LA."

Her words brought a new revelation into the mess. The telepathic IW ahead of him wasn't affiliated with the ones that attacked New York. That group and Yoshida weren't on the same side. There were two factions in play. Ray wasn't sure to be happy or upset.

"I take it ..." Ray drawled, then considered his next choice of words. "I take it, you aren't on the same team as the IWs that hit New York and LA recently, and chased me here."

Portia faced Ashford. His composure had shattered. "Sir?"

"The Federation ..." he grimaced, unveiling his white teeth. "Fuck!"

She moved back to him, heels clicking. "The freeway then?"

An angry corporate nod. "That must have been them, they know he has it." He faced Ray as she stepped aside with arms on her waist. "Well, Mr. Partington looks like you stepped into trouble that extends beyond the LAPD and the Alliance investigators looking for you. If you can't tell me what you saw, at least give us the memory sphere. It's better in our hands than the Federation and their weaponized IWs ... or the Alliance."

"I don't know what happened to it," Ray said. "It was on me before the crash. That's the last time I looked at it."

"Idiots!" Ashford faced up at her. "Did they not search the crash?"

"I guess not. Remember, the real paramedics and LAPD were on their way. We had to extract him quickly."

"Get that memory sphere!"

She nodded obediently and gestured to Ray. "And for him?"

Ashford's composure returned. So did calm in his tone of voice. "Find me a telepath that can deep scan him. If Arianna wants him to live, then she'd better show herself and tell us what she gave him. If we can't discover that memory sphere, then a deep scan of Mr. Partington's head will be necessary." Ashford paused for a dramatic effect. "And it *will* kill him after three or four hours of scanning."

Ray thought back to the text he intercepted from Ashford. He was starting to understand why his interview with Lady M was cut short. Yoshida knew Arianna was arriving with something they wanted and needed to be free to receive it.

Estrella's reboot screen appeared as a line of computer jargon and a flashing cursor. When she opened her eyes, after minimizing the notification stating Geoffrey was offline, she was treated to the view of a van's ceiling. Slowly, she got up, shifting her head about, noting the lack of windows in the van, other than the ones up front.

Thirty seconds later, her internal GPS activated. A mini-map appeared in the top right of her eyesight, a top-down map of the Los Angeles freeway with its twists and turns. Someone recovered Estrella after Piper knocked her off the top overpass.

Kneeling beside Estrella, with a Mona Lisa smile, was Piper. The pixie kiwi was spraying nanites over Estrella's body. A new notification informed Estrella about the state of her body. Two nanite swarms from Piper were working to repair her cyberware and heal her flesh. The two spoke no words, just an endless peer into each other's emerald synthetic eyes, and the twisting of Piper's lips. It made Estrella's face turn red.

Upfront, in the driver and passenger seats, sat two men. She couldn't get a facial scan of them, as she only saw the backs of their heads. Their faces in the windshield's reflection, however ... that was different. She zoomed in on that and saw their reflections. The man driving had pale skin, short brown hair and a five o'clock shadow. The other had dark skin and thinly cut black hair, most likely of African descent.

Their facial scans turned up error messages across all lines. They weren't human. They were IWs, unregistered at that. Her first thought was to get up and take them out, Piper too. It was her job and duty as an RW to do so. She chose not to. There was something bigger going on. That, and she was really getting sick of being told what to do, how to act, and getting punished when she didn't fall in line. They were also driving the van. Attacking them would cause them to crash and kill them all, and with no nanites left, Estrella would not last long. The nanites repairing her came from Piper and obeyed commands Piper's AI sent them.

"Welcome back," Piper said, her kiwi accent snapping Estrella's face back to her. "Sorry about the fall, love. Didn't mean to hit you that hard."

Estrella brought up Geoffrey's status. Error messages blotted the view of Piper. She minimized those from her view.

"Your AI took some damage," Piper added. "Don't worry; I got nanites making repairs to it. But he will be offline for an hour or so."

Estrella grimaced. "How did you know?"

Piper showed her why. She pointed at a network cable. One end was jacked into Estrella's head, the other into Piper's. "Sorry for the intrusion. Had to make sure you were still salvageable."

"I don't get you, Piper." Estrella faced away from her.

Piper sat beside her. The slack of the cable connecting the two lowered to the floor. "I'm not that complex."

"You tried to kiss me. Then you tried to kill me. Now you brought me back."

"You sound like my ex-wife." Piper laughed, her face tilted upward.

"Why the cloak and dagger shit? First you want me dead

because I figured out your secret and clued in you were spying on me. And now you want me alive, what gives?"

"We can't trust everyone," Piper said. "After that stunt you pulled, getting into my system, and hiding Ray's phone from me, I placed you on that no trust list. I know you've been trying to figure me out. But I'll tell you this, everything you thought you knew about me, and what's going on, is wrong. Just place those theories in the garbage. Except the spying part, you were kinda right about."

"Really?"

"I'll be honest with you, I bugged your place when I was there. Your arrival in the city, and the connections to the Bald Skulls had me wondering."

She thought back to Piper's dramatic near-death cries when her battery ran low. It was a trick to bring Piper inside her place and bug it. She made plans to search the corner Piper collapsed to, assuming she'd live long enough to go back to her apartment.

Estrella snorted. "You trust me now, though. What changed?"

"You killed the men who were trying to get to me and Ray. That makes you an ally. And now that he's gone, with all my options, I'm going to need every advantage I can get my hands on." Piper licked her grinning lips. "And you're too cute to hate forever—"

"Hold up." One man upfront cut in, the one driving judging by where his voice came from. "Did I hear that right earlier? You tried to get it on with her, Piper?"

Piper's laughing stopped, and the smile turned to a frown, a nasty one. Piper aimed that frown at the pale driver. "Fuck off, Theo."

The second man up front spoke. "It would explain why she insisted we bring her with us." He spoke with a deep African accent.

"Yeah, she's just a fucking RW," Theo said. "I would have left that malaka back there and be done with it. Ya feel?"

Piper moved closer. Estrella did as well, not that she had a choice. The cable was still jacked into their heads. It became a leash. "We need her," Piper replied.

"We need Ray, who I might remind you, is gone, again," Theo said and faced forward, keeping his attention on driving.

"If you guys hadn't fucking lost him in New York," Piper said.

"He fucking ran like a little malaka when I told him to stay still." With one hand on the wheel, Theo patted his pockets. "Fuck, I'm outta smokes. Piper can I bum one off you?"

Piper sighed and reached for her synthetic arm that split open. She pulled one cigarette stored inside it and handed it to Theo. "That's my last one."

Theo lit the cigarette with a spark of electrokinesis aimed at its tip. He took a puff, blew the white smoke out from his lips, and drove with one hand on the wheel. "Thanks, boss lady, I owe you."

Estrella joined Piper, and the two stood behind the two seats upfront. She had a critical question to ask. "Who the fuck are you guys?"

"Go on tell her," Theo said. "If she's as smart as you say she is, she'll figure it out one day, anyway. Might as well be today."

Piper winced, looking uneasy as she faced Estrella. "All right, well, Estrella—"

"You're all from the Federation," Estrella interjected. "Weaponized IWs the world doesn't know about yet. S ranked."

Piper half nodded. "We are weaponized, yes. But not from the Federation."

"You are, Piper. Fuck, you're more than an RW too."

"I'm not loyal to the Federation," Piper said. "Neither is Theo or Bashiir. But, you're right about that second bit. I'm more than what I appear to be. I'm a fusion of an IW and RW. My cyberware is state-of-the art, giving me not only the powers of an RW but enhanced IW abilities. What I am is just a taste of what's coming."

Estrella's arms crossed. "And what's that?"

"And that is, whatever's in the data that was stolen from a Federation facility and made its way to the Alliance."

"The jungle fires in Indonesia," Estrella said as her head put things together. "So, there was something out there. That was really an assault on that facility wasn't it?"

Piper nodded yes. "It's going to affect the way the world sees all IWs."

"Care to elaborate?"

"We don't know exactly," Piper said. "My cyberware was tested and developed in that facility. After it was approved for use, Zhang Industries, the owners of the facility, went to develop a new project based on it."

"Yoshida sent Ray's girlfriend Arianna to get that information, and sabotage the facility," Bashiir said from the passenger seat. "The Federation sent its secret weaponized IWs after her when they tracked her to Munich. They failed. So, they tried again when they learned she was about to arrive in New York with the stolen data."

"We went to intervene," Theo added. "But we underestimated their numbers, and that some were like Piper, IWs with cyberware."

"That was you two then," Estrella said facing the two men up front. "You were the IWs at JFK?"

"We weren't there to kill people," Bashiir said. "We were trying to stop the Federation and prevent Arianna from delivering the data to Yoshida. Things got complicated, and in a panic, Arianna transferred what she learned into Ray's head, and vanished."

"Well, so we think," Piper said. "The blog post he made suggested she transferred it. After that, the Federation IWs went through a lot of trouble to track Ray when they couldn't find her and erase all evidence they're in the Alliance."

"Let me get this straight," Estrella said. "Whoever can send a telepath into Ray or Arianna's head will learn of the Federation's super-secret weapon?"

"Or get their hands on a memory sphere Ray had," Piper said. "Sadly, Ray had it on him when I lost contact with him."

The Federation was in the Alliance for one reason. They wanted what Arianna stole and committed to memory, then transferred into Ray's head when she was compromised. Estrella's worries grew. There was indeed a war brewing, a war to control top-secret research regarding IWs, and Piper's fusion of IW and RW powers was only a small sample of that research.

"I knew Arianna was more than what she was," Piper continued.

"That's why you befriended her boyfriend," Estrella said. "I saw the messages you sent Ray, buttering him up with news tips."

Piper had a Mona Lisa smile aimed at Estrella. "Arianna's father was one of many unregistered IWs we set up in the city."

She grimaced. Norris Kounias, an IW? The more she thought about it, the more she believed it. "Arianna's father's an IW ..." Estrella said. "That makes—"

"Arianna a half-witch." Piper finished for her. "Her mother was human."

And Nobuo knew that. Estrella understood why Arianna's mother got a bullet to the head, and her father didn't. There was ample evidence that suggested he was a hard target for Nobuo when he attacked the Kounias' residence.

"If Arianna's half-witch half-human, how was she able to infiltrate a top-secret corporate facility deep in the Federation? Her powers shouldn't be strong enough, even with training."

"That's why I did what I could to get close to her, by getting close to Ray," Piper said. "Yoshida's policy is to not hire IWs, yet Arianna worked for them as an operative. And she, as we now figured out, is an S ranked telepath, even though she's half-human."

"I guess Yoshida is planning something similar," Estrella said.

"Illegal research into not only the development of S ranked IWs, but augmenting them with some high-end cyberware—"

A force threw Estrella forward. Piper too. Their bodies crashed against the back of the driver and passenger seats. The sound of tires screeching echoed outside the van.

Estrella got back to her feet, just in time to hear Theo yell. "Holy fuck!"

Piper got up. "What is it?"

Theo pulled the van over, rolling his window down. He peeked out, his hands covering his face from the rare trickle of sunlight. Piper and Estrella were outside after sprinting from the back door of the van. The two leaned against the guardrail of the freeway, the whooshing sounds of cars and trucks speeding past were endless.

Estrella saw what grabbed Theo's attention. She had to use the full zoom of her optical scanner to confirm it. It was the triple towers of Yoshida, dominating the downtown Los Angeles skyline. Estrella's zoomed view of one tower caught a glimpse of glass falling from one of its central floors. Tilting her head up, she saw the glow of flames erupting from the building, slowly dissipating. It was the aftermath of an explosion, one of many.

Piper broke the silence. "They're attacking Yoshida."

Estrella faced her, noting that Piper's synthetic eyes were also conducting scans. "The Federation IWs?"

"Has to be," Piper said. "I doubt you killed all the ones chasing us on the freeway. The rest must have regrouped after the paramedics took Ray."

Estrella looked toward the approximate location of the nearest hospital from the viewing on the freeway. She zoomed in onto that too, and it looked fine. And that was a problem.

"If the Federation wants Ray, then why aren't they attacking the hospital?"

She and Piper watched the triple Yoshida towers, then the

hospital. Then the towers. "That's because Ray probably isn't there," Piper concluded.

"The medivac ship didn't make it to the hospital," Estrella drily said.

Piper stormed back to the van. "They must have been paid off by Yoshida to grab him before the real ones showed."

Estrella followed behind, leaped in with Piper, and then shut the barn-like doors. The interior of the van returned to its darkened state. Piper was standing behind the two chairs. Her synthetic hand was resting at the back one, her NC gauntlet hand on the other.

"Theo, get us to the Yoshida towers now!"

Theo sped away, making their van become part of the LA traffic, plowing through the maze of ramps and freeway lanes. After six minutes, the downtown core of Los Angeles dominated the forward windshield, and another sixteen minutes after that, things grew dark when the shadows of the skyscrapers darkened the streets below.

Piper called out to Estrella, she faced her briskly. In Piper's hand were spare nanotubes pulled from the inside of Piper's arm. "If I give you these, promise me you won't try to kill me, love?"

Estrella was with three weaponized IWs, and one of them was augmented with tech that amplified her powers.

Attack Piper and her gang? No, she wouldn't do that. That was just asking for trouble.

FORTY

RAY

"What's that noise?"

Ashford grimaced, standing up from his chair. He moved to the exit of the waiting room, opening the door slowly. Beyond stood the three armed men who escorted Ray from the rooftops. Ray heard Ashford whisper something to them, something about checking it out. Three thumping boots dispersed when the order was given.

Rumbling shook the foundation of the building. It had everyone on edge, Ray too. He had serious doubts the LAPD was storming in to save him, not while he was on corporate property. Another rumble and surge of worrying thoughts hit. Whoever was causing it had hostile intentions to Yoshida and Ray.

The third shake of the building nearly threw Ray off the couch.

Fire alarms blared and panicking feet left offices and cubicles. Portia helped Ashford to his feet, using her hands that sprung to life with white light. Her telepathic powers were at work.

"We have to go," she said to him. "Right now!"

She dragged him by the arm to the exit. He opted to reach for Ray like he wanted to grab him and put him in his pocket. "We can't leave, Mr. Partington!"

"Call for a team to secure him." She had him near the exit in two seconds flat. "The two of us can't be here now, trust me on this!"

They vanished beyond the door, joining with the fleeing office staff. Ray stood up to do the same. Two armed security personnel had other plans. Their combat-gloved hands pushed Ray back. The unit to secure him was quick.

They weren't quick enough to escape from their death.

The walls crumbled. Explosions and their violent blasts flung Ray to the floor. The body of the first guard spun around. It was his last act in life before his body turned to bits of bones, arms, legs, and flesh plastering the floor, ceiling, and the debris of the walls. A white line of light hit his partner. Blood and gore sprayed everywhere. It looked like a monster ate the two men and then vomited up their remains.

Screaming erupted. Ray wasn't sure from where at that point as he hid behind the couch. He felt the building shake again, smelled smoke, and then heard another explosion. Half the ceiling above him came down and around him. When the dust had cleared, and the deceased remained idle, Ray peeked from his cover.

Something totaled the waiting room and most of the offices on the floor. Ray left the room and tracked across the debris into the hall. Ahead was a gaping hole in the wall, it looked like a bomb went off. Wind rustled the hair of the dead office staff that didn't make it to the emergency exit fast enough.

Ray stood at the massive hole. He tried not to look down. He was about a hundred and fifty stories up, give or take five stories. Heatwaves blurred his view of the Los Angeles skyline, as the winds picked up in speed. No, they weren't winds. Something was generating whatever it was that made his hair, shirt, and pants wave.

A gunship with the logo of the LAPD lowered into view. It hovered outside next to the gap. Its targeting scans shined dotted laser light across Ray's face, its smoking hot Gatling guns, and primed missile launcher were ready for action. It was a ship used by SWAT.

This was the cause of the blasts. Why would the LAPD do this, he wondered?

LAPD, it wasn't them. It had to be the Federation. They hijacked this SWAT vehicle. It was the only logical explanation. Whatever it was Arianna put in his head, they wanted it bad, Yoshida wanted it bad. Everyone that wanted it was ready and willing to kill to get it, and it seemed they were getting desperate. They might've reached a breaking point if they stole a SWAT gunship. Or maybe the Federation really doesn't want Yoshida to know what's in Ray's head.

Either way, standing at the massive hole in the wall, while a gunship acquired Ray as a target, was a fucking terrible idea.

"Oh, shit!" was Ray's parting words before he ran.

He nearly tripped over a body missing its lower half and gushing blood. Ray wanted to vomit when he saw their intestines dangle in the draft caused by the gunship.

The gunship followed him from outside. They fired no bullets. They still needed Ray's head in one piece, and the rounds the gunship had already fired showed it had the power to rip a human to pieces with multiple shots.

An elevator door came into view amidst the smoke and flames. Massive bullets fired from the gunship shot ahead of Ray's path, destroying everything it touched. By the time the barrage was over, the floor ahead of Ray was gone. A three-story drop and a lot of mangled rubble awaited him below. And that was the good news. The bad news was that there wasn't much of an elevator left when he looked at it.

Ray had to find another way out, and it had to be deep within the floor he was on, behind as many walls as he could put between him and the ship. As long as it could scan his presence via the windows or gaping holes, it would taunt him, forcing him to stay put until they took him.

He heard crying from the maze of cubicles he ran past. Not everyone was killed. He wanted to stick around and help, but the office workers were in danger because of his existence. The sooner he left, the sooner the Federation would leave. He pushed deeper into the floor. The gunship tracked him until there were too many walls, blocking all scans.

Ray was inside some executive office, safe for now. Fear made him shut and lock the door. On the desk was a computer, its screen was still active. The user that fled didn't log out and said user had high admin privileges. Ray typed frantically on the keyboard, forcing the screen to display surveillance footage from the cameras that were still operational.

He found the medivac ship he rode in on, idling on the rooftop. The crew didn't leave, but judging by their panicking movements, they were preparing to take off soon. Typical corporate medical personnel. People were dying and could have used a ride out to the hospital, and the medivac crew was making plans to take off because it wasn't in the contract to stick around. And sticking around was exactly what Ray needed them to do, at least for another five minutes as he made his way back up. That medivac brought him here, and he was going to make them bring him out.

He found an intact elevator linking with the rooftops. It wasn't far from the office he hid in too. Ray moved out, slowly unlocking the door, and slipping out into the cubicle-filled workplace. He was glad he did it slowly. To his left were the Federation black op operatives with assault rifles in their glowing hands. They were primed and ready to use their powers.

Ray saw a glimpse of the gunship when he peeked around the corner, keeping low from the patrolling IWs. It hovered beside one of the many holes in the walls and shattered windows, its side door flipped opened, releasing hordes of operatives inside, onto the floor. Ray's journey to the elevator had to be quick and silent.

A turn to the left nearly put him in the sights of two IW black ops members with their heads moving from left to right. Ray made a right, then a left, and then a left, the cubicle maze was longer than he thought. A holographic plant-covered him from behind, he hoped the power keeping it flickering didn't cut.

The elevator doors came into view, then slid open. His finger mashed the rooftop's button eight times in two seconds. It seemed like an eternity for the doors to slide shut. It felt even longer for the ride up. It made Ray's breathing erratic.

He saw the medivac parked on the rooftop when the elevator doors opened. It didn't leave, though its thrusters were blazing with blue light and heatwaves. Its door was still open. He ran to it, screaming and pleading for them to take him.

"The fuck?" one paramedic yelled.

Ray ran aboard. Freedom. They could take off now. They didn't. He found out why the painful way with a wrench to the back of his head. Ray went down to the cold floor.

"Get him out of here! We won't get paid if he's still with us."

Two men grabbed him, one for each arm. Ray saw the rooftop from the opened door. The paramedic stood ready to toss him out. Animal fear wasn't having that. A newfound surge of strength empowered Ray's arms. He fought off the grip of one man, using his newly freed hand to punch the one still holding him. He felt his knuckles crack from the blow. The pain didn't register. Every sense in his body told him going back inside the tower would be the end.

With both hands free, he strangled the closest man, digging his thumbs into their throat. He was grabbed from behind. A swift elbow from Ray got him loose from that. He found the wrench that clubbed him, picked it up, tossed it, and sent it spiraling into the face of a third paramedic that came for him. The third paramedic went flying back upon impact, knocking over a tray. Ray's phones, glasses, and tablet littered the floor. He would need those. He went diving for them, quickly stuffing them into his pockets.

Then he regretted it.

The two men from behind jumped him, clobbered him senseless until his arms and legs went limp. He felt the pain this time. Ray came to, rolled his sore body to face the sky, and watched as the medivac took off, leaving him and everyone else stuck in the Yoshida tower behind. At least he got his stuff back.

He beamed and leaped back to his feet while accessing his botnet. The medivac was a vulnerable object. And there was an app that would give him remote control of it, the same he used to remote control cars on the freeway not long ago.

He stood waiting for the botnet to crack the medivac's password.

39%.

68%

98%

He was almost there—

Two missiles and an explosive blast turned the medivac into burning debris that tumbled and burned to the streets below. The hacking app on his phone beeped a connection lost error message to the medivac. *Yeah, no shit.*

The gunship came into view and hovered eerily as it watched the remains of its target sprinkled down in flames. Its forward end turned to face Ray once again, aiming its red laser targeting equipment. Ray bolted for the elevator before it got any ideas.

Now what?

His hacking app connected with the internal network of the Yoshida towers. He used it to download various floor plans for the building. The main security room caught his attention. It was a perfect place to look before he leaped, something he needed to do with every step. As tempting as it was to ride the elevator to the ground floor, he had a feeling there'd be Federation IWs waiting to electrocute him with their powers. It was best to hack the surveillance systems first.

Getting into the security center was easy, its doors unlocked with a push of a button on his phone. Inside was an octagonal room, empty except for screens covering every inch of wall space, and a central computer terminal. IWs occupied the lobby watching the primary entrance, and rows upon rows of unmoving elevators. Other floors, including the one he was on, had the black ops IWs searching for the lone hacker.

Ray brute-forced his way into the main security computer. The screen ahead of him flashed a message informing users that a critical security threat had breached the building. When he clicked the 'Okay' button, a new prompt appeared on the screen. The vitals of all Yoshida security personnel in the building had flatlined. The computer asked Ray if he would like to activate the assault robots as a backup.

Y/N?

He typed Y.

The assault robots sprung from their recharging alcoves. They looked like four-legged creatures sporting twin Gatling guns for hands. They were programmed to gun down anyone except those that were a registered employee of Yoshida, RW, or a family member. Luckily for Ray, Arianna listed his name as a significant other. He sighed, he missed her, IW or not. He had to find her, and he had to learn what her real motives were. Whatever it was she did, Yoshida forced it upon her, this he was certain.

He hacked the assault robots programming, removing the 'don't kill RWs' variable from its coding. According to Piper, Estrella couldn't be trusted, and he was fairly certain Piper was dead by now. If she wasn't, she'd be here to get him out of this mess by now—

"Ray!"

It was her voice, Arianna's. Ray's heart thumped rapidly.

Arianna was here. Why? Does it even matter why? She won't last long if the IWs get to her before the robots eliminate them. He went running to the door, unlocking it with his phone. Two assault robots accompanied him as protection.

It gave him the confidence to call out her name. "Arianna!"

It didn't matter if the IWs heard him now, the assault robots would take care of them.

"Ray!" she cried out. "Ray! Help me!"

He let the sound of her voice guide him through the office halls. She glanced at him when he found her. Arianna's flawless blue eyes were just the way he last saw them. His robot escort stood at his left and right. It made a frightened Arianna run away.

He put out his hand. "Wait, stop moving!" he cried out and went chasing. "The robots are with me!" *And wouldn't attack you ... why is she running?*

An uneasy feeling hit midway into his chase for her.

"Ray, over here!"

Ray ordered his robot bodyguards to remain as he followed Arianna through a collapsed wall, hoping they wouldn't scare her off. He stepped into a chamber full of computers, and massive cables littering the ground. It was a trip hazard, and he had doubts Yoshida staff regularly worked here. And the more he glanced at the chamber, its eerie red lights, the more he didn't recognize it from the floor map. According to the map he downloaded to his phone, the area they stood in should be empty space, reserved for future expansions. Yoshida made an expansion to the floor, and if he were to guess, didn't bother telling their employees about it.

He hacked one computer. The first images that appeared were biographies of telepathic IWs. It listed some as acquired, others listed as searching for, while a smaller list listed the names as found but not acquired. Avatar 33 was listed as acquired, though, it displayed her real name and profile, Portia Blanchard. Her sister, Vina Blanchard, was on the found but not acquired list.

Ray took a step back from the screen. "Why the fuck would Yoshida have this?"

Arianna laughed at him. He spun around facing her, shocked she was behind when he clearly didn't see her in the room. He discovered why seconds later. Arianna's form changed.

She became an Asian man, with a long ponytail, laughing at Ray. Mental manipulation, Ray saw what the telepathic man wanted him to see, and it was the same strange man he witnessed during the attack at JFK. The man's hand glowed white, then rolled into a fist. Ray felt his body forced to his knees. He couldn't move. Someone else was controlling his mind.

The man brandished a katana from its rest at his side. The blade shined with indigo light, a nanite katana.

"Raise your chin, Ray," the man said. "I just need your head, and nothing else. So, let's make this nice and clean, eh?"

Ray lifted his chin for the man. He had to because the man said so.

FORTY-ONE
ESTRELLA

Theo parked the van in front of a no-parking sign. Nobody cared. Estrella and Piper sprung from the van's rear door first. Theo and Bashiir followed behind. The four of them wielded assault rifles that were hidden under tarps in the van, and that was only half of their arsenal. Twin pistols were holstered to Estrella's body, still wearing the red bike suit. She wasn't sure of the extra heat Bashiir and Theo were packing but imagined it to be similar to Piper, like the twin SMGs dangling behind her lace robe coat as it fluttered in her wake.

The four marched across the street. The Yoshida Corporation's central lobby was ahead, and above that, the chaos that ripped apart a bunch of floors on one of the three towers, a hovering gunship, now deploying quadcopter drones.

Estrella grimaced while looking up. "That explains why the SWAT armory was attacked," she said. "And why the ship disappeared; the Federation IWs hijacked it."

The remains of walls and glass ruined the garden below the tower. It was a shame too since it was a real garden, not some fake holographic one.

Estrella didn't see or hear any emergency vehicles. Between LAX, the freeway and now this, the LAPD, fire department, and paramedics had their hands full. They'll be there soon, but not soon enough. That's where Estrella and her new associates came in.

Up the concrete steps and into the lobby the four went. It was a mess. Before the destructive makeover, the lobby had polished black tiles and wide pillars keeping the high ceiling up in place. A glossy reception counter was ahead, and behind that were halls that took you to three distinct chambers, and in those were the elevators servicing the three other towers. Today? It was full of broken glass from the windows and doors up front, bullet holes put mean cracks in the black pillars. Estrella didn't see anyone at the welcome desk asking what the four were doing there.

Five dead Yoshida security personnel had to be stepped over when the four moved forward with caution. Four assault rifles had their safeties taken off when they came out. Bullets busted back and forth further up. Then came electrokinesis balls. Then came searing jets of flames. IWs were fighting someone. The four kept moving, crunching the glass and debris below their feet.

"I don't like Yoshida," Theo said. "But it looks like, for now, we're all on the same side as those malakas."

"Agreed," Piper said. "Keep their security teams alive if you find any. They're fighting the Federation IWs."

The gun busting sounds subsided. Someone was reloading Estrella figured, the IWs must have hit their cooldown phase. The four arrived at the first set of pillars, taking cover behind them. Estrella looked beyond, down the halls toward the chamber leading to the elevators they went seeking. Four-legged assault robots walked over the bodies of fallen IWs and Yoshida security guards with their brains blown out. Those that took it to the chest had their lungs blown out.

The forward scanners of the assault robots got a nice look at

Estrella. Several Gatling guns roared in unison. She went diving for new cover before the pillar she stood at exploded.

"What the fuck!" She got to her feet, ran, and took cover at a new pillar.

Everyone's rifles went to select new targets. "I thought the robots were part of the building's defense?" Piper asked.

Estrella nodded. "They are ..."

"Then why did they turn on you?" Piper ducked. A salvo of bullets aimed for her face forced that. She opted to remain prone. "And me ..."

RWs were a product line of Yoshida. The assault robots shouldn't have attacked. True, Piper wasn't owned by Yoshida, but her hacked profile should have registered her as corporate-owned property, like Estrella.

The lobby got loud again. An uncountable number of assault robots came charging in blazing their twirling twin Gatling cannons, the recoil made the robots shake violently as they slogged closer.

Theo returned fire and clenched his fist. His bullets curved around the pillars toward one robot. Only two out of the six rounds he fired missed. "Are they hacked?"

He may be correct. Geoffrey spoke, his systems returning online just in time too. *I cannot connect remotely with any of the robots.*

And if Geoffrey, a Yoshida designed and developed AI, couldn't link with the robots, then for sure, someone applied their hacker's touch. More bullets soared back and forth. The lobby was slowly turning into a warzone, worse than the one they walked into. Theo mixed up his attacks, shooting first, and then discharging twin beams of electrical currents from his glowing purple hands. One robot toppled over and erupted with sparks and smoke. Too bad more left the elevators. Too bad there were Federation black ops IWs still at large. It was a three-way gorefest.

Estrella ran for new cover, her Defense Matrix soaked up seven rounds to the chest and torso.

"Piper," Estrella called out when she rested her back against a new intact pillar. "Can your AI link with the robots?"

"No, remember, I'm not officially using Yoshida software."

I may be able to establish a link via nanites, Estrella. But it would require a consistent physical connection.

That meant walking up and touching a robot without dying.

Estrella shouted the message back amidst the roars of gunfire and pyro and electrokinesis blasts from Theo and Bashiir. "Piper, Geoffrey thinks he can connect with the robots." Estrella pointed her barrel at the largest assault robot in the group, the field commander, issuing wireless commands to the smaller robots. "I'm going to link up with that big motherfucker over there."

Piper's face peered from her pillar cover. "You're crazy!"

"And you and your goon squad's gonna cover me."

"I do not see any other option," Bashiir said as he ducked to reload. "There are bound to be more assault robots inside. If we cannot deactivate them, then we have nothing."

Piper pointed at Bashiir and Theo. "You two keep the IWs busy. I'll go with Estrella."

Estrella and Piper's synthetic arms split open simultaneously. Both women pulled and injected a booster shot of nanites into their leg. Theo charged his glowing hands with surging electrokinesis energy and faced the remaining Federation IWs. Bashiir dropped his weapons to the floor, undid his top and pants as his hands glowed orange. Biokinesis turned him into a ferocious lion. It impressed Estrella, especially the speeds he moved at, charging at the IWs. The crossfire rounds couldn't target him, and neither could the blasts of pyrokinesis flames, or hydrokinetic water cannons aimed at Bashiir.

Screams from the first IW mauled to death by the king of the jungle echoed. It was the signal Estrella and Piper were waiting for. They left their cover, running for the robots. Theo ran to support

Bashiir, his body covered in a barrier of electricity deflecting all hostile actions thrown at him.

Estrella's rifle blazed. One robot collapsed in a mess of parts. She reloaded. Two robots targeted her. She hit the overdrive, and using her newfound speed, dodged the slow-motion bullets, or straight up outran them. The wall appeared, so she leaped up to it, and wall-ran across it, lining up the perfect shot at one robot's targeting sensor. A single bullet made it blind, and unable to be a threat. Overdrive ended as she had to conserve her nanite count. Estrella's boots were on the ground from that point on. She checked her swarm count via her combat HUD.

Nanite swarm(s) remaining: 2

Behind her, Piper used psychokinesis to pull fractured pillars to orbit her. Her nanites enveloped them, disassembling them, turning them into gray goo, only to reform them into barricades. Piper covered behind her newfound protection. Her rifle blazed again, and she didn't miss—it's kind of hard to when you could curve your bullets. Two robots turned into a wreckage of metal and sparks.

Estrella was jealous. "Wish I could do that!"

"Like I said, I'm the future," Piper roared as she lowered herself to reload. "And whatever Ray has, will develop version 2.0 of me."

Estrella was shot three times. Her defenses held. She grimaced when she saw it reduced the four nanite swarms powering Defense Matrix to two. She couldn't avoid losing more. She returned fire with her rifle until it clicked. The rifle's ammo status showed the number 0 on her the HUD. She was empty. No worries. She confirmed Geoffrey had copied the rifle's patterns, and dropped it, reaching for her twin pistols.

Estrella ran and slid across the floor, then made a brief over-drive surge with pistols in each hand. She lined up and clapped down the robot to her left, and then the second robot to her right simultaneously with her duel wielding action. She cut the over-drive ability early like before and checked her swarm count.

Nanite swarm(s) remaining: 1

That too drained more nanites than she would have liked.

Geoffrey, show me my battery life.

The charge remaining for her battery appeared in her vision as she dove again, avoiding gunfire, and taking cover behind a shattering pillar. 72%, she liked that number.

Can you have my life support nanites give an extra boost to my utility ones?

I can, but be advised, this will drain your battery faster.

Do it, I need every advantage going forward.

A confirmation screen showed the change was made. Estrella's life support nanites worked two jobs now. One job was to keep her alive, and the second was to transfer their power to her failing utility bots as they continued to maintain her Defense Matrix. It should slow down the number of swarms losing power and dying, maybe even resurrect a few dead nanites.

The trade-off was her life support nanites had less energy, forcing them to return to their internal charging station, taking power from her battery. A new way for Estrella to die became part of the equation, no battery power. She faced her synthetic arm and was glad she brought a spare cell inside. She hoped she'd have the chance to swap it out.

Back to the battle.

Three robots were left, including the command one. Piper held one in place, snapping its four legs with psychokinesis, then had her nanites take it apart. A pool of gray goo oozed across the shrapnel covered floor. Two more left. Piper kept the last robot distracted, luring it to her by throwing debris with psychokinesis. She gave Estrella a nod, take out the commander.

Estrella ran for it, her twin pistols blazing and brightening the red leather biker suit she wore. Spent shell casings ejected with each pull of her trigger. She heard each one ding to the floor in her wake. Gatling rounds hit her. Her Defense Matrix held while her battery power dropped fast as a result, 67% now. She kept running, taking aim at its combat scanners.

When she neared it, Piper told her to jump. So, she did. Estrella felt the force of Piper's psychokinesis hold her, making her leap fifteen feet in the air with one vault. Fifteen fucking feet. Where was Piper her whole life? They'd make a perfect strike team back in Estrella's mercenary days.

"Go, go, go!" Piper cheered.

Estrella landed on the back of the four-legged mechanical monster. It responded by jerking its body, trying to shake her off. Its parts whizzed and roared, but Estrella's cyborg strength and grip helped her hold on. Her NC gauntlet grabbed into its head, the location of its CPU. She brought up her abilities list, and selected Nanite Hack.

Her last free nanite swarm released from her gauntlet, drilling tiny holes into the robot. Once inside, they worked quickly to reprogram and rewire the robot. But first, they needed to sever its link to the Yoshida network security grid.

Meanwhile, the holographic black cat of Geoffrey appeared beside her, unaffected by the movement of the bucking robot trying to throw her off.

I have access to its network. The robot continued to rock. Estrella felt her body move up and down too many times. *Please remain still. Sudden movements of your gauntlet will break the connection.*

How about you keep this fucker from moving?

I am trying my best, Estrella.

After two minutes, the beast's motor functions ceased. She felt the data flow into her.

Confirmed, Ray hacked all the robots in the building, reprogramming them to attack everyone on sight that wasn't on Yoshida's payroll or family list.

The fuck? Why?

Most likely because he was scared and was unaware we had entered. A crawl of computer code blinded her. Geoffrey was processing new data. *He's on the 150th floor, however the robots there are going offline quickly.*

Estrella thought back to the hovering gunship they saw on their way in. *The gunship.*

They know he's there.

You can control this right?

As long as you remain touching it, yes. Your nanites are the bridge I need to operate this—

Clear this lobby of all remaining hostiles.

As you wish.

Estrella repositioned herself, riding the robot as if it were a horse. Geoffrey's hologram remained as they both faced forward, watching the light show of IWs powers flash. "Bashiir, Theo, fallback!"

Geoffrey, Estrella, and the robot's CPU were all one mind working together. She ordered it come to life and walk past an impressed Piper, and into the IW crossfire of Theo and the remaining Federation black ops IWs, and a pissed-off lion ripping someone's arm out from its socket, smearing its face crimson. When Estrella and her robot were in range, Bashiir and Theo ran for cover.

The twin guns twirled and roared. The remaining hostiles in the lobby launched backward in a spray of red and body parts. Blood squirted rapidly from the stumps that used to have a head or hand attached.

Estrella looked down at the lion Bashiir had become and Theo. "Ray's on the 150th floor, go get him."

Theo glanced up at Estrella and nodded at the ride. "That fucking thing isn't fitting into the elevator with you ridin' it, yo."

She grinned. "I'm going up another way." *Geoffrey, take us outside.*

The katana man came within reach of Ray, stepping over several clusters of power cables. His nanite infused katana still glowing with indigo light, its blade aimed at Ray's neck. Ray wanted to run but couldn't. The katana man told him to get on his knees and lift his chin, so the impulses in his head made him do as asked. Telepathic mind control sucked.

In the background, the various alarms blared nonstop. Warning of fires, indications of critical security threats, signals that the assault robots had been destroyed. There was so much racket in the chamber, the strange place that shouldn't even be in the building to start with.

The katana man stopped, while grasping the hilt of his katana, pulled back and went to make the swing. Ray couldn't close his eyes. The man didn't tell him to do so.

His feet felt vibrations on the floor, then another. The gunship had found something else to shoot at. A blast rang, and it was enough to throw the katana man off balance, and then reconsider his actions. Whatever was happening out in the halls wasn't what he had planned. Gatling cannons were discharging, and its sounds were close, much closer than the gunship. Something else got off and entered the floor. Ray wanted to think it was an assault robot, it sure as hell sounded like one.

The katana man moved to the collapsed wall, through which the two men had gained access to the strange computer room. If Ray could move, he would have turned to see what he was doing.

He heard the man grunt. A loud one. "Piper, you backstabbing bitch!"

A section of the chamber collapsed, weapons fire from an assault robot the apparent cause of that. Ray was free to move, bullets flying overhead, beside, and dangerously close to him and the katana man was probably the reason for it. Even bad guys had to have their moments of fear, strong enough to break their concentration. And telepathy required a reasonable amount of mental focus.

The katana man drew a pistol and returned fire. The robot fired back, its weapons fire focused on the man. Dust and smoke partially obscured the battle the katana man and the robot were engaged in, Ray couldn't make out exactly was happening. One bullet grazed the katana man's arm when he went to switch cover behind a wall that was intact.

His weapon dropped to the floor. A new storm of bullets prevented him from retrieving it. Not Ray though, he ran, dove, and grabbed the weapon. It forced the katana man to counter using his powers, his glowing white hands forcing half the bullet spray to stop, turn around and return to its sender, the robot. The robot stopped shooting, and it didn't sound like it was walking either. Crackling sounds of sparks spraying were probably the reason.

Ray had a clear shot at the katana man. He took aim, told his shaking hands to stop doing that, and went to pull the trigger. He hoped the katana man's psychokinesis powers were on cooldown. If they weren't, then Ray was going to regret it.

His pistol cracked three times. The katana man's hands held up before the three rounds. They stopped in midair. He plucked one and put it to his face, gave it a look, then faced back at Ray.

"You know, this could have hurt me, right?"

He wasn't on cooldown. Ray ran, firing blindly, and his missed bullets shattered the computer screens and cables that lay about. He felt a force tug at the weapon, the hands of psychokinesis were pulling it out from his grip. The psychokinesis force wasn't strong enough. The pressure the katana man had to deal with limited his powers. It'd explain why he didn't use mind control again as he was nearing his cooldown. With the robot out of the picture, Ray had to keep up the pressure and force him into it.

The screen on Ray's pistol flashed its ammo count. He had to conserve bullets. He had no spare clips. Those were on his katana-wielding attacker. With a slash of his blade through the air, the katana man launched the debris of the wall hurtling at Ray. One metal beam slapped Ray's forehead. It sent him hiding behind a computer console.

The footsteps of the katana man echoed, and then stopped to step over a cable. "You're just delaying the inevitable, Ray, just like your friend Jax."

Ray snorted. "You must be Nobuo I take it?"

"Why yes. How did you know?"

"That assassin you sent to my hotel didn't have his phone secured."

"Then you must see you can't stop the revolution."

Ray faced the pistol. He placed the barrel to his head, his hands shaking violently. "What if I blow my brains out?"

"Both you and I know you won't do that," Nobuo said then laughed. "You love Arianna too much to make her suffer that kind of loss."

He was still holding the shaking pistol to his head. "Someone's done their homework."

"I'm a telepath, what did you expect?"

"If you can read my mind, why not just take this stuff out of it?"

"You know damn well why."

The conversation he had with Ashford reminded him why. Celia buried Arianna's gift deep within his brain. Only a powerful S ranked telepath stood a chance at getting it, and Nobuo was it, only he was allied with the Federation.

Ray had lowered the pistol. It wasn't until it tapped the floor he sat on that he realized what had happened. "What the fuck is in my head?"

The footsteps paused for a second. They resumed. Nobuo had to step over more power cables. "The solution to the problem IWs worldwide face."

"And that is?"

"Freedom."

"Freedom from what? The Federation? Because you know, if that's the case why not just work with us? The Alliance and European Union would love nothing more than to topple of the Federation. No need to cut my head off too."

"Words like that are exactly the ones the Federation told us." The sound of Nobuo's voice felt closer. Ray looked for another place to run. There wasn't any. "Federation, Alliance ... they are no different. They're all driven by humans."

"You want independence for all IWs."

"It's high time humans became tools used for war, while witches and warlocks sit up top, issuing the orders—"

"Malaka!" The sound of electrokinesis discharge crackled. If Ray's back wasn't pressed up against the console, he would have gotten a good look at Theo's entrance. "You talk too much man!"

When he felt it was safe to stand, he did. Theo stood with his hands aimed at Nobuo, zapping him with twin bolts of electricity. A lion roared; it was Bashiir. When Theo's powers entered the cooldown phase, Bashiir sprinted forward, leaping up to maul Nobuo as he staggered from the electrical shock. Bashiir missed.

Nobuo slipped through, what looked like, a hole he cut in the air. Ray's pistol, Bashiir's jaws, and Theo's drawn rifle couldn't spot any sign of him. Theo approached Ray.

"You two love to make an entrance, huh?" Ray said to him.

"You call that an entrance?" Theo said with a chuckle. "You ain't seen nothing yet, malaka."

Theo showed Ray what was beyond the collapsed wall.

FORTY-THREE
ESTRELLA

The four giant legs of the robot were in motion again. This time, it moved to the broken remains of the glass doors and windows. Piper silently leaped aboard, using psychokinesis to make her jump high. Estrella felt Piper's hands wrap around her waist, holding her from behind.

Estrella flushed. "Piper, go with your people!"

Piper giggled. "I don't take orders from the new girl."

"Really? 'Cause your friends did. Now go join them."

The robot was outside now, covered by the darkness of the sun-blocking towers of downtown Los Angeles. There wasn't an emergency vehicle in sight. Given what they experienced, that might have been a good thing. Estrella had the robot make circles around the property. Cars on the roads slowed to observe. They should be speeding away.

"I wanna know exactly how you plan on getting this up?" Piper asked.

Geoffrey, find the ship. A messy trek through the front garden found it. It was still hovering next to the tower that took the brunt of the assault. *Get its attention.*

Geoffrey relayed the order. The mechanized joints holding the twin Gatling cannons lifted, taking aim at the drifting ship shooting into the tower, creating random explosions here and there. The flames expanded. On Estrella's mark, the guns snarled. The cars in the streets moved thirty over the speed limit after that.

The rounds firing up hit the ship, tearing holes through its central section. Sparks flared. A second barrage followed up. The gunship was no longer shooting the building. It dove, firing rounds at them. Geoffrey had got its attention.

Piper snorted. "Smart girl."

"Last call to get off, Piper."

She felt Piper's arms around her loosen. Then felt the injection of a nanotube hit her back. Estrella's nanite count increased to one. "I got more nanites than you. I think you'll need them for this."

Estrella grinned. "Smart girl."

From behind, Piper's hand in her NC gauntlet held onto Estrella's gauntlet. It made her sweat. "It's like we're a perfect match."

"Uh." Estrella was at a loss for words.

"Relax," Piper chucked. "I'm transferring my nanites to your glove. It should help with its operation."

She is correct; her nanites are surrendering their control to me.

The gunship plunged, taking random shots at the group. Its bullets missed when Geoffrey ordered the robot to run into the streets. Plumes of soil from the garden flung up in their wake. Piper grabbed a network cable from her arm and jacked into Estrella's head. Their heads were connected again via a short wire. A prompt informed Estrella of the users in her head.

My AI and yours can share computing power too, Piper's digital voice echoed in Estrella's head. *Should speed things up.*

Pleasure to meet you at last, Geoffrey. Piper's AI voiced.

Geoffrey sounded pleased. *Akane, your assistance is much appreciated in this matter.*

Please be aware that my construct is not Yoshida in origin.

Understood, sharing with you all security codes and operational patterns of this unit's operating system.

With both their nano powers combined and the gunship at a lower altitude, Estrella made her attack. Geoffrey and Akane's computing kept the robot highly agile in the roads. An exchange of twisting Gatling gunfire ensured. Only the streets and the gunship got hit. Cars approaching the battle U-turned and sped away. Vehicles parked at the side of the road were turned to a flaming mess of scattered parts and glass.

Palm trees crackled and burned, the streets trembled whenever the robot had to make a jump, leaping over the wreckage of a parked car. Missiles exploded with bright red flames; the robot's guns took aim at the missiles seconds after they launched from the ship. The heat from the blast seared Estrella's flesh. Her Defence Matrix held, but she saw a drop in her battery life, down to 56%.

She felt Piper's chin rest over her left shoulder. She wouldn't be surprised if Piper was enjoying the physical contact. *Seriously?*

They dodged another salvo of missiles. The van they'd arrived in turned to blackened slag. *Your hair's in the fucking way,* Piper said. *I can't see shit.*

Another spray of Gatling fire from the robot destroyed the ship's cockpit, and it crashed to the street, making a small crater. The ship was still intact, but not operational. Estrella had the AI duo walk the robot to the ship's main troop deployment hatch. Gatling fire shot it open as the robot stepped inside and found the cockpit, or what was left of it.

Estrella opened her synthetic arm, handing Piper a network cable which she pulled from it. The second network jack on Estrella's head allowed her to connect to the ship's ruined cockpit dashboard. Piper had run off briefly to make it happen, shoving aside the smoldering IW pilots. She climbed back on the robot, holding Estrella's gauntleted hand, resting her chin on her shoulder.

She felt her mind become more machine than RW. There were two network cables plugged into Estrella, her NC gauntlet was feeding nanites into the robot, and she had multiple digitized voices in her head, including two advanced AIs. The sights and sounds outside the shot open ship's door moved; Geoffrey took control of the gunship. They were airborne and ascending to the 150th floor, fast.

The gunplay resumed, this time in the air. Multiple quadcopter attack drones, loyal to the Federation, noticed the gunship was no longer under their control. The dogfighting and rolls were intense as the triple towers of Yoshida and the rest of the Los Angeles skyline stood as idle witnesses. Little by little, the quadcopter drones with their annoying machine guns exploded into tiny bits of molten metal and flames, raining down on the streets below.

Estrella gritted her teeth. Her head was in pain. *You okay?* Piper's digitized voice asked.

This is taking its toll on me.

Keep at it, we're almost through.

We might have to chance it and just run in.

No, it's too dangerous. Piper's synthetic hand held Estrella's, her fingers locking in with hers. She gave it a shake of encouragement. *You can do this Estrella. I believe in you.*

We. Estrella corrected her.

Without Piper and everyone else, they wouldn't have made it this far.

Estrella took a quick breather, her mind issuing orders to pilot the ship away from the three remaining quadcopter drones. Piper was now holding both her hands, the wind blowing in from the opened entrance whipped her black hair about and Piper's pixie hair too. Estrella felt Piper's long red highlighted bangs tickle her cheek and neck, mixed in with the warmth of Piper's breathing on her neck.

It was encouraging. It was making Estrella smile. It made her destroy a drone. And then another. One was left.

You got this, Estrella!

The final drone appeared in Estrella's sights, one of many clusters of windows populating her eyes. Geoffrey pulled the trigger. She watched with anticipation as the red tracer light soared to the drone. It exploded when contact was made. The skies were clear.

Carefully, the ship piloted and hovered next to the gaping hole in the building, exposing the interior of the office space to the outside world. The dead office workers and mangled security personnel made Estrella wretch. The Federation slew innocents in the crossfire, all because Ray had information in his brain he didn't ask for.

Justice had to be delivered.

The gap between the ship's entrance and the exposed and war-torn 150th floor was less than a meter apart according to scans. Estrella jerked her head backward. The sudden pull back forced the second cable in her head out from the ship's cockpit dashboard. There was no time to retrieve that cable as it dangled from her head. She had the robot face the entrance and jump into the building.

A small team of Federation IWs survived the bullet barrage from the assault robots Ray deployed. They didn't last long when Estrella and the gang found them and exploded into chunks of warlock flesh and bones. The gore gave the walls a new look.

The robot Estrella and Piper rode faced away, its four legs crawling about, taking them on a journey through the office halls. Estrella ran optical searches for Ray; she directed Piper to do so as well. Neither of the two scans produced good results.

Estrella smashed her synthetic hand on the robot. It left a dent on its hull. *Where the fuck is Ray?!*

She found a familiar face further in, past a collapsed wall. It was Nobuo. A quick battle ensued with Gatling gunfire exchanged for pistol shots from Nobuo. A bullet grazed Nobuo's arm, and he dropped his weapon. Ray grabbed it. They found him. The final barrage of bullets was stopped in midair thanks to Nobuo's white glowing hands.

He sent the massive rounds back at the robot Estrella and Piper rode.

It exploded upon impact.

Ray laughed at the surprise Theo showed him beyond the wall. He saw Estrella and Piper, and they waved to Ray. The two sat on top of the remains of a command robot full of holes and spraying sparks. He took back what he said. Estrella and Piper were the ones that made the entrance.

Theo grabbed Ray's arm. "Let's get you out of here, shall we?"

Ray shook him off and went running back to the computer console.

"Not yet." He typed quickly on the keyboard, bringing up the profiles of the IWs on it. All of them were telepathic. Theo stood with Ray eying the screen. "I want to know why the fuck Yoshida would have a database like this." Ray pulled up a new screen. "And what is the Avatar program?"

Theo grimaced. "Don't we all, but—"

"I'm not leaving," Ray cut him off, his hands still controlling the computer. "I think Arianna's disappearance has to do with this. I'm pretty sure Yoshida never intended to have anyone to make it this deep into this building, let alone reveal its presence in the floor plans. Just give me five minutes!"

Ray got one minute.

Nobuo returned, cutting a hole through space and time again with his nanite blade.

"Holy fucking shit!" Theo roared, lifting his rifle.

A 360 wide psychokinetic push sent everyone flying backward. Three bodies, one of them a lion, crashed into the computer screens and equipment. Sparks flared from the parts that were damaged. Nobuo was back, and he gave his shimmering katana a twirl, then resumed his previous task. He asked politely for Ray to stand and walk to him with his chin raised, telepathically.

Ray did what Nobuo told him to do. Vibrations trembled across the floor. Ray caught a glimpse of the ruined robot Estrella and Piper rode, limp to the secret computer chamber from the corner of his eye. As sad as the robot looked, it was probably faster for Piper and Estrella to ride it forward than running. He hoped they got there on time.

Nobuo aimed his blade to Ray's neck. "Now, Ray, where were we?"

Nobuo didn't catch Estrella and Piper's surprise attack. Some telepath he turned out to be. It gave Ray hope. The two witches entered the fray, leaping off the robot. Its guns were in pieces dangling about. Estrella was wearing a tight red biker outfit, and the glow from the red lights above gave it an unforgettable shine. A single network cable was plugged into her head but not connected to anything else and it swayed with her movement. Piper had one too.

Estrella's twin pistols cracked, laying down covering fire, and breaking Nobuo's hold on Ray's brain. Ray was free yet again and assisted with his gun. Piper blasted with her dual SMGs. Ray saw nothing but bullets fly, and computer screens explode during the violence. Nobuo laughed.

Debris was flung forward when Nobuo pointed at it. Piper deflected it with a wave of her hand, forcing it to orbit her before she launched it back to Nobuo. His indigo glowing katana cut it in half. A horizontal slash cut the second and third hulks of rubble Piper's psychokinesis sent. Ray fired his gun, but his bullets floated in the air ahead of Nobuo then dropped. Estrella's bullets did the same. A slice through the air and Nobuo vanished. He slipped into the temporal void again. When Nobuo returned, he stood behind Piper. A slash and a splash of red pushed her to the floor. Piper wasn't moving, and she didn't scream when it happened.

Estrella and Ray were next.

Estrella went into overdrive, running so fast all Ray saw was a wave of red and black run for Nobuo. His katana hit nobody, but rapidly kicked boots and flying fists from the red and black blur staggered him backwards. Ray shot again, still nothing. Cables from the floor rose and knotted around the colorful blur. It forced Estrella's overdrive to an end. She stood still, trapped, her limbs bound by the cables that took life and tied her up. Her nanites turned the cables binding her into goo, she snapped back when free, sending a second swarm at Nobuo.

Nobuo screamed at first, waving his hands, trying to swat the nanite swarm away. His flesh burst into flames. This was it. Or was it? His glowing hands thrust forward, and psychokinetic winds blew out the fires. He was perfectly fine, then he slashed his blade again. A computer screen came off the wall toward Estrella. She didn't see it coming. Ray leaped her way, pushing her to safety.

When the two got to their feet, they stood back-to-back. Nobuo had vanished again into a portal. Estrella reloaded her pistols and tossed a clip for Ray. He was back in action. The two spun, searching for signs of his temporal portal, eyes moving around rapidly, backs still pressed against each other. Ray wanted to check Piper, he also wanted to look at Theo and Bashiir, as neither of them moved from the floor where they fell.

"Ray," Estrella said. "You're a very hard man to find and talk to."

Ray smiled, not that she could see it. "You know, I was open to talk when we first met," he said. "But you told me to fuck off, so ..."

"I told you to go fuck yourself."

"Fuck off. Fuck myself. It's the same shit!"

Nobuo was back. Ray and Estrella stood shoulder to shoulder firing their pistols rapidly. Invisible forces held their bullets idle in the air, and a slash of Nobuo's blade scattered them. A leaping cleave from Nobuo came next. Running was pointless as they'd still be in range, and Estrella knew it. She pushed Ray over and stood above him, lifting her synthetic arm up like it was a shield.

Ray looked up just in time to see Nobuo's blade slice Estrella's arm and then slice again. Half her synthetic arm hit the floor in three smoking pieces. He saw a fountain of sparks erupt from the severed wires within the fraction of her arm still attached to her body. It was a grim reminder of how much of a machine Estrella was, compared to Ray. She didn't flinch or cry out in suffering, her ability to experience true pain with her left arm was gone the day she sold her soul to Yoshida.

She sprayed Nobuo again with her nanites, and again his body convulsed. It bought Ray just enough time to get to his feet, retreat, and watch as Nobuo slashed again. Estrella went down like Piper with a vertical gash down the middle of her torso. It exposed blood mixed with metal and wires. Estrella refused to give up and reached for the remains of her arm. They hit the opposite ends of the room after three kicks from Nobuo.

Nobuo twitched. Whatever it was Estrella ordered her nanites to do, continued working, wreaking havoc on Nobuo muscles. He struggled to hold his blade steady to finish Estrella off. Ray shot him again, and the bullets froze in the air. Nobuo's psychokinesis powers were unaffected. Ray cursed.

Everyone was down except Ray, and he knew once Estrella was dead, he would be too. Ray reached for his phone, pulling it out and searching for a vulnerable object. At that point, he didn't care what it was. He needed something.

An icon hovered over Estrella's body. Her AI was still operating and labeled a vulnerable target. Not that he'd try to hack it. His phone gave him a quick peek at her AI's status. Estrella's battery was low, 11% to be exact, as her Defense Matrix ate up her power to keep her nanites alive longer. Ray grimaced when a similar icon flashed over Piper's body. She too was a vulnerable device. That meant her AI was still active.

Ray ran for Piper, and he felt the eyes of a staggering Nobuo watch him. Nobuo was still struggling to work his muscles, fighting off Estrella's nanites that would eventually lose power. Once that happened, it was over. Ray kneeled, rolling Piper's body over. Her chest, despite being drenched in blood with sparking wires coming from the wound, was still moving. She was alive.

"Piper?"

She didn't respond. She looked to the ceiling, and he noticed her head still had a network cable attached. He plugged it into his tablet, worked the keypad, and powered his botnet on, looking to gain access to her AI. It wasn't necessary. A holographic raven perched itself on the top edge of his pad. Akane granted Ray access.

A chat window opened, and Piper's text-only words appeared on his tablet's screen.

Piper Taylor: Fuck, fuck, fuck ...

Ray typed his reply.

DigiSamurai69: Estrella won't last long. She needs more nanites and a new battery.

Piper Taylor: We spent most of them getting to you. She might have a spare in her arm.

DigiSamurai69: Her arm got sliced to pieces. I don't know where he kicked it.

Ray looked down at Piper's synthetic arm. He pointed at it.

DigiSamurai69: Got anything in there?

Piper Taylor: One nanotube and I need you to inject me with it. I need first-aid treatment from it.

DigiSamurai69: What good is that when he finishes her then us off?

There was a pause. No new words showed on the screen. Ray double checked the network cable. It was still plugged into the tablet and Piper's head. New words appeared.

Piper Taylor: Promise me something, Ray.

Her arm opened, granting Ray access to the nanotube and battery. He grabbed them and then typed his reply.

DigiSamurai69: What?

Piper Taylor: The stuff in your head. Make sure people like him don't get it. Not even a taste of it, or what's in Arianna's head too.

He smiled and typed a quick response.

DigiSamurai69: Then you need to stay alive and help me with that.

Piper Taylor: And if I don't, it will be up to you. Please, keep that data away from them. I don't want my daughter inheriting the world he wants to make.

Ray grimaced and waited for Piper's next text words.

Piper Taylor: So, promise me that? Promise me she won't have to live through that.

He typed his final words to her.

DigiSamurai69: I promise.

Ray unplugged from Piper's head. He stood with a nanotube in one hand and an RW battery in the other. Nobuo's capability to move correctly was returning, as was his strength to thrust down and stab a slowly crawling one-armed Estrella, while the other crackled with sparks. Deep breathing banished Ray's fear.

Ray had to become a hero if he were to have Arianna back in his life.

He ran to Estrella while a muscle twitching Nobuo stood over her and struggled to hold his blade still. A psychokinetic force punched Ray in the face. He got to his feet and kept running. Ray wasn't mind-controlled which meant Nobuo was entering cooldown. He had this. Another psychokinetic punch hit, this time to his gut. Ray felt like vomiting. He got to his feet. A punch to the face, and he tasted blood. He kept going, nothing else mattered.

Ray smothered Estrella with his body. Nobuo would have to stab him first, then her. He quickly injected Estrella with the nanites, tossed the used tube away, then looked up. The katana's edge was inches away. Ray parted Estrella's long hair, finding the back of her neck, and battery slot. The spent battery came loose after fighting with the switches for three seconds. He tossed it out of Estrella and saw her body go limp. That was about to change when he inserted the new battery—

Ray's fingers snapped. The pain made him scream. Nobuo was breaking every bone in Ray's hand. He dropped the battery, tried to grab it, and felt his arm break in three places. Rolling off Estrella's body, he went searching for the cell. He found it with his one working hand.

Ray couldn't move. It felt like a force was holding him down by the neck, choking him. His air supply was fading, and his neck was contracting on its own. He failed the promise he made to Piper. It surprised him his neck didn't snap like his hand and arm. He must have rolled out of range for the bone-breaking stuff he figured.

It gave him hope. Estrella's neck and opened battery slot were still within arm's reach. Ray reached over with the battery in hand, twitching from the pain and air loss. He missed the slot, then tried again, and missed, then again, almost got it, but missed. It clicked into place on the last attempt, and he felt the battery tray retract inside Estrella.

Her glowing emerald eyes sprung open with life.

"You're a brave man Ray," Nobuo said. "Not very smart, because if you were, you'd have run away when you had the chance. But, staying behind to help your friends, that's a very brave thing to do."

He couldn't see much but figured if Nobuo could speak so clearly, then his motor functions were about to return. Or, they already had.

Ray waited for his death and grunted his last words at Nobuo. "Fuck you."

FORTY-FIVE
ESTRELLA

Life came back to Estrella's vision. She checked her battery charge, the sole reason she collapsed, as it was still tied to the nanites supporting her Defense Matrix. 100%, she grinned and ordered the one nanite swarm within her to use first aid and make repairs to her body. She didn't wait for them to finish.

Estrella was back on her feet with cyborg speed. She kicked Nobuo's arm, and his blade fell to the floor. She dove and grabbed it with her one remaining hand. Nobuo tried to grab it back. She rolled across the floor and cables to safety, leaped to her feet, and spun around, making a low horizontal slash in Nobuo's direction.

"Nobuo," she snorted. "You've overstayed your welcome; I think it's time you ..." She sliced swiftly across his abdomen. "... split."

Blood poured from Nobuo's split in half belly like a gushing waterfall. His upper body fell backward, while his lower remained standing until Estrella kicked it over.

Off to the side, she saw and heard Ray grumble as his body returned to normal, save for the broken bones. That would take longer to heal.

Estrella checked the status of the nanites healing her, they weren't finished, but she was stable for the time being. She could afford to spare some. She divvied what remained of the swarm into thirds. Ray got a third with her spray from her gauntlet and she ordered them to repair his bones. She limped to Piper with her one arm and gave her a spray, also ordering them to perform first aid, the best they could. Two minutes later, life returned to the pixie kiwi's face. A Mona Lisa smile was Estrella's reward.

Ray stood up and leaned his body against an active computer console. He typed on it with one hand, while the nanites continued repairing the bones in the other. Estrella grimaced and stayed with him while the sounds of sirens echoed the distance. They needed to escape before Piper and her friends got taken down by RWs.

She grabbed Ray with her remaining hand. "We need to leave."

"Wait."

Estrella viewed the screen he was looking at and the dozens of faces flashing on it. Ray held his phone plugging one cable into it and the computer. A download progress bar moved on the phone's screen.

She gave the screen a second look with narrowed eyes. "I know some of these people. They're kidnap victims of the Bald Skulls, all of them. Why the hell is Yoshida keeping profiles on them?"

The faces of the family of three Estrella protected on her first day appeared. It was a list of unregistered IWs with telepathic abilities, a list of those to capture, and those that had been. Arianna and her father Norris' names were on the captured list. It made them both cringe.

"Project Avatar," he said when that name flashed. "Yoshida is just as dirty as these Federation IWs."

And so were the Bald Skulls. The gang that was supposed to be dead, Yoshida, and the top-secret stuff stuck in Ray's head were related. As interesting as the find was, they had to leave, download finished or not.

"We really need to go," Estrella said.

"Another minute," Ray replied, his eyes locked on to the 35% download progress.

"In another minute Yoshida PMCs might storm this place and kill everyone who saw things they shouldn't have."

He faced her. "You know this for a fact?"

Estrella shrugged. "I'd rather not find out the hard way. But the cops are coming, meaning Yoshida's PMC got the call." She pointed at the screen. "And this is some serious classified shit nobody was supposed to see. Let's keep that image."

Ray pulled the cable from his phone. She saw the download error screens flash. The two went to check up on Bashiir and Theo. They were alive, just out cold. They dragged their bodies back then checked up on Piper. She slowly got to her feet, a section of her damaged body already repaired by the nanites.

Piper couldn't walk straight and wobbled about, almost losing her balance. Estrella came running for her, holding her up straight. She heard her giggle. Looking up, she saw that same Mona Lisa smile that warmed her chest.

"I wasn't kidding, new girl." Piper ran her fingers across Estrella's face. "You're breathtaking."

———

Estrella couldn't stop gawking at her left hand. It looked better than the old one she lost days ago at the Yoshida towers. The arm too. It had slightly more storage space than the last. According to TT, who replaced her arm, it should be stronger as well. She'd have to watch her temper. Smashing her fist on a desk might snap it in half with ease.

She was at the police station, having returned from an eventless patrol of the IW district. The LAPD had fears that there might be violence in the wake of the Federation foiled plans to stir up chaos.

A lot of body bags were needed for those IWs, and people might have gotten the wrong idea of Estrella's actions.

Estrella froze when she saw Piper's workspace. The pixie kiwi never returned to work. Police staff were clearing out her stuff into a garbage bag. She convinced them to hand Estrella a photo Piper had of her daughter. It was the least she could do for her.

Peters stopped Estrella when she went to the water cooler for a drink. It was hot out, and the long bike ride back to her place was bound to dehydrate her. It was best to hydrate now.

He pointed at her left arm. "How's the arm?"

She glanced at it for the ninth time that day. "Feels like nothing happened." She stretched her fingers.

Estrella drank her cup of water as she moved toward the exit. Peters followed. "Still no word on the whereabouts of Partington, Taylor, or those IWs working with her."

"Yeah," she said and sipped. "They ditched me just before you guys found me."

Peters sighed. "Still can't believe Piper was a Federation spy this whole time."

"Still can't believe Ray and his girl were working for them." That was a lie of course. But she was going to play along with that story. The news following the incidents labeled Arianna, Piper, and Ray as wanted terrorists. *Yoshida must have put the government up to it. If those three are prime suspects, the whole nation will be looking for them.*

That would be my guess as well, Estrella.

Wasn't talking to you, Geoffrey.

Oh. I cannot tell the difference between you communicating with me and thinking internally.

You and I are gonna have to work on that more going forward ...

The two walked past holographic wanted posters for Piper, Ray, and Arianna. The news blamed them for everything that happened in New York, and recently in Los Angeles. Scapegoats, something to feed the fake news outlets, while Yoshida and the Alliance calmed the growing tensions between them and the Federation. It was the fault of Piper, Ray, and Arianna, not the Federation as Ray tried to tell people. At least there was no war, not yet. Alliance aircraft carriers in the Pacific stood on alert, waiting for the order. The Federation's navy was likely doing the same.

Estrella idled, facing the exit. "I'm gonna clock out now, if that's okay."

Peters crossed his arms. "Can you remain on call? Yoshida hasn't sent us new RWs. We're stretched thin."

"Ah fuck, do I have to?" She tossed her empty cup into the recycling.

"You know how Yoshida would respond if we reported an RW complaining?"

"They'd cut off my battery and nanite supply."

"Yep."

"I also saved them from a whole lot of shit."

"And they don't care. You're just a product doing its job." She grunted loudly and went for the exit. "So that's a yes, Rodriguez?"

"Whatever." She didn't bother to face him.

Once outside, Estrella walked to her motorcycle. The humid air baked her skin as she left the embrace of the AC of the station. The heels of her boots clicked, and then slowly diminished from existence when a black limo pulled up ahead of her. Its rearmost window dissolved.

A woman's voice called to her from within the darkened limo. "You need a lift back home with us."

Estrella pointed to her motorcycle. "Finally got my wheels, so no."

"That wasn't a question." Cigarette smoke escaped the opened window.

She stepped away from the limo, but it kept pace with her. The woman inside wasn't taking no for an answer. Estrella stopped and looked into the limo. She saw a classily dressed woman sit cross-legged, smoking a cigarette attached to a long cigarette holder. There was nobody else inside.

What's the worst that could happen?

Estrella got in, took a seat, and watched as the opened window returned into existence, darkening the interior of the limo. The AC cooled her skin and the buildup of moisture that was forming. The cigarette smoking woman sat ahead of her. Her lace-gloved hand put the cigarette holder to her lips. She took a puff then exhaled a cloud of white smoke. Estrella couldn't smell it, oddly enough. She ran a facial scan on the woman and got error messages on all lines.

"Don't bother with the scans," the cigarette smoking woman said. "I paid good money to keep my face off the database."

"Didn't know that was possible ... or legal."

"When you're high on the corporate ladder, anything is."

Estrella arms crossed, leaning back on the chair. It was comfy. "Yoshida?"

"Miss Yoshida," the woman said. "Or you can call me—"

"Lady M." Estrella sneered. "I've read about you. Was starting to think you were an urban legend."

"I'm real, and I'm also real fucking pissed to learn Yoshida, my business, my source of income, has gone in the direction it did recently."

"And what direction is that?"

"You damn well know." She puffed again and blew the smoke out elegantly. "Your hacker friend Ray is good, but he didn't wipe out all the surveillance in the Yoshida towers."

"This about project avatar?"

"Amongst other things, like what's inside Ray's head that will change the world." Lady M reached for a glass of whiskey, putting it to her glossy pink lips. She pulled the glass away, placing it on the holder next to her. "I have new orders for you, RW."

"Orders? Since when did I take them from you?"

"Did you forget your body is corporate property? You work where we tell you to work since you're a product we lease out to our customers, whether it's the LAPD, private mercenaries, or the fucking military."

"But, I'm special."

"You are." Another puff, and another plume of smoke that had no scent. "I want you to investigate the sins Yoshida's been keeping away from me. I don't care how you do it, just get it done. If you require a team, build one. Want to work solo? That's fine too. Need funding? Talk to me. I wasn't informed of the avatar project, Arianna's real purpose in the company, the shit in Ray's head, nothing. Don't even get me started on how Piper managed to get false paperwork that she was produced by us as well. If Yoshida's conducting black ops work without my knowledge, then you will be the black ops witch I use without theirs to shut it the fuck down."

"Straight to the point." Estrella liked her.

"Thought over in my head a dozen times last night how I would tell it to you."

"I got one request from you I'll need before I do anything."

"Tell me."

"There's a funeral for an RW in Buenos Aires I'd like covered. Her name is Lee Yu-Mi, goes by the name Yumi."

"Email me details, and I'll make it happen."

Estrella liked her even more. "What about the LAPD?"

"Fuck them, they don't own you, we do. I don't want you policing the streets for rowdy IWs or unregistered ones. I need you digging deeper into this. The Federation IWs, Ray, Arianna, and unsanctioned Yoshida operations. Who's bad, who's good, and who needs to go."

"I hear Ashford's dirty."

"So did I, but without proof I can't do anything. That's where you come in. Figure it out before war breaks out and we all fucking die because of it."

"Thought we had the war drums broken?"

"For now, but it'll be a matter of time before this pops up again. Unless you figure it out."

"I guess I'm in." Estrella shrugged. "Not that I had a choice."

"Good." The neon glow from the outside world shined through the windows, painting Lady M's face purple. "Now, any idea what became of Ray and Piper? You two were working together from the feeds I saw."

"They ... ditched me afterward."

"Did you let them?"

"What do you think?"

"Don't know, because you all left the range of the one working camera after you left that hidden computer lab." Estrella chuckled. "So, can we shake on this and get it over with?" Lady M offered her hand to shake. Estrella reached for it and felt nothing. Estrella's hand went through her like she was a ghost. Lady M laughed. "Do you really think I was going to appear physically for an RW?"

"So that's why I can't smell your cig smoke."

"To recap, get this done, give me a list of what you need. And do a good enough job and I might just pay for your freedom. I hear Buenos Aires is your favorite city."

Estrella loved her.

She hated the idea of once again slaving away in life because the corporations said so. But loved the feeling of knowing the chains that bound her had been loosened. Estrella's freedom drew closer.

Her imagination conjured an image of Yumi sitting beside her. The imaginary Yumi gave her a hug and thanked Estrella. Yumi now had a resting place. She told Estrella to swing by and visit when she got her freedom.

"Malakas! This place is too small."

"We're leaving tonight, Theo, so don't worry."

Ray sat back on a futon within Estrella's living room, his home since the attack on the Yoshida towers. Same with Piper, and her team, Bashiir, and Theo. They were all fugitives residing in the dark as the random waves of neon from the windows pulsed.

"Thank fuck for that ..." Theo kicked his feet up on the kitchen table, reclined, and gestured at Ray. "What do we do with him?"

The front door beeped; someone had unlocked it. Estrella entered wearing a short black skirt and a lace sleeveless top. She shut the door and keyed in its lock via the panel. "What are we chatting about today?" she asked.

"We will be getting out of your hair soon, Estrella," Piper said.

"Good." Estrella rubbed her hands together, making her penta-gram shaped jewelry jingle. "Hiding four wanted people in my apartment is making me paranoid, yo."

"Thanks for letting us crash here by the way," Ray said to her.

She said nothing, just looked at him then back to Piper. "You taking Ray?"

Piper shrugged. "That depends."

"Oh, I'm not sitting around waiting for my name to get cleared." Ray sat up quickly from the futon. "If you've read my previous news articles, then you'll know I'm a truth seeker. Finding Arianna isn't enough for me. I want to know exactly what is going on and why. The world has a right to know."

Estrella crossed her arms and faced him. He almost forgot the left one was sliced off days ago. "Guess that means you haven't found her?"

Ray pulled out his tablet, waving Estrella to sit next to him. She did, a bit too quickly, making the futon bounce him. She looked at his screen and the results of his hacking.

"Nothing yet," Ray said. "But I connected with old hacking partners from around the world. They've all reported that the Federation has an APB on Arianna. She's alive and they know it."

Estrella nodded, the glow from her eyes reflected off the tablet's screen. "And like you, she's got the data they want."

"I'm just an easier target to get to," he said. "Whatever that data is ..."

"Didn't you say something about having a part of it copied into a memory sphere?"

"I lost that sphere after the crash. We don't know exactly what's in my head, other than it involves the development of a weapon."

"And as I said before," Piper chimed in, her body wrapped in a black and brief lace outfit leaning against the wall, "my creation was the last project they worked on, before they started what's in your head. So, my cyberware is also the foundation for it."

"So," Estrella mumbled. "We're looking at a weapon that could enhance the power of an IW, making them just as deadly as they were during the war."

"Or worse," Ray said. "Nobuo spoke of wanting to free IWs worldwide."

"That's going to be your next mission then, Piper?" Estrella said facing her. "Find Arianna?"

Piper nodded. "Most likely. We find her and we can learn exactly what she discovered and maybe get the data out of Ray's head so he can sleep well at night."

Bashiir broke his silence from the couch he was sitting on. "The Federation and Yoshida have no idea where she is. How do you plan on doing that?"

"Still working on that part ..." Piper said, wincing.

"We need to find Arianna's father, Norris," Ray said. "He went missing the same night Arianna returned to the Alliance. The two must have made contact, which led the Federation operatives to their house."

Estrella concurred with a nod. "We find the people holding Norris, and hopefully Arianna."

Ray faced his tablet, bringing up the partial download he got from Yoshida. "And maybe get an insight into what this avatar project is." Ray had only got the names of the people on the list. Yoshida purged everything else when they took control of the towers. He flicked through them again, unable to understand why Arianna and her father were on it, and unable to understand why everyone was an unregistered telepath. "Still don't know why Yoshida cares so much about them."

Piper wandered to him, eying the tablet screen. She made a face, and Ray saw it. So did Estrella. Piper knew something, she faced Theo and Bashiir. "I think it's time we told Rodriguez and Partington."

"I guess ..." Theo scratched his head. "They've already gotten in this deep."

Piper's heels took her a few steps back, leaving Ray and Estrella alone sitting on the futon together. The two looked at Piper and her team watching them.

"Tell us what?" Ray asked.

"There have been some things we didn't share with you," Piper said. "About us and the IWs on that list."

Estrella spoke up with raised eyebrows. "Such as?"

"There's more to us IWs apart from being registered or unregistered."

Ray snorted. "So, tell us then."

"That's going to be a rabbit hole you might not leap out of," Piper said. "Are you sure you want to go down there?"

"Yes," Ray said without a second thought. He powered down his tablet, tossing it beside him on the futon. "I am and hope you do too Estrella?"

"Nobody can know what we're about to tell and show you," Piper said. "Not even those in Yoshida or the Alliance, even though they're in clear conflict with our enemies. Understand?"

Ray nodded. "I understand."

He glanced to Estrella sitting next to him. She looked worried, fidgeting her lace-gloved hands. She sank them into the futon's soft mattress. Her response was taking too long, and he wanted to know why. He hoped it had nothing to do with the limo ride home Estrella took. Ray glimpsed her walking away from the limo moments earlier when he hacked the building's surveillance.

Did Yoshida get to her?

Ray faced her. "Estrella?"

"Okay, I'm in," she finally spoke. "What's this secret world that's being kept hidden from us, Piper?"

EPILOGUE

ASHFORD

The tower the Federation IWs hit was still undergoing repairs, twenty-four-hour ones at that. If the construction workers wanted to have jobs tomorrow, then they needed to answer the call Yoshida made. Case in point, it was after 9 p.m. Darkness had fallen over Los Angeles and the dazzle of neon glow and expensive hologram ads came back to life.

Ashford stood in his office watching the sights unfold. His office was in the tower furthest away from the attack. Nobody in the corporation knew of his involvement, and those that witnessed him, in that tower, weren't able to speak anymore.

He took a puff of his cigar. He'd been waiting for this moment since Arianna had returned to the Alliance. It was the smoke of victory. His phone rung, its ringtone giving sound to the silent and dark office, as he stood at the floor-to-ceiling windows watching the repair team work.

He put the phone to his face, audio-only. Understandable.

"Report."

Ashford gave his report while eying the reflection of Ray's memory sphere sitting on his desk behind him. "We found Mr.

Partington's memory sphere in the wreckage of the medivac and have extracted the memories on it."

"Excellent."

"It's not everything that was in Mr. Partington's head, however. About thirty percent if that. We'll still need to find him or Ms. Kounias, if she's even alive, for the rest of it."

"Maybe, maybe not. They took her father alive for a reason, bait to capture her."

"We cannot remotely connect with her brain. But we now know what the Federation had contracted Zhang Industries to build. We can now get started on reproducing their findings."

"How long?"

"Four months."

A sigh came from the phone. "It will take us years to get to the level of development they were at before Arianna destroyed it. They might restart the project and beat us to it."

"I'm diverting every resource we have into fast-tracking this."

"Will it be enough?"

"It fucking better be! I've scrapped a lot of promising projects to do that. Give us three or four months, and we should have something we could test. From there, with a bit of luck, we might catch up. Though, if we can find Mr. Partington or Ms. Kounias, that'd be better."

"Ms. Kounias ..."

"We can't connect with her mind. She's no longer an avatar at this point, just Ms. Kounias."

"Have you come up with a contingency plan if Ms. Kounias isn't alive? Didn't you say someone buried the memories in Partington's head?"

"We'll need a top tier S ranked telepath to deep scan Mr. Partington's head. Something we don't have, but the Federation does."

"Then we need to get that."

Ashford laughed. "Good luck with that. It's clear the Federation has been training IWs for warfare in secret, while we in the Alliance and the rest of the world sat around playing fair and following the rules. There is no high S ranked IWs in this country that isn't a black op agent working for the Federation, let alone telepaths."

"Make it happen, Ashford. I'm counting on you."

"Of course," Ashford said. "I won't let you down ... Mr. President."

The call ended.

"That sounded promising."

Ashford faced away from the window, locking his gaze on the sultry figure of Avatar 33, known by her birth name Portia Blanchard, sitting cross-legged at the edge of his desk. He owed her a lot for getting out of that tower alive.

He grinned and puffed his cigar. "It is, Avatar 33, it is." His hands stroked her white hair, and his nostrils inhaled the fragrance of her perfume. She was a doll that did whatever he asked of her. "You're the top avatar now. Find Mr. Partington or Ms. Kounias, and," he held his phone out, loading a picture of an RW that caught his attention, "Lady M hired this RW to investigate us. See to it she doesn't get far."

Portia glared at the image. "What's her name?"

"Estrella Rodriguez."

AFTERWORD

Thanks for reading! If you enjoyed this story, please leave a review, and help another reader discover this and experience the same ride you did. The more people picking this up means I'll be able to release future books in the series faster.

This book was something that I spent decades on, admittedly, I spent most of that time not working on it. I came up with the idea for it back in the early 2000s when my hair wasn't turning gray. I miss those days. When I made my publishing debut back in 2016, I wrote Splintered Galaxy and shelved Cyber Witch, thinking it was something I'd never publish.

Since I was convinced Cyber Witch wasn't coming out, I poached several ideas from it, incorporating them into Splintered Galaxy. Those that read it might have noticed the similarities between psionic abilities and the abilities featured in Cyber Witch. Never mind the fact there were several cyberpunk moments in the Splintered Galaxy Universe, the ideas I had for Cyber Witch inspired some of those moments.

Even Contaminated Souls borrowed ideas from Cyber Witch. My original vision for Piper's character was that she would be a feisty Japanese woman who had past links with the Yakuza. If you read Contaminated Souls, you'd know how familiar that sounds. Reika from Contaminated Souls was the original Piper from Cyber Witch. The Piper we got in Cyber Witch had to be completely rewritten.

And now, here I am putting out that book series I said I'd never do. A lot of changes to the original story had to be made, so it wouldn't seem like I was just recycling story ideas, when in reality, I had been taking ideas from Cyber Witch, which was at the time, an unpublished story of mine.

Well, that's enough rambling so I'll stop it there. Once again, thanks for reading, and be sure to leave a review.

NEXT TIME ON CYBER WITCH: 2082

Estrella and Ray continue the search for Arianna after Piper reveals the secret world around them. Meanwhile, in the Federation, someone wants answers for the actions of Nobuo. And if they have to travel to Los Angeles to get it, they will.

Next up: Specter Protocol - Cyber Witch: 2082 book 2

KEEP IN TOUCH

What's the best way to learn of my new releases? Subscribe to my mailing list. Don't worry, I'm not a fan of spam, you'll only get emailed my new releases or promos.

http://eepurl.com/cuJS-L

Another way to learn of my new releases is to follow me on Amazon by visiting in the link below, then hitting the follow button on the page that loads.

https://www.amazon.com/Eddie-R-Hicks/e/B01MZoPPKQ

ALSO BY EDDIE R. HICKS

Cyber Witch: 2082

Cyber Witch

Specter Protocol (February 2020)

Digital Coven (TBA)

Psychic Rush (TBA)

Contaminated Souls

Kiss of the Demon Girl

Wrath of the Demon Girl

Awakening of the Demon Girl

Deception of the Demon Girl

Nemesis of the Demon Girl

Liberation of the Demon Girl

Splintered Galaxy Universe

Splintered Galaxy

Celestial Ascension

Uprising of the Exiled

Equilibrium of Terror: Part 1

Equilibrium of Terror: Part 2

Edge of the Splintered Galaxy

The Siege of Sirius

Celestial Incursion

Unsanctioned Reprisal

Hallowed Nebula

ABOUT THE AUTHOR

Eddie R. Hicks is a Canadian author known as a man of many talents, and for good reason. He's educated in media arts, journalism, and culinary arts, and now he writes dark and sexy science-fiction thrillers such as the Splintered Galaxy series.

If he's not working with skilled chefs in the restaurant industry, baking an epic red velvet cake for the hell of it, or playing video games, then he's in front of his computer doing what he always dreamed of doing since he was a kid: storytelling.

facebook.com/EddieRHicks

twitter.com/EddieRHicks

Printed in Great Britain
by Amazon